Dianne Blacklock has been a teacher, tra[...] out chick, and even one of those anno[...] you avoid in shopping centres. Nowadays she tries not to annoy anyone by staying home and writing. *Three's a Crowd* is her sixth book.

www.dianneblacklock.com

Also by Dianne Blacklock

Call Waiting
Wife for Hire
Almost Perfect
False Advertising
Crossing Paths

DIANNE BLACKLOCK

Three's a Crowd

MACMILLAN
Pan Macmillan Australia

First published 2009 in Macmillan by Pan Macmillan Australia Pty Limited
1 Market Street, Sydney

Copyright © Dianne Blacklock 2009

The moral right of the author has been asserted.

All rights reserved. No part of this book may be reproduced or transmitted by any person or entity (including Google, Amazon or similar organisations), in any form or by any means, electronic or mechanical, including photocopying, recording, scanning or by any information storage and retrieval system, without prior permission in writing from the publisher.

National Library of Australia
Cataloguing-in-Publication Data:

Blacklock, Dianne.
Three's a Crowd/Dianne Blacklock.

ISBN 978 1 4050 3942 0 (pbk.)

A823.4

Typeset in 12.5/14 pt Bembo by Post Pre-press Group
Printed in Australia by McPherson's Printing Group

Permission kindly granted by David O'Doherty/Sponsongs for reproduction of *Very Mild Superpowers*.

Papers used by Pan Macmillan Australia Pty Ltd are natural, recyclable products made from wood grown in sustainable forests. The manufacturing processes conform to the environmental regulations of the country of origin.

The characters and events in this book are fictitious and any resemblance to real persons, living or dead, is purely coincidental.

*To Joel, Jeska, Pat, Zac,
Dane and Claire*

Acknowledgements

I must begin this time with a correction. In the acknowledgements of my previous book I included what I thought was a witty line, though at my dear son Dane's expense, which was all well and good until he didn't get the joke! It was promptly clarified and understood, but then it occurred to me that I had been quite remiss in not acknowledging that he in fact provided a great deal of inspiration for that book, as the character, Will, and his cohort were initially modelled on Dane and his rather colourful bunch of friends. I stand corrected, and take this opportunity to give them their due. Thanks guys!

For this book, Dane and his fiancée, Claire, were back in the country, and were a willing and helpful sounding board whenever I needed it. As were Joel and Jeska, and Patrick and Zac, as always. And as always, Joel and Jeska were amongst the first readers of the first draft, and they provided fantastic and insightful feedback. I am lucky and grateful to have such a creative brains trust on tap.

Love and thanks are also due to all my family and friends, whose support and encouragement are never taken for granted, I hope they know. I would like to add a specific thankyou to Lesley McNiven for chauffeuring me around the eastern suburbs while I scouted locations, and for her endless encouragement and loyalty.

And thanks always to my Pan Macmillan family: the marvellous Cate Paterson, the brilliant Julia Stiles, the wonderfully efficient Louise Bourke and the tireless Jane Novak, to name but a few. I also want to mention how much I appreciate and value the camaraderie of my fellow authors, including Ber Carroll, Liane Moriarty, and especially the very generous Tony Park (who writes fabulous novels set in Africa), and his lovely wife, Nicola – two friends I can always count on to stay the distance.

Which brings me finally to you, the reader. I know I say it every time, but it means more to me with every book. The emails, the messages on my website, those of you I've had the pleasure of meeting, have given me such joy and encouragement. I would sit down at my desk on some of the hottest days last summer, my fingers actually numb from RSI, feeling a bit overwhelmed by my looming deadline, and there would be an enthusiastic note from one of you in my inbox. I can't tell you how motivating that is for me, and I can't wait to hear what you think of this one.

December

'What are you wearing tonight?'

Rachel shoved the door open with her hip and backed into the hall. 'Ah, I dunno, Lexie, I haven't thought about it. I'm just walking in the door now.'

Her head hurt. The traffic had been a nightmare, even by eastern suburbs standards, and the bus seemed more crowded than usual, not that it had stopped the driver barrelling along like he was at the helm of nothing more substantial than a skateboard. Rachel was still not used to the way the buses bounced up and down the hilly streets and careered around hairpin bends. How they didn't take out whole rows of parked cars or just plain tip over was a feat of physics clearly beyond her intellectual capacity to comprehend. Arriving home in one piece always felt something of an achievement.

'I was going to wear my wide jeans with that new top,' Lexie was saying. 'You know, the peasant-style one, with the deep frill? I can wear it low on the shoulders, and with the right jewellery it looks pretty dressy, but, with the jeans, not too dressy. See? Perfect.'

'So wear that.'

'It's too hot for jeans now. And I don't think I have a skirt that will quite . . .'

Rachel kicked her shoes off into her bedroom and tuned out. She just couldn't get that interested in clothes; she thought about them the way some people think about cars – something to get you from A to B. She didn't like shopping either. Or jewellery. She didn't dislike it, she just wasn't all that fussed about it. She was obviously missing some fundamental feminine gene. She leaned against the doorjamb and surveyed the state of her room. Bugger. The clothes strewn all over and spilling out of her laundry hamper reminded her that she hadn't done any washing on the weekend. Saturday she didn't get around to it, because in Rachel's universe that's what Saturdays were for – not quite getting around to things. She needed that one day when she didn't have to get things done, or be anywhere at any given time, or do anything to some arbitrary schedule. Rachel had spent last Saturday not quite finishing the newspaper, strolling down to the beach but not going in for a swim after all, stopping to chat with neighbours she bumped into on the way back from the beach, and saying yes to their offer of a beer, and then staying for another, and then, okay, just one more, and later, watching heaps of good clips on YouTube. Well, she watched heaps of clips, some of them were really good.

'But then I worry that cropped pants might be too casual ...'

Sunday it rained so the washing didn't get done. A more organised person would plan for such a contingency and, before taking that walk down to the beach, would have thrown on a load of washing. Easy. But it would have spoiled the very carefree nature of Saturday, even if it meant she didn't have enough clothes to get through the rest of the week. A more organised person would also have probably bought a dryer by now, to replace the one that had broken down earlier this year ... or was it last year? Hmm, Rachel had a feeling it happened just as summer was coming on, and she thought she could get away without it, so that would make it last year. She sniffed under her arm now to see if she could get away with staying in the clothes she'd had on all day. She grimaced. That was the other thing she'd never got used to – the pong on the bus. Especially in this weather; there was a reason they called it 'stinking' hot. If only everyone attended to their own personal hygiene a little more rigorously, Rachel might get away with pushing the boundaries occasionally with hers. She wondered if a squirt of perfume would do the trick.

'Rachel, are you listening?'

'I'm listening to what a stresshead you're being,' she said, side-stepping the fact that she wasn't listening at all. 'I don't know why you're so worried, it's only us girls.'

'Only us girls – and *Catherine*,' Lexie reminded her. 'If I'm not dressed up enough, she'll make one of those comments she always makes, like "Just come from the beach, Lexie?" But if I'm too dressed up, then she teases me about going overboard, like "Who are you trying to impress?" You know what she's like.'

Oh, Rachel knew exactly what Catherine was like, but after twenty-odd years it was water off a duck's back, for the most part. Lexie hadn't known her as long, so she was not fully desensitised yet.

'Yeah well, it's not Catherine's birthday,' said Rachel, 'it's Annie's, and do you think she'd care what you wore?'

She heard the sigh of relief down the phone line. 'You're right. In fact,' Lexie added with a significant bump in enthusiasm, 'that's what I'm going to do. I'm going to choose something that Annie would like.'

Annie liked anything and everything and everyone, but Rachel was not about to stall the horses. 'Okay, so I'll see you soon –'

'Oh, that's why I was calling in the first place,' said Lexie, her voice wavering. 'I talked to Scott almost an hour ago and he wasn't anywhere near ready to leave. They were short-staffed today, poor baby was up to his elbows in washing-up.'

Okay, now Rachel began to feel a little uneasy – being late for Catherine was a whole other box of kettles. As a lawyer, Catherine was accustomed to accounting for her time in billable units of six-minute blocks, and this made her extremely . . . *precise*. That was the polite way of putting it. It also made her extremely intolerant of anyone who kept her waiting. Lexie was giving Rachel a lift, so this was going to make them both late. Not regular, within-reason late, but properly late. And that was not good. Catherine with the black cloud of self-righteousness hanging over her head all evening was no fun at all.

'Maybe I should go ahead . . .' Rachel mused out loud.

'Oh, please no!' Lexie cried urgently. 'Then I'll have to walk in on my own and –'

'Okay, calm down, Lex. What if I grab a taxi over to your place?'

'But I virtually pass your place on the way. And what if Scott gets home while you're in transit? Then I'll have to end up waiting for you, when I could have been heading to your place, and that could add like, another ten minutes, which would totally defeat the purpose.'

She was right. Which meant the entire conversation was also pretty pointless at this juncture.

'Listen, no one's actually late yet,' said Rachel. 'Why don't you just keep getting ready, and if Scott isn't home in time, well, we'll cross that bridge when we come to it.'

That was her preferred modus operandi. In fact, crossing bridges as she came to them was somewhat of a specialty of Rachel's, not that she would recommend it as the most effective game plan. Her lack of preparedness for life's little misadventures had landed her in some less than enviable situations over the years: dropping out of uni with no money and no idea what she was going to do with herself; stranded in more countries than she cared to remember with no money and no idea what she was going to do, and married to a man she didn't love, with no idea . . . Suffice to say there was a recurring theme. She had a feeling her epitaph would end up reading, *Here lies the girl who finally met a bridge she couldn't cross when she came to it.*

'So back to my original question,' Lexie was saying, 'what are you wearing?'

Rachel sniffed under her arm again. She smelled like the 361 bus. No, she wasn't going to get away with it. She stooped to pick up a top off the floor. 'Something Annie would like, remember?' Something clean would do for Rachel.

'Oh, yes, that's right,' Lexie chirped. 'Hold on a sec, Rachel . . . Scottie!' she shrieked. 'You're here, I love you! Scott's home,' she said breathlessly into the phone.

Rachel's ears were still ringing. 'Yeah, got that. Crisis averted then.'

'So I'll see you at ten to, or maybe quarter to?'

'Sure,' said Rachel, knowing it was highly unlikely she'd see her any time before seven. 'Prank me when you're on your way and I'll wait for you down on the street.'

Lexie hung up the phone and tossed it on the sofa as she rushed forwards and leaped up into her husband's arms, straddling him around the waist with her legs. She loved that he was such a big tall man, and he could hold her up in his arms like this with barely any effort.

'Come on, Lex,' he groaned. 'It's been a long day.'

'Oh, poor baby,' she cooed. 'How can I help?'

'By getting down off me,' he said, giving her a quick kiss on the lips before depositing her back on her own two feet.

She pouted up at him.

'I've been on my feet all day, hun,' he sighed, walking past her into the living area, where he threw himself onto the sofa. He frowned, lifting himself up slightly as he reached under his back and pulled out the phone. He placed it on the coffee table just as Mia came waddling out from the playroom. She let out an excited shriek when she spotted her dad, which alerted four-year-old Riley, who came flying through the doorway and launched himself across the room, easily overtaking his baby sister, to land with a thump on his father's chest. Mia squeaked 'Up! Up!' and Scott scooped his arm around her to lift her into the fray.

'Riley, Mia, take it easy, Daddy's had a hard day,' Lexie said in her mother's voice. She had been quite amazed how quickly she'd picked up that tone. She'd never been in a position of authority over anyone; she had always got by on being sweet and obliging. But that approach did not work on a recalcitrant toddler, and Lexie had heard herself quite unexpectedly one day using The Tone. And it worked, what's more. It was not the first thing about motherhood that had surprised her. Or delighted her. Lexie was in her element, she felt this was what she was born to do. She'd never said that to anyone, of course. Except Annie. Annie understood, she always understood. It had been a godsend having her next door when the babies were born. Lexie didn't know how she was going to get by without her there now.

She gazed down at her beautiful son and her beautiful daughter and her beautiful husband, as he tickled, and blew raspberries, and generally delighted his children, and Lexie counted her blessings.

'Well, I know where I come in the scheme of things,' she declared, planting her hands on her hips.

'What?' said Scott, looking up at her.

'Couldn't wait to offload me, and you let the kids clamber all over you.'

'Come and join us,' he invited expansively. 'Clamber all you want. I just had to get off my feet, Lex.'

She softened. 'Do you want me to take off your boots for you?'

'You don't have to do that.'

'But I want to.'

She pulled off his elastic-sided boots, and his socks, remembering how her brother used to tease her, chasing after her and waving his smelly socks in her face, how she hated smelly boys. But nothing about Scott was smelly. Oh, sometimes he smelled a bit strongly of the kitchen, depending on the special of the day at the café. But mostly Lexie loved the smell of him, loved everything about him. She gave his feet a quick rub. 'Better?'

'Thanks love.' He looked up at her. 'What time have you got to leave?'

She glanced at her watch. 'Oh God, I better hurry!'

'Where you going, Mummy?' Riley called after her as she dashed for the stairs.

'Mummy's abandoning us to go out with the girls,' Scott told him.

Lexie frowned, taking a step back. 'Don't say it like that,' she admonished him. 'Riley, sweetheart, you're having a special night with Daddy, and Mummy's having a grown-up night with the girls.'

'Bor*ringg*!' Riley declared, clutching his stomach as though he was in pain.

'Exactly,' said Lexie. 'Now I have to get ready, and I don't even know what I'm going to wear!' she trilled, taking the stairs two at a time.

Twenty minutes and as many outfits, or at least variations, later, Lexie came downstairs in a simple flowered shift and strappy sandals. The more times she'd changed clothes, the hotter and more flustered she'd become, and in the end she settled for the lightest, coolest thing in her wardrobe. She only hoped she didn't look like she was going to the beach.

'How do I look?' she said, walking over to the kitchen where Scott was arranging vegetable crudités on a plate.

'Great,' he said, without raising his head.

'Scott Anthony Dingle! You didn't even look at me then!'

He glanced across at her, poker-faced. 'I don't need to, because you always look beautiful.'

She raised an eyebrow as she sidled over to him, snatching a carrot stick.

'Why do you care anyway?' asked Scott. 'You're only going out with the girls. Or is that just a cover and you're really going out to pick up?'

'Yep, that's it, you sprung me,' she quipped, crunching into the carrot.

'Just try it,' he said, stooping to plant a kiss on her neck. 'You smell good.' He straightened again, considering her. 'And you look good enough to eat, really.' Scott's biggest compliment.

'Not too casual?' Lexie persisted. 'I don't want to look like I'm going to the beach.'

He frowned. 'What does it matter? It's just the girls, loosen up.'

Lexie shrugged, avoiding his eyes.

Scott shook his head. 'It's Catherine the Great, isn't it? I don't know why you girls put up with her.'

'Don't say that,' said Lexie. 'I know she can be a little . . . prickly, but she means well . . . and she has a good heart.'

'Why do people always say that about someone who's a real –'

'She's had a hard life,' Lexie interrupted him. 'You know she started with nothing.'

'Yeah, yeah, teenage mum, did it all on her own, I've heard it before,' said Scott. 'Doesn't give her the right to be a bitch.'

'Honey,' she chided in a low voice, glancing across at the children, but they were absorbed in something on the TV. Scott just didn't like Catherine and nothing Lexie could say was going to change his mind. So she decided to change the subject instead. 'I put the fans on up in the kids' room. It was so hot up there. I don't know how we're going to get by without aircon this summer if it's this hot already.'

He looked at her sideways. 'We'll get by just the same as we always have, Lex.'

'I'm only thinking of the kids.'

'We got by when we were kids, even you, Miss Richie Rich,' he added. 'No one had airconditioning in their houses back then, and everyone wasn't dying of heat exhaustion.'

'I know,' she agreed begrudgingly.

'We either believe in global warming or we don't, Lexie. And if we do, then we have to take personal responsibility, even when it's inconvenient or uncomfortable.'

'I know, I know,' she surrendered, holding up her hands. 'You can stop the lecture.'

They couldn't afford airconditioning anyway. Lexie adored

their pretty little house, tucked away in a pretty little street in Clovelly. She'd had so much fun decorating it when they first got married. They didn't have much money then either, but Scott's dad and a couple of his brothers had all the trades covered, so they were able to do a cheap but effective makeover of the kitchen and bathroom. The rest was achieved with lots of spak filler and paint and elbow grease. Her parents had kept wanting to pay for this or that, but Lexie refused. Scott would never have accepted it anyway. Instead she pored over her mother's interior design magazines and scoured the wholesale outlets and created a home that was chic and comfortable for a fraction of what it could have cost.

When Riley came along the house worked beautifully, at least while he was only crawling. But with the addition of Mia things were getting, well, cramped. The children had to share a smallish bedroom; there was no longer space for the charming rocking chair Lexie had found at a garage sale, or the display unit housing all their baby mementoes and special books. The room had become very utilitarian: Riley's bed, Mia's cot, storage for their clothes. They had even had to resort to one of those padded mats on top of the chest of drawers as a change table. Worse was the impact downstairs; Lexie finally had to surrender the dining space she had created off the kitchen, where sliding doors opened up onto a courtyard draped with fairy lights. The setting of so many fun dinner parties became instead a playroom, and the dining table was moved into the living area, making everything just that bit tighter, and entirely ruining the illusion of space Lexie had worked so hard to achieve.

It didn't matter, not really, only that Lexie had a little secret. She'd only ever told Annie, because as usual Annie was the only person she knew would understand, but she desperately wanted more children, at least one, maybe two. She didn't think Scott would be against the idea in theory – he loved kids and he'd come from a big family himself – but there was no way they could fit another child into this house, nor could they afford a bigger house, not if they wanted to stay in the eastern suburbs. And they really didn't have a choice about that, with Scott's café smack bang in the centre of Coogee. Scott was already sensitive about being able to provide for his family. Lexie remembered the first time he came to her house to meet her parents. He had been gobsmacked, to put it mildly. 'Look at this place! I knew your dad was a doctor, but Jesus, Lexie, you guys are seriously rich.'

She'd denied it at the time; she knew people who were 'seriously rich' and they weren't in that league. She watched him desperately trying to impress her parents, telling them the café was just the first step on the way to owning his own restaurant. 'You never told me that,' Lexie said later. He merely shrugged. 'Every chef dreams of having his own restaurant.'

As nothing had ever come of it, Lexie assumed he'd only said it to impress her parents. It didn't bother her, Scott could stay in the café forever, if that's what he wanted. But she wondered if they would ever be able to afford a bigger house, nothing fancy, just something big enough to fit a couple more kids . . .

She leaned against the bench now, watching him. Lexie knew she couldn't broach the subject with him yet. Not until she figured out a way to make it work. 'So, you're right for the kids' dinner?' she asked, sneaking another carrot stick. 'There's some of that pasta leftover that Mia loves.'

'I think I can look after the food part, hun,' he said. 'And aren't you supposed to be going out for yours?'

Lexie roused herself, turning to check the clock. 'Oh my God, look at the time!'

It was exactly one minute to seven as Catherine stepped through the door of the restaurant.

'There should be a booking under Halliday,' she said crisply to the waitress who came forwards to greet her. She hoped Rachel had remembered, Catherine always felt better when she made the arrangements herself.

The waitress glanced at the reservations list and nodded. 'This way, please.'

Catherine followed her through the still half-empty restaurant to a table set for four with a view out across Bondi Beach to the ocean. As she took her seat, she glanced at her watch. Seven o'clock on the dot. Her punctuality was a great source of pride to Catherine. The same could not be said of her friends, unfortunately.

'Can I get you anything while you're waiting?' the waitress asked her.

She probably had a minimum of ten minutes before they turned up, that's if they were anywhere in the vicinity of their definition of 'on time'.

'Do you have a Margaret River sauvignon by the glass?'

The waitress looked thrown. 'Let me bring you the wine list.'

That would take too long. 'Yes, bring the wine list, along with a glass of sauvignon – a Margaret River preferably, or else something from that region. Ask your sommelier.'

The girl gave her a troubled look before scuttling away. They probably didn't have a sommelier here, she probably didn't know what a sommelier was. It was an acceptable restaurant, the food was tolerable, the service adequate, but as usual around here you were mostly paying for the view and the location. It wouldn't have been Catherine's choice, which was no matter tonight, tonight was for Annie. Catherine had accepted over the years that in a group of friends you had to *compromise*, which basically meant she had to lower her standards whenever they went out. It would be nice if that was acknowledged occasionally. They worked around Annie and Lexie – mid-price, sometimes a pleasant surprise, but mostly mediocre. Every so often Rachel complained about not being able to afford a night out at all, so Catherine invariably just covered her, because if they had to stoop to Rachel's budget they'd be eating at one of those roadside kebab stands.

She took out her phone and speed-dialled home, and was eventually answered with a garbled greeting.

'Alice, don't speak with your mouth full.'

'Then how am I supposed to answer the phone?' she said, still munching.

'Swallow before you pick up.'

'What if my mouth's too full and I'd choke if I tried to swallow before the phone rang out?'

'Then you'd have clearly bitten off more than you could chew,' Catherine returned evenly. 'Honestly, Alice, why does everything have to turn into a debate? Try to avoid speaking with your mouth full. It's impolite. Are you having dinner?'

'Nuh, Martin's not home yet.'

Catherine pressed her lips together. He promised he'd be home no later than seven. At times she honestly believed there was no one else in the world who cared about being on time. The waitress placed the wine list and a glass on the table in front of her, and Catherine nodded in acknowledgement before picking it up and taking a generous sip.

'Has he called?' she asked Alice.

'Uhuh. He was just leaving work.'

'Then do your homework, no MSN or MySpace or Facebook or YouTube. And no more eating, Martin will cook dinner when he gets home.'

'I don't want whatever Martin's cooking,' she whined.

'How do you know?'

'Because it'll be totally crap.'

'Don't say "crap", Alice.'

'Okay, it'll be totally disgusting. And besides, it won't be ready till, like, nine o'clock or something, and I'm hungry now.'

'Then eat a healthy snack to take the edge off your hunger. A carrot, for example.'

'I'm gunna make some instant noodles.'

'*Going to* make noodles, Alice,' Catherine corrected her. 'But I wish you wouldn't. They are simply the worst thing, they have no nutritional value and far too much fat and salt. This is the time you have to start watching your weight –'

'Mu-umm,' Alice groaned.

Catherine could never be accused of being insensitive, she knew not to send her daughter negative messages. 'I'm just saying, if you don't keep an eye on it now, it will be harder to get rid of later on.'

'Can I go now?' Alice said flatly.

Catherine sighed. 'Yes. I'm not sure what time I'll be home, so I'll say goodnight.'

'Night.' Alice hung up, and with still no sign of the others, Catherine scrolled through the messages on her BlackBerry as she sipped her wine. She didn't understand why Alice was so persistently obstinate. Catherine knew adolescence was a notoriously difficult time for mother-daughter relationships. She had certainly struggled to relate to her own mother at the same age;

but her mother had aspired to nothing greater than her role of housewife, and her most pressing commitments any given week were to get to the bottom of the ironing basket and to make sure her father's dinner was on the table when he walked in the door at night. Alice had never seen her mother in such a subservient role, and she never would. Catherine was a successful professional woman, she kept herself trim, attractive and stylish. She was a 'MILF'. Catherine had been quite chuffed when she'd first learned of the acronym, as she didn't doubt for a moment that she merited that particular label. In the best way of course; she could never be accused of being mutton done up as lamb. She was even technologically savvy, for heaven's sake. Honestly, she was an excellent role model for anyone's daughter, or son for that matter. Catherine would have loved to have had someone like her as a mother. Alice didn't know how lucky she was.

Nor did she seem to understand that Catherine was only looking after her best interests, because if she didn't watch her weight now it could so easily balloon out of control, and then she would struggle with it for the rest of her life. It was in their genes; her mother had been a dumpy little ball of dough for all of Catherine's living memory. It was only sustained discipline on Catherine's part that had kept her figure trim. She must speak to Martin about serving some simple dishes, healthy and low-fat, but more compatible with an adolescent's tastebuds. Perhaps he could even include Alice in the process. It was a bit of a waste having a man who liked to cook if her daughter didn't care for what he dished up. He already complained that it was barely worth cooking for Catherine, the way she picked at her food; even resorting to veiled hints that she was bordering on an eating disorder, but that was patently ludicrous. She had explained often enough the number of breakfasts, lunches, cocktail parties and what have you that she was required to attend, so she simply had to keep a sensible eye on her intake the rest of the time. It was called self-control. Draining her glass, she had to wonder why Alice hadn't taken after her in that regard. It was all very well to be strong-willed and determined, Catherine would not have made it to where she was if she hadn't been, but you also had to have direction, set goals, practise self-discipline. Alice couldn't stick at anything, and none of her school subjects seemed to inspire or even vaguely interest her. Catherine could handle the fact that she wasn't particularly academically inclined, if only she displayed some flair for art, or music. *Something*. Catherine had even tried to get her interested in joining the rowing team, which had a certain level of prestige, but Alice had looked at her as though she were mad.

What worried her more than anything was that she couldn't picture her daughter ever making anything of her life. She'd end up like Rachel, who'd had so much potential but had frittered it all away because she couldn't buckle down to anything. Catherine couldn't imagine not having that passion, that drive to excel, to achieve, to make a difference. She wanted Alice to experience that, to have a fulfilling life, to be happy. She had one more year to turn it around before she finished school, turned eighteen and, Catherine had the sinking feeling, was beyond her influence forever.

Annie had always dismissed her concerns, assuring her it was normal teenager behaviour. All very well for her to say. Sophie and Hannah were both high-achievers; they diligently completed homework and kept up piano practice without being nagged or threatened; Sophie had been on the rowing and debating teams throughout high school, and Hannah was class captain in her final year at primary school – all with apparently no pressure whatsoever from Annie, or Tom. They were the kind of parents who liked to give the impression they didn't push their kids like everyone else, that their achievements didn't matter to them, that they only wanted them to be happy. Catherine didn't believe it for a second. Achievement was what led to happiness, that's all she wanted for her daughter.

Finally, at twenty-two minutes past seven, Rachel and Lexie spilled into the restaurant, looking like a pair of fugitives. They indicated to the waitress that they'd spotted their table, and proceeded to make their way towards Catherine.

'Sorry we're late,' Lexie blurted as they drew close. 'It was my fault, though really it was Scott's fault. Though really, you can't blame him for being a little late when he was short-staffed. He did his best. Really.'

Catherine was not even going to bother crediting that with a response. She was a partner at one of the largest legal firms in Sydney, Lexie was a housewife and Scott was a cook in a café. Heaven forbid either of them had to cope with anything genuinely demanding.

'I ordered a bottle after fifteen minutes,' she said instead. There was no need to mention the glass she'd had first. 'I hope that's okay with you.'

'As long as I can have a drink right now,' said Rachel, picking up the bottle.

Catherine held up her glass for a refill. 'Have you been in those clothes all day?' she said, looking Rachel up and down.

'No,' she retorted. She'd been in these clothes all day yesterday, but that's not what Catherine had asked, exactly.

Lexie hesitated, her hand on the back of a chair, as she frowned at the place settings on the table. 'Is someone else coming?'

'Not that I'm aware of,' said Catherine, glancing at Rachel.

'Well, then, what's that . . . it's not . . . I don't . . .' Lexie stammered.

'I booked a table for four,' Rachel said.

Lexie snatched her hand away from the chair. 'Why would you do that? Is one of these supposed to be her place?' she cried. 'Where am I supposed to sit?'

'She's not a ghost, Lexie,' Catherine sighed.

'And if she were, she'd be a friendly ghost,' said Rachel, gently moving Lexie aside. 'Why don't you sit over next to Catherine and I'll sit here opposite you.' That way Lexie would effectively be hemmed in, and she wouldn't have to worry about bumping up against any ghosts, friendly or otherwise.

'I know we're here for her birthday,' Lexie said quietly, taking her seat, 'I just didn't expect there'd actually be a place setting for her.'

Rachel bit her lip. 'I'm sorry, I didn't mean to upset anyone. Just when I rang to make the booking it didn't seem right not to acknowledge her.'

Lexie gazed wistfully at her plate, nodding. 'Because three's a crowd.'

'That's not right,' said Catherine.

Lexie looked at her.

'The saying is "Two's company, three's a crowd", it has nothing to do with four becoming three.'

'Whatever, but the fact is three doesn't work,' Lexie insisted. 'It's wrong. I've heard it's even unlucky.' She sighed. 'How are we going to get by without her?'

'Oh God, you're not going to get all maudlin, are you?' Catherine muttered.

'I wasn't the one who booked a place for her!' Lexie declared indignantly.

'It's okay, Lexie,' Rachel interrupted before it went any further. 'This is the first time we've all been together like this, since ... so maybe we're all a little ... sensitive. And anyway, what is wrong with feeling "maudlin" after somebody dies?' She looked pointedly at Catherine. 'Surely this is the most appropriate time to feel maudlin. Or not. If you don't, that is. Feel maudlin. I mean, you don't have to feel maudlin, you can feel whatever feels right, I mean, you will feel that regardless, but you shouldn't feel bad expressing whatever feeling you happen to be feeling. Maudlin or otherwise.'

Rachel looked at the faces of her friends trying to follow what she was saying. She wasn't surprised they were confused.

'I guess what I'm trying to say,' she went on valiantly, 'is that I reckon whatever anyone is feeling is okay, acceptable, appropriate, at a time like this. And we should support each other ... in feeling however we feel.'

'Fine,' Catherine said, but Rachel knew she was dismissing the notion in the same breath. 'But think about it this way, what would Annie want us to do?' She paused for effect. 'Would Annie want us to sit around moping? Would she want us to wallow in those feelings? I don't know about you, but I doubt that very much. You know how she was, she'd want us to get something positive from this experience, learn from it, even grow from it.'

Rachel glanced at Lexie, who now just looked guilty, or perhaps ashamed.

'Fine,' Rachel said, mimicking Catherine's dismissive tone. 'But maybe it takes time to get to that point. First you have to be allowed to grieve.' She paused for effect, and to think of what to say next. 'Because, the thing is, grief is like . . . it's like an anchor. If you don't bring it up to the surface, then it's going to hold you right where you are, and stop you from moving on.'

Catherine rolled her eyes. 'Sounds like something Annie would say.'

'Well that makes it very appropriate then, doesn't it?' Lexie blurted.

Rachel looked at her kindly. 'Go ahead, Lexie, tell us what you're feeling. We want to know, don't we, Catherine?' She sensed Catherine's silent groan, but chose to ignore it.

Lexie sighed. 'I just miss her,' she said plainly. 'That's all. I mean she lived right next door. I keep thinking I see her out of the corner of my eye when I go out the front. It just feels so empty in there now.'

'How's Tom?' asked Catherine. 'We haven't heard from him since everything –' she was about to say 'died down' but caught herself in time, '– *settled* down.'

Lexie shrugged. 'I've barely seen him, or the girls. You know they left straight after the funeral to stay with his family up north, and then a few weeks ago they came home. I let them be at first, you know, give them space to settle back in. But before I knew it they were gone again.'

'Gone? Where?' asked Catherine.

'Back up north again,' Lexie explained. 'I didn't even talk to Tom, he left a note and the house key in my letterbox. You know, could I water the plants, collect the mail, that kind of thing. Anyway, he said he was sorry he missed me, that they'd probably be gone till after Christmas.'

'That's very odd,' Catherine remarked. 'Why did they come back at all, did he say?'

'Sophie had to sit her school certificate,' said Rachel.

'How do you know that?'

'Huh? Oh . . .' She faltered. 'He must have said it at the funeral, or sometime. But she's in Year 10, and the exams were only the other week.'

'Which means her formal would be any day now,' said Catherine, thinking. 'Why would they come all the way back for the exam and then not stay for the formal?'

'Maybe Sophie didn't want to go,' Rachel suggested. 'She just lost her mother, after all.'

'Nonsense, it would be the best thing for her, take her mind off her troubles,' said Catherine. 'Tom really should be asking for advice about this kind of thing. Why didn't he call me, for example? Alice is one year ahead of Sophie, I've been through all of this.'

'You haven't been through losing your spouse,' Lexie muttered.

Catherine either ignored that or wasn't listening. 'Actually, I'm surprised his firm is letting him get away with this,' she went on. 'There are things you can suspend temporarily, but after this long they'd have to do something. For his sake let's hope they've brought in a locum, because God help him if they just shared his clients around to the other associates.'

'Why do you say that?' Rachel frowned.

'Isn't it obvious? If they can redistribute his workload, they can get by without him.'

'Oh, come on. He just lost his wife. They wouldn't be so callous.'

'Don't be naive, Rachel. It's a law firm, not a welfare agency. And given the current economic climate, they'd be looking for excuses to shed staff . . .' Catherine drummed her fingernails on the table as she sipped her wine. 'Frankly, he's being reckless. It's not like Tom.' She stopped drumming. 'You don't think he's seeing someone up there, do you?'

'What?'

'An old high-school flame perhaps? Widowers have quite the pulling power.'

Lexie was shaking her head vehemently. 'There's no way he'd be seeing someone else, it's far too soon.'

'Not for a man,' Catherine said wearily. 'They jump right back in the saddle.'

Lexie looked horrified. 'How can you say that?'

''Cause it's true, sadly,' said Rachel. 'Sean was supposedly heartbroken when we split, but he barely had time to change the sheets before he was seeing someone else.'

'I think this is a little different, Rachel,' Lexie said, adopting an almost reverential tone. 'Annie and Tom were . . . *Annie and Tom*! They were such an amazing couple, everyone thought so. I'm sure he's absolutely lost without her.'

'Which is why he needs to fill the gap,' Catherine agreed. 'Men are not like women in that respect. The more pain he's in, the more he'll need to block it out with someone else.'

'Tom will never be able to replace Annie,' Lexie insisted, 'they were perfect for each other.'

'To all appearances,' added Catherine.

Now Rachel was frowning. 'What do you mean by that?'

'Just that no one ever really knows what goes on behind closed doors.'

'Why would you say something like that?' said Lexie, blinking back tears. 'If Tom's behaving recklessly, and not like himself, it's because he's devastated, not because he's having an affair!'

'Lexie,' Catherine interrupted calmly, 'it wouldn't be an affair. He wouldn't be cheating on Annie, she's . . . gone.'

Lexie gasped. 'That's exactly the word he used. You didn't hear his voice, on the phone that day, he could barely get it out . . .' Nor could she now, her own voice breaking at the very thought of it. 'I couldn't believe what I was hearing. Annie couldn't have *died*, she had the flu. I talked to her only the day before, when she asked me to pick up the girls from school. She was just feeling a little dizzy and lightheaded, she didn't want to drive . . .'

'Yes, we –'

Rachel cleared her throat, giving Catherine a pointed look across the table. Yes, they had heard it all before, but it didn't matter, Lexie needed to go over it. Again. So Catherine needed to button it.

'And even when Tom called that night, late, remember?' Lexie went on, 'to say he was taking her to the hospital, I wasn't worried. I just thought he was being a bit overly cautious. He said Annie was wheezing so badly she couldn't sleep, and he thought they might be able to give her something to open her airwaves, that she couldn't go all night like that. She was already in the car when I went next door, that was the last time I saw her, through the window of the car.'

Lexie could see her now. Pale and drawn. She had raised one hand briefly, before putting it to her mouth as she broke into a fit of coughing.

The girls were in bed asleep, Tom just wanted someone there

in case they happened to wake. Lexie didn't mind, Annie would do the same for her without blinking. She ended up falling asleep on the couch in their living room. It was Hannah who woke her.

'Lexie?' she yawned. 'What are you doing here?'

'Oh, hi sweetie.' She roused herself, looking around to get her bearings. It was daylight. 'Are Mum and Dad back yet?'

'Back from where?'

Lexie hesitated. Hannah was twelve, the younger of the two girls, and a little excitable. Lexie didn't want to startle her. She pulled herself up to sitting. 'Well, Hannah, your dad took your mum to the hospital –'

'What?' That woke her up.

'Just to get her checked out,' Lexie reassured her. 'That cough was really starting to bother her, making it hard for her to breathe, and you know there are no doctors' offices open in the middle of the night, and the hospital's only up the road . . .' She didn't know what else to say. She really had no idea why they were taking this long. 'So they might have put her on a nebuliser, maybe, you know, like they do for people with asthma when they have trouble breathing?'

'Does Mummy have asthma?' asked Hannah.

'I don't think so, but she might have some of the same symptoms, and so they might treat it the same –'

Her mobile phone started to ring in her pocket. 'Just a sec, sweetie,' said Lexie, reaching for it and flicking it open. 'Hello?'

'What's going on, hun?'

'Oh, Scott, I don't really know. They're not back and I haven't heard anything.'

'I'm going to have to get to work, Lex, it's already seven.'

'Oh sorry, you're late –'

'It's okay,' he assured her. 'I called Josh, and he was going to open, but I can't leave him on his own for much longer.'

'No, of course. You should go, just bring the kids in here. I'm sure Tom and Annie can't be too much longer.'

Lexie decided to proceed as normally as possible, helping the girls with breakfast and their school lunches, while Riley and Mia were occupied in front of the morning cartoons – something Lexie did not ordinarily allow, but today was somewhat out of the ordinary. She kept expecting Annie and Tom to walk through the door any minute, but as the clock ticked closer to the time the girls would have to leave, there was still no sign of them, no word.

'I think we should stay home and wait for them,' Hannah said finally.

'Don't be a baby, Hannah,' said Sophie, using her authority as the older sister. 'I have to go to school today, we've got debating practice at lunchtime for the finals this Friday.'

Hannah bit her lip. 'Can't we ring Daddy and find out?'

'You have to turn off your mobile in a hospital,' said Sophie. 'And Dad would totally let us know if there was anything wrong. No news is good news, isn't that right, Lexie?'

Lexie agreed and, spurred on by Sophie's pep talk, she hustled Hannah along, and the two of them left the house in ample time to catch their regular bus. Lexie took Riley and Mia back home and got on with her day. From time to time she would glance out the front window, or listen for noises next door. She'd heard horror stories about overcrowding in emergency departments, but this was getting a little ridiculous. Surely Tom would have given up and just taken her to a doctor now that it was normal business hours.

As the afternoon wore on, Lexie wondered if she ought to pick up the girls from school. But she was certain Tom would have phoned if he needed her to do that, and if she drove there and the girls weren't expecting her, she'd never find them. They could already be on the bus, or Tom might have arranged for them to go home with someone else. She just wanted to do something useful. Lexie got to thinking about what Annie would do in a situation like this. She wouldn't panic or make a fuss, and she certainly wouldn't interfere; she would do something thoughtful but practical. Lexie was resolved then, and she set about making a casserole for their dinner so Tom would have one less thing to worry about when they did eventually make it home.

However, as dinner time approached and still no one had showed up next door, Lexie had worked herself up into quite a lather by the time Scott arrived home from work.

'I don't understand why you don't just give Tom a call,' he said.

'I don't want to seem anxious, or over the top.'

'But you are, sweetheart,' Scott said plainly. 'Give him a call, put your mind at rest.'

'But he might not have his phone on in the hospital.'

'Only one way to find out.'

Still she hesitated, and in the end, Tom beat her to it.

'Tom,' Lexie said, relieved. 'I've been so worried. What on earth went on at that hospital? I can't imagine how long they must have kept you waiting. Why didn't you just take her to her doctor's?'

There followed what felt like the longest pause. Lexie was beginning to think the line must have dropped out.

'Tom?'

'She's gone, Lexie.'

'Where to?'

'No . . . um, Annie's . . . she died.'

'What? That's impossible, Tom,' she scoffed. 'She has the flu.'

'Yeah . . . they put her on a nebuliser, and apparently it set her heart off into this irregular rhythm, but it wasn't picked up until a nurse was doing a routine check. I think her pulse was too high, or something, and then, I don't know what happened, all hell broke loose, and they were using those paddles, you know?' His voice was breaking up. 'But it wasn't any good. Her heart failed. They worked on her for forty-five minutes. They don't know what happened for sure, there'll have to be an autopsy, but they think she might have had an undiagnosed heart condition, myopathy . . . something, anyway the Ventolin was the worst thing they could have given her. But they weren't to know. And there was nothing they could do.'

'That's ridiculous, of course there's something they can do. She has the flu!' Lexie almost yelled, hysteria creeping into her voice. Scott came into the room. 'Tell them, Tom, tell them they have to do everything they possibly can –'

'It's too late, Lexie.'

Her whole body began to shake violently. She felt Scott's arms around her, supporting her, as he took the phone from her hand. She leaned heavily into him, breathing hard.

'Christ, Tom, I can't believe it. I'm so sorry,' she heard him say after a while. It was real then, she hadn't imagined it. The knot in her chest exploded and she began to sob. Scott tried to hold her up but she slithered down to the floor.

'Yeah, of course, Tom, I'll make the calls,' he was saying, as he crouched down, rubbing Lexie's shoulder. 'Just let us know anything we can do, call any time of the day or night, it doesn't matter.'

'Catherine, are you there?' Rachel asked.

She swallowed. 'Yes, yes, I'm here . . . only . . .' She couldn't talk right now, there was a good chance she was going to be sick. 'Can I call you back?'

'Oh . . . okay.'

Catherine could hear the confusion in Rachel's voice, but she couldn't do anything about that right now. She hurried to the bathroom and quickly checked she was alone before locking herself in a stall and promptly throwing up. She flushed the toilet and walked back out to the bank of basins. She turned on a tap and splashed water repeatedly onto her face. Her hair was held back in a neat chignon but this was going to ruin her makeup. She pulled out a paper towel and dabbed carefully at her face. Not too bad, she should be able to touch it up and no one would be any the wiser.

She took a couple of calming breaths, centring herself the way she'd learned at the health spa last year. Then she walked sedately back to her office and sat down at her desk.

Okay, so people don't just die from the flu, there was obviously some malpractice on the hospital's part. Catherine turned over to a clean page in her notebook and began to write down a series of questions, then she reached for a loose sheet of paper and listed the relevant authorities she would need to contact. She pressed the button on her intercom, summoning her assistant to the door.

Catherine held up the piece of paper. 'Get me these names and numbers, ASAP thanks, Brooke.'

Brooke came forwards to take the paper from Catherine, giving the list a cursory glance. 'Excuse me, Catherine, you are aware it's almost seven pm?'

'So? I told you we'd be working back this evening.'

'Of course,' said Brooke. 'It's just, this list, I don't expect you'd get through to any of them after business hours, they're mostly government departments.'

'Fine, I want to start on them first thing tomorrow.'

'You're in court at nine.'

Catherine breathed out. 'Thank you, Brooke, you can leave me to work out how I organise my time. Just please do as I ask without the commentary.'

'Of course,' she said, retreating.

'And close the door behind you,' Catherine added.

She reviewed what she had written so far, and jotted a few more notes. That was all she could do for now, until she had more information. Perhaps Rachel could fill in some blanks. She picked up the phone and dialled her number.

'Sorry about that,' Catherine said crisply when Rachel answered. 'I was in the middle of something, now I can give you my full attention.'

'Okay,' said Rachel, her voice flat.

'Have you spoken to Tom?'

'No, only Scott.'

'Scott?'

'Tom asked him to make the calls. Lexie was hysterical apparently.' There was a pause before she added, 'I think maybe I should go over there.'

'Of course, you should, that's a good idea. See what you can find out.'

'Pardon?'

'Oh, you know, the details,' said Catherine. 'I would come with you, but I can't get away right now.'

'It's seven o'clock, you can't leave work yet?'

'I'm in court tomorrow morning, Rachel, I can't just sail in there unprepared.'

'Sure . . .' There was a long pause before Rachel spoke again. 'I just don't understand how this could have happened,' she said vaguely.

'Don't worry, I intend to find out.'

Catherine was obviously the only one who could be counted

on to stay focused, get to the bottom of what had happened and instigate appropriate action.

As it turned out, there was nothing at the bottom.

The autopsy revealed that Annie had idiopathic dilated cardiomyopathy, a condition she would most likely have had most of her adult life. The flu had made her weak, and the Ventolin administered via a nebuliser produced a sinus arrhythmia in her heart, which went undetected because Annie was not on a heart monitor. This was not routine hospital procedure for inpatients placed on a nebuliser to treat obstructive airways disease. Ventolin was highly contraindicated when ventricular dysfunction was present, but Annie had never been diagnosed. Apparently the condition would have started to make its presence felt over the next decade, and there was a very high risk of serious, and probably fatal, heart failure in her fifties.

So there it was . . . a sequence of events, so ordinary and routine for anyone else but with such catastrophic consequences for Annie. It could not be undone, rectified, noted on the file so it wouldn't happen next time. There was not going to be a next time for Annie.

Catherine could do nothing to redress the fact of her friend's death, there was no group to support, no awareness to raise, she couldn't even buy a lousy ribbon to pin on her lapel. So instead she applied her considerable energies to the funeral. The family had already chosen the church and cemetery, but that was all they got to choose. She told Tom she would take care of everything, he didn't need to worry about a single detail. He had enough to deal with. As none of his family lived in Sydney they'd all had to stay over at the house – his parents, brother Peter from Melbourne, sister Holly from Newcastle with her husband and kids – so Catherine could only imagine the state the house was in by now. She'd hired a small but elite event organiser who would dispatch a troop of cleaners and caterers to arrive at the house the moment they left for the funeral. They were instructed to prepare simple, elegant canapés, nothing too rich, spicy or pretentious, and nothing hot – this was a wake, not a cocktail party.

The tone should be restrained and refined. And still wine only, sparkling was obviously not appropriate. Catherine then turned her attention to the funeral itself; she liaised with the undertakers and the minister over the order of service, designed the booklets and had them printed, selected music and readings, and booked a string quartet.

Then there were just the flowers to organise, and that was to be her pièce de résistance.

A magnificent hedge of gardenias graced the entire front boundary of Catherine and Martin's home in Queens Park. Over the years the hedge had been nurtured, coaxed, trained and pruned to Catherine's exacting instructions, resulting in a spectacular display of fragrant blossoms every spring. Catherine insisted Annie had a special fondness for gardenias, as she had never failed to comment on the hedge when it was in bloom. Of course she did, it was breathtaking, anyone would comment, not least Annie, who had been known to make kind comments about the sad old pot plants stuck out on Rachel's balcony.

Nonetheless, Catherine arranged to have the entire twenty metres of hedge harvested at dawn on the morning of the funeral, to avoid wilt and discolouration. The blooms were then transported by refrigerated van to a team of waiting florists who worked for several hours to assemble the casket cover, whereupon the same refrigerated van delivered it to the funeral parlour, accompanied by three of the florists, who proceeded to install the delicate and elaborate arrangement into place.

When Catherine left the house later that day for the funeral, the sight of the stripped gardenia hedge had stopped her momentarily in her tracks. It was so bare, like a shaved head. Her public expression of grief.

The result was stunning, the gardenias forming a lacy tablecloth which draped over the entire surface of the coffin. If *Vogue* did a Funeral issue, it would have made the cover.

But somehow the whole thing felt wrong to Rachel. Not that it wasn't perfectly orchestrated down to every last detail – so very Catherine, just not so very much Annie. Lexie had been in such a heightened state of distress all week she had been no use at all, so Rachel had been commandeered into helping Catherine, or rather, following her orders to the letter. She could see it was getting out of hand, and she should have said something, but she didn't really have the wherewithal to take on Catherine right now. She had been in a kind of daze ever since Scott had phoned that night, operating on automatic pilot. It hadn't hit her yet, she decided. She hadn't cried, so surely it just hadn't hit her.

She thought it would at the funeral, but it didn't feel like a memorial to Annie's life, it was Catherine throwing an extravagant party with Annie as the guest of honour. And she certainly was that. The church was packed, which was to be expected when someone died so young, but Annie had always had a way of drawing people to her. She was on first-name basis with local shopkeepers; she struck up conversations with taxi drivers and delivery men and charity collectors, and she had been a regular volunteer at the girls' schools over the years. It seemed as though anyone and everyone who had ever crossed paths with Annie had come to pay their respects. People would say it was a good turnout; they would say – because what else could you say – that it was a lovely service.

But Rachel's heart ached for Tom and Sophie and Hannah, sitting there bewildered in the middle of it all. The girls were clutching simple bouquets of flowers from their garden, flowers their mother had grown, but they didn't dare place them anywhere near the casket to risk spoiling the effect.

Even back at the house any sense of Annie had been stifled, yet the house had always been all Annie – relaxed and inviting, and a little quirky, much like its owner. Every stick of furniture, every item on display, had some history, whether inherited, received as a gift, or even salvaged from a pile on clean-up day. Rachel's flat had been similarly furnished with other people's cast-offs, but Annie had had a knack of throwing it all together. Catherine had begged to differ, remarking aside to Rachel once that tossing a couple of stones and shells collected on a walk into a bowl did not make one an interior designer.

But today the house resembled a film set. Catherine's team had moved furniture to make more room, hidden away all personal items and effects, and instead placed formal floral arrangements on every available surface, alongside large framed photographs of Annie. Her lovely old scrubbed pine kitchen table was concealed under a starched white linen cloth, and her eclectic, eccentric collection of chairs was out of sight, except for a couple of matching ones that must have been deemed acceptable. The intention was clearly that no one was to be sitting around getting too comfortable, but Annie had only ever wanted people to be comfortable in her home.

Much of the time Rachel spent propping up Lexie, who was so fragile she kept dissolving into tears. She had finally turned to Rachel and said in a small voice, 'I don't think I can stay any longer. Do you think anyone will mind? I just need to be with my kids.' Rachel assured her that no one would mind, and Scott was relieved to be able to get her out of there.

The hired help seemed to have everything under control, so Rachel circulated amongst the relatives and family friends she had met on occasion over the years. Tom's parents told her how after the 'dreadful call' they had driven through the night to get to him. They'd left in such a rush they had to contact neighbours the next day to check on their pets, and his mother had to go out and buy a dress for the funeral because she hadn't packed anything suitable. 'You don't actually think straight at a time like that,' she confided to Rachel. They were leaving straight after the wake, dropping Pete at the airport, and then breaking the trip overnight at Holly's. They were anxious to get back home and set up everything nice for Tom and the girls, who were following in a day or two.

Catherine ranged around the place, wineglass in hand, casting her scrupulous eye over the proceedings, hissing orders at the wait staff. As afternoon approached evening, people began to take their leave, and when Rachel saw Tom hugging his parents at the door, she wondered if she ought not go too. But she hesitated; she hadn't really had a chance to talk to him, or the girls; in fact, it occurred to her she hadn't even laid eyes on Hannah or Sophie for some time. She did a quick survey around the living room and was about to check out back when Catherine stopped her in the kitchen.

'Are you after a drink?' she asked, waving a bottle.

Rachel detected a slight slurring of her speech. 'No, I'm right for now, thanks, Catherine. I was just looking for the girls, to say goodbye.' She peered through the flyscreen door out to the garden. 'Is Alice with them, do you know?'

Catherine shook her head. 'I sent her home with Martin a while ago,' she said, filling her glass. 'I think it was all getting a bit much for her, she's never had anyone this close die before.'

If Rachel was not mistaken, Catherine's eyes had misted over. But then she blinked rapidly and drank down half her glass.

'You did a great job today, Catherine,' said Rachel.

'Do you think so?' She looked vaguely anxious. 'I worried I'd gone a little overboard, but I just wanted it to be perfect for Tom. And the girls,' she added quickly.

'I'm sure they appreciated it.' Rachel watched her drain the rest of her glass. 'How are you getting home?'

'I'll call Martin when I'm ready, or else I'll get a cab.'

'Do you want to share one?' Rachel suggested, thinking perhaps the biggest favour she could do for Tom might be to make sure Catherine went home.

But she shook her head. 'No, you go ahead, I've still got things to finish up here.'

'Do you need a hand?'

'No, no, it's all under control,' she said, topping up her glass again.

'Ms Rourke.'

They both turned towards the door where one of the wait staff was standing.

'The bulk of the guests have left, or are preparing to. Is it all right to start packing up our equipment?'

'Well that depends,' Catherine said sharply.

'I'll leave you to it,' said Rachel, slipping out of the line of fire and back into the living room. An informal queue was snaking towards the front door where Tom was pretty well ensconced farewelling his guests. She definitely had time to seek out the girls, and the last place she decided they could be was up in their rooms, unless they'd fled the house, which might have been tempting but was unlikely nonetheless. The layout of Tom and

Annie's house would have mirrored Scott and Lexie's, but the previous owners had done the kind of renovation Lexie could only dream about, giving them a master bedroom and a study/music room on the ground floor, so they could turn upstairs over to the girls. When Rachel arrived at the landing at the top of the stairs, Hannah's door was wide open, but the room was empty. Sophie's door was closed, so Rachel knocked.

'Who is it?'

'It's Rachel.'

There was a pause before she heard Hannah announce, 'You can come in.'

Rachel opened the door tentatively. Sophie was sprawled on the bed, her feet up the wall, while Hannah had arranged a nest for herself out of pillows and cushions on the floor. Although she smiled up at Rachel, her eyes were red and swollen.

'We're hiding out,' she said.

'So I see,' said Rachel, leaning against the doorjamb.

Hannah screwed up her face. 'My head hurts from everyone patting it all the time.'

'I can't stand how they stare at you,' said Sophie. 'They're like people who slow down to look at an accident. What exactly are they hoping to see?'

Rachel decided they probably didn't want her gawking at them either. 'Well, I didn't mean to interrupt. I won't tell anyone you're here.'

'It's okay,' said Hannah. 'You can stay if you want.'

'Are you sure?' Rachel glanced over at Sophie.

She shrugged. 'As long as you don't say anything lame.'

'It's a deal,' said Rachel.

Once the caterers had packed all the equipment into their van, Catherine supervised the placement of the furniture back the way it had been. There were only a few stragglers left, colleagues of Tom's, she gathered, standing out front smoking cigarettes and finishing their beers. Catherine was biding her time, waiting for them to leave. She had barely said two words to Tom all day; she was looking forward to having a quiet drink with him, to see how he was holding up, make sure he was pleased with the way everything had gone today.

She was pouring herself another glass of wine when Tom appeared in the entrance to the kitchen. 'There you are,' he said.

Finally. She smiled her funeral smile, subdued but consoling, the kind of smile one had to master in family law. 'You poor man, you haven't had a moment to yourself all day,' she said. 'Let me get you a glass.'

But he was shaking his head. 'No thanks, Catherine, I'm beat. Listen, Dave has just offered to give you a lift home.'

Catherine took a moment to process that and prepare her response. 'Oh, that's okay, Tom, I need to finish up with the caterers.'

'They've just left,' he said.

'Pardon?' she blinked.

'I told them they could go.'

'Well have they put everything back the way it was? They were under strict instructions –'

'All the furniture is back in place,' he assured her.

'But I had them move some things out to the garage, the extra chairs and –'

'It's okay, I'll get them later, tomorrow.'

'And there's all your things, ornaments . . .'

'The girls will take care of that, they know how everything was,' said Tom. 'Honestly Catherine, you've done more than enough. I don't know how to thank you.'

But she did. 'Have a drink with me,' she suggested.

He smiled awkwardly. 'Thing is, I think Dave might want to get going.'

'That's fine, I can make my own way home, Tom.'

His eyes flickered to the glass in her hand. 'That's probably not a good idea, Catherine.'

'No, I mean I can get a cab.' She paused, frowning. 'When did Rachel leave anyway? She didn't say goodbye.'

'I'm not sure,' he shrugged.

Dave appeared behind him then, rattling his keys. 'Hey Cath, ready to hit the road?'

She was getting pissed off now. No one called her Cath, and

she did not like to be handled. 'Are you sure you're going to be all right alone?' she asked Tom.

'I've got the girls,' he reminded her. 'I think we need some time together, just the three of us.'

That was that then, he'd played his trump card, she could hardly force the issue now.

'Of course,' she said, restoring her composure. 'That's exactly what you need to do, Tom, we'll get right out of your way.' She finished off what was left in her glass as she walked across the kitchen, rinsed it in the sink and upturned it onto the draining board. 'I'll just get my things,' she said to Dave.

'The flowers were so pretty,' Hannah sighed. 'There must've been like a million.'

'There wasn't anything like a *million*, Han,' Sophie refuted.

Eventually Sophie had slid down off the bed to join Rachel and Hannah on the floor. They were both bright, confident girls, though quite different in many ways. To look at especially; Hannah's hair was a riot of honey-coloured curls, while Sophie had the fine, straight, white-blonde hair of her mother. Hannah was bubbly and outgoing and wore her heart on her sleeve. She was much more like Tom, whereas Sophie had a certain level of reserve; not that she couldn't be outspoken, but sometimes Rachel wondered just what was going on in her head.

'Well, there were a lot of flowers anyway,' Hannah was saying. 'But why did they put them in the grave? They just would've got covered up with dirt and then they would've all died.'

'What were we going to do with them?' Sophie asked her sister.

'Maybe we could have laid them over Mum's piano,' Hannah suggested.

'Mor*bid*,' Sophie declared. 'Besides, haven't you noticed all the flowers downstairs? I'm totally flowered out.'

'Gardenias don't last very long anyway, Han,' said Rachel. 'They go brown really quickly, especially if they're handled too much. So in a way, they were perfect for . . . you know, a one-off occasion.' Bugger. She could have put that better.

'You know why we buried her, Rachel?' Sophie said suddenly.

It sounded like a rhetorical question, or at least one she didn't expect Rachel to answer, which was just as well because Rachel didn't have a clue what to say to that.

'Dad thought we wouldn't handle seeing her cremated,' Sophie went on. 'But I think Mum would have chosen to be cremated.'

Rachel paused, glancing at Hannah. She wasn't sure how to respond to that. 'Had she ever said anything to you?'

Sophie shook her head. 'Of course not. She didn't know she was going to die.' She rolled over onto her stomach, propping her chin with her hands and looking squarely at Rachel. 'Dad wanted us to have somewhere we could visit Mum, but I think it would have been against her beliefs.'

'What do you mean?' asked Rachel.

'Well, I'm sure she would have gone with the most environmentally friendly option, and scattered ashes would have virtually nil impact on the environment.'

Sophie had been a mainstay of the debating team throughout high school, she knew how to mount an argument.

'Though I guess those incinerators couldn't be all that good for global warming . . .' Sophie paused, thinking. 'Maybe she would have preferred to donate her body to science.'

Rachel glanced at Hannah; her lip was trembling and she was beginning to look a little dismayed. This didn't seem to be an appropriate topic for conversation right now, but on the other hand, if Sophie needed to talk about it, it wasn't Rachel's place to stop her. Then again, maybe Hannah shouldn't have to listen . . .

The door opened suddenly and Tom appeared. Thank God.

'Thank God, everyone's gone!' he announced as he strode into the room and fell backwards onto Sophie's bed. Hannah leaped straight up off the floor and clambered up next to him, snuggling into his outstretched arm and burying her face in his neck.

'Okay, that's my cue,' said Rachel, getting up.

'No, no, Rach, I didn't mean you,' Tom protested. 'You're not everyone.'

'Still, I'll leave you guys to it.'

'Wait just a sec,' said Tom. He stroked Hannah's hair. 'Hey Hannah-pie?'

She lifted her face. She looked sleepy more than teary, Rachel was relieved to note.

'I'm just going to talk to Rachel for a minute, okay?'

'Sure Dad,' she said, shifting out of his way.

'It's okay, Tom,' said Rachel. 'I can see myself out.'

He ignored that. 'I'll be right back, girls.' He ushered Rachel out onto the landing, pulling the door to. 'Do you really have to go?'

She hesitated. 'Well . . . no, but I think I should, Tom. The girls might need some time with you,' she said. 'Sophie's coming out with some strange stuff, and I'm not sure how Hannah's taking it.'

He listened, nodding faintly. 'Okay, I'll talk to them, but they're going to crash any minute,' he said. 'They're both beyond exhausted.'

'You must be too,' said Rachel.

'Yeah, but I haven't been sleeping that well,' he shrugged. 'And I'm going to need to wind down from today.' He looked at her directly. 'Would it be too much to ask for you to hang around till I get them settled?'

Rachel didn't know what to say.

'Please, Rach,' he added. 'I don't think I can face being alone right now.'

'Of course,' she assured him. 'Whatever you need, Tom. But take your time with the girls, okay? Don't rush them. I'll be here.'

'Thanks, I appreciate it.'

She headed downstairs to the kitchen. The furniture was back in place, but everything looked a little bare. She carried the two chairs in from the hall and placed them either side of the table, then she went to inspect the contents of the fridge. She found an open bottle of wine and took it over to the sink, where a solitary glass stood draining. Rachel gave it a quick rinse under the tap and poured herself a glass of wine. She gazed out the window into the dwindling light and Annie's garden. At least the hired help had left that alone. Rachel wandered over to the screen door and pushed it open, it squeaked as she stepped outside.

There was nothing restrained or formal about the garden, in fact it rather ran riot. Plants had to be hardy this close to the ocean to survive, so there were rosemary and lavender bushes, seaside daisies, some pretty funky-looking cacti, and here and there a quirky little statue peered out from behind the foliage: fairies and goblins and gnomes, put there when the girls were little.

At least half an hour must have passed before Rachel heard Tom moving around in the kitchen. She came to the back door.

'No, stay out there,' he said. 'I'm just gathering supplies.'

'Are the girls okay?'

'Yeah, Hannah was asleep as soon as her head hit the pillow.' He took a couple of glasses from an overhead cupboard and turned around to look at her. 'When I went back in to check on Soph, she was plugged into her iPod. I took the hint. They haven't had a minute to themselves the whole week, and Sophie likes her privacy.'

Rachel nodded. 'Do you want a hand there?'

'Nuh, coming now.'

She held the door open as Tom walked through, his arms laden with bags of chips, a bottle of Scotch, glasses and an ice bucket. He set it all down on the outdoor table.

'Let's get drunk,' he said.

Rachel eyed him dubiously.

'Don't give me that look, not you, Rach,' he sighed, dropping into a chair. 'All day, the "looks" I've been getting, you have no idea.'

'Sophie said something about that.'

'If I cry, people are uncomfortable; if I smile, they're uncomfortable. I spent the day contorting my expression into what I thought people could cope with. It's exhausting.'

'You didn't have to do that, Tom.'

'Oh, but I did. I have a responsibility to everyone to grieve the way they want me to grieve.'

Rachel watched him loosen his tie and undo the top button of his shirt. 'I haven't cried,' she said suddenly.

He glanced at her. 'I won't hold it against you.'

'But you know I thought the world of Annie, and Lexie can't stop crying. What's wrong with me?'

'Nothing,' said Tom. 'That's exactly what I was trying to say. There are these expectations about how you're supposed to grieve.'

'I never seem to get it right,' Rachel shook her head. 'I have a terrible tendency to laugh when I hear something really sad, or tragic, or serious, or just at totally inappropriate times. It's so embarrassing.'

Tom was smiling at her. 'Like at your wedding.'

'Oh no, don't bring that up,' she protested, covering her face.

It was possibly the worst thing Rachel had ever done. Poor Sean struggled valiantly through vows he had written himself, while she struggled just as valiantly, though with less success, to suppress the fit of giggles that had seized her. Half the congregation were shocked and dismayed at the bride's lack of composure, the other half were too busy trying to contain their own laughter.

'See, I'm a terrible person.'

'You're not a terrible person, Rach. They were pretty lame vows.'

'Oh, come on, at least he tried, God love him.'

'Whereas you, you had nothing,' said Tom.

'Don't remind me,' Rachel groaned.

'I never got to ask you what happened back then. Did you go blank or something?'

'No. Apparently Catherine put it on my to-do list, but I didn't see it, or I forgot . . .'

'You forgot to write your wedding vows?'

'I thought they told you what to say,' she defended. 'Why else do you have the guy with the robes if you've got to do it all yourself?'

Tom smiled, gazing at her across the table.

'What?' she asked.

He shook his head. 'I'm just glad you're here. Thanks for staying, Rach.'

'Don't mention it.'

He picked up the bottle of Scotch. 'So, are you going to help me drown my sorrows?'

He was almost too pretty for a man, was Tom. He had big, crystal-cut blue eyes framed with thick curled lashes, high cheekbones, bowed lips, and caramel hair tipped with blond that looked like it had been done by a professional, but Annie insisted he never stepped foot in a hairdresser's, she cut his hair. He'd always had good hair; he wore it longer at uni, surfie-style, his shoulder-length locks bleached bright blond by the sun and sea. Had all the girls drooling over him. Had all the girls, period.

But for some reason he had taken a seat right next to Rachel in their first lecture, their very first day of first-year Law. She probably looked safe, ordinary, non-threatening, despite the fact that she was desperately trying to look ever so cool and like she absolutely belonged there. How anyone thought they could pull that off in first year, Rachel had no idea. But that was the whole thing. She had no idea.

'Hi, I'm Tom,' he'd said as he dropped into the chair. He reminded her of a big friendly puppy.

'Rachel,' she nodded.

'Where are you from, Rachel?'

She was living in college because she didn't have any choice. But she was determined to find an alternative, especially before the end of semester, so her parents couldn't drag her over to London or Madrid in the break.

However, she wasn't going to admit to this guy that she lived in college, it didn't exactly fit with the image she was trying so hard to project. So she just said, 'I'm a local.'

'Cool. I've come down from Crescent Head, do you know it? Up the north coast? So I'm living in college and it sucks. If you hear of anyone looking to share a place . . .'

And that's how she and Tom and a procession of housemates came to share a sprawling old Californian bungalow on the somewhat whimsically named Rainbow Street, for the next two and a bit years, until Rachel dropped out and took off overseas. Tom was the only one who understood at the time. Her parents shook their heads as they wrote their cheques, writing cheques being pretty much the extent of their parenting, and of far greater use to Rachel than any discipline or advice they might have cared to administer. And Catherine thought she was plain mad, throwing away two whole years of a law degree. Not quite two years, Rachel reminded her. She had failed yet another subject, so she was falling further behind. 'That means you'll be taking a lot of classes with me,' Catherine pointed out. She was a year behind Rachel and Tom, but gaining fast. Giving birth to Alice in her

HSC year had created a momentary setback, but setbacks were only ever momentary in Catherine's life, whereas they had a tendency to completely derail Rachel's. She sometimes had the feeling her whole life thus far was one big setback.

Catherine maintained that Rachel had wasted too many years travelling, and that's why she was where she was today. Which was nowhere, in Catherine's estimation. But travelling had suited Rachel; the incredible freedom of drifting from place to place without a plan, finding somewhere to stay for a night, then staying for a month. Or six. And moving on when she felt like it. She had never been happier, except for that brief period at Rainbow Street, and that was a big part of the reason she left. She knew it couldn't last, so she didn't want to get too used to it, too attached, only to watch it inevitably dissolve around her.

By the time she returned from overseas there was no more share house. Everyone had moved on, graduated from uni and into adult life. Catherine was forging ahead with her career and had already managed to fit in a brief marriage and divorce. She had insisted that Rachel be back in time for her second wedding. And Tom was thoroughly settled with a wife and two kids. Rachel suddenly had the urge to catch up to her friends, to settle too, whatever that meant. Perhaps it was time to make a home for herself. That was right about when Sean came along, so she settled for him.

'So, shall we drink to Annie?' said Tom, raising his glass.

'Of course,' said Rachel.

He clinked his glass against hers and they drank, though as the Scotch hit the back of her throat she gasped a little, just managing to swallow it down before she had to cough.

'Are you right there?' Tom asked.

'Just not so used to spirits,' she croaked, clearing her throat again.

'Me either. But this is pretty smooth stuff.' He turned the bottle to check the label. 'Clients give it to me. I keep it for special occasions,' he added, shaking his head ruefully.

Rachel looked at him. 'Well, you got through today,' she said. 'That was no mean feat. And Catherine certainly didn't help.'

He frowned. 'Yes, she did, of course she did.'

Rachel winced. 'I know that, I just . . .' God, she sounded like a bitch. 'I only meant, well, I know what Catherine's like, better than anyone, and I should have reined her in –'

'Hey,' he interrupted her, 'she's not your responsibility. Besides, I'm grateful to her. I realise today wasn't very "Annie", but I wasn't up to organising it,' he went on. 'Let's face it, the only person who'd be able to pull off an Annie-style funeral would be Annie herself.'

He had a point. 'Surely the girls would have liked to have some input?' said Rachel.

'I think they're still in shock, Rach. Perhaps after a while . . .'

She thought about it. 'So maybe you can plan your own memorial, say, in a year's time, just the three of you.'

He was staring out into the garden. 'How are we ever going to get through a year?' he said quietly.

'One day at a time, isn't that what they say?' said Rachel, before wincing again. 'Sorry, I should be able to do better than that cliché.'

'No, all the clichés work,' he assured her. 'It really is like a bad dream, and I do keep thinking she's going to walk through the door any minute. Or that I'll come home and she'll be sitting at the piano with one of her students . . . and everything'll be back to normal. But nothing's going to be normal ever again.'

Rachel watched him staring into space, his eyes glassy. 'You didn't have any warning, nothing to prepare you for this. If you'd known about the condition, or she'd been sick for longer, you'd have had time to get used to the idea.'

'How could I wish Annie had suffered so we could get used to losing her? That doesn't seem right.' Tom shook his head. 'No, I've been thinking about this a lot, and I'm pretty sure this is the way Annie would have wanted it.'

'What do you mean?'

'You know what she was like, she believed in destiny, fate, all that new-agey crap.'

'I take it you didn't share those beliefs?' Rachel said wryly.

He smiled then. 'Not really, but whatever, if this had happened to someone else, she'd have had a whole lot to say about how it was "meant to be", that the person was never destined for long on this planet. All that. The worst part for her would have been leaving the girls without a mother. But worse than that even would have been the idea of putting them through years and years with a sick or dying mother. It would have broken her heart to do that to them.'

Rachel thought about it. He was right. Annie was totally devoted to those girls, they were her life.

'So you see,' Tom went on, 'if she was meant to die young, this is how she would have wanted it – no dramatic build-up, no lingering. Get it over with, and then get on with it,' he said plainly. 'Except she's not here to show us how to do that.'

'You'll figure it out.'

He was shaking his head. 'I just don't know if I'm up to it. It's so hard, Rach, too hard. It's crushing.'

Rachel's stomach began to churn, what was he suggesting? That life wasn't worth living now?

'Can I tell you something I haven't told anyone?' he said.

She swallowed. She didn't really want him to, but she could hardly say no under the circumstances. 'Sure,' she said, before taking another gulp of Scotch.

'What I'd really like to do is just go away,' Tom said plainly, 'somewhere no one knows us, and start all over. Not have to explain, no one would have to know about Annie. Then I wouldn't have to be the dutiful widower.'

Was this all about finding another woman?

'No one expects you to be a monk, Tom,' Rachel said awkwardly.

'No, that's not what I'm talking about,' he shook his head. 'Sorry, I'm not explaining myself very well. The thing is, I'm suddenly a widower. I didn't ask for the role, I wasn't prepared for it, I'd never even considered it, but now I don't have a choice. I've been sentenced to some arbitrary period of misery, of people feeling sorry for me, feeling uncomfortable around me, not knowing what to say. And I don't know either. My life has changed forever and I don't know how to live it any more.'

'It's still your life, Tom,' said Rachel. 'Go away if that's what you need to do.'

'But it's not just my life, that's the thing, it's the girls' as well,'

Tom reminded her. 'And I can't do that to them. They've lost their mother, they're going to need security, and continuity, so everything else is going to have to stay the same.' He glanced at her. 'I'm worried about Soph.'

Rachel nodded. She could see why, if the conversation upstairs was anything to go by. 'Does she have any contact with her father?' she asked tentatively.

Tom looked wounded. 'I'm her father, Rach.'

'Of course, I'm sorry, I didn't mean –'

'I know, but that's the very reason I'm worried about her.' He drained his glass, setting it down on the table. 'She's going to feel like the odd one out now, she doesn't even have the same surname as me and Hannah. That's just the kind of thing Sophie will obsess about.'

Annie hadn't changed her surname when they married, so she had certainly seen no reason to change Sophie's, who was nearly two when she and Tom met. When Hannah was born, it had seemed only fair to give her Tom's surname, and though they had decided it was the perfect time for Tom to formally adopt Sophie, she and Annie remained Veitches, while Tom and Hannah were Macklins. They could never have anticipated a reason to do otherwise.

'She knows where she belongs, Tom,' said Rachel.

'I hope so, she can be hard to read.'

'She's a sixteen-year-old girl, doesn't that make her illegible?' Rachel suggested.

Tom smiled faintly, shaking his head. 'It's such a bad age to lose her mum.' He looked at Rachel. 'You'd know all about that.'

'It's a little different, Tom, my mother's alive, she just doesn't seem to know I am.' She gave him a lame smile. 'Annie has given those girls the most amazing foundation, she was ten times the mother my mother could dream of being.'

'Yeah, she was,' he said wistfully. 'I was in awe of her when we first met, the way she was with Sophie. I think that's why I fell in love with her. She was so patient, and loving, and she was all on her own. Her parents wouldn't have anything to do with her.'

'Did they show up today?' Rachel asked.

He shook his head. 'Didn't even respond to my messages. They believe she's going to hell, you know.'

'Tom –'

'It's true, Rach,' he insisted. 'Fucking fundamentalist freaks. It used to make me so angry, but Annie was never resentful. She said it'd be bad for the girls. So in her heart she forgave them, even if she couldn't understand them, even if it still hurt her so much . . .'

His voice broke then, and he pressed his fingers to his eyes, dropping his head. Rachel didn't know what to say, though perhaps it was better not to say anything, just give him a moment.

Eventually he sat up straight again, clearing his throat and reaching for the bottle. He tilted it towards Rachel, but she shook her head. 'I thought you were going to get drunk with me?'

'I'm still on this one,' she protested, picking up her glass and taking another sip. That went down a little easier. She looked at him. 'You know, Tom, time will heal.' She groaned, slapping her forehead. 'There I go again, where are all these clichés coming from?'

'You do seem to have a certain flair for them,' he observed.

'What can I say? Lack of originality has always been one of my strengths,' she said.

He grinned then. 'Okay, what else have you got? Give me your best.'

Rachel drummed on the tabletop with her fingers. 'Hmm . . . let me think. Well, you've already covered "It was meant to be." What about "Things always happen for a reason"?'

'Got that today,' he nodded, 'a few times. Along with "Something good will come of this."'

'I hope someone told you "You have to keep busy"?' she asked.

'Oh, they did, repeatedly.'

'You're still young –'

'I have my whole life ahead of me,' said Tom, raising his glass and taking a drink.

'Think of all you have to be thankful for,' Rachel added.

'At least she didn't suffer.'

'She was too good for this world.'

'Life goes on.'

'Life is short.'

'Ah, best one I heard,' said Tom, sitting forwards, 'was from this woman, I'd never met her before, I think she said she worked in a health-food shop, or an organic co-op, some place. You know how Annie made friends with everyone, the further off beam the better.' He gave a wry smile. 'Anyway, what was her name? Skye . . . or Summer, something like that. Do you know her?'

Rachel shrugged. 'I don't think so.'

'Anyhow, she got me aside and she launched into this whole extended analogy about grief being like an anchor that will keep me in the same place, while I need to rest and take stock, which is okay for a time, but that when I'm ready I shouldn't be afraid to bring it up to the surface and take it on board, because then it will free me, and I can move on, and go where the tide takes me, or steer my own course, maybe into another safe harbour . . .'

They looked at each other, and then Rachel couldn't help it, her inappropriate-reaction button activated, and though she tried to suppress it, laughter gurgled up through her chest and escaped, unfortunately via her nose first, in the form of a kind of convulsive snort. She tried to cup her mouth and nose with her hand, as if that would stop the deluge. But it was no use. And then Tom started to laugh, openly and loudly, and Rachel gave up, laughing along with him. And the laughter kept coming, in great rolling waves. And every time it subsided they caught one another's eye and burst into peals of fresh laughter all over again. Rachel laughed until her sides ached and her face was wet with tears.

Finally Tom let out a loud sigh, wiping his eyes with the heels of his hands. 'I haven't laughed like that in ages.' He paused and looked across at her. 'Thanks, Rach.'

'Any time,' she said. Then she had a thought. 'In fact,' she added, leaning forwards on the table, 'really, any time you want to have a laugh . . .'

'What are you saying?'

'I'm not good for much,' said Rachel. 'I can't organise things like Catherine does, and I can't cook, or whatever Lexie's doing for you.'

'Cooking,' he confirmed. 'Casseroles and cakes. Coming out of our ears.'

'Okay, I'll make you a deal,' she said. 'When it's all getting too much and you want to have a break from being the grieving widower, call me, or come over, whatever. I'll be at your disposal.'

Tom was listening intently.

'You can laugh, tell stupid jokes, get drunk, be totally inappropriate. Whatever you want. I won't tell anyone.'

A smile slowly formed on his face. 'I'm going to hold you to this, young lady,' he said.

'That's the idea.'

Rachel paced herself much better than Tom, and after he had consumed the best part of half the bottle of Scotch, he stopped making any sense at all and his eyes were struggling to stay open. It took some convincing, but she finally talked him into calling it a night. Getting him inside and into bed was a little more challenging. Just getting him upright was a feat in itself, and he had no hope of walking in anything like a straight line. He leaned heavily on Rachel, and he was not a slight man; lucky for her she wasn't a slight woman.

When they got to his room, he fell forwards onto the bed before she could stop him.

'Tom, roll over,' she said. 'You can't sleep like that.'

He grunted in reply but didn't budge. Rachel kneeled up on the bed beside him and heaved on his shoulder to turn him over. He groaned. She hoped he wasn't going to throw up, that'd be stretching the friendship. She leaned over him and started to unravel his tie.

He opened one eye. 'What are you doing?'

'I don't want you to choke in your sleep.'

He sighed heavily, patting her leg. 'I love you, Rachel. Have I ever told you that?'

'Yes, you have,' she said, lifting his head to slide his tie out. She tossed it aside and started to undo the buttons on his shirt.

'I've always loved you, Rachel.'

'Mm.'

'We used to be best friends, what happened?'

'I left the country and you found your soul mate.'

'Oh yeah.'

She undid the buttons on the cuff of his sleeves and then started on his belt buckle.

'Rachel, are you going to have your way with me?'

She laughed. 'I don't think you'd be up to it, Tommy boy.'

He smiled, his eyes closed, as she tugged to loosen the belt.

'Be gentle,' he sighed.

Rachel removed his belt and stepped back onto the floor, crouching down to take off his shoes. This was not the first time she'd had to perform this particular service for Tom, though it had been a while. Back at Rainbow Street it had been a semi-regular occurrence, getting Tom into bed after a big night; but then, he'd been known to do the same for her on occasion. She peeled off his socks and tossed them aside, straightening up again to look down at him. His eyes were closed, but he wasn't snoring yet. She probably should try and get his shirt off at least, make him more comfortable. She grabbed his wrists and pulled him up to sit, but he couldn't hold himself up, so Rachel quickly dropped to one knee as he slumped forwards, his head landing heavily on her shoulder. She eased his shirt down his back and then started to wrestle one arm out of its sleeve.

'Hey, Tom, can you work with me here?'

He bent his elbow and yanked his arm out and then Rachel was able to slide the shirt off the other arm and let it drop to the floor. And that's when she realised he was sobbing. He brought his arms around her, clinging to her. Rachel didn't move, her back was hurting and her leg was shoved awkwardly against the bed base, but she just held him, stroking his head from time to time, murmuring reassurance. Eventually his sobs subsided and he lurched back to lie flat on the bed.

'Fuck,' he sighed. 'I'm sorry.'

Rachel got up, a little stiff and creaky, and perched on the side of the bed. 'Are you okay?'

'I guess not.' He met her eyes then, taking hold of her hand. 'I'm sorry.'

'Would you shoosh already.'

'Rach,' he said. 'Can I ask you something?'

She squeezed his hand. 'Anything.'

He took a breath. 'Do you think you could stay?'

'Tom –'

'I'm not coming on to you, I just don't want to sleep alone, I hate it.'

'Tom,' she winced, 'I can't, not with the girls here, it wouldn't be appropriate.'

'I thought you and I didn't have to be appropriate?'

'Around the girls we do.'

He sighed, bringing his forearm up to rest on his forehead. 'I'm sorry.'

'Hey,' said Rachel. 'Would you stop saying that?'

He met her eyes again. 'I didn't mean to make you uncomfortable. It's just, the nights are the worst.'

Rachel thought about it. 'I tell you what, I'll stay till you fall asleep.'

'You will?'

She nodded. 'Sure, but you can take your own pants off, I've gone as far as I'm prepared to go.'

She got up and walked around the other side of the bed to the window, closing the blind and drawing the curtains. When she came back, Tom's trousers were on the floor and he was under the doona. He'd left space for her, and Rachel considered her options. She could lie next to him on top of the doona, but that seemed a little too ... besides, she was beginning to feel pretty tired, she didn't want to risk falling asleep. So she propped up the pillow and sat with her back against the bedhead. Tom nuzzled his head in next to her hip. 'Thanks Rach,' he said, his eyes closed.

'It's okay,' she said, resting her hand on his head and giving it a pat.

'We have a deal, right?' he murmured.

'Yes we do.'

Thirty seconds later he was snoring.

Rachel sat there for a while to make sure he was fully asleep, then she carefully eased off the bed and tiptoed out of the room. Out in the kitchen she rang for a taxi, then quickly tidied up, putting the bottle of Scotch out of sight, washing the glasses and popping them away in the cupboard. She didn't want to leave traces of their little party for the girls to see in the morning, and they were likely to be up well before their father tomorrow. She locked the back door and turned out the lights as she crept quietly back through the house. She stuck her head in Tom's room as she passed; he was snoring loudly now. Rachel closed his door, hoping he'd get the chance to sleep off the worst of it, that the girls wouldn't wake him. She briefly wondered whether she should leave them a note, but that might seem weird. It wasn't her place to tell them what to do.

She left through the front door, closing it as noiselessly as possible, then sat down on the front step to wait for the taxi. She felt empty. Sad, of course, but also quite an overwhelming emptiness. Maybe that's what you felt after the funeral of a close friend. She didn't know, she'd never lost anyone this close before.

She couldn't help wondering why it had to be Annie. Surely the world could get by without Rachel far more easily than it could get by without Annie. It's not as though she would ever top herself, but it occurred to her she wouldn't be all that missed if she did. Despite being their only child, her parents would hardly notice; after all, they didn't even live in the same hemisphere, hadn't for more than fifteen years. Not that that would stop her mother from creating a heart-rending anecdote to share at dinner parties, about the loss of her beloved only daughter.

No, Rachel would not be missed, not really. She had no husband, no kids. At work she was entirely dispensable. Annie had two daughters, and they had a close and loving relationship. And she and Tom were happy; they hadn't evolved into the stereotypical bickering couple who'd been together too long. They weren't sickening or lovey dovey either, thank God. They were just solid. Right together. Two halves, all that shit.

Not like her and Sean. He fitted neatly into the category of the 'nice guy' – easygoing, reliable and, in all honesty, a little bland. But he was just what Rachel needed right then. It was all very well wandering solo around the world, but back at home she didn't fit in with her friends. And she felt it. She couldn't hang out with Tom any more because he was part of a couple, and although she could hang out with Catherine, things had changed. She remembered being terribly hurt when she found out they'd all gone out to dinner together one night without inviting her.

Catherine had brushed it off by saying she didn't think Rachel would want to hang around with a bunch of married couples.

So that was that. She needed to find her other half. The story of how she met Sean was not particularly memorable; it was at a party of 'mutual friends', he asked for her number and called a few days later. Their subsequent date was pleasant and Rachel couldn't find any reason not to go out with him. So they became a couple, and got invited out to dinner with their couple friends, and generally fitted in. By the time Rachel realised that birds didn't suddenly appear every time he was near, they were already engaged. She couldn't let him and everybody else down by pulling out of the wedding. Rachel decided it would all turn out okay, she'd grow to love him, and if she didn't . . . well, she'd cross that bridge when she came to it.

The taxi turned into the street and Rachel jumped up to meet it at the kerb, waving madly. She didn't want the driver to sound the horn and disturb anyone. She climbed into the back and gave him her address, settling into the seat as he pulled off again.

As usual, Rachel's preferred strategy left much to be desired, and Sean was devastated when she sat him down one night after four pallid years, when she realised she had not in fact grown to love him but was instead beginning to loathe the very sight of him. But that wasn't his fault, he hadn't done anything wrong, so she just said something vague to the effect that it wasn't working. 'Is it the sex?' had been his first question. Why did guys jump to that straightaway? Reassured on that front, he moved on to 'What can I do to make you change your mind?' 'Can't we work it out?' 'Maybe we should have a baby?'

That was when Rachel fled. Why did people treat babies like some kind of glue to hold a relationship together? Sean was obviously not her other half, they were not a good fit, and no amount of glue was going to hold them together. And certainly not a baby.

Sean quickly got over his heartbreak. Two weeks later he was on the internet happily dating a line-up of willing women. He later told Rachel that breaking his heart was the best thing she could have done for him. 'Chicks dig it!'

Rachel got out of the taxi when it arrived at her block and

walked up the steep drive, and then up the three flights of stairs to her flat. She often wondered why she didn't have better legs considering the heights she had to scale just to get to her front door. As she let herself in, she noticed the light flashing on her answering machine, and she pressed it as she walked past it down the hall. There was a series of messages from Catherine, each more slurred than the last.

Where are you?
Where the fuck are you?
What the fuck are you doing out so late?

She would be unbearable if she found out that Tom had asked her to stay on after everyone had left. Catherine had always been a little jealous of their friendship. She'd had her eye on Tom when they were back at uni, but nothing had ever come of it. Catherine needed to believe that every second man was secretly attracted to her; could barely control himself around her, in fact. Despite appearances, she actually had quite a fragile ego. Rachel knew better than anyone how much the circumstances surrounding Alice's birth had knocked Catherine's confidence, but she would never admit it. Instead she just got pissed off when her flirtatious behaviour went unreciprocated, or worse, unnoticed and she had to find ways to rationalise it; ergo – Tom was not the kind of man who was going to be interested in a woman with a child. He was a good-time guy, he didn't want to settle down. Then Annie came along, with a child in tow, and Tom duly settled down. Rachel could still feel the steam coming off the pages of the letters Catherine had penned to her across the world.

Rachel knew it was not so much that Catherine couldn't get over Tom; she just couldn't get over why he'd passed her over in favour of someone like Annie. Annie had transferred to their university from the Conservatorium when she couldn't cut it there, according to Catherine. Actually, she didn't go back after Sophie was born because of the hours and lack of childcare. In her letters, Catherine had informed Rachel that though she was supposedly some kind of piano virtuoso, Annie became just a music teacher. In fact, she'd added, she didn't even get her Dip Ed, she only ever taught privately so she could be at the beck and call of her daughters. None of it had ever made a scrap of sense to Catherine.

Rachel checked the time; it was too late to call her back now, she'd have passed out long ago. She would wait till the morning to make up something to appease her, but now she was tired and she just wanted to go to bed. If she could find it. She had pulled nearly every item of clothing she owned out of her wardrobe this morning, trying to find the right thing. She usually gave what she wore only a passing thought, if that. But today was different. The standard all-black funeral option didn't feel right for Annie, who never wore black herself. She said it sucked the life out of people. There was a grim irony in there somewhere.

Rachel gathered the pile of clothes up in her arms, looking around for a clean bit of floor where she could dump them for now. God, this place was such a mess, she really needed to spend a weekend bringing back some order. It was just so hard to get motivated. Her flat was in an old building with a tight landlord, so 'rundown' didn't begin to describe it. But it was cheap. You got what you paid for, and if Rachel wanted to live near her friends, on her salary, then this was the best she was going to do. All her furniture was other people's cast-offs, some of it quite decent, particularly anything from Catherine. But nothing went together, there was no unifying theme, no style, probably because Rachel didn't really have any to speak of. And if you didn't have style, you at least needed money, and Rachel didn't have much of that to speak of, either. She had refused to take any kind of settlement from Sean when they split. She had come into the relationship with nothing, that was how she would leave it. He gave her a cheque anyway, because in the end he was still a good guy. It meant she could pay the bond on a flat and connect to all the services without asking her parents for help for once. Rachel didn't mind so much, she figured they owed her something, she just didn't like giving them opportunities to salve their consciences for never being there for her.

Both ambitious, workaholic lawyers, her parents split when Rachel was in her second year of high school. They told her later that they'd kept it together till then for her sake. But they hadn't kept anything together. Rachel understood the term 'cold war' long before she came across it in history class. Her childhood had been like living in the Arctic Circle, only chillier. Her parents couldn't stand living together, they could barely stand the sight of each other. Rachel felt like she'd been holding her breath her whole life, and when they finally broke the 'bad' news, she was able to breathe out with relief for the first time.

'So you're okay, darling?' her mother asked, bearing down on her, pushing her father out of the way.

'Yep,' Rachel replied. 'What happens now? Where am I going to live?'

For a brief, tantalising moment she had imagined herself holding court in her own apartment, with her parents taking turns to come and visit her. But she knew that was an impossible fantasy. She was only thirteen after all.

And so then the real fun began. The split marriage meant split parenting, which for Rachel meant being split down the middle. They pulled and tugged and fought over her like children with a stuffed toy who'd sooner see it torn into pieces than relinquish their claim. They even changed her name – she became Rachel Halliday-Holloway, which was embarrassing and unnecessary, but her mother insisted her own name be indelibly stamped onto her daughter's; she would have had it tattooed onto her if she could have gotten away with it. Rachel gradually adapted to living between the two warring camps, learning to tolerate her father's new girlfriend, and the one after, and the one after that, while avoiding her mother's incessant grilling about what went on there, with whom and how often. Rachel didn't understand her; the whole marriage she had spent wanting to get away from him, and now that she was, she was obsessed with his every move and overflowing with so much vitriolic spite she was like a snake perpetually ready to strike. It was exhausting. Rachel soon worked out there were two ways she could deal with the situation. Rebel outrageously and create more trouble for them than they'd know how to handle, or keep her head down, her mouth shut, and get through her school years, till she achieved independence at eighteen and wouldn't have to live with either of them, or keep both their names.

Rachel went with the latter option, largely due to Catherine's influence, it had to be said. Catherine had come to their school on a scholarship in Year 7 and she did not take it for granted. She valued the opportunity to rise above the socio-economic level she'd had the misfortune to be born into, as only Catherine could put it, even at the ripe old age of thirteen. Rachel thought her family seemed okay when she finally met them, but Catherine could barely disguise her embarrassment of them. She seriously contemplated the notion that there had been a mix-up in the hospital when she was born, so little did she feel in common with her 'birth family'. But it didn't matter, she maintained, she was headed way beyond their ordinary little life in their ordinary little suburb. She travelled an hour and a half to school and back every day, never complaining; in fact she never even mentioned it so as not to draw attention to the fact of where she did live. She did not want to be associated with the western suburbs; after all, she would not be there for long.

Rachel had never met anyone so disciplined at such a young age, and it certainly had an effect on her, at least back then. If she wanted her independence, albeit for vastly different reasons, she had to work for it. So she hung around with Catherine, and kept up her marks, which kept her parents off her back. All was relatively well until Year 11, when her father accepted a position in the UK and her mother went ballistic.

'What do you think of your precious father now, Rachel? Abandoning you when you're at such a vulnerable stage of your life? When you need him the most? I tried to tell him the effect this will have on you, your self-esteem, your body image, your general sense of worth as a human being. And as for your ability to trust men and have a chance at a healthy relationship in the future, well that's shot. I tried to tell him all this, but do you think he cared? Do you think he even listened? Of course not, because the truth is, and I hate to have to be the one to say this to you, darling, but your father doesn't care about anyone but himself. Duncan Halliday is the most important person in the world to Duncan Halliday.'

Then in Rachel's final year at school, her mother met Victor Castaneda, 'a successful business magnate', as she liked to tell everyone, and after a 'whirlwind romance' he asked her to come back to Spain with him. Suddenly her daughter's self-esteem and the rest were none of her concern. She packed Rachel off to the UK the day she finished her final exams, so her father could 'have a turn for a change'. Rachel was only permitted back in the country when her room was available in college, because her mother had leased out their apartment and moved permanently to Madrid. For the first time in her life Rachel didn't actually have a home to go to. Until she met up with Tom.

She felt a sensation in her chest, a tightening, creeping up into her throat. So here were the tears, finally. Though she wasn't sure if she was grieving for Annie, or grieving with Tom.

She thought about him now, everything he had ahead of him, not least a pretty horrendous hangover in the morning. She was glad she'd stayed tonight, she felt she'd given him some small comfort. She hoped so anyway. Rachel turned onto her side and the tears spilled onto her pillow. Maybe she was not completely dispensable.

The next day

'What are you doing here on a Saturday, Catherine?'

She looked up from her computer. Bill Carlton, one of the senior partners, was standing in the doorway to her office, watching her curiously.

'Probably the same thing you are, Bill,' she replied offhand.

He was shaking his head. 'I'm just calling in to pick up some papers I need for a breakfast meeting on Monday. I'll be teeing off within the hour.'

Catherine sat back in her chair. 'Are you saying you've never worked on a weekend?'

'Of course I've worked on a weekend, but usually in the privacy of my own home, and preferably in slippers.' He held her gaze for a moment longer before he shrugged, turning away. 'Don't work too hard,' he called as he walked off up the corridor.

Catherine pushed her chair back and swung her feet up onto the desk with a loaded sigh. She honestly couldn't say if that exchange had left a good impression or not. There seemed to be a fine line between being regarded as a hard worker or as a machine, and for women the line shifted constantly. She had a sense that Bill felt her place was at home with her daughter on the weekend, despite the fact that he was off to play golf and wouldn't be spending the day with his family anyway.

Well, screw him. Catherine lurched forwards to grab the phone, and sat back again, dialling Rachel's number.

'Oh hi,' Rachel said when she picked up. 'I was going to call you soon. I got your messages.'

'Hmm. Where were you last night?'

'Bumped into my neighbours, you know, the friendly ones?'

'You mean the out-of-work, drug-addled ones?'

Rachel ignored that. Besides, the thread was predicated on a lie, so she didn't want to get into an argument defending it.

'When did you leave Tom's?' asked Catherine. 'You didn't say goodbye.'

'No, you weren't around.' She much preferred it when she didn't have to actually lie to avoid telling the whole truth.

'How did you get home?' Catherine asked.

This was beginning to feel like an inquisition. 'Taxi.'

'Well I was coerced into taking a lift from that slimy friend of Tom's, *Dave*.'

'Did he try something?'

'He wouldn't dare. I gave him short shrift, anyway,' she said. 'So what are you up to?'

'What do you mean?'

'I mean, what are you up to? What do you think I mean?'

'Nothing.'

'You're free then?'

'Well, actually, I'm sorting through my clothes.'

'You are? That's very proactive for you on a Saturday,' Catherine remarked. 'I hope you're making a nice big pile for the charity bin.'

'Then what will I have to wear?'

'You could always go out and buy yourself some decent clothes.'

'Oh, right, that's what I can do with all that spare cash I have lying around,' Rachel quipped.

'Don't get me started on that low-paying, dead-end job of yours.'

'Now why would I be foolish enough to do that?'

But Catherine couldn't resist. 'When are you going to look for a proper job?'

'I have a proper job,' Rachel returned. 'I go to an office, and there are desks and phones and computers, just like grown-ups. They even pay me.'

'You sell bedpans and walking frames.'

'We prefer to call them "life-enhancing products".'

Catherine made a snorting sound.

'Heaven forbid you need anything like that one day, Catherine.'

'I don't care what you sell, I just don't understand why you're selling in the first place.'

'I don't do the selling, I order stock, take inventory, write up invoices –'

'Stop, you're hurting my head, and breaking my heart,' Catherine scolded. 'You could be a lawyer, Rachel.'

'Um, yeah, except I don't have any qualifications.'

'You know I could get you a paralegal job here in a heartbeat.'

'Or I could shoot myself. It's a toss-up.'

'Rachel –'

'There's a reason I dropped out of law, you know, Catherine.'

'Yes, you were restless and immature, but you always wanted to do law.'

'No, my parents always wanted me to do law,' Rachel corrected her. 'I had no idea what I wanted to do, I still don't. So I'll stay in this job until I figure it out.'

'Do you want to meet somewhere for coffee?' Catherine said suddenly.

'Why?'

'What do you mean, why?'

'If it's because you want to discuss what I should do with my life –'

'No, no,' said Catherine. 'It's because I'm bored. I came into the office today to make up for yesterday, but there's not really that much for me to do. I can't even make calls on a Saturday.' She checked her watch. 'We could do lunch. Have you eaten?'

Rachel hesitated. 'What about Lexie?'
'What about her?'
'Shouldn't we ask her too?'
'Why?'
'Because I just don't feel right excluding her.'
'What are you talking about?' said Catherine. 'You and I have coffee together all the time, we don't always ask Lexie.'
'But that was before . . . when Annie was still . . . with us.'
'What's your point?'
'I don't want Lexie to feel like she's not one of us now. That we were only friends with her because of Annie.'
'Well, that's true, isn't it?'
'No,' Rachel protested. 'I consider her a friend in her own right.'
'Yes, of course,' said Catherine. 'I only meant that we did meet her through Annie, that is how we became friends.'

Annie had to be everybody's friend, it seemed to Catherine. So when the young newlyweds moved into the place next door, she couldn't help herself, she had to invite them along to their next get-together. Which was fine as couples – weirdly Martin and Scott hit it off immediately – but it was the tipping point that saw them become 'the girls'. Before that, Catherine had always felt the real nexus of the group had been herself, Rachel and Tom. In fact, with Rachel away overseas for so many years, it was Catherine and Tom's connection that really kept everyone together, until Rachel returned. Then Lexie and Scott became a regular fixture, and before long Sean, and suddenly it was 'the girls' talking babies and children and renovations, while 'the boys' were off talking about whatever they talked about, which had to be more interesting. Catherine didn't like it, though she usually managed to get Tom aside at some point for a little shop talk.

'Look, Rachel,' Catherine said finally, 'you and I have known each other forever, we had coffee together long before we ever met Lexie, or Annie.'
'But if Lexie was to find out –'
'How would she find out?'
'She might,' Rachel defended. 'And then how do you think she'd feel? It is a bit of a sensitive time right now, and she's not

coping all that well. You saw her at the funeral. Scott had to take her home she was so distraught.'

Catherine sighed loudly. 'Fine, if that's how you want it. But she'd have to bring the kids on a weekend. And lunch with two sticky toddlers is not exactly my idea of a good time.'

'So we better leave it,' said Rachel. 'I'm in the middle of all this, and I'm pretty tired after yesterday. I just want to chill, to be honest.'

Catherine felt snubbed, but she wouldn't admit it, or embarrass herself by pushing the point. 'Okay, fair enough. I'll call you through the week.'

She hung up the phone, feeling restless and uneasy. They had nothing planned tonight, and Catherine did not like spending Saturday nights in. Martin relished them, it gave him an opportunity to try out one of his new recipes; he had been blabbing on about it before she left the house this morning. He had his day all organised, starting with a trip to the growers' market, then a drive out to Haberfield, for godsakes, the only place he could get some authentic ingredient or other; Catherine couldn't remember what, she never listened that closely. He also thought he'd probably have a chance of picking up a particular Italian film on DVD that he'd read about.

So although they were having a gourmet meal and watching a DVD with subtitles, it still made Catherine feel uncomfortably suburban. Her parents would probably be staying in tonight, and maybe they'd treat themselves to takeaway Chinese (they still hadn't ventured to try Thai), and a new release from the video store. Catherine wanted to believe she had come a long, long way, but there were moments when she felt a deep sense of dread that she was merely a shinier version of that same western suburbs girl, just with more expensive shoes. Though she rarely let on to such insecurities. Over the years she had developed a virtually impervious outer shell, and she preferred to keep her inner demons tucked firmly away. Rachel knew most of them, though not even she knew them all. She was the only person Catherine mixed with now who had known her back then, except for her family of course, and she was able to keep them at arm's distance. Rachel had been her confidante and, more importantly, her alibi when she snuck off with James. James Barrett from the nearby boys' private school had grown up in privilege and was as worldly as a seventeen-year-old boy could possibly be. All the times she was supposed to be sleeping over at Rachel's she was really sleeping with James, in the pool house of his parents' Point Piper mansion, or the staff quarters – yes, the staff quarters – of their Palm Beach house, while they were off gadding about Europe or Dubai or some other exotic location. They were seriously, obscenely wealthy, and it was like an aphrodisiac to Catherine. It might have been teenage infatuation, but she had never felt so exhilarated. Still hadn't probably. James talked about going to university together, working overseas for a spell, getting married and building their own empire.

Then her period was late. James backed off, almost imperceptibly at first, more obvious in hindsight. They were back at school, the beginning of their HSC year, so she wasn't seeing him quite as much. He said she'd better check it out, but she was too afraid. A week passed and she phoned him, but he wasn't home apparently. His mother said she'd let him know she'd called. There were no mobile phones then, no SMS or MSN or any way to send private messages back and forth. When she hadn't heard from him for more than a week she began to feel desperate. She waited outside his school on the day he had rugby practice so he couldn't avoid her. He looked a little peeved, but he left his friends and walked with her to the train station. He asked her if she'd done the test. She hadn't. He gave her a twenty-dollar note. 'Do it,' he insisted. 'Then come to my house on Friday afternoon.' She went, but she still hadn't done the test. It was completely irrational of course, but her reasoning was that while she didn't know, she didn't have to deal with it. James was annoyed, frustrated, even angry. She started to cry, and he hugged her. And then he kissed her, and then they had sex. And everything seemed like it was going to be all right that afternoon. It was February, hot, golden, summery. He told her not to worry, to have the test and then they'd work out what to do. Rachel went with her to the chemist, and they went back to her place to do it. She remembered shaking so much she had trouble holding the indicator stick still. She burst into tears when the two blue lines appeared.

Catherine called James's house and he came to the phone this time. She told him it was positive, and they arranged to meet at the end of the week.

On the Wednesday night, after dinner, Catherine was working on a major English assignment in her bedroom. Her parents and her brother were watching *A Current Affair* on TV. There was a knock at the door, probably one of her brother's mates, her parents never had any visitors.

She heard voices, a formal tone. Catherine was curious, she came out of her room. James's father was sitting in an armchair opposite her parents, with a briefcase on his lap. Her insides lurched. What was going on? Where was James?

'Evening, Catherine,' said Mr Barrett. 'Your mother and father don't seem to have any idea what I'm doing here.'

She swallowed. 'Me either. Where's James?'

'At home, attending to his studies, like he should have been all along.' He paused meaningfully. 'So do you want to tell them, or shall I?'

Catherine froze. This couldn't be happening. What *was* happening?

'Would you like me to leave the room?' he persisted.

She found her voice. 'I'd like you to leave my house.'

'Catherine,' her mother admonished. 'Where's your manners?'

'Just what's going on here?' her father frowned, but his voice held no authority, just hapless confusion.

Mr Barrett looked pointedly at Catherine. 'You need to tell them, Catherine. It's not going to go away, at least not by itself.'

It still made her sick to the stomach thinking about it. How were her parents supposed to take the news, there in their lounge room, in front of a total stranger? They were in shock, which was the only way Catherine could forgive them for what they proceeded to do. Not that she'd really ever forgiven them, but it was the only way she could abide them at all.

Mr Barrett presented her parents with an 'agreement' which ran to several typed pages, full of legalese and double-talk which would have stumped her parents in the best of circumstances. And these were clearly not the best of circumstances. The Barretts would pay an amount equivalent to the full cost of an abortion, plus an additional sum for 'damages', thus more than meeting their obligations. What Catherine chose to do after that was on her own head, and they would not be liable for any costs whatsoever associated with bringing up the product of a pregnancy they would elect to terminate if the decision was up to them. There was the additional coda that while their son had admitted to having sexual relations with Catherine, there was no incontrovertible proof that the child was in fact his, so all in all, they were more than meeting any obligation that may be deemed reasonable under the circumstances. The settlement was therefore to remain closed and no further action could be taken.

Catherine's parents were not very well educated, they had left school at the minimum age, her father having worked himself up over the years to become a supervisor in a manufacturing plant. Her mother was a housewife. They were caring, but ineffectual. They didn't have a hope against Mr Barrett. And such was their shame and embarrassment at their daughter's indiscretion, they became obsequious to a fault. They tried to assure him he didn't have to pay any money, and they didn't need to sign any papers. But Mr Barrett knew better. They signed the papers and he signed a cheque, and that was to be the end of that.

In a rare display of maternal authority, Catherine's mother promptly carted her off to the doctor, and a due date was determined. It was never openly discussed, but there was no option for Catherine but to have the baby. She'd left it too long in her fear, but her parents were against it anyway, due to some vague moral code based on an even vaguer nominal religion. Catherine knew she would have to inform the school, so she approached her year mistress, a kind and understanding woman, who nonetheless was obliged to follow established protocol. She had no choice but to report it to the principal.

The following week her parents were called to the school to 'discuss' their daughter's predicament. Catherine had always been ambitious, it was she alone who had organised and applied for the scholarship to the school. Her parents had been confounded at the time; why did she want to traipse all the way across to the other side of Sydney when there was a school just up the road? But Catherine was determined, and of course she got her way. But no longer. She was not allowed to sit in on the meeting with the principal, nor was she given any opportunity to state her case. They simply could not accommodate a senior student in her condition, wearing the uniform, turning up at the school every day. As she was due to give birth right on the eve of the HSC, the likelihood of her even sitting the exam was slim, so she would only be wasting everyone's time, attract unwelcome attention, and probably be a distraction to the other girls. The principal graciously assured her parents they would not record an expulsion, as long as no further action was taken or correspondence entered into. Her parents had not the vaguest idea of what such action would be and were once again only too willing to oblige.

Catherine could not bring herself to front up at the local high school, especially in her 'condition'. The Schadenfreude of her old cohort from primary school would be more than she could bear. She kept a low profile, immersing herself in her HSC texts, along with the odd baby manual. Alice was born two days after her due date, and Catherine got straight back on track to complete her HSC the following year. Sometimes, looking at Alice now at the same age, Catherine wondered how on earth she'd done it. Alice was a very good baby, and she did have her mother right there, but she was only a child herself. She supposed her motivation was overpowering — she was so terrified that she would get sucked back into the outer suburbs and that all she'd be able to give Alice was her life all over again. She was determined they would live in the right suburbs, that Alice would go to the right schools, and if anyone ever tried to cross her daughter, they were going to have to deal with Catherine first.

She never expressed her intense and profound heartbreak at being abandoned so soundly by James. She never heard from him again, he never made any attempt to contact her. So Catherine decided that success would be her best revenge. She would never again let herself get in the position where someone could wield such absolute power over her.

Her outstanding exam results assured her entry into a law degree, which she went on to complete with first-class honours. She was courted by all the major law firms, but she made the bizarre choice — at least in the minds of those who knew little about her — to apply for a position with an albeit prestigious firm

Riley happily transferred over to Claire, and Scott crouched down to release Mia from the pram, lifting her up into his arms. 'Bring the pram through here, Lex,' he said.

She pushed it into the far corner of the café, behind a screen that hid the door to the storeroom. Bean East had begun its life more than a decade ago, capitalising on the trend in all things South-East Asian. But the Balinese interiors had become tired and the menu had evolved over time, so a couple of years ago the café underwent a cosmetic revamp, giving it a more streamlined, modern look, using dark timber fittings and solid blocks of colour. The 'east' now had more to do with its location in Sydney, though there remained a vaguely Asian influence in a couple of the wall hangings and the Buddha that kept watch from his post on the counter.

Lexie turned to face Scott. 'Sorry, I should have realised you'd be too busy.'

'It's okay,' he said, stooping to give her a peck on the cheek. 'How are you doing?'

She looked up at him. 'I saw Tom and the girls off this morning.'

Scott nodded. 'I know.'

Tom was taking the girls up the coast to stay with his parents for a while. The girls would miss some school, but it was the right thing to do; they needed to get away, and they all needed the kind of nurture and solace you could only get from family.

'I just couldn't be at home, it felt so quiet,' said Lexie, her eyes becoming moist, 'like she's really gone.'

Scott put a hand on her shoulder. 'Why don't you call the girls, meet them somewhere so you can talk about it?'

Lexie shook her head. 'Catherine can't handle the kids.'

'Well, organise dinner then. Have a girls' night out, I'll stay with the kids.'

She shrugged. 'I think that might make Annie's absence all the more obvious.'

Scott sighed, giving her hair a stroke. 'I don't know what to tell you, hun.'

'You don't have to fix it, Scott,' said Lexie. 'I just wanted to talk.'

'Sorry to interrupt.' It was Claire again. 'I got you a table.'

'Oh, I don't want to take one away from a paying customer,' said Lexie.

'You're not,' Claire assured her. 'There's no one waiting right now. Except Riley. I've set him up at the table. What's Miss Mia going to have?' she asked, giving her tummy a gentle tickle.

'Do you want a smoothie like Riley, Mia?' Lexie asked her.

'Movie yike Ryee,' she nodded enthusiastically.

'Thanks Claire,' said Scott.

She disappeared back into the kitchen and Scott handed Mia over to Lexie while he went to find a highchair.

'Don't you have to get back to the kitchen?' Lexie asked him when he brought one back to the table.

He shook his head. 'They can hold the fort for ten minutes.'

Once Mia was happily ensconced in the highchair with her Mia-sized smoothie, Scott reached across the table to take Lexie's hand. 'Are you sure you won't think about going out tonight? Might cheer you up?'

'I don't think I'm up to it,' she said. 'To be honest, I don't know what's going to happen to the three of us now. I mean, Rachel and Catherine grew up together, they've always been friends. I only came into the group because of Annie. I would never have been friends with the other two, probably wouldn't even have met them in the normal course of things. We don't really have anything in common. I like Rachel, I think we have a genuine connection, but she's so easygoing anyone would get on with her. But Catherine . . .'

Scott covered his mouth with his hand, probably to hide a smirk.

'Don't look like that,' Lexie admonished.

He dropped his hand away. 'I'm not looking like anything!' he protested. 'Go on, what were you going to say about Catherine?'

'Well, we're different, we lead such different lives,' said Lexie. 'I'm not sure how we'll go without Annie there to . . . bridge the gap, I guess. She was like Carrie, you know, in *Sex in the City*. Annie was our Carrie,' she nodded to herself. 'You see, everyone thinks Carrie's their best friend, but you never really know who Carrie considers her best friend. The thing is, she's the centre, the conduit that connects everyone. And Catherine, well . . .'

Lexie screwed up her face, thinking. 'I was going to say she's like Miranda because they're both lawyers, but she's probably more like Samantha – a little full of herself, self-centred, though she is honest, if brutal. I'm probably most like Charlotte, because I'm married with children and totally happy with that. And then Rachel, well, she's a bit like Carrie too, I suppose.' She glanced across at Scott, whose eyes had glazed over.

'Oh, I'm sorry, when did I lose you?'

'You told me I should just listen. So that's what I'm trying to do.'

Lexie smiled. 'You probably think I'm silly trying to relate real life to a TV series.'

'I don't think you're silly.'

'It's just a good analogy, that's all. Especially because there's four of them.' She sighed. 'It's always four, you know, in movies, books, TV shows . . . you think about it. Not just *Sex in the City*, but, um . . . there's *Desperate Housewives* . . .'

'Ah, but wasn't there, like, half-a-dozen *Friends*?' he said.

'That's true,' she nodded. 'And if there were more of us, this wouldn't be such a problem.'

'Why do you say that?'

'The dynamic has room to adjust when there are more people, you can regroup. But with only three, there's nowhere to go.'

'What about *The Three Musketeers*?'

'That story's all about d'Artagnan, the fourth musketeer.'

Scott thought about it. 'There were only three *Charlie's Angels*.'

'But there was Charlie,' Lexie reminded him.

Riley started to giggle and they looked at him looking at Mia, who had managed to open the lid of her smoothie and had stuck her arm in the cup, all the way to her elbow. Scott leaped up and dashed over to the kitchen for a wet cloth. He returned and set about cleaning her up.

'Meth Daddy,' she declared.

'Yes, Mia made a big mess,' he said, tweaking her nose. 'Messy Mia.'

That made Riley giggle again, which in turn made Mia squeal with laughter as she realised she was the star attraction.

Scott sat down again, looking at Lexie. 'Are you going to be okay?'

She nodded. 'I guess all I've been trying to say is that it's just not going to be the same without Annie.'

'Of course it's not,' said Scott. 'How could it be? Things change, Lex, nothing stays the same forever.'

'I wish it could,' she said wistfully, gazing at her children. 'Wouldn't it be wonderful if they were never going to grow up and move away, if they could just stay children forever?'

Scott was shaking his head, smiling indulgently at her. She supposed that sounded foolish, but it was the way she felt. Annie's death had shaken Lexie right through to her core. The funeral was unbearable, and the wake . . . people talking, laughing, drinking wine. What was wrong with them? She even saw Tom smiling. Shouldn't he be shattered? How could he go on? How could any of them go on as normal? It didn't seem right that a person like Annie could be removed from the face of the earth and everything would still go on as before. A person like Annie, who was good, and had never hurt anyone, and who had always been there when Lexie needed her. And Lexie had believed she would always be there, and had imagined all the days stretching off into the future when Annie would be there, when Riley started school, then Mia, all the family birthdays, graduations . . . they would be the family friends in photographs of their every milestone.

But not any more. Things could change in an instant, catastrophically, irreversibly. So Lexie did wish she could stop time and hold her family close to her, no matter how foolish that sounded, or how impossible.

November

'Rachel.'

Lloyd's voice behind her always sent chills. And not in a good way.

'Lloyd.' Rachel swivelled around in her chair to face her direct supervisor looming over her, a man for whom a little power was a disturbing thing. And for whom a little deodorant would not go astray. He really shouldn't wear synthetic fibres.

'You placed an order for twelve cases of Handy Pickers on Tuesday last, correct?'

'If you say so.'

'I don't have to,' he returned. 'The paper trail confirms it.'

So why was he asking her?

'I am therefore forced to wonder if you were aware that we currently have seven cases of Handy Pickers in stock, on hand as it were. And having said that, if you are conversant with the fact that Handy Pickers generally move at a rate of one case per calendar month, tops.'

He looked as though he was expecting an answer, but Rachel had lost track of the question.

'At the same time, we are entirely out of Handy Grabbers, indeed we are waiting to process in excess of twenty back orders for the same.' He paused to take a deep, meaningful breath, allowing Rachel time to consider the enormity of the problem. 'I don't think one needs to be a detective to work out that you have, in fact, confused Handy Pickers with Handy Grabbers.'

Rachel suppressed a yawn. 'There's a difference?'

He shook his head, closing his eyes for a moment to emphasise his disappointment. 'Of course there's a difference, Rachel. Your product knowledge leaves a great deal to be desired. Have you ever thought about taking the catalogue home to study over the weekend?'

'You know, I haven't.' Which was the truth. She had never thought of doing that, it had never so much as crossed her mind.

'Well, I think this calls for a training session in Monday's staff meeting,' he said, jotting a note to himself on the clipboard he carried officiously around with him everywhere. Why didn't he get with the program and get himself a palm pilot like every other self-important middle manager?

Hold on, did he say 'training session'? Rachel winced. She couldn't be responsible for putting the staff through that.

'Lloyd, you don't need to cover it in the staff meeting. I'll take the catalogue home, I'll brush up on my pickers and grabbers, I promise.'

'Good,' he said. 'Then you'll be all set to present it at the meeting.'

'What?' she gulped.

But he was already walking away, and Rachel did not fail to notice the spring in his step. Snide little man. Her phone started to ring and she swivelled her chair around again and reached for the receiver. 'Handy Home Health Care,' she said wearily.

'Rachel?'

She frowned. She knew that voice . . . 'Yes?'

'It's Tom.'

She went blank. And speechless.

'Tom Macklin,' he said after a moment.

Rachel roused herself. 'Sorry, Tom, I just wasn't expecting you to call me here at work.'

'Is that a problem?'

'No,' she dismissed. 'Where are you calling from?'

'My office.'

'You're back in Sydney?'

'Yeah, Sophie had to sit her school certificate,' he explained.

Life goes on. Unrelentingly. Next week it would be two months since Annie died, and Sophie was back sitting exams, and Tom was back sitting at his desk at work. But Annie wouldn't be waiting for them when they came home this evening. What had Tom said, that nothing would be normal ever again?

'How are you all doing?' Rachel asked.

'Oh, up and down,' he said in a weary tone. He was probably sick of having to answer that question. 'It's been good to stay up the coast, away from it all. Mum's been great, except she's always trying to feed us. She thinks food is the solution to everything.'

Rachel smiled faintly. 'It's a pity you had to come back so soon.'

'Well, it has been six weeks,' said Tom. 'Actually, I had intended staying put now till we go up again for Christmas, but Sophie wants to go straight back up there.' Rachel heard him breathe out. 'I'm not so sure it's a good idea.'

'Well, I don't think they do all that much after their exams,' she offered.

'I'm not worried about that,' said Tom. 'But she's going to miss her formal.'

'Does she realise that?'

'She says she doesn't care.'

Rachel didn't know what to say, and she certainly didn't know why Tom was telling her this.

'I'm a bit worried about her, Rach,' he said. 'And I was wondering . . .'

He paused. He paused for so long Rachel was beginning to think the phone had dropped out. 'Tom?'

'Sorry, I'm still here.'

'What were you wondering?' she prompted.

'Well . . .' he hesitated, 'would you mind talking to her?'

'Pardon?' Rachel wasn't expecting that.

'Would you mind talking to Sophie?'

'About what?'

'About why she doesn't want to go to the formal.'

'But didn't she tell you she just doesn't care?'

Tom sighed. 'Yeah, but I think there's more to it.'

Rachel didn't doubt that. 'Why do you think she'll tell me?'

'You're a woman . . . you know about this stuff.'

'But I'm not a parent, Tom.'

'You know more about girls than I do.'

'Why? I don't have any of my own.'

'But you are one.'

'I guess.'

'No, you are,' said Tom. 'I can tell the difference.'

Rachel smiled then.

'Look, Rach,' he went on, 'you get on really well with the girls, they love you.'

'Laying it on a bit thick,' she muttered.

'Is it working?'

She sighed. What was she doing? Tom was asking for help. There was only one answer. 'Sure, I'll talk to her, Tom.'

'Thank you,' he said, clearly relieved. 'Do you want me to come and pick you up?'

'When?'

'Tonight.'

She blinked. 'You want to do this tonight?'

'Why, are you busy?'

'No, I'm free . . .' Just not prepared.

'Sophie's really pushing for us to leave as soon as possible,' Tom explained. 'I don't think I can put her off for much longer without a reason.' He paused. 'Please Rachel?'

She roused herself. So now she was making him beg? 'Of course, Tom, tonight's fine.'

Rachel made her own way to Tom and Annie's – strike that – Tom's. That didn't sound right either. Tom and Sophie and Hannah's? Rather a mouthful. Tom and the girls'? Might have to do for now. This was going to be strange. Rachel was fairly certain she'd never been to their house when Annie wasn't there. Until the wake at least, and then it didn't even feel like their house.

And now Rachel was coming over to talk to Sophie. It felt like such an intrusion. Annie was so close to her girls, so good with them. They had a wonderful relationship, she'd never needed help from anyone else.

But Annie was gone. When was that going to sink in?

Tom met her at the door in bare feet, a T-shirt and board shorts. She was relieved to see that he looked a lot better than he had at the funeral; the time away had clearly done him good. He seemed refreshed, his skin was lightly tanned and his hair had grown out a little; Rachel could see a faint echo of his younger self.

'Is this how lawyers are dressing these days?' she remarked.

He glanced down at himself. 'I'm still in Crescent Head mode,' he said. 'I couldn't wait to get out of that suit and tie today, it felt like a straitjacket.' He stood back to let her in. 'Sophie's up in her room, alone. Hannah's at a friend's, she'll be home for dinner. So, you might as well go straight up, unless you want a drink or something first?'

'No, I'm right.' Rachel frowned, looking ominously up the stairs. 'Does she know I'm coming?'

Tom shook his head. 'I didn't want it to seem like it was a set-up.'

'I think she's going to pick up on that when I ask her why she doesn't want to go to the formal.'

Tom shrugged sheepishly, before giving her an encouraging pat on the back. 'I'm sure you'll know how to handle it.'

Rachel looked at him sideways, passed him her bag and headed up the stairs. She knocked lightly when she reached Sophie's door. 'Hi Sophie, it's Rachel.'

She glanced down the stairs to where Tom was standing, clutching her handbag to his chest as he stared back up at her with an anxious frown. She shooed him away as Sophie opened the door.

'Hi Rachel,' she said, a slight edge to her voice. She was suspicious. 'What are you doing here?'

'Oh, your dad called, said you were back in town. I thought I'd drop in . . . say hi.'

Sophie just stood there, not saying anything. She'd always looked like her mother, but now it was a little uncanny. She had a level of composure quite beyond her years. Rachel had heard it said that when someone loses a parent, they shift up into that generation. Sophie was too young to become the woman of the house, but there was a world-weary look in her eyes that was disconcerting.

'So am I interrupting something?' Rachel tried next. She was running out of openers.

Sophie finally released a groan. 'I'm just catching up on Facebook. The internet connection is so-o-o slow at Grandma's.' She turned around and sauntered back over to her desk. 'She still has dial-up, would you believe?' she threw over her shoulder at Rachel. 'I didn't think that even existed any more. It's like, totally ancient.'

Rachel was relieved to see some semblance of a teenage girl surface again. She ventured a step or two into the room as Sophie plonked down on her chair and grabbed the mouse, clicking it in rapid succession to close or hide whatever was on the desktop. It wouldn't have mattered, Rachel couldn't make out anything from where she was standing anyway.

Sophie swivelled her chair around and swung her feet up to rest on the bed. 'Take a seat, if you can find a spot,' she said.

The bed was covered in various stacks of folded clothes, neat little piles of string bikinis and underwear, and a couple of tops and shorts laid out flat like she was working out what went with what. 'Packing?' Rachel commented rather superfluously as she perched on the edge of the bed.

Sophie nodded. 'We're leaving in the next day or two, I hope so anyway. Dad's got stuff to sort out at work.'

'Yeah, he said you wanted to go straight back up the coast again. All that time without broadband, how will you survive?'

She shrugged. 'It doesn't matter, I think I'm going to close down my Facebook page anyway.'

'Oh?'

'It just seems like such a waste of time. I had heaps of messages, some of them were kind of nice, but most of them were just requests to join some stupid group or do a quiz, like which *Twilight* character am I? I mean, who cares?'

Obviously not Sophie any more.

'How did the school certificate go?' Rachel asked, in an attempt to move on to something she did care about.

'It was okay,' said Sophie. 'It was only three days. I didn't have to do any of the internal exams, they gave me "special consideration",' she added wryly, using her fingers for quotation marks.

'So,' Rachel hesitated, desperately searching for a segue, 'what now that it's all over? Are you going to celebrate?' God, was that the best she could come up with?

Sophie looked her straight in the eye. 'Dad told you I don't want to go to the formal, didn't he?'

'Oh, he might have mentioned it . . .'

Sophie gave her a small, sly smile then. 'You're so totally obvious, Rachel.'

She sighed, leaning back against the bedhead. 'I know, I've never been good at subterfuge. I'd make a really hopeless spy. And I so wanted to be 99 out of *Get Smart* when I grew up.'

Sophie was frowning. 'Is that the one Anne Hathaway played?'

'Oh, in the movie, yeah.' Sophie was going to think she was a bit tragic. 'I was talking about the TV show, I was just a kid . . . never mind.' Back to the subject. She looked directly at Sophie. 'You know your dad's just worried about you.'

'He shouldn't be,' she said. 'He's making such a big deal about

.this, like it's some major rite of passage that I'm going to totally miss if I don't go. But it's just a stupid party.'

'Well, it's a little more than that,' Rachel suggested. 'You don't think it might be fun?'

She sighed, shaking her head. 'I don't know what it was like in your day, Rachel –'

Ouch, she was old enough for a teenager to refer to 'her' day?

'– but it's so over the top now. Everyone thinks they're on the red carpet or something. I don't want to spend all that money on a dress I'm never going to wear again, just so I can boast about where I bought it.'

Rachel thought that sounded eminently sensible. But what if she was just making excuses? Maybe it was because she had no one to go shopping with . . . Tom would be pretty useless.

'You know, Soph, if you need someone to go shopping with you . . .' Rachel hesitated, what was she saying? 'Well, to be honest, I'd be the worst person. But . . .' She thought about it. 'Lexie! Lexie'd be great, and she would love to go with you.'

'It doesn't stop with the dress, Rachel,' said Sophie. 'There's the shoes, the bag, the jewellery . . . you have to get your hair done, makeup, nails, fake tan –'

'Fake tan?' Rachel frowned. 'That's crazy.'

'Tell me about it.'

'You're all fifteen, sixteen, right?' said Rachel. 'Why the hell are you trussing yourselves up like turkeys at Christmas? The people who do all that stuff are desperately trying to recapture the way they looked when they were your age. You guys are gorgeous without all the trimmings.'

'That's exactly what Mum would say,' said Sophie. 'Would have said,' she corrected herself.

Rachel's stomach lurched. Was that good or bad? She wasn't actually arguing Tom's case. Not that he had a case. What was she doing here again?

'Mum would never have approved,' Sophie added.

Rachel hesitated. 'I don't know that that's entirely true, Soph,' she said carefully. 'She wouldn't have wanted you to miss out on one of the highlights of your school years.'

'Well, she did.'

'Pardon?'

'Mum didn't go to her formal,' said Sophie. 'She thought it was a waste of time as well.'

Rachel knew there was a little more to it than that. Annie's family belonged to some fringe sect of an otherwise mainstream religion, and by all accounts she had a pretty austere upbringing. Rachel was quite sure she would never have been allowed to go to anything as potentially debauched as a school formal, whether she wanted to or not. So of course when she came home pregnant after a year of new-found freedom at university, her parents simply and quite thoroughly disowned her. Although they lived on the north-west outskirts of Sydney, Annie had never seen them again; they had never laid eyes on Sophie, or Hannah.

Rachel thought for a moment. 'Look, whatever choices your mum made, I know she would always have encouraged you to make the decision that was right for you.'

'That's exactly what I'm trying to do,' said Sophie. 'It's just not important to me, Rachel. It seems . . .'

She was struggling to find the word, but Rachel knew what she was getting at. 'Insignificant in the scheme of things?' she offered.

Sophie let out a sigh. 'Yeah,' she said quietly. 'Insignificant, and shallow, and frivolous.'

And adolescent, Rachel wanted to say. It was the one time in life when shallowness and frivolity were acceptable, even expected. And Sophie was going to miss it.

'Look, I get it, Soph, I really do,' Rachel said kindly. 'I know that's how it must seem to you right now. But think really hard, if you don't go, do you honestly think you might not regret it down the track?'

Sophie looked at her directly. 'Nope.'

'You seem so certain,' said Rachel. 'All I'm saying is you might kick yourself once the photos are up on Facebook and MySpace, and there's nothing you can do about it then. It'll be too late to change your mind.'

While she was talking, Sophie got up off her chair and walked across to a corkboard on the wall. She removed something and turned around, coming over to stand in front of Rachel. She held out a violet-coloured card, the invitation to the formal. 'Here, you tell me if you think I'll regret not going.'

Rachel frowned, taking it from Sophie's hand. She scanned down the flowery script until her eyes landed squarely on the real reason Sophie did not want to go to the formal.

'You are such a giant doofus, Tom!' Rachel declared when she came back down the stairs and he ushered her into the kitchen.

'Why? What have I done?' he said, clearly baffled.

She thrust the invitation into his hands and folded her arms as he read it, his brow all furrowed in concentration. He looked up after a while and shook his head helplessly. 'I don't understand.'

Rachel sighed loudly. 'Look at the date.'

He looked, but still he didn't appear to twig.

'Tom!' she exclaimed. 'It's Annie's birthday.'

'Oh fuck!' he cried, hitting his hand to his forehead.

Rachel stared at him in disbelief. 'How did you not realise that? What is it with the male brain and dates? There's like a lobe missing or something.'

'Still think I'm hopeless?' asked Tom.

After apologising profusely and berating himself repeatedly, he finally talked Rachel into staying for a beer. They had come out the front and were sitting side by side on the step, where they could glimpse the ocean at the end of the street and catch the evening sea breeze. But more importantly, where Sophie couldn't hear them.

'Not entirely,' said Rachel. 'You do have some redeeming qualities.' She clinked her beer bottle against his.

'Poor kid, no wonder she didn't want to go,' said Tom.

Rachel nodded. 'She has no way of predicting how she's going to feel on the day. Maybe it'd all turn out great, be the best thing for her . . .' She glanced at Tom. 'But you know, to be honest, I can't help thinking it'd be really hard. She'd be all dressed up, you'd be taking photos, it would be so painfully obvious her mother wasn't there. There'll be a lot of times in the future when she'll have to face that, and it'll be hard, but it's too soon right now, too raw, and she's way too young to have to deal with that around her friends . . . who, by the way, she doesn't even feel she can relate to any more, given what she's been through.'

Tom sighed. 'I wish she'd felt she could have said that to me.'

'It would have helped if you'd picked up on the date yourself.'

'Go ahead, rub it in, I deserve it.'

'Yes, you do,' Rachel agreed, sipping her beer. 'So when will you head back up the coast?'

'Probably at the weekend. I should at least put in the rest of the week at the office.' He took a swig of his beer. 'I don't know how this'll go down at work.'

Rachel nudged against him. 'They'll understand. You just lost your wife, for godsakes. What kind of place would it be if they gave you a hard time right now?'

'A law firm.'

'But they're not *inhuman*, surely?'

He looked at her sideways, then took another swig of his beer.

'Well, Tom Macklin, what the hell are you doing working for them if they're that bad?' Rachel demanded to know.

'I sold my soul, Rach, I admit it. And now I have a family and a mortgage, so there's no way out.' He shook his head. 'I never imagined I'd be doing this corporate crap, it was the last thing I wanted to do with a law degree. Remember when we were going to change the world?'

'I remember when *you* wanted to change the world,' said Rachel. 'I was never that big on the idea.'

'So all was right with the world as far as you were concerned?'

'Not at all, I just wasn't cut out for it,' she said. 'I needed to remember to change my sheets regularly before I started trying to change the world.'

Tom smiled. 'You're a funny girl, Rachel Halliday-Holloway.'

'Don't call me that. You know I don't use the double barrel any more.' She paused, considering him. 'What happened, Tom?' she asked seriously. 'When I left you were still this idealistic boy, raring to take on the establishment.'

'You weren't around, Rach, so you missed it,' said Tom. 'But you should have seen how these firms infiltrated the final-year students, seducing us with their graduate programs and fat starting salaries. I thought I'd try it for a year or two. Couldn't hurt, get a bit of experience, some money in the bank.' He paused. 'But life has a way of tying you down. Annie wanted another child straightaway.'

Rachel looked at him. 'Why was that?'

'She worried that if we left it too long Sophie might feel different, set apart. She wanted us to gel as a family. I could see the sense of it, so I went along.' He took another swig of his beer. 'Next time I looked up I was a corporate lawyer with a wife and a child and a baby on the way. And I've been on the treadmill ever since.'

Rachel detected a tone, and more than a whiff of frustration. She wasn't sure what to say.

Tom turned his head to meet her gaze. 'Hey, don't get me wrong, it was great that Annie could be home for the girls, that she had that choice. It just seems to work out that in order for one person to have choices, the other person usually doesn't get any.'

'Everybody's choices come at a price, Tom,' said Rachel. 'Women choose babies, their career goes down the toilet. They choose career, they're loaded up with guilt at leaving their babies. No one makes a man feel guilty for going to work and putting his kids in childcare.'

'True,' he nodded. 'But that works against us as well. Keeps us on that treadmill.' He sighed heavily. 'Now I'm on my own I'm never going to get off it.'

Rachel frowned. 'Are things going to be harder without . . . um, without Annie's financial contribution?'

He gave a half-hearted laugh. 'It wasn't much of a contribution, Rach – she didn't work a lot, you know. And she didn't charge enough when she did. I guarantee she was the only piano teacher in the eastern suburbs who would accept a home-cooked lasagne for payment, or a box of vegies from someone's garden.' He paused, draining the remainder of his beer. 'No, Annie was the primary caregiver, I was the primary breadwinner. That was carved in stone.'

Rachel had never sensed this was an issue in their marriage;

in fact she'd never sensed there were any issues in their marriage. But then again, she hadn't talked to Tom like this while Annie was alive. Annie had never complained about Tom; even when everyone else was having the standard whinges about their husbands not helping out enough, not listening . . . the usual, Annie never had anything to say.

Tom was probably just feeling overwhelmed by the situation. He was perfectly entitled.

He got to his feet, picking up their empty beer bottles. 'I'll get us another, eh?'

'No, I should go,' Rachel said, standing up.

'Really?' He looked disappointed. 'You can't stay for dinner? I was going to defrost one of Lexie's casseroles.'

It was tempting, but she knew she should get out of their way. Tom needed to be available for Sophie if she decided to open up.

'No, really, I have to get going,' said Rachel. 'I've got stuff to do.' She picked her bag up off the step.

'Then let me drive you home at least.'

'Don't be silly,' she said, stepping down onto the footpath. 'Hannah'll be getting dropped off soon, won't she?'

He nodded. 'Are you sure?'

'Absolutely.'

'Okay.' He paused. 'Well, thanks for coming over, Rach, I really appreciate it.'

She shook her head. 'Don't mention it.' She looked up at the house. 'It felt strange, coming here, without . . .'

'Yeah.'

'Maybe Sophie's just not ready yet, Tom.'

'Maybe none of us are.'

She hesitated, not wanting to tell him what to do. 'You should think about marking Annie's birthday somehow with the girls,' she said. 'It obviously means something to Sophie, and probably to Hannah as well.'

'What do you suggest?'

Rachel smiled and shook her head. 'I can't fix everything, Tom,' she said. 'You'll figure it out.' Then she turned and headed up the street.

*

Annie's birthday

'So let's drink to Annie,' said Catherine, raising her glass. 'And remember her fondly on this, the day she was born.'

Lexie was tearing up again, and even Rachel looked a little misty. Catherine needed to move things along.

'So it occurred to me that Annie was the kind of woman who would have liked to have left some kind of legacy, don't you think?'

'What do you mean?' asked Rachel.

'Well, in the same way that she always wanted her life to mean something, I think she'd want her death to mean something.'

Rachel and Lexie were staring at her, unblinking. Uncomprehending. She'd better just spell it out.

'I thought we should each do something positive, set a goal, with Annie as our inspiration. And we can help one another, it can be a bonding experience.'

Lexie and Rachel glanced at each other.

'What kind of a goal are you talking about?' Lexie asked tentatively. 'Do you mean we should run a marathon together or something?'

Rachel pulled a face. 'God, really? Is that what you're talking about?'

'No, no,' said Catherine. 'Unless that's something you've always wanted to do?'

They both shook their heads emphatically.

'And I'd rather die than bungee jump,' Lexie added.

'Or parachute out of a plane.'

'Oh I could so never do that,' Lexie agreed. 'I mean, I wouldn't take that kind of a risk, I have kids.'

'I don't have kids,' said Rachel. 'But there's no way you'd catch me jumping out of a plane.'

Catherine rolled her eyes. 'Excuse me,' she said, tapping her glass with a fork to get their attention again. 'I'm trying to get you to look at the bigger picture here. When something like this happens, you can't help but think about your own mortality.'

'Which is why I don't want to jump out of a plane.'

'No one's saying you have to jump out of a plane!' declared Catherine. She picked up her glass and gulped down half of it in frustration.

Rachel was watching her. She knew the way Catherine worked. She had something specific in mind, but she was trying to lead them into coming up with it themselves so it didn't look like it was her idea. 'Why don't you just cut to the chase, Catherine, and tell us what you have in mind?'

'All right.' She took a breath. 'Do you think if Annie had known what was going to happen to her, she would have done things differently?'

'Absolutely,' said Lexie. 'She never would have taken Ventolin, for one thing.'

'No, I'm not talking about that. I mean, had she known she was going to . . . you know, that she was . . . that she was not long for this world,' Catherine said, grasping for the right euphemism, 'do you think she might have . . . well, done things differently?' she repeated.

'Like what?' asked Rachel.

'Lived her life differently.'

'No way,' Lexie said firmly. 'Annie lived her life on her own terms, it's what I admired most about her.'

'Well, there you go, that's why she should be an inspiration to us,' Catherine declared. 'Can you say with as much confidence that there's nothing missing from your own life?' She leaned forwards. 'If you knew you were going to die tomorrow, what would you do?'

Lexie gasped. 'I'd run straight home and hold Scott and the kids tight and not let them go!'

'Okay,' Catherine sighed. 'Let's not say tomorrow, let's say in one year. Or five even. What's missing from your life? What would you regret that you hadn't done?'

Had more babies, Lexie decided without hesitation. But she wasn't going to say that out loud. She had a feeling it wasn't what Catherine had in mind.

'It's an interesting idea, Catherine,' said Rachel. 'I suppose it gives us something to think about.'

'No time like the present!' Catherine urged.

'I can't just come up with something out of the blue,' said Rachel. 'I need time to think.'

'Then why don't I go first?' Catherine suggested. 'I've given this a lot of thought.'

They both looked at her expectantly.

'Okay, so . . . here's my idea. We need to find Lexie a job and Rachel a man,' she announced, quite pleased with herself.

Now they both looked at her gobsmacked.

'But . . . I have a job,' Lexie protested.

'No you don't,' Catherine said plainly. 'You have a relationship. You're a mother. I don't know why people call it a job, no one's paying you to do it, and all it will leave you with is a gap in your résumé.'

Lexie was speechless.

'I thought you wanted me to get a new job?' said Rachel.

'I do, but with you I had to prioritise. One thing at a time.'

'Well, I'm not looking for a relationship right now,' Rachel said firmly. 'I'm just not . . . in the right head space at the moment.'

'I understand why you feel that way,' Catherine said kindly. 'But it's nothing that a good haircut and losing a kilo or two wouldn't fix.'

Rachel bristled. Despite her own unwavering belief to the contrary, Catherine was no oil painting. In fact she would probably be considered rather plain, if not for the monthly haircuts that cost the equivalent of a week's rent for Rachel. On top of that were even more outrageously priced cosmetics, facials, manicures, pedicures, waxes, eyebrow-shaping, and who knew what other treatments. Catherine was like a car that had been detailed; she came as close to being airbrushed as a living, breathing human could.

Lexie could throw on a shift and sandals, like tonight, and look stunning. Because she was still the right side of thirty and, despite having two babies, she was pretty and perky and . . . well, the right side of thirty.

Annie had been the one with the real style. She never wore what was in fashion, certainly never followed trends, but she was one of those people who always looked effortlessly fabulous, probably because she had seemed so comfortable in her own skin.

Rachel had also turned her back on fashion, though with less successful results. It had evolved during her years backpacking, when most of the time she had no idea of the latest trends – they hardly mattered trekking through Kazakhstan or trying desperately to keep warm travelling around the Netherlands on a bus in the winter. Comfort always won out over style, and that mantra had stuck.

'So, are you up for it?' Catherine was saying.

Rachel considered her from across the table. This was so typical of Catherine; always ready, willing and more than prepared to ferret out the flaws in everyone else, but rarely able to turn the magnifying glass on herself.

'What about you, Catherine?' Rachel said finally. 'You haven't said what goal you're setting for yourself?'

'I don't know,' she mused, sipping her wine. 'It's a little harder for me. I mean, I have achieved, or I'm well on the way to achieving, all the goals I've ever set for myself – career, financial, personal. There's nothing really obvious, but I'll keep thinking about it. I'm sure something will present itself.'

'What about your relationship with Alice?' Rachel suggested bluntly.

But Catherine waved that away. 'Any issues between Alice and I are not going to be solved until she grows up a little. There's nothing more I can do. She's seventeen, I just have to be patient.'

And just like that, as though she was coated in Teflon, the idea slipped away without leaving the faintest impression, not so much as an oily smudge.

'So this is not the best time to be looking for a job, Lexie,' Catherine continued, 'right before Christmas, but we can start to work on your résumé, if you like.'

'Catherine, I haven't even thought about going back to work –'

'That's why you need to start thinking about it,' she insisted. 'Riley's off to school next year, isn't he?'

'But I still have Mia.'

'You'll do far more good for Mia if you set an example of a strong, independent woman. Alice was in day care from when she was a baby. Honestly, you spoil them by giving up any aspirations for yourself so you can be there to tend to their every need. Life's not like that, Lexie.' She shook her head, taking another mouthful of wine. 'Kids today think they're the centre of the universe. That's why they all have such a hard time out in the real world. Some of the interns we get at the firm, you wouldn't believe the way they go on. They expect to be handling briefs from the first day, and they think filing and the like is beneath them. Honestly. Makes my hair stand on end.'

Lexie didn't agree with a word Catherine had just said. Not the intern part, she didn't know about any of that. But she refused to accept that she was spoiling her children by staying home with them, or setting a bad example for Mia. She would have liked to argue her case, she just didn't know how.

'You know what Scott's hours are like,' she said instead, which was just making excuses. 'I don't see how I could work around them.'

'That's my point – why should you?' said Catherine. 'Why should Scott's career come first? I repeat, what kind of example is that for Mia?'

Lexie gave up. She'd never been combative, it just wasn't in her nature.

'Okay, so I propose that we get into it straight after Christmas. We might even get you a date for New Year's, Rachel.'

Rachel blinked. 'What, are you planning on advertising on a billboard or something?'

'Virtually,' said Catherine with a self-satisfied little smile. 'You see, that's a pun. We're going to find you someone over the internet.'

'Are you kidding me?' said Rachel. 'You want me to go out with some internet loser who doesn't have a date on New Year's?'

'Do you have a date on New Year's?' Catherine enquired archly.

'No, but that's by choice,' she insisted. 'I'm over the whole New Year's thing. There's all this pressure to celebrate and do something even if you don't feel like it. And if you don't have anything to do, that's even worse.'

'Well, I wouldn't know about that,' said Catherine. 'We always have several invitations on New Year's Eve.'

'I'm with Rachel,' said Lexie. 'We prefer to keep it quiet on New Year's. Scott usually has to work the next day, so he doesn't want to have a big one. It's just too close to Christmas. It would be different if we could space it out.'

'What are you suggesting, we celebrate the new financial year?' said Catherine.

'I wonder if that's what accountants do?' Lexie mused.

'God, could you imagine anything worse?' said Rachel. 'Celebrating the new financial year in the middle of winter with a bunch of accountants?'

And finally, that raised a gentle laugh.

Catherine picked up the bottle of wine and went to pour herself a glass, till she discovered it was empty. 'Oh. Shall we order another?'

Christmas

Rachel tried to sleep in as long as she could on Christmas morning. Catherine would be here to pick her up around eleven and Rachel didn't like to have to fill in too much time before that. Although she had spent many Christmas mornings alone, she'd never got used to it. There was something inherently sad – why beat around the bush? – there was something *pathetic* about being alone on Christmas morning. Oh, she had places to go and people to be with, but she still had to get out of bed on her own in an empty flat.

She wouldn't admit it to another living soul, she could barely admit it to herself, but she always held on to a secret hope that one of her parents might remember to call on Christmas morning her time. But as it wasn't Christmas Day yet on their side of the world, they wouldn't think of it until this evening, Sydney time. And as Rachel was always still out, all she usually got were the forced festive messages on her answering machine.

The hamper had arrived as always a week ago. The same David Jones hamper her mother ordered for her every year. 'Such a convenient service!' she would declare when Rachel rang to thank her. The tradition had started at the end of her first year of uni; the hamper turned up the day before Tom set off up the coast to spend Christmas with his family. He had invited Rachel to come with him, but Catherine was expecting her, and it was Alice's first Christmas – at least the first one she was vaguely aware of, she'd still been a blob in a bassinette the previous year. The hamper had provided a great source of amusement for Tom. With them living on instant noodles most of the time, the basket full of gourmet delicacies was like something from another world – jars of pickled herrings and English marmalade, maraschino cherries and marinated goat's cheese. And then the more Christmassy fare: tinned ham and shortbread, a pudding, fruit mince in a jar, which Tom disgusted Rachel by tucking into with a spoon. 'Well, it's not like you were going to make pies, is it?' he defended himself. She told him to go ahead and take whatever he fancied, except anything chocolate, and then she made up a smaller hamper to take with her to the Rourkes'. They were ever so grateful and did lots of oohing and aahing, but Rachel had the feeling they were probably no more likely to eat most of the stuff than she was.

Nevertheless, it had become a tradition to divvy up the hamper and bring a share to Catherine's every year. So Rachel had sorted the loot into a couple of baskets, wrapped them in cellophane and tied them with a big red bow. Then she wrapped all the presents for today and, in a rather lame attempt to kid herself, placed them under her very modest tree. She had gone without a tree once, to see if it made her feel a little less pathetic, but it didn't. So the tree was reinstated and the presents placed under it, though she stopped short of putting out sherry and Christmas cake for Santa.

Rachel had been awake for some time before she finally dragged herself out of bed and headed for the shower. She had just enough time to get ready without rushing, but without having to wait around filling in time either.

As she emerged from the shower twenty minutes later, she thought she might have heard the ringtone on her mobile announcing a text message had arrived. Although it was probably only Catherine confirming times, she couldn't help feeling a tiny measure of excitement. Just maybe her dad had thought to message. She flipped open her phone, but she didn't recognise the number as she clicked to select the message.

> How's the hamper this year?
> Save me something.
> Merry xmas, tom and the girls xxx

Rachel smiled. She quickly replied, wishing them a merry Christmas in return, before storing his number into her phone. Although Tom had been her friend originally, she'd never had his mobile number. They didn't have mobile phones back in the day, and when she returned from her travels he was with Annie, and things were different then. It would have been somehow inappropriate to have his number, to call him about social arrangements and the like. Rachel had come back home preparing herself to meet Tom's new wife, but somewhere along the way, Tom had become just Annie's husband.

Rachel was about to give up on drying her hair when she heard the doorbell. Blowdrying bored her senseless, she could never persevere till her hair was completely dry. She went to answer the door and was surprised to see Martin standing on the threshold.

'What are you doing here? Aren't you the cook?' Rachel asked as she accepted his Merry Christmas kiss on the cheek.

'Ah, but you see I'm all organised, it's cooking itself right now,' he explained. 'And you know what Catherine's like when her parents come, let alone Andrew as well. I thought it was best if I just ducked out to get you.'

Which was a discreet way of saying that Catherine had already downed enough champers and orange to make driving inadvisable, if not illegal. Rachel wasn't surprised. It had slipped her mind that Catherine's brother would be there as well, and she had to admit, spending the best part of a day in his company was hardly a drawcard. He was a strange, disappointed, prematurely middle-aged man who felt that life should have given him a far better deal, despite the fact that he had done nothing much to deserve it. He'd married a mousy, whiny woman, but even she had got sick of him and left him for the proprietor of their local video store. Andrew had moved back down from Queensland to live with his parents, claiming the bitch was bleeding him dry and he couldn't afford to do otherwise. He'd probably drink himself stupid today, give Catherine a run for her money. Deck the halls.

'So, are you going to astound us with yet another amazing stuffing recipe this year?' Rachel asked when they were in the car and on their way. Martin was a nice man, a really nice man, he was just a tad . . . well, single-issue. The only thing that really got him going was food: preparing it, cooking it, talking about it. So that was what Rachel talked about with Martin, though she usually regretted it before long.

'Oh, no, no, no,' he said in a mischievous tone, 'there's not going to be any turkey this year.'

'No turkey?'

'It's supposed to be a surprise, but what the hell,' he said happily. 'We're going . . . Scandinavian!'

'Scandinavian?'

'It's one of the most traditional Christmas cuisines,' he informed her. 'The British and their turkey roasts came much later, you know.'

No, she didn't.

'Just wait till you taste my pièce de résistance this year,' Martin went on.

'Wow, what is it?' she said.

'Traditional gravlax,' he announced. 'I had to cure a whole salmon, first time I've ever done anything like it. Did you know, the process takes three days . . .'

Oh no, and he was going to take her, painstakingly, step by step, hour by hour, through all seventy-two of them. Rachel did her best to pay attention for the remainder of the trip. Mercifully it was a short drive and the traffic wasn't too bad, so it didn't feel too interminable by the time they pulled into the driveway.

Catherine must have been watching out for them because she threw open the door as they walked up the front steps.

'Merry Christmas, darling Rachel!' she said expansively, before throwing her arms around her.

Yeesh, how much champagne had she polished off so far?

'Thank God you're here,' Catherine said into her ear. Then she drew back, still holding her hands. 'Well, don't you look nice,' she said in an encouraging tone, as though Rachel was someone getting over a brain injury and re-entering society. Then she touched her hand to Rachel's barely damp hair. 'Hmm, didn't have quite enough time to dry your hair? Never mind,' she went on without waiting for an answer. 'What do you think?' she gushed, stepping back and performing a little pirouette.

She looked like one of those highly stylised women in a 1950s movie or magazine — stunning, but a little surreal, like she was in technicolour. The dress had a tight-fitting bodice and a big full skirt, printed with oversized flowers in reds and greens. She wore exactly matching forest-green shoes, and her mouth was a slash of bright red lipstick.

'It swishes when you move,' was all Rachel could think to say.

'I know, isn't it gorgeous?' Catherine exclaimed. 'I feel like Grace Kelly. Have you got a drink yet? Martin, Rachel doesn't have a drink!' she called.

'Right here, dear,' he said, coming back from the kitchen with two glasses.

'Oh, don't we usually start with champagne and orange?' said Rachel as he passed her a glass of neat champagne.

'Nonsense,' said Catherine. 'It must be at least eleven-thirty by now, and besides, it's Christmas Day! Loosen up, Rachel!' she added, clinking their glasses together and taking a good glug from hers, just as Rachel noticed Catherine's parents and Andrew watching from the sofa.

'Oh, hello, Mrs Rourke, Mr Rourke,' she said, hurrying over towards them. 'Andrew . . . Merry Christmas everyone.' She set her glass down on the coffee table as they all got to their feet.

'Merry Christmas to you, Rachel, dear,' said Catherine's mother, receiving her kiss.

'You both look well,' said Rachel as she leaned over to kiss Mr Rourke on the cheek. She glanced at Andrew. Would she have to give him a kiss? He was making the decision for her, leaning in for the kill. Rachel performed a counterattack, leading with her cheek, so he had no choice but to plant his sloppy lips there. Ick, she wanted to wipe her face right away, but she'd have to wait a tactful moment till he wasn't watching.

'Well you look great, Rachel, just great,' he said. 'Doesn't Rachel look great, Mum?'

'Yes, she looks great,' Catherine butted in. 'And there'll be plenty of time to catch up later,' she added, shooing them along. 'Go and help Martin in the kitchen, won't you lot? Rachel and I need ten minutes together to exchange gifts, okay? It's our tradition. Martin, bring the rest of that bottle in here so we don't have to come looking.'

'Of course, dear,' he said, ushering the others out of the room.

This was the part Rachel always dreaded. It hadn't always been like this; it used to be fun, and sweet, even a little meaningful. Although Rachel always had plenty of pocket money when they were kids, she would never have dreamed of showing Catherine up by buying her expensive gifts. Instead they bought each other candles and cheap costume jewellery from the markets, sometimes a crazy piece of clothing from an op shop. They found secondhand books of their favourite authors, or made each other mixed tapes. Rachel even knitted Catherine a scarf one Christmas. It was pretty bodgy, she was a sloppy knitter, but Catherine wore it regardless.

But now Rachel spent more time looking for Catherine's gift than she did for anyone else's, she spent more money and she certainly expended more angst. Yet she rarely succeeded in finding something that met with Catherine's approval. Perhaps simple, inexpensive gifts were an uncomfortable reminder of a past life, now that she had reinvented herself into someone accustomed to designer labels and luxury brands. But it was more than that – Catherine seemed to take almost personal affront at what she deemed a less than perfect gift, as though it was proof the giver just wasn't trying hard enough. Rachel suspected it was her fragile ego again, needing reassurance that she was special, exceptional even. But forcing someone to buy you a gift seemed an odd way to prove it.

Rachel monitored Catherine's expression as she opened her present now, going into overdrive to explain that it was made from one hundred per cent cashmere, and that it was called a 'shrug', and they were very popular, and you could wear it over almost anything.

Catherine fixed a smile on her face and finally spoke. 'You shouldn't have, Rachel.'

It sounded more like a statement of fact than a declaration of gratitude.

'I'm just not sure it's going to fit,' she went on. 'You know I have very slender shoulders. But you kept the docket?'

Of course, Rachel always kept the docket; she'd known Catherine a long time.

'Now, open yours!' Catherine said, thrusting a large parcel at her.

It was heavy. Rachel carefully removed the elaborate wrapping which Catherine always had done professionally, and opened the box, pushing aside the tissue paper. She lifted out an ugly, carved figure, not unlike one of those Easter Island statues, though in miniature. But it was really heavy, she guessed it was made of stone, or maybe concrete. Was it a garden ornament? She lived in a flat.

The irony of all this was that Catherine rarely bought Rachel anything that she either particularly liked or was likely to use. Not that she'd realise that, because Rachel always thanked her profusely, to the point of gushing. In fact, the intensity of her display of gratitude was generally inversely proportionate to how much she actually liked the gift in question. But it just didn't seem right not to be appreciative of the thought, if nothing else; it went against the very nature of gift-giving. But try as she might, Rachel just couldn't muster up any fake enthusiasm as she stared at the lump of stone in front of her.

Catherine tossed back half a glass of champagne and then began to laugh uproariously. Maybe it was meant to be a joke?

'You should see your face right now!' she said when she got her breath back. 'I knew you wouldn't know what to make of it. But it's perfect, wait till I explain. He's the Javanese god or something – of *sexual* potency.'

'You have got to be kidding me.'

'No!' Catherine exclaimed. 'Isn't he just divine? He does grow on you, I promise, I had him sitting on my dressing table all week. Anyway, it's just meant to be a bit of fun, even though it was hideously expensive. I thought he would make an ideal mascot for our internet search.'

'Hmm, we'll see about that,' Rachel muttered, settling him back into his box.

'Uh-uh,' said Catherine, wagging her finger. 'I'm not going to let you welch on our agreement.'

'I don't remember agreeing to anything.'

Catherine laughed loudly again and threw her arms around Rachel. 'I'm so glad you're here, it makes it so much easier to put up with them,' she said, cocking her head in the direction of the kitchen.

'Maybe we should go and join them?'

'In a minute,' she dismissed. 'Do you have to go to the Dingles' later?'

Rachel nodded.

'You could get out of it,' Catherine said, taking her by the hands. 'Just message Lexie and tell her you promised me you'd stay.'

'I don't want to get out of it,' said Rachel. 'It's fun.'

Catherine was shaking her head. 'You're too nice for your own good sometimes, Rachel. Though I guess you do have that smorgasbord of Scott's brothers to perve at, pity they're all taken.'

They heard footsteps coming down the stairs, and then Alice appeared. She gasped when she saw Rachel. 'Mum! You said you'd call me when Rachel got here!'

'I'm not the concierge, Alice.'

'Hi sweetie! Merry Christmas,' said Rachel, getting to her feet. 'You look great!'

'I think that top's a bit tight,' Catherine muttered.

Alice ignored her mother and instead made a beeline for Rachel, giving her a big, unreserved hug. Rachel adored Alice; she was the only child she had known since birth, when she was barely more than a child herself. She had been terrified to even hold her at first. Babies were scary, vulnerable, breakable, and Rachel didn't trust herself with something so precious. But when she got back from overseas, Alice was a fully-formed little person, and that was when they really bonded. They could have conversations; they could read books together, play games. Alice used to come for sleepovers whenever Catherine needed a babysitter, which was often, but Rachel didn't mind, she loved it. Maybe it was because she was an only child too. Rachel had observed throughout her life that only children had a certain connection; nobody but an only child could really understand what it was like to be one.

'I have something for you,' said Rachel, stooping to pick up a long thin tube wrapped in Christmas paper. At least it was still fun giving Alice presents.

Alice gave a little squeal as she tore off the wrapping and twisted the end of the tube open. She carefully drew out the poster from inside. 'Omigod!' she squealed again, unfurling it. 'No way! This is awesome, Rachel! Where did you find it? I haven't seen posters of these guys anywhere!'

'I had to order it online from the US.'

'Who on earth are they?' said Catherine, turning up her nose. 'I've never heard of them.'

'Wow, Mum, I'm surprised, because you're like, so totally immersed in the Jersey indie scene.' Alice rolled her eyes. 'This is so totally cool, Rachel, thanks heaps!' she cried, throwing her arms around Rachel's neck.

'I hope you don't think you're going to be putting that up in your room,' said Catherine.

Alice turned to look at her. 'What difference does it make to you? It's my room.'

'I didn't have the interiors designed by the most prestigious firm on the eastern seaboard to have cheap posters ruining the walls,' Catherine said airily.

'Fine,' Alice retorted. 'I'll put it on the back of my door then.'

'Alice, the doors are custom-made from reclaimed river red gum. You're not hammering tacks into them.'

'Chill, Mum, I'll use Blu-Tack.'

Catherine sighed. 'We'll discuss this later.'

'No we won't!' Alice spat.

'I beg your pardon, Alice?'

'We never "discuss" anything, you just say no. It's total bullshit.'

'Alice –'

But Alice had grabbed the poster and stormed back over to the stairs. They stood watching as she stomped loudly on each individual step until she was out of sight.

Catherine turned to glare at Rachel. 'Well, thanks for that.'

*

Rose Bay

'I wish you didn't have to go so soon,' Lexie's mother lamented as she wrapped slices of ham in foil.

'Mum, it's nearly four o'clock,' said Lexie, 'and we've been here since nine this morning.'

'But Dad called, he'll be on his way shortly,' she persisted. 'It was a boy, by the way. Name of Finn, I think he said.'

'Oh, I love that name. I'd like a Finn.'

She bit her lip. 'Lexie, no, think about it. He'd be Finn Dingle, that's too awful.'

'Mum, don't start.'

'All the trouble I went to when you were born so that your name would be strong and beautiful and you could wear it with pride.' She shook her head. 'Tamblyn's not that easy, there are a lot of names that don't go with it. Alexa Tamblyn was perfect, but as we found out soon enough, you just weren't an Alexa. You were the cutest little poppet, smiling all the time, with that adorable cap of curls and those big round eyes. And everyone was calling you Lexie before long, and I gave in, because it suited you so well. And Lexie Tamblyn had a certain ring.'

Her mother took a deep, wistful breath. Here it comes, thought Lexie, steeling herself.

'Why you had to take Scott's name is beyond me. In this day and age. And now the children are saddled with it as well.'

'Whether or not I took his name, the kids would still be Dingle,' Lexie pointed out. 'Unless you'd prefer Dingle-Tamblyn.'

She grimaced as Scott stuck his head around the door. 'The kids are all strapped in the car, how are we doing here?'

'Who's watching them?' asked Lexie.

'Everybody. They're all waiting out there to see us off.'

'Okay, that'll do, Mum,' said Lexie, closing the lid of the esky.

'But there's some —'

'Mum, you've packed up enough leftovers to feed us for a week,' Lexie insisted. 'And we really have to get going, we still have to pick up Rachel on the way.'

'Okay,' she surrendered. 'I only wish we didn't have to divide up Christmas like this. Why can't all your family just come here, Scott?' she added as he picked up the esky.

He looked sheepish. 'There's too many of us, Sally.'

'The more the merrier as far as I'm concerned.'

'Mum, we're going to see you tomorrow for Boxing Day brunch,' Lexie reminded her. 'But now we have to go or we'll be late.'

As they drove away with a toot of the horn, Lexie glanced over at Scott. He always had the same expression leaving her parents' place — a little put out, on edge — he certainly never seemed relaxed. Sometimes it got to her; she wished she could reassure him that her mother's biggest issue with him was that he had a silly-sounding name. But she wouldn't tell him that, of course, because that would probably hurt his feelings.

'You okay?' she ventured after a while.

He shrugged. 'My family's important to me too, you know, Lexie.'

'I know that, honey,' she insisted, touching his arm. 'We won't be late, I promise I won't get stuck talking to Catherine.'

'It's not that, I'm not worried about being late,' he said. 'I'm just saying, my family's important too. Just as important as yours.'

'Of course they are. I love your family, Scott, you know that.'

He sighed heavily. 'Yeah, I know. It's just . . . never mind.'

Lexie watched him, wondering if she ought to draw him out, get him to say what was on his mind. But it was Christmas. Maybe there was another way to approach it.

'Well, I was glad to get out of there,' said Lexie. 'I don't think I could have sat listening to Monica for much longer.'

He glanced at her. 'Yeah?'

'Wasn't she driving you up the wall?' Lexie went on. 'The way she kept saying, "When are you two going to take a trip overseas?" She knows we can't afford it, it's just rude. How would she like it if I said, "When are you going to get on with it and have a baby?"'

'I think your mother takes care of that line of questioning,' Scott said with a smile. 'Poor old Eric never has a lot to say.'

'Because he can't get a word in between Stephanie and Monica trying to outdo each other.'

The rivalry between the sisters-in-law was obvious, despite the sugar coating they tried to put on it.

'Don't you find it hilarious?' Lexie paused to clear her throat. 'When I was in Utopia,' she began, affecting a pompous accent, 'I found the service truly marvellous. Ooh, then you must go to Nirvana, my dear, it's on the way to Shangri-la, before you get to Xanadu.'

Scott was grinning, shaking his head. 'You're a nut.'

They pulled up at lights and he turned to look at her. 'Do you wish you could do some travelling?'

'No,' she said simply.

'Really? You were sitting there pretty wide-eyed while they were talking, asking lots of questions.'

'I was just being polite,' Lexie dismissed.

'So you don't have any urge to travel?'

She shrugged. 'Maybe one day. But the kids are too little. And you couldn't leave the café anyway.'

'Does that bother you?'

Lexie shifted in her seat to face Scott. 'What are you getting at?'

He sighed. 'I just wonder sometimes if you wish things were different, when you look at Monica, with her clothes and her cars and her trips . . . and you're . . . tied down here, because of the café and the kids.'

'Scott Anthony Dingle. Don't you even say it! Don't even hint it! I can't imagine my life without you and the kids, and I wouldn't want to!' Lexie was shaking her head as she sat straight in her seat again, folding her arms. 'Imagine saying that, on Christmas of all days!'

She could feel him staring at her. She looked across at him and he had a big wide grin on his face.

'What?' she asked.

He leaned right over and kissed her soundly on the mouth. 'I love you.'

'That's more like it.'

Lexie had sent a text message about twenty minutes ago to say they were packing up at her mum's, so Rachel didn't imagine they could be too much longer. And it wouldn't be a moment too soon as far as she was concerned. Lunch had been a strained affair, to say the least.

Catherine was pretty well sloshed, and her mood had become increasingly erratic as the day wore on. Alice sat with her chin in her hand, pushing the food around her plate with a fork and grimacing. Rachel couldn't blame her. There was smoked mutton and venison, salted cod, herring – lots of herring, smoked, pickled, in a salad. There were potato pancakes and turnips, black bread, roe, and the much-lauded gravlax. It was rather odd food to be eating on a typical Australian summer day, though she supposed the customary turkey roast was an odd tradition as well. But at least it *was* tradition. It might have been different if either Catherine or Martin had a Scandinavian background, but neither of them did, so Rachel had to wonder what had possessed them to go with this theme. And who were they trying to impress? It certainly wasn't working on this crowd.

As Martin carried out one platter after another, Mr Rourke would ask hopefully, 'Is this the turkey then?' or 'Will this be the ham?' or just 'What's this then?'

'Your father's not all that keen on fish,' Mrs Rourke muttered repeatedly.

'So, no turkey?'

Catherine finally snapped. 'No! There is no fucking ham or turkey! There is, however, delicious and frightfully expensive gourmet food that Martin has gone to a lot of trouble to prepare. It's *Scandinavian!*'

Rachel sighed with relief when the doorbell finally rang. 'That'll be Lexie,' she said, jumping up from the table. She quickly did the rounds, saying her goodbyes while Catherine tottered out to the front door.

'Lucky you,' said Alice when Rachel got to her. 'You have a means of escape.'

Rachel laughed nervously and gave her a hug. She wished she could kidnap her, she could only imagine the fun Alice would have at the Dingles'. 'I'll see you soon, chook. Merry Christmas.'

'Easy for you to say,' she grumped.

Rachel quickly gathered up her things and hurried to the door.

'Really,' Catherine was insisting drunkenly, 'we've got so much food, Lexie, you should come in and have a plate with us.'

'The kids are in the car —'

'Bring them in as well,' Catherine slurred, leaning on Lexie's shoulder. 'I'll go out and have a word to Scott.'

'No Catherine,' Lexie stopped her. 'It took us longer to get away from Mum's and we're running a little late. Scott's getting agitated, so —'

'Ah, tell him to go fuck himself.'

'Catherine!'

'You've really got to learn to stand up for yourself and stop taking so much shit from him, Lexie.'

Lexie looked perplexed. 'But . . . I didn't . . . I don't . . .'

'We really have to go,' Rachel broke in chirpily. 'Thanks again, Catherine, it was great.' She gave her a swift, firm hug and a kiss on the cheek. 'I'll call you next week.'

Then she grabbed Lexie's arm and propelled her down the front steps and up the path to the car.

'My God, she was so —'

'Pissed,' Rachel finished for her. 'It's Catherine's default position at Christmas.'

'Not just at Christmas,' Lexie muttered.

They walked out past the shorn hedge of grief and Rachel smiled when she saw their car. 'Ah, look at that! A normal, happy family on Christmas Day, what do you know? I was beginning to think there was no such thing.'

Lexie had a funny look on her face. 'You think of us as a happy family?'

'Lexie, you guys are so perfect you belong on a Christmas card.'

She broke into a teary smile. 'I haven't even wished you a Merry Christmas yet,' she said, hugging Rachel.

Scott tooted the horn lightly and they bent to look at him inside the car. He beckoned impatiently.

'Should we tell him to go f—'

But Lexie covered Rachel's mouth with her hand.

*

Walking into the backyard of the Dingles' house in Maroubra was always the highlight of Christmas Day for Rachel, at least for the last few years since she'd been invited to join them. While she was married to Sean they had always called in to Catherine's in the late morning on the way to Christmas lunch with Sean's family, which was an unremarkable but pleasant enough affair. The first Christmas after they separated, Rachel was beginning to feel a little lost. Annie and Tom were going up the coast as usual; and with her brother and his insufferable wife coming down from Queensland, Catherine had decided to pack up her family and head as far as possible in the opposite direction. So much to Alice's horror, they were spending Christmas in Tasmania. There had been a moment's awkward silence when everyone was discussing their plans and it became obvious that Rachel didn't have any.

'Great! That means you're free to spend Christmas with us!' Lexie had exclaimed happily. Rachel tried to beg off, thinking that was the polite thing to do when the invitation had only been extended out of politeness, but Lexie wouldn't hear of it.

'My mother adores having extra people at Christmas, you have no idea. And the Dingles, well, to be honest, they wouldn't even notice an extra person. But they'll love having you.'

That year Rachel had experienced possibly the loveliest Christmas of her life, as it turned out. The Tamblyns were delightful, particularly Sally and Keith, who, for the first time in more years than anyone could remember, did not have lunch interrupted to go deliver a baby, and thus declared that Rachel was a good-luck charm and should join them every year for Christmas. And the Dingles were a revelation. They were a big, rowdy bunch who actually seemed to enjoy each other's company. Scott was the youngest of four brothers; there was a Chris, an Adam and a Mitch, Rachel had never quite mastered who was who but they forgave her, seeing as their mum rarely got their names right either. They appeared to love their wives and adore their kids, who ranged from teenagers all the way down to toddlers. Rachel had no way of knowing who belonged to whom because they all mixed together so seamlessly.

'There's my girl,' Scott's dad, John, greeted her expansively when they arrived, giving her a big bear hug. 'Well you just get more beautiful every year, Rachel.'

'Leave the poor girl alone, Ding,' said Jenny, Scott's mum. 'She doesn't want an old bloke like you slobbering all over her.'

Rachel adored them, she wished they could adopt her, she wanted to belong to this family. They lived in a post-war brick house perched high on the crest of a hill, with a view to the ocean from the second-storey extension. There was always an absurd amount of food. Rachel was usually too full, but this year she tucked into the turkey and ham like a junkie who'd been deprived of a fix. Beer and wine flowed, everyone sported those ridiculous flimsy paper hats from their Christmas crackers, and sharing the enclosed bad joke was mandatory. It was all set to a soundtrack of sentimental Christmas standards playing on a constant loop through speakers someone had set up on the upstairs balcony, facing out to the yard. At least until one of the teenagers would surreptitiously change the music, the 'oldies' would eventually notice and Bing Crosby would be promptly reinstated, singing 'White Christmas' all over again from the start.

Night cricket was another Dingle Christmas tradition, played after dinner, once everyone actually felt capable of standing up. Rachel was always one of the first to get out, she was so bad at ball sports. She definitely blamed that on being an only child. Sitting here watching the Dingles, she couldn't help fantasise about how different her life might have been if she'd had even one sibling. Just to have someone else who shared her genes, her history, her parents . . .

Lexie was bowled out and she came over to sit beside Rachel at the far end of the table. 'Everything okay?' she asked.

'Of course,' she assured her. 'I just love watching them, they have such a good time together. I'm still waiting for Jenny and John to offer to adopt me, you know.'

Lexie looked at her. 'Have you heard from your mum or dad?'

Rachel shook her head. 'They're just getting up on their side of the world. They'll probably call soon, leave a message on my answering machine.'

'Must be hard not having your family close by.'

Rachel didn't want to spoil Lexie's illusions by suggesting

that even if her parents lived in the same street they would never be close.

'Do you know how lucky you are, Lex? You have two wonderful families.'

'Actually three,' she corrected her.

'Of course, what am I saying? You have your own little family as well.'

Lexie gave a faint shake of her head. 'I do know how lucky I am, Rachel, and frankly it scares me.'

'Why?'

'Sometimes I think I have too much, and that something will have to be taken away from me.' She turned to face Rachel. 'I mean, look at Annie and Tom – the perfect couple, the ideal family. What did they do to deserve what happened to them?'

'You can't think like that Lexie,' said Rachel. 'Some people don't "deserve" tragedy, just as some people don't deserve love and happiness, more than others.'

That was her silent dread. She'd dealt with it in therapy, years ago, but she had to keep reminding herself nearly every day. It wasn't some intrinsic personal flaw that made her little more than an afterthought to her parents. She had to believe that, or else what was she supposed to make of her life now? That she was alone because she didn't deserve to be loved, while Catherine deserved to have someone who doted on her hand and foot, no matter how she treated him in return? Or even that Tom deserved to lose his beloved wife?

'Shit happens,' Rachel went on, 'and it doesn't discriminate. Do you think some poor kid born in Africa is less deserving than some kid born up the road from here?'

'But that just makes me all the more worried,' Lexie said, wide-eyed. 'I don't deserve all this more than that poor child in Africa, and it could all get taken away so easily.'

'Yeah, it could, but it probably won't,' said Rachel. 'And worrying about it isn't going to help. You should just enjoy it, Lexie, every moment. And never, ever take it for granted.'

*

January

'Boy, when you say "in the new year", you don't muck around, do you?' said Rachel as she opened the door to Catherine. It was January 2, Rachel had managed to hold her off until now with vague excuses, hoping she'd drop the internet dating idea altogether. It wasn't much of a strategy, Catherine did not give up easily.

'Take some of this stuff from me, will you?' she said, dumping a heavy box into Rachel's arms.

'What is this?' she frowned.

She pushed past Rachel, lugging bags over both shoulders. 'It's Elvis, the sex god I gave you for Christmas. You left him at my place, and we're going to need him tonight. He's our mascot, remember?'

'Hmm.' Rachel followed her down the hall into the living room. 'Did you say "Elvis"? Isn't he supposed to be Javanese?'

Catherine shrugged. 'I don't know any Javanese. Elvis seemed to suit him.' She looked around. 'Honestly, Rachel, how do you get the place into such a mess when you're only one person?' She dropped her bags into one of the armchairs and started bustling about, gathering up newspapers which were lying around. 'Where's your recycling bin?'

'No, I haven't finished with those,' Rachel protested, coming over to wrest the pile of papers from Catherine's hands.

'What are you going to do with them?'

'I still have stuff to read, articles to clip.'

'You clip articles?'

'Yeah.' Well, she thought about clipping articles. And sometimes she actually did. Then she didn't know what to do with them.

'What do you do with them?' Catherine persisted.

Rachel groaned. 'What's it to you?' She walked over to a corner of the room and dropped the newspapers on the floor in a pile.

Catherine was shaking her head. 'You're going to turn into one of those old ladies in a house full of junk, stacks of newspapers and collections of empty jars ... And cats, you'll have cats everywhere, and the council will come around and impound them.'

Rachel folded her arms. 'Thanks for that cheery glimpse into my future, Catherine.'

'Don't worry, I wouldn't actually let any of that happen to you.'

'Oh, that's so nice, you'll stop council from taking away all my cats?'

Catherine ignored that. 'We are going to get your life back on track. Starting with putting you out there again,' she added, sliding her laptop out of one of the bags.

'Why did you bring your computer? We can use mine.'

'You're still connected to the internet?'

'Ye-ah!' She said it like it had two syllables and she was a teenage girl. But that's how Catherine made her feel sometimes. 'I pay my bills, Catherine, I'm not as useless as you seem to think I am.'

'Okay,' she said, holding her hands up in surrender. 'Doesn't hurt to have another computer between three of us.'

Rachel frowned. 'Who else is coming?'

'Lexie, of course. She's been held up waiting for Scott – as usual.'

'You asked Lexie?'

'I thought it'd be fun. So did she.'

'Yeah, fun at my expense.'

Catherine turned to face her squarely, hands on hips. 'Well, someone's certainly got an attitude,' she scolded. 'You were the one who wanted me to include Lexie in everything.' She gave her head an exasperated shake. 'Look, I know this is hard, that's why I'm trying to inject a little fun into it. But Rachel, this is not just about you not having a boyfriend, this is about you avoiding a relationship. I think we both know that's what you've been doing, and maybe for good reason. But your time is up, you've got to start to put yourself out there, and whether you like it or not,' she pointed in the direction of the computer, 'this is how it's done these days.'

This was what really annoyed Rachel about Catherine – she had this infuriatingly accurate insight at times, at least where other people were concerned.

'But you'll be pleased to know I brought something to ease the pain,' she said, plucking a bottle of champagne out of a cooler bag.

Ah, another of Catherine's gifts; she could always be relied upon to bring the booze.

'I'll get some glasses,' said Rachel, turning for the kitchen.

'Make sure they're clean,' Catherine called after her.

When Rachel returned with freshly rinsed champagne flutes, Catherine had set herself up at the coffee table, sitting cross-legged on a cushion on the floor, shoes kicked aside, her glasses perched on the edge of her nose, while Elvis stood sentinel over her laptop. 'Well, flutes even? Wonders never cease.'

Rachel grabbed the bottle and began to tear off the foil. She really needed a drink.

'So I've been doing some research,' said Catherine. 'You have to approach this like a business.'

'Sounds romantic.'

'There's nothing romantic about it at all.'

'Super!' Rachel exclaimed, popping the cork.

'No, I mean of course the romance will come, it should come. But if you let romance get in the way of finding a partner, you may overlook some extremely viable prospects.'

'"Viable prospects". Now I'm getting hot.'

There was a knock at the door so Rachel put the bottle down and sauntered up the hall to answer it.

'Hi, Happy New Year!' Lexie chirped, lurching at her with a kiss and hug. 'Sorry I'm late, you didn't start without me, I hope?'

'No, I've just opened a bottle.'

'I brought one too!' she said happily, raising hers. 'This is going to be fun.'

For the spectators more than the participant, Rachel thought dully.

Once they were ensconced in front of duelling laptops at either end of the coffee table, their glasses charged, Catherine commanded their attention.

'Okay, Rendezvous is by far the most mainstream, respected site, so that's the best place to start. 'So type in r-e –'

'I know how to spell rendezvous, Catherine,' said Rachel.

'Okay, but don't forget the .au or else you'll end up on the American site.'

'Nothing wrong with that,' said Rachel. 'I might hook up with George Clooney.'

'Yeah, George Clooney is on Rendezvous,' Catherine said deadpan. 'Besides, he's gay.'

'He is not,' said Rachel.

'He *so* is not,' Lexie agreed. 'I don't believe that rumour for a second.'

'Whatever, he's not in the ballpark,' said Catherine. 'Now the idea is to browse first, get a feel for what's out there. Enter your basic search parameters – I'm thinking . . . thirty-five to fifty –'

'Fifty? I don't want someone that old.'

'George Clooney is pushing fifty,' Catherine reminded her.

'Yeah, but he's clearly an exception,' said Rachel.

'Okay, forty-five,' she revised. 'Within fifty kilometres of your postcode, looking for a short- or long-term relationship . . . now, press enter and off we go!'

Rachel propped her chin in her hand as she scrolled down through the opening lines. '*Love is friendship on fire* . . . What does that even mean? Oh, here we go, *Looking for that exceptional lady with eyes of fire.* Fire is hot, obviously. Ha, I made a pun.'

Catherine rolled her eyes. 'Here's one – *Having achieved everything in life, the only thing missing now is you. Are you the one to share with me the best of what life has to offer?*'

'Wanker,' Rachel grunted. 'If he's achieved everything in life, how come he's on the internet looking for a date?'

'Oh my God!' Lexie exclaimed, wide-eyed. 'Listen to this – *It's cold outside, rain is falling and wind is lashing the trees. Inside it's warm, the fire is glowing and I've poured two glasses of red. One for me and one for DOT DOT DOT!*'

'You're making that up,' said Catherine.

'Sadly she's not,' said Rachel flatly, before taking a gulp of her champagne. 'This is a really bad idea, Catherine.'

'Look,' she said, 'unless they're in advertising or marketing or something, you can't expect them to be good at writing a catch-phrase. Click on one you like the look of and read his entire profile.'

They went silent for a while, sipping their drinks and perusing the talent, for want of a better word.

'They're all accountants,' said Rachel after a while.

'How do you know that?' asked Catherine.

'Hello! They're all "professionals" in "financial services".'

'Well, given the global financial crisis, maybe they're trying to avoid the term "investment banker" or "stockbroker".'

'Or "retrenched",' Rachel muttered.

'What is it about *The Shawshank Redemption*?' asked Lexie, frowning at the screen. 'It's like, everybody's favourite film.'

'It's a good film,' said Catherine. 'Nothing wrong with that.'

'And why do all these big chunky boofheads call themselves "athletic",' Rachel wanted to know.

'I noticed that too,' said Lexie. 'And they're all after girls who are "slim" or "athletic". I bet their idea of an athletic girl is different from their idea of an athletic guy.'

'Listen to this one,' said Rachel. '*My ideal partner would be slim, blonde or fair hair, shoulder length, five/five to five/nine in height, feminine, toned but not muscular, and wear a nice perfume.* Could he be more specific?'

'He's just being efficient,' said Catherine. 'He knows what he likes.'

'Unlike this one,' Rachel went on. '*Looking to settle down and live life at a frantic pace.*'

'I'm confused,' said Lexie.

'You're not the only one,' said Rachel. 'He goes on – *Someone who knows how to have fun, but also show restraint. Must have a wicked side but be well balanced.* And schizophrenic, clearly.'

Lexie started to giggle.

'You're both bringing a very negative vibe to this whole thing,' said Catherine.

'Hold on, I think I've found the one!' Rachel declared. '*I do bonsai and am interested in camellias and heritage species roses.*'

'Oh, dear,' said Lexie. 'Why would you admit to that if you were trying to get a date?'

'It could be worse,' said Catherine, 'he could be into trains.'

'I wasn't finished,' said Rachel. She cleared her throat importantly. '*I am also interested in light railways and their history. I have constructed a steam railway in my garden which combines several of my hobbies.*'

They looked up from the computer screens then, meeting each other's eyes, and that was it. All three broke into uncontrollable fits of laughter, until Rachel was rolling on the floor, Lexie had tears running down her cheeks and even Catherine couldn't catch her breath.

She was the first to recover, however. 'I promise you, I've heard so many stories about people finding their perfect match this way. We just have to persevere, surely we're going to have to get to the good ones soon.'

So the three of them resumed their positions and focused on the screens again.

'Hey, here's a catch,' said Catherine. 'This one signs off with *No frumps with too many lumps please.*'

Rachel and Lexie gasped.

'What's he look like?' Rachel asked.

'He's got a head like a shin of beef.' Catherine often reverted to her suburban roots when she had a few drinks under her belt.

'What exactly does a shin of beef look like?' Rachel asked her.

'I don't know,' said Catherine. 'My mother used to say it all the time.'

'Listen to this,' said Lexie. '*And ladies, when I say "slim", I mean size eight to ten, not twelve to fourteen.*'

Rachel was topping up their glasses. 'Okay, what I don't get is, are there actually women who would read that and sigh with relief that they're an eight to ten and therefore in the running? If there are, they need a good slap around the head.'

'That's a little politically incorrect, Rachel,' said Lexie.

'Well, I didn't mean it literally.'

Lexie blinked. 'Don't you mean the opposite? You meant it "literally" – like in a book, like literature. It's made up.'

'No, it's the other way around.'

'Is it?' She looked at Catherine for confirmation, and Catherine nodded. 'God, now I feel stupid.'

'You shouldn't,' Rachel reassured her. 'People do it all the time. It's one of my bugbears.'

'We could put that in your profile,' said Catherine. 'I'm just bringing it up now. *Must literally know the meaning of literally.*'

'And be able to spell and punctuate.'

'I'm with you there,' said Catherine. 'You know, even fully grown, fully qualified lawyers are writing emails like teenagers now. No capitals, they don't even seem to have a clue what an apostrophe is.'

'Don't get me started,' said Rachel.

'Anyway, I think this might be the best way to go,' said Catherine. 'You put up your profile and they can come looking for you.'

'So you're saying if we build it, they will come?'

'Here's hoping.' Catherine raised her glass and took a drink, before setting it back on the coffee table. 'Okay, so there are a couple of standard boxes we have to tick before we get creative with your blurb. Postcode, height –'

'I don't know how tall I am,' said Rachel. 'At least not in metric.'

'You're the same height as me,' Catherine dismissed, keying it in.

'Am I?'

She nodded. 'Since high school.'

'Oh.'

'Body type is next . . . I think we should go for *a little bit overweight*.'

'No she isn't,' Lexie protested.

'Define "a little bit overweight",' said Rachel. 'I mean, how long is a piece of string?'

Catherine frowned. 'What are you trying to say?'

'Just that isn't everyone a little bit overweight?'

She shrugged. 'I'm not, Lexie isn't.'

'But people always underestimate their weight, and how much they drink, stuff like that. It's an accepted fact, doctors actually allow for it,' Rachel added knowingly.

'So are you saying that if you put *a little bit overweight*, they'll assume you're a sumo wrestler?'

'Maybe.'

Lexie was reading off the screen. 'I think you should just put average,' she decided.

'But when they meet her . . .' Catherine left the rest to their imaginations, and Rachel's imagination was seeing herself in a sumo-wrestler costume.

'Look,' she said, trying to hang on to the rapidly diminishing shreds of her self-esteem, 'according to some chart somewhere, maybe I am strictly above my ideal weight, but compared to the population around me, I think I'm pretty average.'

'Actually, that's a good point,' Catherine nodded. 'The general population is becoming more obese, so you probably are average. I'll go along with that.'

Somehow Rachel didn't feel like it was a victory.

'Next is *Don't have children*, obviously, but we should tick *Want children*, I assume?'

Rachel shrugged. This was getting serious. 'I guess.'

'You don't want kids?' asked Lexie, trying to hide her horror at the idea.

'No, I do, I suppose, I mean, that's normal, right? It's just hard to imagine, the way my life is right now.'

'It won't be when you meet the right man,' Lexie said encouragingly.

'Which is the object of the exercise,' Catherine murmured, reading the list on the screen. '*Education level* – well, I suppose we can fudge it and say *university*, even though you never graduated. *Occupation level* – *clerical/admin*. Hmm, that's probably not going to look good – why are you just doing clerical work if you have a degree – but what can we do?'

Open another bottle, Rachel decided, getting up. They'd emptied the first.

'Oh, don't open that for me,' said Lexie when Rachel came back from the kitchen with the bottle she'd brought. 'I have to drive.'

'Well, I don't,' said Catherine. 'Pop the damn thing.'

'How are you getting home?' asked Rachel.

'I'll call Martin, or a taxi.'

'I can give you a lift,' Lexie offered, getting to her feet. 'Do you mind if I make myself a cup of tea, Rach?'

'Sure, if you don't mind teabags?'

'That's all we have at home,' she assured her, walking over to the kitchen.

'Philistines,' Catherine muttered. She picked up the glass Rachel had just filled and proceeded to empty half of it. '*Political persuasion?*'

'Left-wing, you know that.'

Catherine winced. 'But I don't think you should admit to it. Some people might think you're a communist.'

Rachel was shaking her head. 'I wouldn't be interested in anyone who thought left-wing meant communist,' she said. 'Yeesh, Catherine.'

'But you want to keep your options open, don't you?'

'That's what I was trying to do with the weight thing.'

'But that's different,' said Catherine. 'You can hide your political persuasion.'

Rachel was over it. All this scrutiny was getting a bit much. She left the blurb largely to Catherine, who was suddenly much less concerned with telling the truth. She excused it on the basis that the checklist was like the nutritional analysis panel on the side of a box of cereal, while the blurb was like the front of the box – colourful, attractive, eye-catching; where you could get away with the suggestion that eating the cereal would change your life, though no one really believed that. So she transformed Rachel into a vibrant, gym-toned intellectual who liked discussing the latest subtitled film showing at the Dendy over a soy latte in an inner-city café. She attempted to avoid the more obvious clichés, but it proved almost impossible. Of course Rachel wanted someone who could make her laugh, who liked good conversation over a nice meal, walks on the beach. She did, however, stop short of mentioning pina coladas and getting caught in the rain.

When her profile was finally lodged and active they had a drink to celebrate; Lexie even accepted a splash in her glass so she could toast to Rachel's imminent success.

'You don't look all that excited, Rach,' she remarked, looking at her.

'Oh, it's just the whole shopping-list approach,' she cringed. 'I mean, whatever happened to just meeting someone and hitting it off? Catching someone's eye across a crowded room, or waiting in the same line to order coffee and striking up a conversation, getting stuck in an elevator with a total stranger . . .'

'What kind of books have you been reading?' Catherine grimaced.

'I just don't think it's very romantic to have a checklist you mark off first.'

'And that's how you ended up with Sean.'

'Oh, for heaven's sake,' Rachel scoffed. 'People did meet each other before the internet, Catherine. What about you and Martin?'

'To be honest, I did have a bit of a checklist. I didn't want infatuation to cloud my judgement.'

'You were infatuated with Martin?' Rachel couldn't imagine Martin arousing feelings of infatuation in anyone.

'That's what I'm saying,' Catherine sighed. 'I wasn't going to be influenced by infatuation, passion, raw attraction, it only leads to heartbreak; whereas a cool-headed, pragmatic approach can lead to contentment and a solid partnership.'

Lexie was making no attempt to hide her horror this time.

'Don't look like that,' said Catherine. 'When you get older and you have a few failed relationships behind you, you'll think differently.'

'I'm not going to have a few failed relationships behind me,' Lexie insisted. 'I'll still be with Scott.'

'Yeah,' Catherine nodded faintly, thinking about it, 'you probably will.'

Lexie felt proud, but looking at the expression on Catherine's face, she was not so sure she meant it as a compliment.

'How did you and Scott meet?' Rachel asked. 'I'm not sure I've ever heard that story.'

Catherine gave Rachel a dark look as Lexie's face lit up and she leaned forwards.

'Oh, it was just wonderful,' she swooned. 'It really was love at first sight, I wouldn't have believed it could happen, but it did.'

'Wow, this'll be good, go on,' Rachel urged.

'Well, I was at Coogee beach with a couple of girlfriends after our final exams in third year, and we decided to get some lunch, and we walked up to this new café that had just opened.' She grinned. 'I don't have to tell you which one. And there he was,' she sighed the entire phrase.

'That's it?' said Catherine.

'Well, no, of course not,' she said. 'I mean, I was totally gone, hook, line and sinker, there and then, the whole shebang.'

'Okay, we get it. What did Scott do?'

'Oh nothing, you know Scott.'

'When does the love at first sight part kick in?' asked Catherine.

'With me!' she insisted. 'As soon as I saw him I knew he was the one, and that was that.'

'Okay, but what about Scott?'

'Well, he took a little longer. I went back to that café every day for a week, and finally he said, "Weren't you here yesterday?"'

'And the day before, and the day before that, and —'

'Go on, Lexie,' Rachel interrupted Catherine.

'So I said "Yeah."'

'And then what?'

'Well, the following week —'

'You kept going every day for another week?' said Catherine.

She nodded. 'So he spoke to me again. This time he said, "Do you live near here?" And I said, "Why do you ask?", and he said, "'Cause you come in here a lot." And so I said, "That sounds like a pick-up line."'

'What did he say to that?'

'Nothing, he just smiled, in that coy way of his.'

Catherine groaned. 'This is the longest love at first sight story I've ever heard.'

'Nearly there,' Lexie assured her. 'A few days later some of my friends were having a party, and well, by then, we were having little exchanges when I'd go in, you know, "Beautiful day", "What have you been up to?" or "Where are you off to now?" and so I said there's this party, and would he like to come, and, well, the rest is history.'

'Thank God for that,' Catherine declared, before draining her glass. 'I was beginning to think you two were never going to get together.'

Rachel smiled. 'It's a lovely story, Lexie.'

'Not really one of the best love at first sight stories I've ever heard,' Catherine muttered.

'That's true,' Lexie agreed. 'That title belongs to Tom and Annie.'

Rachel thought about it. 'You know, I don't think I've ever heard how they met.'

'Haven't you?' said Lexie. 'Annie used to talk about it all the time. She used to tell her girls like it was a fairy tale, you know – "Once upon a time . . . " It was so sweet.'

'I don't remember it being all that remarkable,' Catherine sniffed. 'Didn't they just run into each other on campus?'

'Exactly!' said Lexie. 'In fact, literally! He *literally* ran into her.' She gave a little laugh, clearly pleased with herself. 'Well almost. Annie was walking Sophie to the childcare centre at the uni and she came around a corner and Tom was flying along on his bike, and so he had to swerve to avoid crashing right into the stroller. Can you imagine?' Lexie gasped, shaking her head. 'Anyway, he lost control and flew right over the top of the handlebars and landed in a hedge.'

Rachel had a chuckle at that mental image. 'No wonder he never told me that story.'

'Well,' Lexie continued, 'Annie felt so bad, even though it wasn't her fault, and she helped him up out of the hedge, apologising the whole time, checking if he was all right, that he hadn't broken anything. But then Sophie started to cry at all the commotion, and Tom just brushed himself off and went over to the stroller, and he crouched down in front of her and before long he'd not only stopped her crying, he made her laugh. Annie said she fell in love with him right there. And could you blame her? Sophie's own father had never had anything to do with her.'

'That's another story I never got to hear,' said Rachel. 'I tried to ask Tom about it once but he got a bit touchy. What did happen to Sophie's biological father?'

'He dumped Annie when she told him she was pregnant,' Catherine said bluntly.

'To be fair,' Lexie countered, 'they were very young, and she had only gone out with him a couple of times. They barely knew each other. Annie thought she was obliged to tell him, but when she saw how petrified he was by the very idea, she wasn't going to push it. So she went home to tell her parents, and they disowned her.' Lexie shook her head. 'Poor thing, she had no one she could really count on until Tom came along.'

'On his bike, nearly running them over,' Rachel prompted her.

'Oh, right,' Lexie resumed, 'so he walked them to the childcare centre, and he waited for Annie and walked her to her lecture, even though his own lecture had started like, half an hour before.'

'Yeah, well Tom wasn't exactly known for his punctuality,' said Catherine.

'And then he was waiting for her at the childcare centre that afternoon,' Lexie went on. 'And he had this funny little hand-sewn giraffe for Sophie, which he'd picked up at a Community Aid Abroad stall set up on the library lawn that day. She still has it, you know.' Lexie continued as though she was talking to herself, staring into space. 'And he walked them home, pushing his bike the whole way, and Annie asked him if he'd like to come in. And he stayed for dinner, and well, they were inseparable from that day on.' Her eyes started to well. 'I don't know how he's going to get by without her.'

'Is he back yet?' Catherine and Rachel asked in unison. They glanced at each other.

'Oh, yes,' Lexie stirred. 'Sorry, I forgot to tell you, that's partly why I was late tonight. When I left the house he was out front unpacking the car. They just got back this afternoon.'

'How is he?' asked Catherine. 'How are the girls?'

'I didn't see the girls, they were inside and I couldn't hang around for long,' said Lexie. 'But he seemed okay. Tired from the drive, he said.'

'I should give him a call,' said Catherine and Rachel in unison again. They looked at each other, a little warily this time.

Lexie was nodding. 'We're really going to have to look out for him. And the girls. I think Annie would have wanted that, don't you?'

'Of course we'll look out for Tom,' Catherine almost snapped. 'Don't forget Rachel and I were friends with him well before Annie came along.'

Rachel didn't know why she was being so touchy about it, and she certainly didn't know why it had turned into a competition.

Catherine was distracted then by something on the computer screen. 'Well, would you look at this,' she said. 'Cupid has already sent you three arrows.'

'The lingo is unbelievable,' said Rachel. 'What, do they think we're twelve?'

'Come on, let's take a look,' Catherine insisted, shifting her laptop so they could all look at the same screen. 'Let's try *Handsome Guy* first, he sounds promising.'

She clicked on the link and his profile came up.

'Okay,' said Rachel, when the other two hadn't said anything, 'the only thing attractive about him is his sense of irony.'

'Maybe that's it,' said Lexie helpfully. 'Maybe he's just being ironic?'

'Still, he has a head like a shin of beef and nothing in his profile that even vaguely interests me.'

'Okay, let's move on to contestant number two, shall we?' said Catherine, clicking on the link. 'Well, there, he doesn't look too bad.'

Rachel screwed up her nose as she skimmed his profile. 'Too sporty.'

'Oh come on, Rachel, a lot of guys are going to have some interest in sports. You can't cull them on that basis.'

'Why can't I? If they're allowed to cull on dress size, I can do what I like.' She looked a little closer. 'Nuh, he likes bike-riding. Men in fluoro lycra,' she shuddered.

'Third time lucky,' Catherine said patiently, clicking the mouse.

They all sat quietly reading the profile. Rachel couldn't find anything wrong with him, she was hoping one of the others would.

'Well he seems nice,' Lexie said finally.

'Yes, he does, he's not even all that into sports,' Catherine pointed out. 'And he sounds quite sensitive, the way he talks about he and his ex not being suited, that it's no one's fault, and now he just wants to move on. Sounds a bit like you and Sean,' she added, nudging Rachel. 'And look, no kids, that's a plus.'

'Why?' Lexie frowned.

'I don't mean in general,' said Catherine. 'But if he had kids it just means he has to have a lot more to do with the ex wife, which is always complicated, let me tell you. I see it every day.'

'So what happens now?' said Rachel, as though a doctor had just given her unpleasant test results.

'You could be a little excited at least,' Catherine suggested.

'This is the best I can do,' Rachel assured her.

'All right, well, you have to send an arrow back –'

'For crying out loud.'

'– which will let him know you're interested, and put the ball in his court.' Catherine studied the screen. 'Ooh, and he's online now. You might get an immediate response.'

'He's online now? How can you tell?'

'There's a kind of indicator light in the corner, see?'

Rachel pulled a face. 'That's creepy.'

'Why is it creepy?' said Catherine. 'You're online now. He has to be online if he just sent you an arrow, think about it. Look, you can even chat online.'

'No way I'm doing that.'

'Why? It might be fun with us all here!' Lexie chimed in.

'No, I can't think on my feet like that. And I don't even know the guy.'

'It could be how you can get to know him.'

'Perhaps, if I was a teenager.'

'Fine,' said Catherine. 'Do you want me to go ahead and just send the arrow?'

'Sure,' she said. 'I'm going to get another drink.'

In the time that took, *Philosophy Guy* had sent back an actual written message. Catherine read it out to her.

His name was Phil, hence the moniker; he liked her photo, he said she had a nice smile; he worked in IT, which he found quite stimulating. Rachel was not exactly bowled over, but at least he used correct spelling and punctuation, Catherine pointed out.

She proceeded to act as scribe, as all three of them composed a reply, which ended up sounding more like an interrogation.

He gave some sketchy answers, claiming it was difficult to get to know someone over email. There was a little more to-ing and fro-ing, but Rachel lost interest, so she left Catherine to deal with him. By the time the second bottle was finished, Rachel had a date for the following Friday night.

'That happened really fast,' she said, her head spinning, though that could be attributed to the champagne.

'Damn straight,' Catherine said proudly. 'If I keep going at this rate, I'll have a job for you by next week, Lexie.'

*

The day after

'What would you think if I went back to work, Mum?'

'Lexie!' Her mother looked up from the stack of sheets she was searching through. They had embarked on their annual post-Christmas sales expedition. Her mother always waited a polite interval, at least until the first week in January; rushing to the shops before that was simply vulgar, she maintained. Lexie used to enjoy these trips, the buzz finding designer labels at a fraction of their pre-Christmas price. But after a while she started to wonder why a dress selling for eighty dollars could ever have been worth five hundred.

These days she just wondered where everyone got the money. Weren't they absolutely bled dry after Christmas, like her and Scott? And the level of frenzy seemed, well, a little vulgar as well. Not that her mother ever behaved in a frenzied manner. She always had a plan and a very specific list, which she rarely strayed from. It wasn't a bargain, she had always told Lexie, if you didn't need it in the first place. So it was the time of the year she replaced or topped up her linen, flatware and glassware, and began to stock up on gifts for the coming year.

'Why, darling,' she was saying, 'do you want to know if I can mind the children? Because I'd be only too thrilled. We'd have to work it around some of my commitments, but I'm sure it can be done, and honestly, anything to help. Your father and I have been so worried.'

Lexie's face dropped.

'What's the matter?'

'You're pleased?' she said. 'I was hoping you'd be horrified, or at least disapproving that I'd leave the kids so young.' If she wasn't even going to get support from her mother's generation, where would she get it?

Sally looked at her daughter's crestfallen face. 'Let's take these to the register. I think it's time for coffee.'

Twenty minutes later they were ensconced at a table at a nearby café, and Mia was occupied with her babycino. Lexie had not dragged Riley along today. Mia was still young enough to go in the stroller, but it would be unfair to expect poor Riley to trudge around behind them all day, so she had arranged a play date with a friend from his preschool, who was starting big school with him at the end of the month.

'So what's this all about?' Sally asked her daughter. 'Why did you ambush me with that question?'

'I didn't ambush you, Mum.'

'Lexie, there was obviously an agenda attached. And as I was not informed of that agenda, I gave you an honest answer instead of telling you what you wanted to hear.'

Lexie sighed. 'I didn't mean to ambush you, Mum. I thought you wouldn't approve of me going back to work, and I wanted someone to be on my side.'

Sally frowned. 'Okay, I'm still not following you. What exactly are you talking about?'

'It's just been . . . suggested to me, by some quarters, that with Riley going to school this year, I should think about going back to work.'

'This is coming from Scott?'

'No, of course not!' she insisted.

'Well, it's not exactly a crazy idea, darling.'

'But you stayed home, Mum, for all three of us. And not just till we went to school.'

Her mother, in fact, had never had a 'job', according to Catherine's criteria, because she'd never been paid for the tireless work she did for various charities and organisations.

'It was different for me,' said Sally. 'Your father had a good income, darling, a very good income. You know that. And the hours he worked made it almost impossible for me to consider working.'

'It's the same with Scott.'

She thought her mother was going to choke on her latte.

'I just mean his hours are difficult to work around,' Lexie explained. She knew the income was no comparison. 'The early starts, weekends . . .'

'Weekends aren't really the issue though, are they, sweetheart?' her mother pointed out. 'It just means he has a day off during the week when he could be with the children if you were working.'

'But then we'd get no family time at all.'

'That is a good point,' Sally agreed. 'And something to be taken into account, certainly. Do you remember how difficult it was with your father?' She shook her head. 'No matter how carefully we scheduled birthday parties and family get-togethers, some woman would always go into labour at the most inconvenient time.'

'I finshed Gammar,' Mia announced.

'I'll get her –'

'No, no,' Sally waved her off. Lexie sat back, sipping her coffee, watching as her mother gently and lovingly, and always so patiently, cleaned up her granddaughter, then lifted her over onto her lap and let her rest her head against her pale cashmere cardigan and play with her necklace. It was only costume jewellery; that was one lesson Sally had learned early on, when Riley had closed his little fist around a string of antique pearls she was wearing, and tugged. The entire family had spent the next hour on their hands and knees, searching for the pearls, which had scattered into every corner of the room. An errant pearl showed up every so often for probably the next six months.

Of course at the time her mother had dismissed it. She was always so patient, so forgiving and understanding of the little mishaps – and not so little ones – that children were prone to cause. Lexie's childhood had been idyllic for the most part. It was true, they didn't see an awful lot of their father, but she understood very early on that babies didn't arrive politely during business hours. It wasn't his fault, he wasn't putting his job before his family and neglecting them; he'd certainly prefer not to have to drag himself out of bed at three in the morning in the middle of winter to stand in a room while a baby virtually delivered itself. But that's what he had to do, so that he was there on the occasions when things were not so easy or straightforward, when the fate of a baby or its mother depended on his expertise, when his presence in the room was the difference between a happy ending and a tragic one.

So her mother had to be the rock of the family, the centre. And she performed her role so well that it was all that Lexie wanted to do when she grew up. Despite her expensive private-school education, despite her better than average results, she did not want to follow Monica or Eric into medicine. Family pressure, albeit gently applied, made it impossible for her not to at least try. She'd never actually told anyone that she didn't want to be a doctor, so how were they supposed to know? Lexie didn't like to let anyone down, so she dutifully enrolled in a Bachelor of Medical Science and dutifully kept her grades up so that she would be eligible for the postgraduate medicine program. And then she walked into Scott's café. Lexie would never forget the day she first laid eyes on Scott, working behind the counter in the open kitchen, tall and gorgeous, with a smile that had simply turned her insides liquid. There was no other way to describe it. He still did it to her to this day.

So Lexie did not take up the offer she received in the new year to proceed to Medicine; instead her bachelor degree qualified her for a position as an assistant in a medical lab. Her parents were stunned, to say the least, and although Lexie insisted it had nothing to do with meeting Scott, and that she'd never wanted to do medicine anyway, she knew they would always believe that she had simply fallen in love and lost all perspective. Which was why Scott was so sensitive around them. They were always polite to him, unfailingly, but he wasn't stupid, and he knew how it must have looked to them. He'd tried to talk Lexie into continuing with her studies, but she managed to convince him at least that it was genuinely not what she wanted to do. Still he remained tentative about the future, not daring to suggest that they might actually have one together until he felt he could offer her the kind of future that would meet with her parents' approval. So Lexie had had to be the one to propose, or she would have been waiting a long time.

And now she was blissfully married, with two beautiful children, and the only thing that could make her happier would be to have more beautiful children. And to be able to be with them full-time while they were little, and take them to the park, and play make-believe, and walk them to school, and cut the crusts off their little sandwiches, and never miss a single moment.

She gazed wistfully across at her mother. 'I want to be like you, Mum.'

Sally looked up from Mia. 'Well, that's one of the nicest things anyone could ever say.'

'But it's true. I want to be a good mother, just like you.'

'You are a wonderful mother, Lexie,' Sally assured her, 'and I'm so very proud of you. But times have changed. Even if your father had had an average-paying job, I still probably wouldn't have gone out to work. Houses were so much more affordable. It's so difficult for young couples now, I don't know how they manage. Most women have to work, whether they want to or not. In a lot of cases they want to, and that's fine too. You know, when I was at the planning meeting for the breast cancer benefit the other day, there were so many little toddlers running about, someone said we might have to think about organising a creche. It was just like years ago, running the fundraising committees for the school and the like, when we all had our own children underfoot. Now it's the grandchildren.'

She sighed contentedly, gazing down at Mia, and Lexie accepted she wasn't going to get the kind of support she was hoping for, although she did appreciate the kind of support her mother was only too happy to give.

'I've been meaning to ask,' said Sally. 'How is Tom next door, and the girls? You haven't mentioned him lately.' She shook her head sadly. 'Poor man, I think of him often, losing that beautiful wife. And the girls, losing their mother! It doesn't bear thinking about.'

Lexie replaced her cup in its saucer. 'They only got back yesterday. You know they've been up the coast nearly the whole time since the funeral?' Lexie paused with a tremulous little sigh. 'I went in this morning with a casserole, but he said I shouldn't bring any more.'

Tom had explained that Sophie was going through a vegetarian phase, 'and Hannah and I just can't keep up. There's still some in the freezer, from . . . you know, before we went away.'

'I just want to help, Tom.'

'I know you do.' He had smiled down at her. 'But you've got enough on your plate with your own kids. And you've been great, Lexie, I really appreciate it. But we're doing fine. Really.'

Lexie sighed now. 'I feel like he's keeping up a brave face for us all. I wish I could just get him to open up, I want him to feel free to be able to talk about it. But I don't know how to approach it. I can't keep taking him food now that he's specifically asked me not to, but it's a bit forward for me to invite him in for a cup of coffee, like I would Annie.'

'Exactly,' Sally agreed. 'You can't treat him the way you would a girlfriend, it's not appropriate, and I daresay it would only make him feel uncomfortable.' She paused, thinking. 'Why not get Scott to ask him down to the pub for a drink?'

'Pardon?'

'He'd probably feel more comfortable talking to a man, over a beer. It's what they do.'

'I don't go to the pub,' said Scott that evening, 'and I don't think Tom's much into the pub scene either.'

'There's a scene?' asked Lexie. 'You have to be "in" it, you can't just go occasionally?'

Scott sighed, stretching his legs out in front of him. They were sitting outside, after dinner, letting the kids have a bit of a run around in the fresh air before they put them to bed. It was too hot inside.

'I wonder where all the Christmas beetles have gone?' Scott mused.

'Christmas is over.'

'No, I haven't noticed them around this year. They used to be everywhere when we were kids, remember?'

Lexie shrugged. She didn't want to talk about Christmas beetles, she wanted to talk about Tom.

'Maybe it's because of global warming,' he went on. 'Someone should look into that, write a paper. "Global Warming and the Demise of the Christmas Beetle". That'd get people's attention.'

Lexie was getting frustrated with the beetle talk.

'As I was saying –'

'I'm not going to ask Tom down to the pub, Lex,' Scott said plainly. 'It'd be weird.'

'Then get a six-pack and go and knock on his door.'

'Lexie,' he groaned.

'What's wrong with that?'

'I've never done it before.'

'You've never had a beer with Tom?' she rebuked, eyebrows raised.

'Of course I have, with other people around, in a group situation,' said Scott. 'Not just me and him. We wouldn't have anything to talk about.'

'You could ask him about Annie.'

'Christ, Lexie, blokes don't do that.'

'You spend time with Martin alone.'

''Cause Marty's a massive foodie, that's all we talk about. I wouldn't ask him how it's going with Catherine. I don't want to know, quite frankly,' he added.

Lexie was shaking her head. 'I don't get it. How can you spend so much time with someone and not talk about anything personal?'

'You don't get it because you're a woman,' he said. 'You could stand for five minutes on a bus stop with someone you'd never clapped eyes on before and know everything about them before the bus pulled up.'

'You act like there's something wrong with that,' Lexie said airily. 'It's actually a good thing, Scott, probably why women live longer. I know I'm going to bring Riley up to be different. To be able to share his feelings, and to listen.'

Just then Mia's voice rang out in the twilight. 'Ryee, Ryee!'

She was running after him, her little legs unable to keep up while he skipped and hopped and bolted out of her reach.

'Stop Ryee! Yissen me, Ryee!'

Scott grinned. 'Good luck with that.'

Friday

At ten minutes past eight, Rachel walked in through the doors of *sandbar*, which was so hip it didn't need a capital letter. Catherine said she should aim to be just a little late, she definitely did not want to be the one sitting there waiting for him. But, she reminded her, a little late was probably what Rachel considered on time . . .

'. . . so scrap that idea. Try to be on time, what you would consider to be on time.'

'I'm hanging up now,' Rachel had said into the phone.

'Wait on, what are you wearing?'

She sighed. She was going to have to admit she had given the issue more consideration than usual. She had even gone shopping. Practically unheard of.

'I bought a new top.'

'Well, well,' remarked Catherine. 'Someone's going to a lot of trouble.'

'Shut up.'

'So what's it like?'

'It's green . . . ish. With a kind of pattern.'

'But what style?'

'I don't know, little sleeves, v-neck, the sales girl said it was very "in".'

'Of course she's going to tell you that,' said Catherine. 'More important is whether it suits you, Rachel, whether it has the right cut for your particular figure faults. Why didn't you ask me to come shopping with you?'

Because Catherine was the worst person in the world to go shopping with; she wanted to dress Rachel like an uptown lawyer, which suited neither her taste nor her budget. More than once shopping with Catherine she had ended up buying expensive clothes she had never worn.

But Rachel didn't say any of that. She just said, 'Because I'm the worst person in the world to go shopping with, I know it, and there's no need to put anyone else through the ordeal.'

'Where did you buy it?' Catherine continued the inquisition.

'I don't know. From a shop.'

'Well, I didn't think it was from a roadside stand, though I wouldn't put it past you. Was the "shop" in Westfield at Bondi Junction?'

'Yep.'

'Well it's probably okay then.'

'Thanks for your blessing, but actually I am quite happy with it; it doesn't make me look fat, and I think the colour suits me.'

'Does it show some cleavage?'

'I don't have any cleavage, Catherine.'

'Oh, you do too. Wear a push-up bra.'

'Like I'd have a push-up bra.'

'I bought you one last birthday,' she said flatly.

'Oh.' Whoops.

'I can see that gift was appreciated,' Catherine harrumphed. 'Try it, you won't regret it.'

But standing here now, inside the entrance of *sandbar*, Rachel was very much beginning to regret it: not just the push-up bra, but the money she'd wasted on the top, and the whole thing. A rowdy group burst through the door behind her, sweeping her further into the room, into the midst of what seemed like acres of brown skin and bleached hair, very short skirts and even shorter shorts showing off long legs, flat bellies and lots of tattoos. She didn't belong here. Wasn't the whole point of internet dating that you could avoid pick-up places like this?

'Rachel?'

Her stomach clenched. The voice was right behind her. She turned around slowly. It was him all right.

'Phil?' she smiled awkwardly.

'I saw you walk in,' he said. 'You're even prettier in person.'

Yeah right. Well he was shorter in person, but she probably shouldn't say that.

'I managed to get us a table,' he said. 'This way.' She followed him to the far side of the room, weaving around all the taut, tanned, tattooed bodies. He looked his age, and he was dressed a little on the conservative side. What made him choose this place? They arrived at an empty table in the corner.

'Can I get you a drink?' he asked.

She noticed a half-full glass of beer on the table and remembered one of the 'first date' tips she'd read on the Rendezvous website. *Don't let him buy all the drinks, in fact, buy your own drinks if you feel at all uncomfortable or uncertain. And while we're on the subject of alcohol, take it easy.*

'You've already got a drink,' said Rachel. 'So I'll get this one myself.'

They were lining up three deep at the bar, but Rachel didn't mind the wait. Give her a chance to gather, regroup, catch her breath . . .

What was wrong with her? Nothing had even happened. God, she was such a coward. Or was she? Wasn't it just the whole set-up? It was so artificial. He seemed all right, but how could she really know? This was so much worse than a first date – all the nerves and anxiety, without the initial spark of attraction that had made it seem like a good idea at the time. Instead, you just had all the discomfort of a first date while you were trying to see if there was a spark. It was the wrong way around.

If she could have made a run for it, she would have. But she had to fulfil her part of the deal. She'd entered into a social contract right there, in black and white, on her computer screen, when she agreed to at least meet the man. Rachel wondered if there was a minimum-time clause?

All too soon she was sitting opposite him, nursing her drink, smiling awkwardly as they made their way through the standard repertoire of small talk. How was your Christmas and New Year? Did you have far to come? How did you get here? Traffic? Weather . . .

Shit. Now what?

'So, have you been on Rendezvous long?' Phil asked.

'No, that was my first time when you made contact. You're my first date,' she added chirpily.

'Ah . . . well.' He was nodding, like that meant something.

'So how about you?' Rachel asked. 'How long have you been doing this internet dating thing?'

'Oh, a while,' he nodded again. He nodded a lot, didn't say much though. And he seemed like he was carrying the weight of the world on his shoulders. Was this the persona he was trying to cultivate? If so, it did nothing for Rachel. She preferred someone a little more upbeat, who could have a laugh at themselves, not take things quite so seriously.

Hmm, maybe she did have a shopping list after all.

'I'm trying to find my way, you know?' Phil was saying. 'Life takes us along unexpected paths, we don't always end up where we thought we would.'

'But don't you think that's half the fun?' said Rachel, trying to lift the mood. 'It's one of the things I liked most about travelling . . . not having a plan, going where the road takes you.'

'What I was trying to say,' Phil resumed, as though her input was merely an interruption, 'is that with all the best intentions, things just don't always go the way you'd hoped.'

What was he going on about?

'I loved my wife very much when I married her.'

Here we go.

'And in my heart of hearts, I intended to be with her till death us do part.' He paused. 'But is it right to bury all feeling, all desire, all longing to stick to some antiquated rules about what is right?'

Rachel shrugged.

'We didn't have sex very often.'

And she didn't want to know that!

'Now we don't at all.'

'Pardon? Aren't you separated?'

'Well, yeah, but when you live in the same house –'

'I'm sorry,' Rachel had to interrupt. 'You still live with your ex wife?'

'It's the simplest thing for now, till I figure out what to do. Don't want to upset the applecart before it's absolutely necessary.'

What did that mean?

'You don't have children, do you?' Rachel thought she should check.

He shook his head. 'No, but I hope to one day. Very important to me. Not so much to the wife.'

'You mean your ex wife, don't you?'

'Well, we haven't made any legal moves,' he explained. 'Just emotional ones.'

Cripes.

'We've been moving away from each other for a long time, making our own lives.'

'So she knows you're on an internet dating site?' said Rachel.

He hesitated. 'Not as such.'

What the hell did that mean?

'Do you know where the ladies' is?' Rachel asked suddenly.

'Oh . . . probably near the men's, I suppose, you have to go up the stairs at the back.'

As Rachel got to her feet, so did he. 'I'll get you a drink while you're gone. Was that Chardonnay?'

She wanted to say No! I don't want you to get me a drink, I don't want to sit here any longer and listen to your crap. And I certainly don't want to see you again. Ever.

But all she said was 'Yeah.' Even though it wasn't Chardonnay.

The bathroom was sufficiently far away to give her time to think up a strategy. It was also mercifully empty. Rachel supposed it was still relatively early: the toilets didn't begin to get overcrowded and overwrought till later in the night. She stood at the basins, staring at herself in the mirror. Why couldn't she just be a grown-up and go back to the table and calmly say that it was nice to meet him but she didn't see this going any further. But the idea was anathema to her. This was why she'd ended up married to Sean; she'd never been good at confronting difficult or awkward situations, she'd never learned how. But this guy was a creep; he was basically either looking for a mistress, or for a leg-up out of an unhappy marriage, too gutless to actually leave and risk being on his own. Yet she was the one standing here feeling anxious and awkward and cornered. She should have organised some kind of bail-out plan with the girls – a phone call at a designated time, a secret code, the pretext of some kind of emergency that would require her to leave at once. That was gutless too, and besides, Catherine probably wouldn't have played along, she'd expect her to deal with it, one way or another. Rachel glanced at her watch – how much longer would be considered reasonable? Perhaps just one more drink would do it?

She touched up her lipgloss and flicked back her hair, before taking a deep breath and walking sedately to the door. As she opened it, she saw an incredibly familiar back heading into the men's room opposite.

'Tom!' she cried.

He spun around. 'Rach, hey,' he grinned widely, coming towards her. 'Fancy meeting you here.'

She felt so incredibly relieved she threw her arms around him and hugged him tight. 'I'm so glad to see you, Tom, you have no idea.'

'What's up?' he said, pulling back to look at her.

She released him then. 'I'm on this stupid internet date –'

'What are you doing dating over the internet?' he frowned.

'It was Catherine's idea,' she dismissed.

'That'd be right.' He rolled his eyes. 'You let her push you around too much, Rach, you've got to stand up to her sometimes.'

'Fine, but that's not going to help me right now,' said Rachel. 'This guy's a creep, he's married —'

'Why did you accept a date with a married man?'

'I didn't know, obviously!' she insisted. 'He's just gradually let it unfold that he's only "emotionally" separated from his wife. They still live together, and she has no idea that he's internet dating.'

Tom was shaking his head. 'Dickhead.'

'I don't know what to do.'

'Tell him you're not interested in dating someone who's married. It's pretty simple. You do have the moral high ground.'

She bit her lip. 'I know, I should be able to do that, but I'm hopeless at confrontation.'

'So nothing's changed, eh?'

She gave him a lame look. 'Thing is, I don't know anything about this guy, he might get weird, he might follow me after I leave . . . I don't know.'

'Exactly,' Tom agreed. 'Let this be a lesson to you, my girl. Internet dating,' he shook his head. 'Would you like me to help?'

She winced. 'Oh, I couldn't ask you to do that . . . Could I?'

'You're not asking, I'm offering. In fact, I think I might have to insist.'

'Really?'

'Really,' he said, thinking. 'Whereabouts are you sitting?'

'We're in the back corner, over on the right as you come in through the door.'

He nodded. 'All right, I'll come and find you soon, just go along with whatever I do, okay?'

'What are you going to do?'

'Haven't figured that out yet, but go along with it, whatever it is.'

Rachel felt so much better as she made her way back to the table. Phil was looking a little despondent as she came closer, perhaps he was thinking she'd done a runner. But then again, he'd looked despondent before she left as well.

'Hi,' she said, taking her seat again. 'Toilets are miles away. Thanks for this,' she added, raising her glass and chugging down a couple of mouthfuls. She would not have been quite so cavalier if she didn't know Tom was on his way to rescue her. God, Catherine would have a fit if she heard it put like that, but Tom was a mate, a friend, he was just bailing her out like a girlfriend would. Anyway, she probably wouldn't even mention it to Catherine.

'So what do you do for a living, Phil?' she asked, to pass the time.

'We discussed that in our emails,' he replied, a suspicious frown putting a dent in what she just noticed was a very wide, high forehead.

'Of course,' said Rachel. 'I'm being too general.' She took another gulp of her wine. Her mind had gone blank, she'd already erased Phil from the 'need to know' banks of her memory. Come on, Tom. 'What I meant is,' she resumed, 'tell me more about your work, what do you actually do, day to day?'

He still looked a little peeved, but she could not have cared less. He launched into a lengthy monologue about systems administration, and Rachel's attention drifted. She wondered what was going on in his marriage to make him seek out women on the internet. Was he just bored? Cripes, listening to him drone on now, Rachel couldn't imagine what his wife was like if she was the boring one.

She hoped instead she was a firecracker, frustrated with his blandness. Perhaps she nagged, which was the only recourse left to her, or worse, maybe she just ignored him. One thing, Rachel was certainly not surprised she didn't want to have sex with him any more.

'Rachel.'

Finally, that was Tom's voice behind her. She must not look relieved, though she wasn't sure what expression she was supposed to have just yet.

'I don't believe this,' he continued as he came around beside her, staring down at her.

'What?' Give me a clue.

'You said you wouldn't do this any more, Rachel.'

She opened her mouth to speak, though without any idea of what she might say.

'No, no excuses.' He held up his hands. 'You're either committed to making this work or you're not, and it isn't fair to keep stringing me along while you decide what you want.'

He turned to look directly at Phil then. 'Sorry, mate, I guess she didn't tell you she's married.' He glanced at her hand. 'She's not wearing her ring, so how would you know? She wears it so little she doesn't even have a mark, see?' he added, picking up her hand and waving it across the table at him.

'Tom!' Rachel snatched it away again. She thought that was a nice touch.

'And I'm sure she hasn't told you that she's made a hobby of picking up men. Now I admit, I'm no saint, I've had some anger issues, and a few of those guys didn't come out of it so well, but I've been getting it under control, and we're really trying to make it work. At least I thought we were.' He paused ominously. 'This really hurts, Rachel. And when I get hurt, you know I express it as anger, that's what the therapist said, remember? If you don't come home with me now, I can't be responsible for what I might do.'

'Tom, you can't threaten me –'

'No, you should go,' Phil blurted. It was the most animated she'd seen him all night. 'Do what he says.'

Rachel sighed dramatically, leaning down to pick up her bag from the floor, before standing up and swinging it over her shoulder with a flourish. Tom stood watching her, his arms folded in front of his chest, his face stern. Somehow she had to stop herself from laughing until they got out of sight and out of earshot.

'Sorry about this, Phil,' she said.

But he was just shaking his head and holding his hands up in surrender mode.

Tom held out his hand and Rachel feigned a moment's hesitation for good measure, before putting her hand in his. Then he turned and walked determinedly through the crowd. She didn't look back at Phil, she didn't want to risk giving the game away.

They pushed through the main doors and stepped out into the night air. Tom turned to her, a twinkle in his eye.

'No,' she whispered loudly. 'He might not be far behind us, keep walking.'

Tom kept hold of her hand as he negotiated the traffic and

led them across the road to the promenade edging the beach. They continued at a brisk pace for the equivalent of a block or so, as Rachel kept checking over her shoulder to make sure they weren't being followed. Finally, when she was satisfied they were free and clear, she pulled her hand out of Tom's and gave his shoulder a thump.

'Ow!' he exclaimed. 'What was that for? I just rescued you.'

She was grinning up at him. 'You crazy, crazy man! I could barely keep a straight face. Where did you get all that?'

'I've watched my share of bad soaps,' he said proudly. 'I was pretty good, eh?'

Rachel laughed. 'You might have made him turn over a new leaf.'

'Then my work here is done,' he said, brushing his hands against each other theatrically.

Her face dropped then. 'Oh my God, oh no, Tom!'

'What's wrong?' He looked concerned. 'Did you leave something behind, your phone?'

'No, but I made you leave!' she cried. 'I'm so sorry. You should go back in, I'll be right now.'

'Nuh,' he shook his head dismissively. 'I can't go back, what if he's still there?'

Rachel bit her lip. What was Tom doing there anyway? It was none of her business, but she was curious to know who she'd dragged him away from. 'I feel terrible, hijacking you like that. I've ruined your whole night.'

'You've salvaged my night,' he corrected her. 'And you didn't hijack me, I offered, remember. To be honest, I was glad to have an excuse to get out of there.'

'Oh? Why is that?' she asked, trying not to sound nosey, as they started along the path again at a more relaxed pace.

'I was with a few of the guys from work,' he explained. 'They've been threatening to take me out, I knew they were thinking it would "do me good".' He gave her a sideways glance. 'When they got wind the girls were gone for the night, they wouldn't take no for an answer.'

'They were trying to rescue you,' said Rachel. 'But won't they worry where you got to?'

'No, I told them before I left,' he said simply.

She looked up at him. 'What did you tell them?'

'The truth — that a friend was stuck on a disastrous blind date and needed a way out. They looked a little uncomfortable at first, till I added, "friend of the wife's", and then they looked really uncomfortable and were only too happy to send me on my way.'

'Well, I appreciate you helping me out. I don't know what I would have done if you hadn't come along.'

'Oh, he looked pretty harmless,' said Tom. 'The worst he could do was bore you senseless, probably.'

She smiled.

'You can do a whole lot better than him, Rach.'

She looked up and he was watching her.

'You look nice tonight,' he said.

Rachel stared down at the path, feeling her cheeks go hot, but she doubted Tom would notice in the dim light.

Suddenly he was in front of her, walking backwards so he could face her. 'Hey, I've got an idea.'

'What?'

'Let's go back to your place and be wildly inappropriate.'

She stopped in her tracks, staring up at him wide-eyed.

'You know, like you said, if I ever want to be inappropriate and pretend I'm not a widower for a night, you're my girl.'

'Oh,' she said, recovering. 'Um, okay then. If you really want to.'

'I really want to, and you promised, and I rescued you, so you owe me.'

She folded her arms. 'Okay, you made your point. Would you like to come back to my place, Tom?'

'Got anything to drink?'

'Um, I think,' she said vaguely.

'We'll pick up something on the way to be safe.'

At the bottle shop en route to her place, Tom insisted on buying, amongst other things, a bottle of vodka and one of Kahlua and a large carton of full-cream milk so they could make White Russians, like the old days. It had been their special-occasion drink back at Rainbow Street. They used to pool their meagre spending money and buy really cheap vodka, but always genuine Kahlua.

They tried a cheap coffee liqueur once, but it ruined them, so never again. Rachel was pretty sure she hadn't had a White Russian since, and she wasn't all that sure she wanted one now.

But when they arrived at her flat, Tom decided it was the perfect way to kick off. Although she tried to point out that play had actually already started, he went ahead and mixed the drinks and handed her one.

'To old friends,' he declared, raising his glass in a toast before taking a gulp. 'Ah, brings back memories.' He stepped out of the kitchen into the living area. 'So does this.'

'What?' she said, looking around.

'You still live like a uni student, Rach.'

'Shut up, I wasn't expecting company.'

'You still have to live here.'

She thumped him on the arm again. 'Listen, it's all very well for you, you've got a wife to –' She gasped, covering her mouth with her hand. 'Oh shit, Tom, I'm sorry, that was really –'

'Inappropriate?' he said, plonking down on the lounge. 'That's what tonight is all about, isn't it?'

Rachel took a large gulp of her drink.

'Besides, Annie wasn't all that big on housework. I pulled my own weight.' He looked over his shoulder at her, before patting the seat beside him. 'Come, sit, tell me about this internet wild-goose chase you're on.'

She breathed out then. Good, change of subject. She walked around the lounge. 'I told you, it was Catherine's idea,' she said, sitting down next to him.

'And if Catherine said you should jump in a fire . . .?' He raised a fatherly eyebrow at her.

'It's not like that. She just got a bee in her bonnet after –' This time she managed to stop herself before she made yet another faux pas.

'After what?' Tom prompted.

'Oh, after I couldn't remember the last time I'd been out on a date.'

'And why is that?'

Rachel frowned. 'Because it's been a long time,' she said, stating the obvious.

'No, I get that,' he said. 'But why has it been so long since you've been out on a date?'

She shrugged. 'No one's asked me.'

'I don't believe it.'

'There's a man drought. Don't you read the papers?'

'No one's come on to you at all?' he persisted. 'In how long?'

'Oh, maybe some guy's chatted me up in some bar, some night, but let's just say there haven't been any "genuine expressions of interest".'

'Bet there has.'

'Well you'd lose.'

'I don't think so,' he said, planting his feet on the coffee table.

She glanced at him. 'What are you trying to say, Tom?'

'You would have had plenty of "expressions of interest", but you don't give a guy the time of day.'

'What?'

'It's true. I've seen you in action, and I'm one of the walking wounded.'

Now she turned her head all the way to look at him straight. 'What on earth are you going on about?'

'I had a huge crush on you for years.'

'You did not.'

'Why do you think I came and sat next to you the first day at uni?'

'Actually I've always wondered about that. Why did you?'

He just looked straight back at her.

'Oh, come off it, Tom. We were mates, we clicked, we had the same sense of humour . . .'

'Yeah, you're right, I could tell all that just by looking at you,' he said deadpan. 'Guys don't approach girls cold because they think they might have a good sense of humour, Rach.'

She frowned. 'You didn't . . . not because . . . no, Tom, I'm not one of those girls that guys notice.'

Tom just looked at her. 'You were – in the parlance of today – *hot*.'

She shook her head with a nervous laugh. 'You are so full of it, Tom Macklin. A girl knows if she's hot.'

'In my experience, hardly ever,' he said. 'The girls who think they're hot are generally not. The ones who have no idea of the effect they're having . . . they're the ones you fall for.'

Rachel grunted. 'So why did you have a different girl every weekend?'

'Hey, I was a twenty-year-old red-blooded male, and it was on tap,' he said. 'Besides, you never took me seriously.'

'And I'm not about to start now,' she muttered.

'Despite all the times I asked you out,' he continued over the top of her.

'You never asked me out,' she protested.

'I asked you out all the time,' he insisted.

'When, where?'

'The pub, the movies, for a meal.'

She was shaking her head. 'We were housemates, we went out together all the time like that. I asked you out just as often.'

'But I bought you presents.'

'What presents did you ever buy me?' she scoffed.

'Caramello Koalas,' he said, meeting her eyes directly. They had sunk down further in the lounge now, shoulder to shoulder, their feet side by side on the coffee table. 'Remember?'

She used to love Caramello Koalas, and Tom did bring her home one pretty much every time he went to the shops. Once he even got her a Caramello Koala showbag from the Easter Show.

Tom was watching her intently, their faces were close.

'Why do you think I never got serious about any of those girls?'

He was baiting her, the second she said 'Really?' he would burst out laughing and cry 'Gotcha!'

'You broke my heart when you went away,' he said in a low voice.

No, don't be tempted, don't take the bait. Change the subject.

'Hey,' her eyes lit up. 'I just remembered something. You are going to love this!' She jumped up and ran into the hall.

'What is it?' he called after her.

'You'll see.' She walked back into the room carrying a squat black speaker and a microphone.

'Is that what I think it is, B1?' said Tom, getting up off the couch.

'If you're thinking karaoke,' she grinned. 'I almost forgot I had it, I haven't used it in years.'

'This is brilliant.'

'And you don't know the best part,' she said. 'Here.'

She dumped it into his arms and he set it down on the coffee table, while she crouched in front of her CD stack. 'Here it is.' She twisted around, holding up a CD. '*The Best of Queen – Karaoke Edition.*'

'You're kidding me,' he said, taking it from her to read the back. 'This is too good.'

The playlist read like a soundtrack to the evening so far. 'Under Pressure', 'Somebody to Love', 'Another One Bites the Dust', 'We Are the Champions', 'You're My Best Friend'. Rachel couldn't remember exactly how to set the machine up, but between the two of them they worked it out eventually.

They sang and danced and mugged their way shamelessly through the entire repertoire, chugging straight from a bottle of wine that they swapped for turns on the microphone. By the time they got to the finale – 'Bohemian Rhapsody', what else? – they were leaping around the room, standing on the couch, jumping over the coffee table, and doing a very good job of behaving totally inappropriately. After the classic head-banging segment, and the final crescendo, they collapsed onto the floor, singing the last couple of lines into the microphone together, the poignant denouement, lying on their backs, gazing into each other's eyes. The music came to an end, the only noise in the room was the sound of their breathing. Tom was still staring at her. Rachel smiled, her heart pounding in her chest. And then he was drawing closer, and he lifted his head, and he brought his lips down onto hers, and his tongue was in her mouth, and they were kissing! Rachel was in shock for a moment, but then something happened, she started to kiss him back, eagerly in fact. And that was the pattern from then on: brief moments of awareness, of thinking, What the hell? This is *Tom*! were obliterated as they kissed and caressed and frantically tugged at one another's clothes, their bodies grinding up against each other, till Rachel heard herself cry out.

*

She woke with a start. What a *dream*. Where the hell did that come from? As she caught her breath she gradually became aware of a sharp blade of pain slicing through the centre of her forehead – the result of too much alcohol and not enough sleep. She closed her eyes. If she could just get back to sleep she'd be okay. She wouldn't have to live through the next few hours, and she'd wake up feeling a whole lot better. Not great perhaps, but vastly improved. But something wasn't quite right. She was naked under this sheet. Rachel didn't normally sleep naked, even if she only wore a singlet and undies. She couldn't remember getting into bed last night; in fact, the last thing she could remember was karaoke; after that it was a blur, further muddied by that disconcerting dream which had woken her just moments ago, and which she certainly did not intend to revisit. Did Tom actually leave? She couldn't remember seeing him out. Maybe he'd crashed out on the couch? It was all very foggy, but it didn't matter right now. All that mattered was getting a few more hours' sleep. Breathe deep and steady . . . lose yourself to it. Her head was feeling heavy, this just might work. But not lying on her back. She had to assume the position. She rolled onto her side, stretching her top leg over . . .

And then she screamed, leaping from the bed and dragging the sheet with her in one frantic move.

'Tom! What are you doing here?'

'Rach, inside voice,' he rasped. 'Please.'

'What are you doing in my bed?' She held up her hand to block his naked body from her line of sight. 'With nothing on!'

He squinted, glancing around. 'You've got the sheet.'

'Well do something! Cover yourself!'

'You've got the sheet, Rachel,' he repeated.

And she was certainly not giving it up. She glanced around the floor and stooped to grab her bathrobe, tossing it at him. He gathered it around himself.

'What's going on, what are you doing here . . . still?' she asked weakly, knowing what the answer had to be but dreading him saying it out loud nonetheless.

He didn't need to say it, the expression on his face was enough.

'Oh God.'

'It's okay, Rach,' he said, propping himself up on one elbow.

'No, it's not, this is not okay . . . this is . . .'

'What?' he said gently. 'This is me, Rach, and it really is okay. Come over here,' he patted the bed, 'let's talk about it.'

'No!' she exclaimed.

'Why not?'

'Because . . . because you, you're . . . and I'm . . . and this is not supposed to happen . . .' And then it struck her. She swallowed. 'Tom, did you use something?'

'What?'

'Did you use some protection?'

'Ah, no,' he frowned. 'But don't worry, you won't catch anything from me, I haven't been with anyone . . . since . . . you know.'

'That's not what I'm talking about. I'm not on the pill.'

That woke him up. 'You're not?'

She shook her head.

'Why not?'

'I'm not in a relationship,' she shrilled. 'I didn't think I needed it.'

He lay back flat on the bed. 'Shit.'

Rachel insisted she had to deal with this immediately. She had never been much good at keeping track of her cycle, but her period had finished a week or so ago, or thereabouts, so she was somewhere in the middle, and she couldn't take the risk of ignoring this and hoping for the best – there was no crossing this bridge when she came to it. She remembered vaguely that the morning-after pill had to be taken within . . . was it twenty-four or forty-eight hours? Damn, she couldn't think straight. And she couldn't put it off. She just wanted to get the whole thing over with, with as little fuss as possible.

But that was not going to be so easy. Tom insisted on coming to the clinic with her; in fact, he would not take no for an answer. Rachel knew that if she tried to argue the toss with him they would end up talking about what happened, and she certainly didn't want to go there. So it was easier just to let him come along. He was dressed and looking a little brighter when she emerged from the shower – he must have washed his face in the kitchen sink. And he'd made coffee.

'Rach, we have to talk about this,' he said, handing her a cup.

'No, we don't, we really don't.'

'Rachel . . .'

'Just drop it, Tom.'

'Why?'

'Because it's embarrassing.'

'You don't have to be embarrassed with me.'

'Well, I am. So deal with it.' Rachel closed her hands around the coffee mug, holding it to her lips and taking small sips as her eyes blurred. This was going to ruin everything. She turned away to gaze out the window at the brick wall of the neighbouring building. Now whenever they saw each other it was going to be awkward, they wouldn't be able to look each other in the eye, they wouldn't be able to be friends . . .

'We'll grab a taxi to my place so we can pick up my car, okay?'

'No,' she said firmly, turning her head but not looking at him. 'What if Lexie's around, what if she sees us?' Her voice caught in her throat. 'This is a fucking nightmare.'

She felt his hands on her shoulders and she jerked away from him, spilling her coffee. 'Oh fuck,' she sobbed.

He took the cup from her and put it in the sink and grabbed a tea towel to wipe her hands.

'Don't,' she whimpered.

'Stop it,' he said gently. 'Your hands are trembling.' He pressed the tea towel into them and held them firmly between his. 'Rach, you're my friend. Let me be yours.'

She lifted her eyes then to meet his, and they filled with tears. Tom folded his arms around her and held her close, and Rachel cried into his chest, letting herself pretend for a moment that he was still her friend, that nothing would change.

'It's going to be okay,' he said after a while. 'Trust me.'

She took a deep breath and stepped back from him, wiping her eyes.

'Come on,' he said, 'we'll get my car, it'll make things easier.'

'I don't want to risk going near your place, Tom.'
'Don't worry, you won't have to.'

He instructed the taxi driver to pull up around the corner from his house. 'Can you wait here for a few minutes, please? My friend will stay in the car.'

'Sure.'

'I'll be right back,' he said to Rachel, getting out of the taxi.

He returned not more than five minutes later. She saw his car pull in across the road, and he got out and walked back over to the taxi. He bent to speak to the driver, handing him some cash through the window. 'Does that cover it?'

'Yeah, with change.'

'Keep it.'

He opened the passenger door for Rachel and she stepped out. He went to put his arm around her as they crossed the road but she reared away from him. 'What are you doing?'

'Sorry.'

They drove in silence to the clinic, but it wasn't awkward so much as surreal. Rachel felt like she was still dreaming, but now she was only too aware that the images flashing through her mind had never been a dream. She had blocked them at first, startled, thinking they were some sort of latent fantasy, and she really did not want to explore what that was about. But now she wanted to understand what had happened, how it had happened, and so she opened her mind up to remembering. It had started out on the living-room floor, but who had started it? Did she come on to him, or did he come on to her? No, he kissed her first, she remembered now, the shock of it, but it didn't last long. Soon enough she was responding with voracious abandon like some sex-starved adolescent. God, it was excruciating. Rachel knew they were consenting adults and all that, but it felt wrong on so many levels. Annie had died only a few months ago, and Rachel was already hopping into bed with her husband. She wasn't going to judge Tom, he probably needed some sexual release, he was a bloke, after all. But he could get that with someone else, anyone else, not a mutual friend of the family. Rachel should have shown some restraint. Some respect. She should have been the responsible one. And if only she had been a bit responsible, he wouldn't be escorting her to the sexual-health clinic right now to get a dose of the morning-after pill. The whole thing was just tacky.

'Are you okay?'

Rachel stirred, looking across at Tom. They were parked in the carpark of the clinic, and he'd turned off the engine.

'Yeah, sure.' She fumbled for the door and stepped out into the glaring sunshine. She had forgotten her sunglasses.

They had to wait for a long time, forty minutes at least. Rachel felt tired, so tired. She could have curled up to sleep right there on the hard vinyl bench. But surely it couldn't be much longer. She would sit through the indignity of the interrogation by the doctor, get the pills and go home and draw all the curtains and blinds, and then she would sleep until it was over.

Her name was finally called and Tom stood up as she got to her feet.

'Forget it, Tom, you're not coming in there with me.'

'But –'

'No,' Rachel said firmly.

He sighed. 'Okay. I'll wait here.'

The doctor was kind and sympathetic; Rachel didn't know why she had assumed it would be awful. She told Rachel that next time she didn't need to come to the clinic, the morning-after pill was now available at chemists' over the counter.

'There's not going to be a next time,' Rachel said flatly.

'Why do you say that?'

'It just feels a little . . . sordid or something.'

'That's an interesting term to choose.'

She shrugged. 'It's just the circumstances.'

The doctor smiled kindly. 'We hear everything in this place. Women who wake up next to someone they've never seen before, sometimes more than one –'

Rachel blinked. 'No, it's nothing like that. My friend is out in the waiting room, I've known him since . . . for a long time. It's just complicated.'

The doctor considered her. 'In my experience things are rarely anything but. You're a healthy young woman with normal urges. And shame is an entirely pointless emotion.'

As they walked out of the building back to the car, Rachel felt a little calmer, while Tom seemed more agitated.

'So, which type did she give you, the double or the single dose?' he asked.

Rachel thought about it. 'Um, well she only gave me one pill, so I guess it's the single dose. How do you know about that?'

'I read a brochure while I was waiting for you,' he dismissed. 'So she talked to you about side effects?'

She nodded.

'She went right through your medical history then?'

'Um, she asked a couple of questions . . .'

'About your mother? She should have asked you about your mother as well, any history of blood clots, that kind of thing?'

Rachel was frowning.

'Well?' he prompted.

'She didn't ask about my family history. I don't think it's relevant, Tom.'

'Of course it's relevant,' he said, raising his voice. He turned to look at her. 'Fucking doctors and their fucking offhand attitudes.'

It suddenly hit her. Rachel could see the fresh, raw pain right there in his eyes.

'I don't want you to do this, Rachel.'

'Tom –'

'You can't take medication when you have no idea what side effects it might have. You could have a reaction . . .'

'It's okay, Tom. I've taken it before,' she lied.

'You have?'

'Yeah, once, overseas. I was fine. A bit of nausea and cramping, that was all.'

He breathed out heavily, leaning back against the car and rubbing his eyes. Rachel just wanted to go over and hug him, but she couldn't do that any more. Everything had changed.

He got his keys out of his pocket and pressed the remote lock. 'Okay, but I'm staying with you tonight.'

'Tom, you can't –'

'Don't worry, I'll sleep out on the couch, but I'm not going to leave you alone.'

'What about the girls?'

'Hannah was staying the weekend anyway, and I called Soph while you were with the doctor. She had plans tonight, she wanted to stay at her friend's.'

Rachel frowned, thinking. 'Are you sure she's all right? You know where she'll be?'

'Of course.' He opened the door for her. 'I'm not going to argue about it, Rach. I'm staying, end of discussion.'

She climbed into the car and he closed the door again. He was completely rattled, she could see it now; something like this could really throw him. Had really thrown him. She had to let him do what he needed to do.

She just wished she could take it all back. If only she hadn't seen him at *sandbar*, if only she'd had the guts to walk away from Phil herself. But if she'd had the guts to do that, she would have had the guts to tell Catherine in the first place that she didn't want to look for a date on the internet. So she wouldn't have been at *sandbar* and she wouldn't have bumped into Tom and he wouldn't have come back to her place ... And how had things gotten so out of hand anyway? Fragments of conversation were finding their way back to the surface of her memory. He said he used to have a crush on her. Did he really say that? Was she remembering it right? Rachel felt immediately self-conscious, throwing Tom a sidelong glance, worried somehow he would know what she was thinking.

He looked over at her. 'What?'

'Nothing,' she said, staring straight ahead again.

He was only teasing her last night, about the crush. That's all it was. She remembered now. Mostly.

'I'm just going to call in here,' he said, pulling up outside a small group of shops. 'Your fridge is like some kind of science experiment, Rach. If we're hunkered down for the weekend, I'm getting in fresh supplies.'

Rachel would normally have put in a protest, but she let him go. She watched him through the window, chatting away to the shopkeepers, charming them. He'd always been a charmer, Tom.

Everybody loved him, Rachel included. But never in that way, she never even vaguely considered herself in contention. But she suspected she had never been closer to anyone in her life than when they lived together at Rainbow Street. People who knew them at the time said they were like brother and sister, but that didn't seem to describe it for Rachel. Maybe because she'd never had a sibling she didn't really understand the relationship, but Tom didn't feel like a brother to her. Others said they were like an old married couple, but they got on so much better than any married couple Rachel knew back then.

Tom returned to the car with two bulging bags and put them on the back seat. He was rustling around in one of them and Rachel turned to see what he was doing.

'Ah, here it is.' He tossed something into her lap.

It was a Caramello Koala. Rachel's heart skipped a beat. She stared down at it as he got back into the driver's seat.

'Thanks,' she said quietly, without looking at him.

'My pleasure,' he replied, starting up the engine and pulling out into the flow of traffic.

Rachel rolled over, stirring from a deep sleep. She wondered what time it was. The room was dark, but the blinds and curtains were closed so it was hard to tell. Her head felt clearer, that was a good sign. She was trying to decide if she felt nauseous or just hungry. She climbed out of bed and went over to the window, opening the curtains and pulling up the blind. It was dusk. She slid the window open and breathed in the salt air, looking out across the rooftops to the ocean and the violet sky. It was a little cool for January, which was a blessing today. All in all she didn't feel too bad.

Then she heard movement out in the kitchen, and she remembered she still had Tom to deal with. She'd slept with one of her best friend's husbands. She'd slept with one of her best friends. How did one deal with that? It's not as though she could jump on a plane and disappear to the other side of the world.

She walked tentatively down the hall and into the living area. Tom was standing at the sink, washing up. Great, now he was cleaning up after her, as if she didn't already feel uncomfortable enough.

He looked around then. 'Hey,' he said warmly, reaching for the tea towel over his shoulder and wiping his sudsy hands. 'How are you feeling?'

'What are you doing, Tom?'

'Just washing the containers I cleaned out of the fridge.'

She sighed, leaning against the doorjamb. 'You didn't need to do that.'

'Someone had to,' he said.

Was that a glimmer in his eye? Were they going to get through this after all? He certainly looked more relaxed. Rachel decided to play along. Maybe they could actually pretend nothing had happened. Maybe they could fool themselves that everything was back to normal. It was worth a shot.

'Wow, what is that?' she said, peering over at the stove. 'Smells great.'

'It's chicken soup.'

Rachel's eyes grew wide and she couldn't help grinning. 'You are kidding me, you didn't make chicken soup?'

He slung the tea towel over his shoulder again. 'Get real. They were selling it at the deli where we stopped. Said it was homemade fresh every day. I think it may even be kosher.'

'Whatever, it smells good.'

'Want some?'

'I can get it.'

He put his hands on her shoulders and turned her around. 'Just go, sit, I'll bring it out.'

She did as she was told and he appeared shortly after with a bowl and her stable table, and a giant smirk on his face.

'You own a stable table,' he said. 'I thought only old people owned stable tables.'

She took it from him. 'Old people and people who don't have a dining room,' she said airily, as she positioned it comfortably on her lap. 'Don't knock it till you've tried it.'

He passed her the bowl of soup and a spoon, and then he took a seat at the other end of the couch.

'You're not having any?' she asked.

'I've already had two bowls. Had to ward off the hangover hunger pangs.'

She nodded, tucking into the soup. 'It's good.'

'So you're not feeling any nausea?'

She shook her head. 'I feel fine.' She slurped another spoonful of the soup. It really was good. 'You know, Tom, there's no need for you to stay. I'm absolutely fine.'

'I thought we'd settled this.'

'But –'

'Rachel, any side effects you're going to have might not kick in for up to twelve hours, they say. I'm staying,' he said flatly.

'Okay.'

He got up. 'Shall we see what's on the telly?'

'Sure.'

He picked up the remote and pointed it at the TV, and Rachel noticed then he was dressed in a T-shirt and long shorts. He hadn't been wearing those this morning. 'You've changed your clothes,' she remarked.

'Yeah, I picked up some stuff when I went to get the car,' he said, sitting back on the couch. 'And I hope you don't mind, I helped myself to a shower.'

'As long as you didn't clean it.'

He grinned. 'No, it was quite clean.'

'Hmm, see, I'm not a total loss.'

He gave her an odd look and seemed as though he was about to say something, but then he turned his attention back to the TV. 'Okay, it's that time of the year. We have cricket, or tennis, or cricket, or *CSI* re-runs.'

'Tennis,' said Rachel.

He glanced at her. 'I thought you didn't like sports?'

'I don't, but I find tennis very . . . meditative, don't you reckon?' she said. 'You know, the tock . . . tock . . . tock . . .' She tipped her head from side to side in time. 'And the scorer guy up in his throne –'

'The umpire?'

'Yeah, him, he has all this power, I love it. He can scold the players, he can even tell the crowd to be quiet. I keep expecting him to say "Off with their heads!"'

Tom smiled, flicking over to the tennis just as a rather stunning South American–looking player was serving, stretching one arm up high as he gave the ball a powerful slam, at the same time exposing a tempting glimpse of taut brown abs.

'And the guys are definitely hotter,' Rachel added.

Tom nudged her leg with his foot. 'What if I said that?'

'If you said that I'd think you were gay.'

Sunday

Rachel had emerged out of a deep sleep a little while ago and had been contemplating getting up, but she wasn't in any hurry. Then the phone started to ring. She'd left it in its charger out on the hall table, and she wasn't about to leap out of bed to try to get to it in time; she'd let the machine pick it up. But then she heard footsteps in the hall, and she remembered Tom was here, and oh God! He wasn't going to answer the phone, was he?

'Tom!' she cried urgently, scrambling to get out of bed.

He burst in the door. 'What is it? Are you all right?'

'Were you about to answer the phone?' she demanded, coming around the end of the bed.

'Christ, Rachel, I thought something was wrong,' he said, visibly relieved.

'Were you going to answer the phone?' she persisted.

'I didn't want it to wake you.'

'Tom!' The ringing finally stopped. 'You can't answer my phone at . . . whatever time it is on a Sunday morning.'

'Sorry, I wasn't thinking.'

Catherine's voice came over the answering machine. *'Well, I've had about enough of this. Where are you, Rachel? If you're still in bed, then pick up! I've been trying to call you since yesterday, don't you ever listen to your messages? Why do you even have an answering machine? Is it just so you can screen calls? Mine, in particular?'*

Rachel groaned. 'I better get this.' She stepped into the hall and grabbed the phone mid-sentence as Catherine continued her rant. 'I'm here.'

'Well, thank God for that,' she said. 'Did you get my messages yesterday?'

'No, I didn't even check the machine. I got . . . caught up with something.' She looked up at Tom, still standing there in the doorway. She waved her hand to usher him out of the way. He nodded, mouthing 'Sorry' before turning back down the hall.

'And you had your mobile phone off the whole time?' Catherine was saying.

Rachel walked into her room again, closing the door behind her. 'Um, no, I don't know, did I?'

'Well, it kept going straight to the recorded message saying you weren't available.'

'It's probably flat,' Rachel replied, falling back on the bed.

'Honestly Rachel, you're hopeless,' said Catherine. 'How did you not realise that by now and recharge it? What's going on? Where have you been? I was ringing to find out how the date went . . . Hold on a minute! Is that it? Did things go *really* well –'

'God, no,' she baulked at the idea. 'You think I'm going to spend the night with a guy I just met?'

'Well, if you hit it off . . .'

Catherine had a confidence about sex that Rachel found a little confronting; she sometimes wondered if Catherine had any boundaries at all.

Like she could talk, after Friday night.

'The date was an absolute disaster, Catherine. Turns out Phil's married.'

'*Married* married?'

'What other type of married is there?'

'You know, end-stage married, nominally married.'

'Well I don't know what any of that means,' she returned, 'but he claimed to be "emotionally" separated, though he still lives with his wife, and apparently she has no idea of his internet shenanigans.'

'Look, some people need to explore their options before they make such a radical change in their lives,' said Catherine matter-of-factly. 'Think about it, when a person decides, for whatever reason, to leave their job, no one expects them to quit outright before they've checked out their prospects and made some enquiries, at the very least. In the majority of cases, people find another job first before they give notice.'

So that's how Catherine justified her modus operandi. She always had someone waiting in the wings, ready to escort her out of a relationship that was floundering. Although publicly she had always made out that one followed the other, in consecutive order, she'd admitted drunkenly to Rachel one night that there was usually an overlap, that a dalliance had begun before she'd got around to ending the existing, unsatisfactory relationship. The thing was, Catherine was just incapable of being alone, it threatened her self-image too much. She needed the attention of a man to fan her ego.

'Well, be that as it may,' said Rachel, 'there was no spark with Phil, no connection at all. I persevered through a couple of drinks and then I called it a night.'

'Really? I didn't think you had it in you to be so assertive.'

'I can be assertive, it wasn't that hard.'

'So he mustn't have been all that interested either.'

Rachel knew Catherine didn't mean to offend, but sometimes her bluntness was a little hard to take, and Rachel certainly wasn't in the mood for it today.

'Well, now that we're all caught up,' she said, 'I better get on with my day.'

'Hold on one minute, I won't keep you from your busy schedule for much longer,' Catherine said, laying on the sarcasm with a trowel. 'I had another reason for calling.'

'What's that?'

'You know how we were talking with Lexie that we really need to watch out for Tom?'

Rachel's heart dropped into her stomach. Thank God video phones had never taken off in a major way.

Catherine didn't wait for an answer. 'He's just as bad as you, I've been trying to get him all weekend as well. You don't happen to have his mobile number, do you?'

God, for a minute then she thought she was going to ask her if she knew where he was. 'Ah, yeah, I might.'

'But it'll be on your mobile and it's flat, so send it to me when you recharge. Oh, but you'll probably forget ... Don't worry, I'll send you a reminder.'

'Rightio.'

'Anyway, my idea is to have the two of you over for dinner.'

Now Rachel's heart was giving her indigestion.

'With the girls, of course,' Catherine went on. 'That's really the whole point of it. Even though there's a year between them, Sophie and Alice have always got on well, and I think Alice, being the older one, could really be someone Sophie could confide in, you know, in a big sisterly way. And then of course Tom definitely needs someone to talk to about bringing up the girls now, and there's nothing I can't tell him.'

'Then what do you need me for?'

'Don't be like that, Rachel.'

'I'm not being like anything,' she insisted. 'I think what you're saying is great, and you should have Tom over for dinner and discuss parenting and all that. But I'll be like a shag on a rock, there's nothing I can bring to the conversation.'

'Look, without you it'll just be the three of us, with Martin, and that's, well, you know, three never works. I was thinking of having it one night when Martin was busy, but then who'd cook? And the thing is, Tom's comfortable with you, you have that whole brother-sister thing going on.'

'Yeah, just like you and Andrew.'

'Hah! Anyway, it will make it a nice relaxed evening for everyone.'

Hah!

'I just want to give Tom an opportunity to really open up.'

Hah hah ... *hah!*

God, how was she going to get out of this? 'Will you be inviting Lexie as well?'

'For crying out loud, Rachel, what is it with this obsession about including Lexie in absolutely everything? She lives next door to Tom, she sees him all the time. And I'd have to ask her *and* Scott, and the whole tribe. It would be an entirely different kind of evening with toddlers running amok, "relaxed" not being one of the words anyone would employ to describe it.'

'Well, then I shouldn't come either, Catherine,' said Rachel. 'You have a perfectly valid reason to ask Tom and the girls over, but if I come too, for no good reason, then we are specifically discluding Lexie, and I'm not comfortable with that.'

Good. That ought to do it.

'Rachel,' Catherine said, 'is there something you're not telling me?'

She could write a book. Or at least a rather salacious short story.

'Is it being around Tom that's unsettling you?' Catherine persisted. 'Do you feel weird because of Annie?'

Weird didn't begin to describe it.

'If that's the case, I think you have to put aside your own feelings and try to imagine how it is for poor Tom. He's suddenly not part of a couple any more, and he's probably not getting the invitations they used to. You've been through this, Rachel, you should understand. And dare I say, it would be a lot harder for him, under the circumstances. People are probably awkward around him. I wonder how he spends his weekends when the girls are off with their friends?'

Cleaning out my fridge.

'He needs to be around people he feels comfortable with, who he has some history with, so he can be himself. Now, I'm sure you can find a way to reconnect with him, which is all the more reason you should come. So it's settled,' she said, wrapping up her one-sided argument. 'I'll let you know the details after I've spoken to him.'

Rachel wouldn't argue with her now, she'd come up with an excuse when the time came. 'Fine, talk to you later.'

She hung up the phone and sat up, thinking about what to do about Tom. Because something definitely had to be done about Tom. They'd had the loveliest time last night. The awkwardness had largely dissipated, and sitting there together, watching the tennis and making stupid jokes, adding commentary, improvising their own scoring system, was like slipping on a pair of old shoes, easy and comfortable. But Rachel realised she had to draw a line and finally be the responsible one. Tom was operating from a lonely, probably frightened place after losing the wife he adored. His obsessive need to take care of her was simply an attempt to make up for what he hadn't been able to do for Annie. It was like penance. But enough was enough. She had to give him absolution and send him on his way. She stood up and walked determinedly out to the kitchen.

Tom looked around as she came into the doorway. 'I made coffee,' he said brightly. 'How are you feeling?'

'I'm feeling fine. Completely normal, no symptoms at all.' Which was a tiny lie, because she'd actually been getting mild period-type cramps since she woke up, but she wasn't about to tell Tom, he'd be calling an ambulance.

'That's great, Rach, I'm glad to hear it,' he said, passing her a mug of coffee.

She took a sip and put it down on the bench. 'Tom,' she said firmly, 'it's time for you to go now.'

He opened his mouth to say something but she jumped in first.

'No, no, the tables have turned. No discussion, you have to go home.'

'Okay, I will, in another hour or so, once I can see you're really all right now that you're up.'

'I'm really all right!' she insisted. 'And you have to go.'

He looked a little nonplussed. 'What is it, because I nearly answered the phone? I promise I won't do that again.'

'No you won't, because you're not going to be here.'

He sighed, folding his arms and leaning back against the bench. 'Are you mad at me?'

'No, of course not,' she insisted, softening. 'I really appreciate that you stayed, Tom, and I really appreciate what you did on Friday night –' Oh bugger '– you know, at the bar, rescuing me, and all that,' she stammered.

'Rachel, we haven't talked about –'

'No, we haven't, and we're not going to.'

'Are we just going to act like it didn't happen?'

'I think if we can pull that off, it's the best course of action.'

He looked at her for what felt like a long time. 'You're sure you're okay with that?' he said finally.

And then it struck her. Tom was feeling just as awkward, obviously. And maybe a little guilty as well. Not that Rachel thought he should feel guilty, not at all, but he probably couldn't wait to get out of here and he was only trying to do the decent thing and not hurt her feelings. Well, that was a relief, to clear the air, to know where they both stood.

'I'm absolutely okay with that,' Rachel assured him. And she was, she didn't feel a thing, a little numb if anything.

'Because I'd really hate it if we couldn't be friends, Rach,' Tom said seriously.

'Don't worry,' she said. 'And I'll prove it. Only a friend can tell another friend to piss off and give them some space.'

He smiled widely then. 'Do you mind if I finish my coffee?'

'Oh, okay, if you must.'

Thursday

Lexie sat staring at the computer screen, supporting her chin in the palm of her hand. Another email had arrived from Catherine, hounding her for her past employment details, dates, referees and the like '... or else how do you expect me to put your résumé together?'

Lexie sighed. She had hoped that if she just ignored the emails, Catherine would eventually lose interest. But she had underestimated her tenacity. She was like a dog with a bone. Lexie couldn't understand why this was so important to her. One thing was becoming increasingly clear, she was going to have to confront Catherine eventually, or else be confronted by Catherine, which was more likely. Either way, Lexie needed to have her position clarified in her own mind if she had any hope of defending it. And the fact was, her position was as clear as mud. That was really the issue at the heart of things. It wasn't that she was so afraid of standing up to Catherine – though she could certainly do without that – it was that being cornered this way had made her realise she didn't know what she was going to do with her life for the next few years, and beyond that. She knew what she wanted, but was another baby even an option, realistically? She needed to know for sure, because it wasn't something she could put off indefinitely.

But what did Scott want? Who knew? Certainly not Lexie. Lately he'd been working so hard, often getting home barely in time to kiss the kids goodnight. He was run off his feet at the café because they always erred on the side of understaffing every shift in an effort to save money. Sometimes they tried to call up a casual when they got too busy, but casuals were hard to find on a beautiful summer day. And all the time costs were going up – food, electricity, rates – and Scott was worried that it would be the rent next. He was running around like a mad thing putting out fires, but had he stopped to think about where he wanted to be in five years? Ten? Two?

They needed to talk. They hadn't really talked about the future since before Mia. *Well* before Mia. It used to be all about the future all the time, making exciting plans: the wedding, buying the house, the renovations, deciding when to try for a baby and then falling pregnant the very same month. Once Riley had arrived safe and healthy, and they got past the blur of the first few months, they talked about a reasonable space between kids, because having an only child had never been an option for either of them. So they settled on the month she'd go off the pill.

And they hadn't talked since.

There was never any time. Well, they were just going to have to make time, Lexie decided, or more to the point, Scott was going to have to make time. There were more important things in life than the business. She picked up the phone and called the café. Scott answered.

'Hi, hun, how are you? How are the kids?'

'We're all okay, we miss you.'

'Me too.'

Lexie couldn't help feeling it was all a bit perfunctory.

'So, I was thinking,' she began, 'why don't I get the kids off to bed a little early tonight, and you and I can have a nice dinner, just the two of us. I'll open a bottle –'

'Can't Lex, I'm going to be late, I was just about to call.'

'Late, again? What is it this time?'

'I haven't balanced the books for December yet, and January's almost over. I have to keep track of where the business is at, it's just too unstable at the moment.'

'Okay, well, why don't you bring the books home? I could help, we can sort it out together.'

'Nuh, it's quieter here, and besides, everything's on hand. If I tried to pack it all up to do it at home, I'd forget something for sure. I'll feel better if I just stay until I get it done.'

'We have to talk, Scott,' Lexie said plainly.

'What? Why? What's going on?'

'That's what we have to talk about,' she said. 'What is going on? I feel completely shut out, Scott, I need to understand what's happening with the business and how it's going to affect our future.'

There was a pause before he answered. 'Lex, I just got through telling you how stressful things are, and you want to load all this on me now? Make me answerable to you?'

'No, that's not –'

'Jeez, honey, I like to think of you and the kids as the nice, easy part of my life and that coming home is like coming to an oasis.'

That's how her mother had always made things for her father. She said it was important that home was the one place he didn't have any responsibility, or stress, or demands on him. 'Of course. I'm sorry, Scott, don't worry about anything here, just do what you have to do.'

'Thanks for understanding.'

'Do you want me to keep some dinner for you?'

'No, there's food I can finish off here.'

'Do you want to say goodnight to the kids?'

'Sure, put them on.'

Lexie stood by while the kids babbled on to their father; she felt chastened, but also a little uneasy. When she took the phone back off Riley, Scott had already hung up.

'Okay, just another five minutes and then bathtime,' she said, walking back inside. She really felt like a glass of wine, but Lexie didn't like to drink when she was the only adult here with the kids. She peered out through the glass doors, where they were playing happily in the sandpit. It hadn't been as hot today, there was a fresh nor'easter rolling through the house, expelling any hot air still lingering from the middle of the day. The kids should sleep well tonight.

It'd be okay to have just one glass.

Perched on a kitchen stool where she had a clear view into the back garden, Lexie took a sip of her wine as she picked up the phone and dialled Rachel's number. She needed to talk to someone, and easygoing, non-judgemental Rachel was the best listener she knew. After Annie.

'Hi, it's Lexie,' she said when Rachel picked up.

'Hi Lexie, what's up?'

'Oh, nothing, just haven't seen you for a while. What have you been up to?'

'Nothing, nothing at all. Same old . . . you know how it is.'

'Hey,' Lexie remembered, 'didn't you have that date?'

'Oh yeah.'

'So how did it go?'

'Nowhere,' said Rachel. 'He was married.'

Lexie gasped. 'No!'

'I'm afraid so.'

'Is that allowed?'

'No one's checking ID or anything,' said Rachel. 'I guess they can do whatever they can get away with.'

'That's terrible. What are you going to do?'

'What do you mean?'

'Well, can you report him or something?'

'To be honest, I don't think anyone would give a damn,' said Rachel. 'In fact, I've heard since that these sites can be a real hangout for married men on the prowl.'

'I'm sorry but I think that's disgusting, it shouldn't be allowed. They should vet the whole process.'

'But when you think about it, Lex, it's no different to any pick-up place, they're full of married men trying to hide their wedding rings while they chat up girls.'

For a moment Lexie softened, thinking of how lucky she was to have Scott, and how she really had nothing to complain about.

'So what about Catherine's plans for you?' Rachel was asking.

'That's part of the reason I was calling, actually.'

'Oh?'

Just then a siren wail emanated from outside, followed by Riley's voice. 'Mum-*mmy*! Mia got sand in her eyes. *Again*!'

'Oh, damn,' she muttered. 'Can you hold on just one minute, Rach?'

'Sure.'

Lexie dashed outside and scooped up Mia, restraining her arms at the same time. Mia was too little to understand that rubbing her eyes with sand-encrusted fingers only made matters worse. Lexie quickly dealt with the offending sand under the kitchen tap, before popping Mia on the bench, holding a wet facecloth firmly over her eyes. She grabbed the phone again.

'Sorry about that, Rach.'

'No problem.'

'Scott's not home and we're on the verge of crazy hour.'

'Why don't you call me back, or I'll call you later if you like?'

'Actually, I was going to ask, are you free Saturday? Maybe we could meet for coffee, or even lunch?'

'Sure, where did you have in mind? I'll let Catherine know.'

Lexie hesitated. 'The thing is, I'll have to bring the kids, and you know how she is around the kids.'

'Uhuh.'

'I really just wanted to sound you out about something, there's no need to bother Catherine with it. I know she's a very busy woman.'

'Okay then.'

Lexie got the feeling Rachel was a little uncomfortable. 'You know, why don't you just come here? That way the kids'll be occupied and we can have a nice chat.'

'All right. What time?'

Saturday

It was close to three o'clock when Rachel walked around the corner into Lexie's street. She had insisted that Lexie not put on lunch, she had enough to do with the kids. A cuppa and a bickie would be sufficient. She couldn't imagine what this was about, what Lexie wanted to 'run by her'. Rachel had no idea what she could offer, apart from a listening ear. Lexie was clearly missing Annie, and Rachel couldn't help but think she would prove to be a poor substitute. Annie had always appeared to possess boundless patience, Rachel had noticed it particularly in the way she was with her kids, or anyone's kids for that matter. She never seemed to get ruffled. Rachel vividly remembered a hot, sticky afternoon at Tom and Annie's house, Lexie heavily pregnant with Mia, and Riley playing up something shocking. Scott must have been at work and Lexie was close to tears trying to cope with Riley on her own. Finally Annie had gone over to him and crouched down, whispered something close to his ear and then took him by the hand and led him inside the house. Ten minutes later they had returned to the back garden; Riley was calm and he remained that way for the rest of the afternoon. It was almost as though she'd cast a spell on him.

As Rachel drew closer to their house now, she saw Tom's car in the drive, which meant he was probably home. She hadn't spoken to him since last weekend. Every time she thought about calling him, talking to him, seeing him, it freaked her out. She wished things could be different, because she really wanted to call him, talk to him, see him. Something had happened last weekend, and it wasn't the sex. It was spending time with him, mucking around, being mates again. She felt like she had got her best friend back, only to ruin it by sleeping with him. She was never going to be able to look at him the same way again. And the longer she left making contact, the more awkward it was likely to become.

Nonetheless, she scooted past his house and straight over to Lexie's door, huddling inside the alcove out of sight as she knocked, glancing over her shoulder like she was being followed. Or like she was insane.

Lexie opened the door, smiling widely, with Mia perched on her hip. 'Hi Rachel! Look who's here, Mia. It's Aunty Rachel. Say hello to Aunty Rachel.'

But Mia was playing coy today, burying her head into her mother's neck with an obstinate grunt.

'Mia —'

'It's okay if Mia doesn't feel like saying hello,' Rachel reassured her. She was all for teaching children manners, but she often found the trouble parents went to to coax their tiny tots to perform, or conform, a little awkward for everyone involved.

'She's overdue for her N-A-P,' Lexie explained, standing back to let Rachel through. 'I wanted to keep her up till you got here so that she could S-L-E-E-P while we talk. Riley won't interrupt quite so much.'

This was beginning to sound serious.

'You know what?' she went on. 'I'll put her down right now. Just go on through, make yourself at home. Riley's out there playing.'

Rachel heard Mia begin to grizzle as Lexie mounted the stairs, revealing her fate. She walked out into the living area, immaculate as always. How she did it with two little ones was beyond Rachel.

'Hi Riley,' she called, spotting him in the playroom as she put her bag down on the kitchen bench.

He looked up, contemplating her with a slight frown.

Rachel took a couple of steps closer. 'Don't you remember me? I'm Rachel.'

'I know who you are,' he said in a bored tone, returning his attention to the Lego model he was building.

Hmm, knew her, wasn't that impressed by her. Story of her life.

Rachel was perched on a kitchen stool flipping through a magazine when Lexie reappeared.

'Did you get yourself a drink?' She skittered over to the fridge. 'I should have said there was cold water. You would have been thirsty after your bus trip.'

She bustled about as she spoke, placing a coaster and a tall glass in front of Rachel and pouring icy water from a stainless-steel jug.

'Thanks, I was fine.'

'So, coffee?' she chirped.

'Sure. If you're making it.'

Lexie turned around to fire up the coffee machine, or whatever it was you did with the things. Rachel was a total coffee pleb; while she enjoyed a good cup of coffee as much as the next person, she was happy to drink instant, an admission she would never make in mixed company, of course.

Lexie prattled away about the kids, and Scott working so hard, and the kids, as she made the coffee, opened and closed cupboard doors, scuttled back and forth from the fridge, and a few minutes later, an elegant afternoon tea appeared before Rachel's very eyes – there was coffee, a little tray of sugar cubes piled into a pyramid, a plate of miniature cupcakes, all individually decorated, a basket of those homemade cookies encrusted with big chunks of white and dark chocolate, and what looked like a lemon-curd slice arranged on a green glass platter.

'Lex, you shouldn't have gone and bought all this.'

'I didn't,' she shrugged. 'I made it.'

Rachel's eyes widened. 'You made all this?'

'Don't worry, I didn't do it all today,' Lexie dismissed with a smile. 'Just the slice. I make the cookies all the time, the kids love them, and they keep quite well in sealed containers. The cupcakes last longer, because you can freeze them, so I always have some on hand.'

Rachel examined them up close, tiny little cupcakes with perfect dollops of creamy icing and a variety of toppings: a drizzle of gooey caramel, chocolate shavings, nuts, glazed fruit, a swirl of passionfruit. They were like miniature works of art.

'They're all different flavours, right?' said Rachel, in awe.

'Yeah, I make batches of different kinds, that way I can defrost a selection.'

'Do you freeze them with the icing and everything?'

'No, I just slapped that on this morning. It takes no time.'

She was clearly a freak.

'Do you make these for the café?'

'No way,' Lexie shook her head with a smile. 'I just like to bake. Scott would never let me do anything for the café.'

'Why not?' Rachel picked up one of the cupcakes with caramel. 'Doesn't he think they're good enough?'

'Oh, it's not that, he thinks my parents would be horrified if they thought I had to help out.'

'I don't get it,' said Rachel, taking a bite of the cupcake. 'Oh my God,' she warbled, her mouth full. 'This is fantastic.'

'You know how he's always worried that my parents think I married beneath me, and that he's not good enough?'

Rachel swallowed. 'I can't imagine your parents would think that way.'

'They don't,' she insisted. 'I mean, if they were going to be disappointed with anyone, it would be me, because I didn't continue with medicine. But I know they love me, and they just want me to be happy, and they know Scott makes me happy, so they love him too. That's the way it works with them.'

Rachel was eyeing off the cakes again. 'What's the passionfruit one?'

'Well, passionfruit,' said Lexie, 'with cream-cheese icing.'

Rachel sighed.

'Help yourself,' Lexie insisted. 'They're only bite-size.'

Rachel was not going to be able to resist. 'What did you want to run by me?' she asked, picking another.

'Oh, yes,' said Lexie. 'Well, ever since Catherine started pushing me about going back to work –'

'Don't let her get to you,' said Rachel, before popping the cake in her mouth. She had to stop herself from moaning audibly.

'I won't, but the thing is, I do feel like I'm at a crossroads.'

'Mummy?' Riley had wandered in. 'What's up there?' he said, pointing to the top of the bench, which was just out of his line of sight.

Lexie excused herself while she got Riley a cookie and some juice and set him up on a little table out in the playroom.

'You were saying you're at a crossroads?' said Rachel when Lexie returned.

'That's right,' she said, sliding back onto a stool. 'I do want to stay home with the kids, but Scott is working so hard, and I wonder if I shouldn't be contributing financially, but I don't know what I'd do. Catherine keeps forwarding me ads for lab assistants, but I don't want to go back to that. I never wanted to do it in the first place, but when I didn't go ahead with my medical degree, that was all I was qualified for.'

'Then what do you want to do?'

'I don't know,' Lexie shrugged.

Rachel looked at her. 'Come on, if you could do anything?'

She hesitated. 'I'd like to have another baby.'

'Oh.' Rachel wasn't expecting that.

'You think I'm mad, don't you?'

'Of course not.' She glanced around. 'I'm just wondering where you'd fit another baby. You've only got the two bedrooms upstairs, right?'

Lexie nodded. 'I know, we can't have another baby living here, and we can't afford to move. Maybe we could if I went to work, but then, I wouldn't want to go to work and leave a new baby.'

'What does Scott have to say?'

'See, that's the thing,' said Lexie, 'we haven't talked about it.'

'Don't you think that's where you should start?' Rachel suggested.

'I know, you're right. But he's so stressed out lately, we never have any time to talk.'

Rachel wasn't sure what to say, so she picked up another cupcake instead. 'Are you sure he wouldn't think about stocking these at the café. They are seriously good.'

'Thanks,' she said despondently.

Clearly she didn't want to talk about cupcakes. 'Look, I'm probably the worst person to talk to about this. I've never even figured out what I want to do when I grow up, so what would I know?'

'But you've done so much with your life,' Lexie insisted. 'You're so worldly, you've travelled all over, even lived in other countries, and you've worked all kinds of jobs. I haven't done anything.'

Rachel was a bit taken aback by Lexie's impression of her. She was worldly? Not just some uni dropout who bummed her way around the world in a series of low-paying backpacker jobs and who still didn't have anything vaguely approaching a career?

'Come on, Lexie. You're raising two beautiful children, and you run this house like a pro, and frankly, you cook like a pro.'

'It's just a hobby,' she shrugged.

Rachel really had to lay off the cupcakes – eating them and talking about them.

'Okay, let's think about this logically.' Although it was hardly her strength. 'You know what you don't want to do, you do not want work in a lab, so you have to tell Catherine to drop it. You don't need the pressure, or the distraction, frankly.'

'You're right. That's what I'll do.' She paused, giving Rachel a plaintive look. 'Would you mind being there when I tell her?'

'Of course, we'll do lunch one day or something. You know, Lex, you shouldn't let Catherine intimidate you. She's just bossy and she thinks she has the answers to everyone else's problems, even though she can't see the gaping issues in her own life. The interesting thing about that is, she doesn't want to see them, that'd be way too confronting.'

'How did you two ever become friends?' said Lexie, shaking her head. 'I've never understood it. You seem so different.'

'Well, I guess we are now,' said Rachel. 'But we've known each other since high school, we had a lot more in common back then.'

'Oh, like what?'

Rachel thought about it. 'Having parents we couldn't relate to, I suppose.'

'You and every other teenager.'

'That's true,' Rachel smiled. 'But she was a good influence on me, she was the reason I got through high school. She was so sure of herself, so sure of the future.'

'Hmm . . .' Lexie raised an eyebrow. 'Catherine doesn't come across as the eternal optimist to me.'

'Well, the whole drama around the pregnancy really knocked her badly,' said Rachel. 'You've heard the story, haven't you?'

Lexie nodded.

'I think it made her determined not to let anyone screw her over like that ever again. And look, she had a baby when she was just a schoolgirl, that's got to be so hard. She had to sink or swim, and sinking would never have been an option for Catherine. So I guess she had to become pretty tough to get where she is today.' Rachel paused, thinking about it. 'I don't know, I was away for so many years, and of course we kept in touch, but when I came back she'd definitely changed. We didn't really have much in common any more.'

'You've stayed close though,' Lexie commented.

Rachel wondered how close they really were these days.

'I guess once you get past a certain age you stay friends out of habit,' she shrugged. 'Anyway, you shouldn't be worried about Catherine. You need to be talking to Scott.'

'I know, you're right. He's just so busy at the moment.'

'Things quieten down a bit at the café after Australia Day, don't they?'

Lexie nodded.

'So don't stress, one step at a time, everything doesn't have to be settled by tomorrow.'

'You're right, of course.'

Rachel had never been told she was right so much in one conversation.

Lexie gave her a grateful smile. 'Thanks for listening, Rachel. I just have all this stuff going round and round in my head till I can't think straight.'

'Happens to the best of us, Lex,' Rachel assured her. 'I'm glad you called, you know. You should call, any time, even if you just want to chat, whatever.'

'Thank you, I appreciate that,' said Lexie. 'I've been feeling a little lost since Annie . . .'

'Of course, you two were so close.'

Lexie nodded. 'We had coffee like this all the time, she was only next door. A day hardly went by that we didn't speak to each other, maybe just in passing, but she was always there if I needed to talk. She always listened.' Lexie looked across at Rachel. 'You know, this is probably going to sound strange, but I really miss not being able to talk to her about this, about grieving for her. I know she'd say all the right things. Does that make sense?'

'It does actually,' said Rachel. 'Tom said something similar to me once, he said he didn't know how they were going to get through this without Annie to show them the way.'

'He said that?' Lexie smiled wistfully. 'That's sweet. And sad.' She looked at Rachel. 'What do you miss about her?'

She wasn't prepared for that, and she felt so guilty now even thinking about Annie, she went blank. 'Um, well . . . I liked it when all of us were together, the four of us. I miss that.'

'Me too,' Lexie agreed. 'It's just not the same without her.'

'It's not. But we will readjust over time, Lexie,' Rachel assured her. 'We have to, because we need to be here for each other. Annie would want that.'

Lexie nodded. 'You're right.'

Again? This was some kind of record.

They chatted amiably for another hour or so, mostly about the kids. Rachel was happy to let Lexie talk while she continued to sample the wares. Riley wandered in from time to time, but he was not interested in joining them, Rachel clearly held no attraction. She had never held much sway with littlies, she always seemed to get on much better with older kids. It was an observation that made Rachel a little nervous about having children of her own; if it was ever going to happen, she wished the stork could deliver them once they'd turned, say, twelve.

She eventually decided she had better get going before she risked falling into a diabetic coma. Lexie walked her up the hall to the door.

'How are Tom and the girls?' Rachel couldn't resist asking.

'Well, Sophie and Hannah don't seem to be around all that much,' said Lexie. 'I suppose they're keeping busy in the holidays with their friends. Tom has to work, after all.' She paused at the door, resting her hand on the lock. 'But sometimes when I have to get up to Mia in the middle of the night, I see a light on next door. I don't think he's sleeping very well, poor thing.'

Rachel felt an involuntary pang at the mental picture of Tom sitting up on his own at night, wandering around the house perhaps, not wanting to go to bed alone. She remembered that night after the funeral, when he wanted her to stay till he fell asleep . . .

Lexie was opening the front door. 'Oh, speak of the devil, there he is now. Tom! Hi!' she waved eagerly.

Rachel couldn't move. She wondered if there was any way to avoid him. What was she going to do? Duck out the back? She was being ridiculous. And now Lexie was watching her, standing frozen in the hall.

'What's wrong?' she asked.

'Oh, nothing, I was stopping to think if I'd left anything behind.' Could she be more lame? 'No, I reckon I'm all set,' she smiled, coming forwards.

'Look who's here,' Lexie turned to call out to Tom.

She really didn't have to make an announcement of it. Rachel stepped out through the front door as Tom walked around from the other side of his car, holding a soapy sponge and a garden hose, wearing only a pair of board shorts. Great.

'Hi Rach,' he called out with a broad smile.

'Hi there,' she nodded. 'Washing the car?' she added superfluously.

He looked amused. 'Your powers of observation are quite phenomenal, Rach.'

Lexie giggled, then she cocked an ear towards the house. 'Ah, that's Mia waking up. I'll leave you guys to it. Thanks again, Rach,' she said, giving her a quick peck on the cheek. 'We'll talk soon, okay? See ya, Tom.'

And she vanished into the house, the door closing behind her. Rachel looked over at Tom, who had ditched the sponge and the hose and propped himself against the boot of the car, waiting. She had to talk to him, at least for a polite minute or two.

'You parents are odd creatures,' she said, for the sake of saying something. 'I couldn't hear a sound then, but Lexie heard her own child from the floor below, through a closed door. Yet other times, Mia can be yelling *"Mummy! Mummy! Mummy!"* at the top of her lungs, tugging at her skirt, and she doesn't seem to hear it at all.'

Tom smiled. 'It's one of the very mild superpowers you get when you become a parent.'

'Mild superpowers?'

'Yeah, everyone can't be a superhero, Rach, but we all have our own special powers. Things like . . . being able to judge whether furniture will fit through doorways. Or being able to get pens working again. That's a very useful mild superpower.'

Rachel couldn't help smiling then. 'What on earth are you talking about, Tom?'

He grinned back at her. 'It's from a comedy song the girls played to us a while back. We all had to work out what our very mild superpowers were. Sophie's is always knowing how a movie's going to end.'

'That could get annoying.'

'You're not wrong – we had to impose a gag order on her so

she wouldn't spoil the ending for us all the time. Now she writes it down, just to prove that she knew it all along.'

Rachel ambled slowly over towards him. 'What's Hannah's?'

'Oh, hers is good,' he said. 'She finds money, everywhere, all the time, on the footpath, in the sand even. Ever since she was tiny. Just coins, but she often finds gold ones.'

'And what about you?' asked Rachel. 'What's your very mild superpower, Tom?'

He smiled. 'Peeling.'

She frowned.

'Hardboiled eggs, mostly. That's what started it. The girls were amazed how I could peel the shell off a hardboiled egg in a couple of pieces, clean.'

'That is impressive,' Rachel agreed. 'Can you do oranges and apples so the peel is all in one piece?'

'Of course,' he said with a dismissive shrug. 'Peeling is my very mild superpower.'

She smiled, and they fell silent for a moment. Rachel wondered if she should ask what Annie's mild superpower was. Maybe this had only come up since . . . no, it sounded like it was part of their family folklore. But it might upset him? Though it could upset him more if she was ignored. Surely Tom would say something . . . After a while, Rachel couldn't stand it any more.

'Well, I must have been standing behind the door when they handed out the very mild superpowers,' she said finally.

'Oh, come on, you're being modest,' said Tom. 'What about your talent for stating the obvious?'

'Does that pass for a very mild superpower?'

'When you do it so well . . .'

Rachel was standing in front of him now, trying to avoid staring at his bare chest. Well, not just his bare chest, his whole bare torso – his board shorts were sitting quite low on his hips. She looked away down the street.

'You should have a shirt on, you know,' she blurted suddenly.

'Pardon?'

'Or sunscreen at least,' she remarked. 'It's hot out here.' Or was it just her?

'Was that a display of your very mild superpower again?' he asked. 'Or are you channelling my mother?'

'I'm just saying, you don't want to get burned. That sun is hot.'

'Oh, do you want to come inside? I'll get you a drink.'

'What?' Rachel's eyes flew up to meet his.

'Do you want to come in for a drink?' Tom repeated calmly.

'Oh,' she hesitated, 'are the girls home?'

He shook his head. 'No, they're both off for the weekend again. Their friends' mothers insist on having them stay all the time. I think they worry they're not getting fed properly or something.' He gave her a crooked smile.

'Does that bother you?'

He shrugged. 'As long as the girls are happy. It's nice for them to get a bit of mothering, I suppose. Whatever they need . . .'

Rachel couldn't help feeling they needed their father more than other people's mothers, but it wasn't her place to say so.

'Catherine called about dinner next Saturday night,' said Tom.

'Oh?'

He looked at her. 'She said you knew about it.'

'Um, she mentioned something last week,' Rachel said vaguely. 'Nothing definite.'

'You will come, though?'

'Did you say next Saturday?' She screwed up her face, looking skyward, like it took a great deal of concentration to sift through her packed schedule. 'No, Saturday's no good actually. I'm busy.'

His face dropped. 'You're kidding? I only said I'd come because you were going to be there.'

'Why? What's wrong?'

'Well,' Tom sighed, 'I don't really have that much in common with Martin.'

'You're both lawyers,' she reminded him.

He shrugged. 'And Catherine, well, you know, she can be a little . . . intense.'

Rachel could hardly argue with that.

'I thought it'd be more relaxed with you there,' he said. 'You can't get out of what you're doing?'

She hesitated. 'Could be a little awkward.'

'It's not another internet date, is it?'

'No, no,' she assured him. 'I've given up on that.'

'Glad to hear it,' said Tom. 'Maybe I should call Catherine back and reschedule?'

Bugger, then she'd have Catherine on her back, grilling her about what she was doing that was so important, and Rachel wasn't that good a liar. She was obviously going to have to do this sometime or another, after all she was the one who insisted that they act like nothing had happened.

'I'll see what I can do,' she said finally.

'Great, let me know, okay? We'll pick you up if you like.'

Rachel nodded. 'Anyway, I better get going.'

'If you wait ten minutes till I rinse off the car, I can run you home.'

She waved him off. 'No, I'm fine, it's five minutes on the bus.'

'Are you doing anything later?'

'Huh?' she blinked.

'You want to go see a movie or something?'

'No!' she blurted, a little too adamantly, she could tell by the look on his face. 'It's just, I really can't. I've got . . . a thing.' She glanced at her watch without seeing the time. 'Oh, and I'm really going to have to rush, get home, get ready, you know . . .'

He nodded. 'You're a regular social butterfly.'

'That's me,' she said, walking away backwards. 'I'll let you know about next week, as soon as I sort it out.'

'I'd appreciate it.'

'See ya,' she said, raising her hand in a wave before turning to hurry up the street. She didn't look back at him again. She couldn't. He'd seemed a little . . . well, forlorn, for want of a better word. Some friend she was. He was going to be alone for the weekend, as was she, and she couldn't even bring herself to go to a movie with him.

Yep, she was the one who'd insisted that they act like nothing had happened.

It was a lot easier to make resolutions like that when he was wearing a shirt.

*

Wednesday

Catherine turned into the driveway, anticipating that delightful sense of relief she almost always felt arriving home. She'd had very strong ideas about what she wanted for this house and had worked closely with her architect; she got the impression he felt a little too closely at times. But Catherine was a self-avowed control freak, and she wasn't about to apologise for it. She had lived in a number of period homes to date, and while she loved their grace and proportions, she was over it. She craved clean lines, smooth finishes, hallowed spaces; she wanted it to be an almost Zen-like experience walking through her front door, like living in a work of art.

'Fuck!' She gritted her teeth. Martin had parked his BMW in the driveway, far enough back so that he blocked the entrance to both garages. He was probably going out again, but the moron could not think to park out on the street so that he didn't block her. No, that would involve using his head. Well, she would stop here, and he could waste his own time moving her car out to shift his.

She'd had a rotten day and she was in a foul mood. She could feel the niggling beginnings of a headache, and that pissed her off even more because she needed a drink, and if a headache was really coming on, a drink would only make it worse. But she was going to have a drink regardless.

She let herself in through the front door, slamming it behind her and dumping her briefcase on the hall table. She strode down the hall, shedding her jacket and tossing it over the back of the sofa as she passed through the living room and out into the kitchen, her heels clattering on the travertine the whole way.

'Hello darling,' Martin greeted her, poised over the chopping board.

'Your car's blocking the garage,' she snapped, heading for the fridge.

'Oh, yes, I'm expecting a call from the video shop. I booked that new film I was telling you about –'

'Fine,' she cut him off, grabbing a bottle of wine. 'You can put my car away when you're done.'

'Of course,' he replied calmly. 'How was your day?' he ventured.

'Dreadful. And I don't want to go over it.' She turned her back on him to get a glass from the cupboard.

'Okay, well, I bought a lovely piece of salmon this afternoon. I actually popped down to the fish market after work. And I'm going to bake it, with . . .'

And on he droned. Catherine tuned out, as she usually did when Martin started talking food. Why he persisted she had no idea, she had never shown any interest in cooking, and less in eating. It was okay when they were entertaining, but when it was just them, she couldn't give a flying fuck. She poured herself a large glass of wine and replaced the bottle in the fridge, picking up the glass as she turned around to face Martin. He was still rabbiting on.

'I'm going to sit outside for a while,' she said, cutting him off again.

'Oh . . .' He looked a little taken aback. Then he sighed. 'Right then, I'll just get on with it, I suppose.'

Catherine turned for the doors out to the terrace.

'Oh, I nearly forgot,' said Martin, stopping her. 'Alice wanted to talk to you about something when you got home. She's up in her room, she's waiting for you.'

'Well, Madam can come and find me if it's so important,' she said, stepping outside. Although it had been a hot day, it was pleasantly cool out here under the shade of the flourishing grapevine. The jasmine had finished flowering for the season, but the air had the sweet scent of freshly mown grass. The gardener must have been today.

Catherine took a long drink before setting her glass down on the wrought-iron table and taking a seat on one of the matching chairs she had imported from France. She had wanted to recreate a Mediterranean loggia out here, despite the architect arguing that it was not in keeping with the modernist lines of the house. He had designed a Japanese-style garden on the original plans, but Catherine had rejected it out of hand. She knew what she wanted, and she always got her own way. She needed greenery, lots of it, and while she liked order, a raked pebble garden was a little too anal, even for her.

She breathed deeply, closing her eyes. She ought to know by now to schedule meetings with the spiteful Mrs Alannah Cresswell earlier in the day so she had time to recover. Catherine generally enjoyed her work. Securing generous settlements for women tossed onto the seconds pile was immensely satisfying, even where there had been little hardship involved. It was Catherine's belief that men should be made to pay a fair price for 'moving on', usually into the arms of a younger woman. If they broke any other kind of contract, restitution would be expected and duly forfeited; it should be no different in a marriage contract. Of course she got the greatest satisfaction the more heartless the moving on, and the younger and blonder the replacement. But every now and then, a certain kind of woman turned up – more often than not the blonde replacement – who was nothing but a gold-digging opportunist. She would generally latch on to a wealthy man, take delight in watching his marriage fall apart in her wake, and then proceed to revel in the lifestyle he provided, contributing nothing, but then considering herself due for a share of his wealth when she inevitably became bored with her middle-aged husband with a paunch and thinning hair. Catherine was not in the position to judge, she had an obligation to her firm to get the best possible settlement for the client they were representing, regardless of the circumstances. But she hated it. She felt it undermined the rest of her work, and Alannah Cresswell was just the type of money-grubbing, pretentious little upstart who made her blood boil.

She picked up her glass and took another long drink as Alice burst through the door.

'You could've told me you were home already!' she accused.

'So I could be the recipient of such a charming welcome?' Catherine returned archly.

'Sorry Mum, hi Mum,' Alice groaned in a monotone as she sauntered over and dragged a chair out from the table, scraping it across the flagstone paving. She slumped down into it, facing her mother.

'Sit up straight, please Alice.'

Alice sighed dramatically, squaring her shoulders into the back of the seat. 'I have something important to ask you and you have to promise you'll give me a fair hearing.'

'When do I not give you a fair hearing?'

Alice almost rolled her eyes. 'Okay, here it is. Travesty is playing at the stadium and I know you don't like big outdoor concerts, and you think I'm too young, but the last time I asked was a full year ago, and I am seventeen now, after all. Anyway, tickets were like, impossible to get, but now, it's so totally amazing, because Lottie —'

'Who?'

'Lottie . . . Charlotte Campbell, you know her, Mum. You were like, totally impressed when you found out who her dad was.'

'Mm . . .' Catherine recalled now. Her father was Douglas Campbell, the CEO of a major investment bank, one that had survived the crash with both its stocks and its reputation intact. Catherine had been taken aback when he'd shown up one Saturday afternoon to pick up Charlotte — a rather nondescript little thing, it had to be said — dressed in grubby clothes as though he'd been working in the garden. Catherine had paused to wonder just who they were letting into the school these days, but she had impeccable manners so she invited him in and even offered him a drink while Charlotte got her things together. Out of politeness, and not a little curiosity, she had asked him what he did for a living. 'Yes, I know who Charlotte is.'

'Well, her dad's got some kind of VIP passes, she can take three friends, and it's in a roped-off area, totally safe, and Lottie's mum's going to take us and everything, and you so have to let me go or I'm seriously going to die.'

'You're not going to die, Alice.'

'Oh, come on, Mum, give me a little poetic licence.'

Catherine was vaguely amused, she just wished these things weren't the be-all and end-all to Alice. At her age, Catherine was pregnant; concerts and the like faded into insignificance. She understood from then what was really important — working hard, getting ahead, not letting anyone get the better of you — and she believed it had stood her in good stead. Not that she'd want Alice to get pregnant to learn those important life lessons, heaven forbid, but she wouldn't mind if her perspective was a little broader than the latest teenage fad.

She had to admit though, she was not against the idea of Alice cultivating this friendship with Douglas Campbell's daughter.

'When is this gala event?' she asked.

'Saturday night,' Alice said hopefully.

'This Saturday?' said Catherine. 'Well, I'm sorry, darling, but this Saturday is impossible. The Macklins are coming for dinner.'

'So?' Alice said, a look of crazed disbelief on her face. 'Did you even listen to a word I just said, Mum? This is Travesty, and I have been, like, their biggest fan *forever*! These are VIP tickets, this is totally a once-in-a-lifetime thing! Don't you get it?'

Catherine shook her head with a knowing smile. 'Alice, you're seventeen. Let's hope there are far bigger things to look forward to in your lifetime. And of course I "get" that you're disappointed, but I'm afraid there's nothing we can do. This was organised more than a week ago.'

'But it doesn't matter if I'm not here.'

'Of course it matters. I expressly included the girls in the invitation so you could all catch up before school goes back.'

'Can't we just make it another night then?'

'No, Alice! That is the height of bad manners, shunting people around because you get a better offer. How would you like to be treated that way?'

'I wouldn't care if someone had a good reason,' she insisted. 'I bet if you rang Tom and got him to check with Soph, she would totally be on my side.'

'Well I'm not going to ring Tom, obviously. Of course they'd agree with whatever you said, you'd be putting them in an untenable position.'

Alice went to protest further but Catherine spoke over her.

'Look, you will have many more opportunities to go to many more concerts. As much as you think this is the end of the world, it's far from it, and sometimes in life we have to choose to do what is right over doing whatever we feel like. At your age I was already pregnant with you, and my adolescence came to an abrupt end, but I made the most of it —'

'Why do you always have to bring that up!' Alice cried. 'Just because you went and got yourself pregnant —'

'I didn't "get myself" pregnant, young lady,' Catherine

interrupted firmly, raising her voice with control. 'It takes two, it's just that all too often one party gets left with the consequences.'

'What does this even have to do with anything?' Alice demanded. 'It's so unfair, having me is your excuse for everything.'

'Alice –'

'I wish you never *had* had me, you should have got rid of me while you had the chance!'

'Now you're being ridiculous.'

Alice got to her feet. 'It would be better not to have been born than to have you as a mother!' She went to stomp off, but Catherine rose from her chair and caught her by her arm, gripping it tightly.

'You ungrateful little brat,' she seethed, her face close to her daughter's. 'When I witness this kind of behaviour from you I have to wonder why I did bother keeping you. You can forget about concerts, parties or anything else for the foreseeable future.'

'You can't do that!'

'Oh yes I can,' said Catherine. 'I'm grounding you for first term at least, until I see some evidence that you have your priorities straight.'

'I hate you,' Alice hissed tearfully as she wrenched her arm out of her mother's grip and dashed for the door, running inside.

Catherine stood there, breathing hard, clenching her nails into the palms of her hands to stop them from trembling. Why did Alice push her like that? She made her so angry, made her say things she didn't mean. She picked up the glass of wine and drained what was left. But her hands were still trembling.

She turned and walked back into the house.

'Oh, dinner's almost ready,' Martin said timidly.

'I can't eat,' she said, crossing directly to the fridge.

'Come on, Catherine, you have to eat something.'

'Don't you start at me as well.' She grabbed the bottle of wine she'd opened previously and headed across the room.

'I'm going to have a bath,' she barked over her shoulder. 'And I do not want to be disturbed for anything.'

*

Saturday

'Listen, I need you to get here a little earlier, Rachel,' said Catherine down the phone line.

Something was up. Rachel could hear it in her voice. 'Oh? What for?'

'Miss Junior Drama Queen is staging the tantrum to end all tantrums, claiming that while she might have to be here tonight, I can't make her talk to anyone or be pleasant, or even polite. I think she's going to make the most of this opportunity to embarrass me.'

'What happened, Catherine?' asked Rachel, knowing there had to be something. Alice was a sweet girl at heart. She wouldn't be mean just for the sake of it.

'Oh, I wouldn't let her go to some silly concert tonight. She was offered a leftover ticket at the last minute and so I'm the worst person in the world because I expect her to fulfil a prior commitment. Aren't I a monster?' she said deadpan.

Rachel realised she was getting a very edited version, but she wasn't so sure she wanted to see the bits left on the cutting-room floor either. 'What do you expect me to do, Catherine?'

'Just talk to her. You have a lot more chance of getting through to her than I do right now.'

Why did everyone think Rachel had all the answers all of a sudden? This was becoming a disturbing pattern, and it was also a little overwhelming. She had always considered herself a good listener, but that was because listening only required just that – to listen, nod in appropriate places, make the odd encouraging comment. She felt hopelessly unqualified to actually solve other people's problems.

'What do you want me to say to her?' she asked Catherine.

'Oh, you know – "You'll be hurting Tom and the girls more than you'll hurt your mother", blah, blah, that kind of thing,' she dismissed. 'I just want you to make sure she comes down to the table, minds her manners and spends an adequate amount of time with the girls.'

'God, I dunno, Catherine, how do you expect me to do all that?'

'Look, underneath it all Alice doesn't want to upset Sophie and Hannah, but she needs a way to save face. If she thinks I had to bring in reinforcements, she'll believe she's scored some kind of victory over me. She'll have her win.'

Wow. Tonight must be important to Catherine if she was prepared to let Alice score points over her.

'Well,' said Rachel, 'Tom was going to pick me up –'

'Then give him a call and tell him I needed a hand, but don't let on about anything. I'll come and pick you up. How soon can you be ready?'

At five pm Rachel came down the stairs of her building to wait for Catherine, a full two hours before Tom would have been picking her up. It was going to be a long night. Once again she had found herself paying a little too much attention to what she was going to wear. That was also becoming a disturbing pattern, but she really wasn't in the mood for Catherine's criticism. She wanted to be comfortable, but also feel good about herself, and the top she'd bought for her internet date filled both criteria. And Catherine hadn't seen it yet. Tom had, but that didn't matter, men never remembered what women wore.

'Well, you look nice,' said Catherine when Rachel got into the car. 'Is that the top you bought for your blind date?'

'Yep,' said Rachel, clicking her seatbelt into place.

Catherine pulled out into the traffic. 'How is that all going, by the way?'

'What?'

'Rendezvous. Are you getting lots of "arrows"? Any worth pursuing?'

'Oh, I haven't had time to check lately,' Rachel dismissed. She had not, in fact, even looked at it again since the night Catherine set it up.

'Well, don't leave it too long,' said Catherine. 'Tick tock.'

'What's that?'

'Your biological clock. Though mind you, the mood I'm in, there are far worse things that could happen in your life than not having children.'

When they arrived at her house, Catherine shooed Rachel immediately upstairs to deal with the recalcitrant. Rachel knocked on her door.

'Hi Alice, it's me, Rachel.'

There was no answer, so she knocked again, and called a little louder. 'Alice!'

When there was still no answer, Rachel thought about her options. It was probably better to let herself in than go back down to Catherine, who was likely to come up and storm the Bastille, which would not get things off to a good start.

'Alice,' she said loudly, as she opened the door a little way. She stuck her head around tentatively to see Alice splayed out, tummy down, on the bed, her head cradled in the crook of one arm as she clicked away on her laptop with her free hand. An ergonomic nightmare. Rachel spotted the culprit cord trailing from her ear into the computer. No wonder she couldn't hear her knocking. She moved into Alice's peripheral vision, finally getting her attention. Alice jumped up, removing the earphones at the same time. 'Hi,' she said, a little flustered.

'Sorry, I did knock . . .'

'It's okay,' she dismissed, making a series of rapid clicks on the keyboard before closing the laptop.

'I didn't mean to disturb you.'

Alice lifted one eyebrow. 'Mum sent you up here, didn't she?'

Rachel intended to play it straight, at least as straight as possible. 'Yes, she did.'

Alice slid the laptop off her bed and onto the floor and shifted to make room for Rachel. 'You might as well sit down.'

'Thanks.' She walked over to the queen-size bed. It was what you would call a lavishly appointed room – all the furniture and woodwork had been custom made from that rare timber Catherine was so taken with. There was a long, sleek slab of the stuff running the length of one wall, supporting a desktop computer at one end and a good-sized flat-screen TV at the other. Two identical doors on the right led to an ensuite and a walk-in robe. She had everything a girl could want, but it had always reminded Rachel of a hotel room. There were some nice touches – the deep aubergine bedspread topped with a pile of gorgeous pillows, the rather funky bedside lamp and designer clock radio that looked like a piece of modern sculpture – but there was a distinct absence of girlie paraphernalia, no posters, no clutter. Catherine's orders.

Rachel sat on the bed and propped a couple of pillows behind her back. 'So, how are you?'

Alice pursed her lips. 'What did she tell you?'

'That you're upset about not being allowed to go out tonight, and that she's worried you're going to make it unpleasant for Sophie and Hannah just to get back at her.'

'Did she tell you where I wanted to go?'

'She said it was a concert.'

'Yeah, a Travesty concert, you know how much I like them. And it was a VIP ticket, Rachel, we were going backstage and everything.'

Bugger, the stakes were high. 'Your mum just felt because it was last minute –'

'I asked her on Wednesday, Rachel.'

'You did?' Bloody Catherine. Rachel had got the impression it had all come up today, that's what 'last minute' suggested to her.

Alice was watching her. 'What did she tell you?'

This was delicate. 'She didn't specify.'

Alice groaned. 'Typical. Why does she do this, Rachel? It's like she just doesn't want me to have a good time. She didn't get to have a good time when she was my age, because of me, and so now she wants me to pay for it.'

'Oh, I don't think that's it, Alice. I think it's more that she's scared the same thing will happen to you.'

'How am I going to get pregnant under parental supervision in the VIP stand at a rock concert?'

'I don't mean she's scared you'll fall pregnant. I think she's scared you'll miss out on opportunities –'

'Like going to this concert,' said Alice.

Rachel wasn't going to get anywhere making this about the fairness or otherwise of missing the concert. Especially because she happened to agree with Alice on that point. But she could not take sides. That would only make things worse.

'The thing is, chook, I understand you're upset and disappointed, but that's between you and your mum. Tonight she just wants to do something nice for Tom and the girls.'

'Crap, she just wants to suck up to Tom and flirt with him all night. She's so embarrassing.'

'She's not going to flirt with Tom,' said Rachel uncertainly.

'Come on, Rachel, you know what she's like. If there's a good-looking guy around, she has to have his attention.'

'You think Tom's good-looking?'

'Yeah,' she shrugged. 'Well, *I* don't, you know, he's way old, but yeah, he's good-looking. And he's a pretty cool guy. It sucks what happened to Annie. They were like this perfect, sitcom family. It's *so* totally unfair.'

'Hmm. That's why it's not really fair to make them uncomfortable tonight,' said Rachel. 'They've been through enough already, don't you think?'

Alice slumped back against the pillows next to her. 'I don't even know what I'm supposed to say to them.'

Rachel realised there was more to this than just missing out on a concert. 'You're not alone there, honey. No one knows what to say to them. But I'll tell you something Tom told me, just between us.'

'What?'

'He can't stand it when people treat him differently, or they're awkward around him. And he feels like he can't be himself, like he's not allowed to laugh at a joke, or have fun, or whatever, because it'll seem inappropriate. I bet it's the same for the girls.'

'Wow, I never thought of that. How much would it suck, being so self-conscious all the time?'

'That's right. Sophie and Hannah have lost their mum, they shouldn't have to lose their adolescence as well.'

'But what if they want to talk about it?' said Alice. 'I would totally not know what to say.'

Rachel thought about it. 'You know what my strategy is when I don't know what to say?'

Alice looked up at her, unblinking.

'I don't say anything, I just listen. I've realised lately it's quite a skill. In fact, I think listening might be my very mild superpower.'

Alice started to laugh. 'No way, how do you know about mild superpowers?'

She shrugged. 'It's from a song, isn't it?'

'You're funny as, Rachel.'

Rachel didn't know what she was as funny as, but she decided to take it as a compliment.

'So, how did you do in your school certificate, Sophie?' asked Catherine.

The evening was going along quite well, all things considered. Alice was behaving herself, and Tom and the girls had arrived on time, all of which had clearly put Catherine in a good mood, that and the copious glasses of wine she was downing at a record rate. She seemed nervous, almost desperate to impress. But perhaps Rachel was only thinking that because of what Alice had said.

For his part, Tom was being very attentive, the perfect gentleman in fact. Although he'd barely made eye contact with Rachel all night. Really, she was starting to wonder what she was doing here.

'She got all band sixes,' Hannah piped up proudly, but Sophie frowned at her.

'That's impressive,' Catherine remarked, 'especially considering all you've been through. Your mother would be very proud of you, Sophie.'

Sophie's cheeks flushed crimson. 'The school certificate's not that hard, Catherine.'

'Tell that to Alice. She didn't get any band sixes, did you even get any band fives?' She glanced fleetingly at her daughter before she took another slurp from her glass. 'What subjects are you taking for your HSC, Sophie?'

'Oh, um, well, English, of course. It's compulsory, but it is my favourite subject. And I'm doing the extension unit as well.'

'Is that the one where you have to do a creative piece of writing?' asked Catherine. 'You and Hannah have always been so creative.'

'In music, maybe, not so much writing. That's not the extension unit I'm doing, you can't pick that up until Year 12 anyway.'

'Are you going to take that unit, Alice?' Tom directed towards her, leaning forwards on the table.

'I'm doing the same as Soph,' she muttered.

'English Advanced?' asked Sophie.

She nodded.

'What do you think about the area of study?'

'Totally dodgy.'

'I know!' said Sophie, becoming animated. 'I've always done okay at English, but I just don't get it.'

'You just have to learn to talk the talk,' said Alice. 'It's way crap.'

'Language please, Alice,' said Catherine.

'There's this pretty cool blog,' Alice went on. 'It's run by this dude who did his HSC a couple of years ago, and it's turned into this massive forum where all these Year 12s ask questions and explain stuff and you can totally understand it. I can show you if you like.'

'That'd be awesome.'

Alice jumped to her feet, but Catherine cleared her throat.

'Excuse me, Alice, we haven't had dessert yet.'

'Oh, I'm so full, thank you, Catherine,' said Sophie. 'I don't think I could fit dessert in.'

'Well, you are a very sensible young woman, Sophie,' said Catherine. 'That's why you'll keep that lovely slender figure.'

'To be honest,' Tom chimed in, 'I'm pretty impressed that a couple of teenagers want to skip dessert to check out something related to their school work.'

'You're absolutely right, Tom,' Catherine gushed. 'Go ahead, girls.'

'Can I come too?' Hannah jumped up.

'Yeah sure,' said Alice.

Hannah came around behind her dad's chair and wrapped her arms around his neck, whispering something in his ear. He broke into a broad smile. 'Of course, honey.'

'Love you, Daddy,' she chirped, planting a kiss on his cheek before running off to join the other two.

Tom turned to watch them disappear up the stairs before looking back at Catherine and Rachel. 'Hannah told me that she was pretty sure she could still fit dessert in, and would I mind saving her some.'

Catherine staged an affected laugh. 'Oh, Tom, your girls are absolutely delightful. You're doing such a good job with them, despite what you must be going through.'

'I don't know, Catherine,' he shrugged. 'Their mother left them in pretty good shape. I just hope I don't screw it up from here on in.'

'If you want my advice,' said Catherine, clearly chomping at the bit to give it, 'you'll have to keep a close eye this next year or two, particularly on Sophie. She's a very smart, sensible girl, but there are so many temptations and distractions out there these days. And everything seems to come at once! Why is it that the same year they are sitting their HSC, they are finally allowed to drive a car and get into licensed venues? It's madness.' She knocked back the rest of her glass of wine.

Martin returned to the table; he'd been quietly going back and forth, clearing away the dishes from dinner, like some nineteenth-century manservant. But he seemed happiest keeping a low profile.

'Oh Martin, darling,' Catherine said, placing a hand on his forearm, 'I think we should serve dessert out on the terrace, it's such a beautiful evening. What does everyone think?' Her eyes swept past Rachel's to land on Tom's.

'Sounds great,' said Tom. 'Do you need a hand with anything, Martin?'

He was shaking his head, but Catherine answered for him, almost like he was a ventriloquist's dummy. She even rested her hand on his back as she spoke. 'Oh, Martin loves it, don't you, Martin? He's right in his element. He'd secretly love to run a restaurant, wouldn't you, Martin?'

She stood up, which brought Tom to his feet, and she linked her arm through his. 'Come along, Rachel,' she said over her shoulder. 'And what about an after-dinner drink, Tom? A liqueur, port, or we have a delicious cognac. It's a Hennessy Paradis, frightfully expensive, you must try it.'

'Actually, would coffee be too much trouble?' he asked as they paused at the door out to the terrace. 'I'm driving.'

'Nothing is too much trouble for you, Tom,' Catherine gushed. 'Martin, coffee for Tom, and you and I will stick with the wine, eh, Rachel?'

Bad luck if she wanted a fancy cognac. Catherine led Tom out onto the terrace and Rachel glanced at Martin. 'Are you sure I can't help?'

He shook his head emphatically. 'She'd kill me if I let you lift a finger.' Then he winked. 'But you know I enjoy it.'

'Well, I'll take the wine out at least,' said Rachel, grabbing the bottle and both their glasses.

It was never easy to get away from Catherine when she'd had a few. Hannah rejoined them after a while, searching out her dessert. Once she had finished she grew visibly more tired; she draped herself across her father's lap and started to fall asleep on his shoulder. Tom made moves to leave a number of times, but Catherine kept veering the conversation off in another direction. Eventually Sophie and Alice came downstairs, and when Sophie finally pulled up a chair behind Tom and leaned her head sleepily on his free shoulder, he had to be firm.

'Thanks so much for tonight, Catherine, it's been lovely, but I really need to get these girls home to bed before I have to carry them to the car, and they're way too big for that now.'

They seemed to get a second wind on the drive home, however.

'Omigod!' Sophie exclaimed once they had pulled off up the street. 'How drunk was Catherine at the end? She could barely stand up.'

'Or talk straight,' added Hannah.

'She still managed to slobber all over you, Dad.'

'Eew,' cried Hannah. 'That's gross.'

Tom glanced across at Rachel. 'That's enough, girls, a little respect,' he said. 'We've just been guests in Catherine's home, sat at her table, eaten her food.'

'That Martin cooked. What did her last slave die of?'

'Sophie, what are you saying, that it's okay for the woman to do all the cooking but not the man?'

'Okay, okay,' said Sophie. 'But why is she so mean to Alice? It's like she can't stand her own daughter.'

'No, that's not it,' said Rachel. 'Catherine is just so driven and ambitious, she gets frustrated when people aren't like her.'

'Who'd want to be like her?' said Sophie.

'Soph,' Tom warned.

'Dad, give me a break. Are we supposed to pretend she's a great role model or something?'

'No, but she is an old friend of Rachel's, and mine, and your mother's. And she was nice enough to invite us over and you don't return the favour by gossiping about her the whole way home.'

'We're not all the way home yet,' said Hannah.

'Very funny, Han.'

'I can't help myself, I'm a very funny girl,' she said airily.

'Funny-looking, more like,' said Sophie.

'I'll give you both funny in a minute,' said Tom.

The girls burst into shrieks of laughter.

'That is such a Dad thing to say,' said Sophie.

'That's nothing,' said Tom. 'Keep it up and you'll both be laughing out of the other side of your faces.'

That set them off again.

'What does that even mean?' Hannah cried.

'We'll be laughing out of our ears!' exclaimed Sophie.

And on they went, suggesting all the body parts out of which one could possibly laugh, punctuated with increasingly hysterical bouts of laughter. It was infectious, of course, and before long Rachel was laughing so hard she could barely breathe, and Tom was wiping tears away with the back of his hand while trying to keep his focus on the road.

They'd finally calmed down by the time he pulled up in front of Rachel's block. He turned off the engine and undid his seatbelt. 'I'll walk you in.'

She snorted. 'Don't be daft.'

The girls giggled in the back seat.

'Sorry,' she said. 'That's very chivalrous of you, Tom, but I assure you I can find the door myself.'

'All right, if you say so.'

Rachel turned around in her seat. 'Bye girls, it was really great seeing you.'

To her surprise they both lurched forwards and kissed her on the cheek, Hannah hooking one arm around her neck as she did so.

Then, as Rachel turned back, Tom leaned across and gave her a peck on the cheek as well. 'Night Rach,' he said. 'See you soon, I hope.'

She got out of the car and closed the door, stepping backwards and waving. They all waved back, but Tom didn't start up the engine. He was obviously going to wait for her to go inside. She turned and walked quickly up the driveway and out of sight. She was digging around for her keys in her bag under the light at the entrance when she heard footsteps approaching up the drive. She looked around to see Tom coming towards her. It gave her a fright.

'What's the matter? Is something wrong? Did you leave the girls in the car?'

'They're okay,' he said, stopping in front of her. 'I told them I'd just be a minute, that I'd forgotten to tell you something.'

'What is it?'

He took a deep breath. He seemed a little nervous. 'The thing is, Rach,' he lowered his voice, 'I haven't been able to stop thinking about you, about the other night.'

Her heart missed a beat. 'Tom –'

'No, listen to me. You said that if we can act like nothing's happened, that's for the best, and we didn't need to talk about it. Well, seeing you tonight, wearing that top again . . .' He paused. 'I couldn't even look at you, Rach. Obviously I can't act like nothing's happened, so we're going to have to talk about it. That was the deal.'

Rachel's throat had gone dry. Damn that she'd put it like that, and that he remembered it word for word, and that he was a lawyer, and that he could mount a case for the defence.

'I don't know, Tom,' she shrugged. 'What's the point?'

He dropped his head with a sigh, looking down at the ground for a minute, before raising his eyes to meet hers again. 'I'll come round tomorrow afternoon, we'll discuss it then. You owe me that much.'

'What about the girls?' she said, clutching at the only straws left to her.

'They'll be off with their friends or whatever, they'll be fine for an hour or two.'

Rachel thought about it. Two hours alone in her flat with Tom. No way. But clearly he wasn't going to let her renege.

'Okay,' she said, 'but not here, I'll meet you down at the park, at Bronte.'

He pulled a face. 'Rach, it's crowded there on a Sunday. How are we supposed to talk?'

'That's my best offer, Tom. Take it or leave it.'

Sunday

Rachel walked down the hill towards Bronte Park. It was a bright, sunny January day, there were people everywhere. Good, that part had gone to plan. And she was prepared. She had thought it all through; in fact, she'd thought of little else since Tom left last night. She knew what to say to put him straight, she'd gone over and over it, even rehearsed it out loud in the shower this morning. He would see the sense of her argument, and she would be so firm, so confident, that he would have nowhere to go.

She crossed the road into the park and walked down the path towards the beach, surveying the general area. It really was packed; all the picnic shelters were occupied, and there were groups of picnickers scattered all across the grass. She heard a whistle and looked around. Tom was leaning against the railing of the promenade edging the beach, dark glasses shielding his eyes, his hand lifted in a wave. She walked over towards him.

'Great spot for a quiet chat, Rach,' he remarked wryly as she approached.

'Let's walk for a while then,' she suggested.

He shoved his hands in his pockets. 'Okay.'

They strolled along for a minute or two while a noisy throng of teenagers approached and passed them.

'So,' Rachel spoke first. No use delaying the inevitable. 'You called this meeting.'

He hesitated. 'Can't we go somewhere?'

'We are somewhere,' Rachel said flatly. 'Just get on with it, would you, Tom?'

'Okay.' He took a deep breath. 'Like I said, I haven't been able to stop thinking about that night.'

Rachel didn't respond, she'd let him do the talking for now, get it off his chest. See where he was coming from.

'And I'm not just talking about where we ended up. I said some things . . .'

Where was this headed?

'. . . you know, earlier, before we . . .'

'Don't worry,' she stopped him. She didn't want to recount the events in detail. 'I don't remember much.'

He took her arm then and turned to face her, propping his sunglasses back on his head. 'What do you mean, you don't remember much?'

'Just that. We were pretty drunk, Tom.'

He frowned. 'I remember everything, I wasn't that drunk.' He looked put out. 'I remember what I said, and I knew what I was saying. I'll repeat it all if you like.'

She shook her head. 'Come on, Tom, you know we can't . . . this is not . . .' God, she didn't want to put it into words what this wasn't and what they couldn't do.

'Rachel, I think if you were honest you'd admit there's something between us —'

'No, no, no,' she insisted. 'You can't go there.'

'Why not?'

He was looking earnestly down at her, still holding her arm. She had to stay focused. It was time for her speech. Suddenly a cyclist whooshed past, barely missing them. They needed to get out of the way. Rachel glanced around.

'Let's sit over there,' she said, slipping her arm out of his hold and walking off the path and onto the grass. Tom followed, dropping down onto the ground and reclining back to rest on his elbows. Rachel sat bolt upright, her legs tucked underneath her, facing him.

'Okay, I've thought this through very carefully, Tom,' she began, 'and I believe there are a couple of things going on here. I think a lot of it has to do with you wanting to go back to a time before

Annie, a time that probably feels safe, and where, in a sense, metaphorically I suppose, you're not going to bump into her, if you get what I'm saying. That has to be less painful.'

Rachel couldn't tell what he was thinking, his eyes were hidden behind the sunglasses again, but the set of his jaw seemed a little grim. She cleared her throat, continuing. 'And then when, you know, when you came with me to the clinic, well, that obviously triggered some very difficult memories, but at the same time it must have seemed to you that you were getting the chance to put something right, to make up, in some small way, for what happened to Annie, where you were helpless to do anything. So now you feel responsible, or bonded, the way people feel when they save someone's life. Not that you saved my life, it wasn't that serious, of course.' She was beginning to blather. She needed to get back on track. 'I guess what I'm trying to say is, there are a lot of complex feelings all tied up in this, clouding the issue, making you think you feel things that you really don't.'

He sat up then, leaning closer to her. 'What the fuck are you talking about, Rachel?'

She blinked. 'What?'

'Don't patronise me, I'm not an idiot. You bloody women think you have the monopoly on emotional insight, that men are all adolescents.' He shook his head. 'Tying all this into my feelings for Annie, and what happened to her, you're doing what everyone else wants to do – pigeonholing me as the grieving widower, deciding what I should feel and when. I didn't think I'd get that from you, Rachel. And I certainly don't need it from you.' He got to his feet abruptly, but he wasn't finished. He lifted his glasses and glared down at her. 'You know what?'

She squinted up at him, shielding her eyes from the sun with her hand. She was always forgetting her frigging glasses.

'Even if there's an element of truth in what you're saying, so what? You're right, feelings are complicated, we don't always know where they come from or why. But I know what I feel,' he said, his voice becoming hoarse, 'and you don't have the right to analyse the crap out of it and make it something less than it is.'

He turned and took a few steps, before he stopped to look back at her. 'You want to analyse something, then take a good, hard look at yourself, Rachel. Why are you doing this? Is it because you can't get on a plane and run away this time?'

Then he turned again and strode away up the grassy slope. Rachel sat where she was, her heart racing, her head spinning, her eyes fixed on him until he walked out onto the street and she lost sight of him.

It wasn't relevant, what he was referring to. It had happened so long ago, and it didn't mean anything, they had both been so drunk. Why was he bringing it up now? It was the night before she left, they had a farewell party at Rainbow Street. Everyone they knew came, and others they didn't, not because Rachel was leaving, but because there was a party. That's how it worked back then. All the student share houses were party houses, there was always something on every weekend, and that weekend the excuse was that Rachel was flying out the next day to London, via Bangkok. She didn't want a big thing at the airport; her flight was too early anyway. She had planned to go alone, by taxi, but Tom wouldn't hear of it. He was coming to see her off, but only him, she had even managed to fob off Catherine. As the party wore on through the night, and people started dropping like flies all over the house, Rachel was still wide awake and wired. She told Tom she wanted to stay up all night, she could sleep on the plane tomorrow. So they sat outside in the backyard, just the two of them, drinking White Russians and talking and laughing about God knows what. Silly stuff. And of course, inevitably, she started to cry. And Tom held her, and comforted her, and told her how much he was going to miss her, and that she was his best friend. And then they were making out on the damp, hard ground. It must have been three or four in the morning. After a while Tom pulled her to her feet and led her inside, without a word. They went to his bedroom first, at the back of the house, but it was taken, so they walked up the hall to hers.

Rachel's mouth was dry. The sun was hot, and her legs, still tucked underneath her, were starting to go numb. She stretched them out, rubbing her calves, wiggling her toes. The memory that she'd spent years suppressing was coming back with a vengeance, so vivid she could almost feel his skin against hers, his mouth. She remembered indulging in the moment, allowing herself to feel what it would be like to be loved by Tom. And she remembered holding him close afterwards as they drifted off to sleep, spent, his head nestled in the crook of her neck, and that he'd said, 'I don't want you to go.'

She'd woken with a start after an hour, maybe two, she didn't know exactly, but dawn was breaking. She eased herself out of his arms and slipped off the bed. Fortunately Tom slept like a log; Rachel was forever having to wake him up in the mornings when he slept through his alarm. She was all packed; too bad if she'd forgotten anything, she wasn't going to double-check now. As long as she had her passport and her wallet, that was all that really mattered. She crept out of the room and up the hall, quietly letting herself out of the house. She slung her backpack over her shoulders and walked through the hazy dawn, all the way down to Anzac Parade, where she had more chance of hailing a passing taxi. When she arrived at the airport it was still too early to check in, so she found one of the bathrooms where she could take a shower and change her clothes. She was first in line at the check-in counter when her flight opened, and she didn't wait for it to be called at the gate, she went straight through Immigration and waited on the other side where only passengers were allowed.

Not that Rachel actually expected Tom to follow her. That was the whole reason she left like that, so they didn't have to face each other, feel awkward, feign excuses, fumble for the right words that would let him off the hook. Because although Tom clearly had some affection for her, and she didn't doubt he would miss their friendship, he would never seriously consider someone like Rachel. He had girls lining up around the block, beautiful girls she could never compete with. Besides, she and Tom had something else, something better. Up to that point they'd shared an intimacy all the sharper because it had never been consummated; he couldn't hurt her, let her down. Abandon her. And that meant more to her than anything.

So in the days before email and other forms of instant communication, Rachel was able to keep her distance, writing him a jolly postcard after a couple of weeks, with a few words to let him know she was safe and well, but with no return address. She finally included that after three more such postcards, and when

Tom wrote back to her he made no mention of their last night together. It was in the past, forgotten, almost like it had never happened.

Until the poison pen letter had arrived from Catherine with the news of Annie. Rachel had never told another living soul that she had cried herself to sleep that night, scrunching the letter up to her wet face, till it disintegrated, leaving odd little ink marks on her cheeks.

She put it down to homesickness at the time, that she was missing out on all her friends' milestones, but it was entirely her own choice. She could have come home for the wedding – she had money, and she was only working casually in a bar. She could have come home any time she wanted, but she didn't. She stayed away till Tom was well and truly married, with a couple of kids. When she finally did return, she quickly hooked up with Sean and became one of the girls. And Tom was just someone else's husband, and that worked for her.

Rachel hoisted herself up off the grass, stiff and weary, and wandered back down to join the promenade. She didn't want to go home, she didn't know what she wanted to do. She'd follow the coastal walk for a while, clear her head. She'd never seen Tom so angry. He said he felt patronised, and maybe that was fair enough, though it certainly hadn't been her intention. She had to find a way – without upsetting him again – to get him to see the truth in what she was saying. His memory had tricked him into actually believing he'd once had a crush on her and, even more absurd, that she'd broken his heart. Oh, she remembered he'd said that the other night, but she took it for what it was. Extreme nostalgia brought on by drinking White Russians and listening to old Queen songs. Rachel had been wrong to indulge him; she'd virtually handed him a pair of rose-coloured glasses to glorify the past and diminish the real, true, once-in-a-lifetime love he had found with Annie, which he was clearly now terrified of living without.

She couldn't get out of her head what Catherine had said the night they'd gone out to dinner for Annie's birthday: that the more bereft Tom felt, the more likely he would be to rush in to try to fill the void. Well, Rachel couldn't be that person for him. She wasn't that strong.

She looked around, taking in her surroundings. She was probably no more than a block away from Tom's street. She couldn't avoid this, there was no plane to catch to far-off places, much as she might wish there were. She wasn't good at confrontation, Tom had said it himself. But this was not going away by itself; it would remain percolating under the surface, infecting their friendship and, worse, stifling his grief. The deal was over, she wasn't going to let him be 'inappropriate' any more. A good friend, a true friend, would help him deal with his grief, and make it safe for him to do just that.

Her resolve renewed, Rachel headed for Tom's place. She didn't even know for sure that he had gone home, but she had to try; she didn't want to put it off or she might lose her nerve.

She walked briskly up the street, praying that Lexie would not suddenly appear out front of her house and think Rachel was coming to visit her, a perfectly reasonable assumption to make. But she made it to Tom's front door undetected and gave it a firm couple of knocks, despite a slight tremble in her hand. She couldn't hear any movement inside. Damn, what if he hadn't come home? She knocked again, loudly, insistently, and then she heard footsteps, and a muffled, 'Coming.' Her heart was in her mouth as she made out his silhouette approaching through the frosted glass. Then the door opened. His face registered surprise, but it was quickly tempered by the anger still festering in his eyes.

Rachel's chest was heaving. So much for resolve, she could feel tears rising in her throat, and she realised she was going to choke up if she tried to speak. Tom still hadn't said anything, he was just staring at her.

She swallowed hard. 'I didn't want to leave things like that,' she rasped, cupping her hand to her mouth to clear her throat. Tears were stinging her eyes. Pull yourself together. She looked up at him. 'I didn't want you to be angry with me,' she said, but her voice broke up.

He drew her inside and closed the door as he folded his arms around her. 'I couldn't stay angry with you, Rach,' he murmured, holding her tight as she dissolved into sobs.

This was not the way it was supposed to go. But maybe it was okay, just for a minute, while she got herself together. He held her close and stroked her hair, softly kissing the side of her head as he shushed her, swaying her gently in his arms. Rachel felt his cheek against hers, his lips close to her ear, his breath on the skin of her neck. It was giving her goose bumps. Okay, enough. 'Tom . . .'

He lifted his head to look at her, cupping her face in his hands, his eyes gazing steadily into hers.

'Rachel,' he breathed as his mouth sank onto hers. She gasped. This wasn't a dream, they were really kissing. Her heart was pounding as he pressed her up against the wall, his body so close she felt melded to him. This was not supposed to happen, but the sensations were overpowering, his mouth, his tongue, his lips, leaving hers now as they trailed down her neck. Rachel arched her head back, opening her eyes . . .

'No!' She pushed against his chest. 'Tom, we can't –'

'It's all right,' he whispered, 'the girls aren't here.'

'But Annie is.'

He blinked. 'Well, we won't go into the bedroom.'

'Tom, she's everywhere!'

He sighed, leaning his forehead against hers, catching his breath. 'Okay, wait here,' he said, breaking away from her and rushing down the hall.

Rachel stood there, breathing hard. This was getting out of hand, she had to put a stop to it. He reappeared, rattling his car keys.

'Tom, this is not why I came here,' said Rachel. 'We have to talk.'

'All right,' he said, grabbing her hand as he opened the door. 'We'll talk back at your place.'

'Tom,' she stood her ground. 'I mean it.'

He looked at her squarely. 'You want to talk here? With Annie all around?'

She hesitated. 'You promise we're going to talk?'

'Cross my heart,' he said, leading her through the door.

'No, wait,' she said, pulling her hand out of his. 'I don't want to get into the car with you, what if Lexie sees us?'

He sighed. 'Fine.' He thought about it. 'You walk down the street, I'll pick you up at the corner.'

She frowned, biting her lip. It was all so . . . clandestine.

'Go on, scoot,' he said, giving her a gentle push out the door. 'I'll give you a head start.'

He was right, they couldn't stay here. Rachel scuppered quickly out through the front gate and down the street, not looking back towards Lexie's house. As she hurried to the corner, she began to have second thoughts. How had she let that happen? She could still feel his lips on her face, her neck, it sent a shiver through her body just thinking about it. And now they were going to her place? Oh, this was bad. She was really going to have to be firm with him. They had to *talk*.

'Rachel!'

She looked up. Lexie was pushing the pram across the road towards her, holding Riley by the hand. Oh shit.

She had reached the kerb, and was negotiating the pram up onto the footpath. How was Rachel going to play this? She took a deep breath, walking sedately to meet her.

'Hi! What are you doing here?' Lexie beamed at her.

'Well, I was . . . in the neighbourhood,' she began, 'and, actually, I just called by your place, but you weren't there, obviously,' she added with a nervous laugh.

'No, I just took the kids for a paddle, but we're heading home now, so come on back.'

'Oh, I better not,' said Rachel, consulting her watch and shaking her head regretfully. 'See, now I'm out of time.'

Lexie frowned. 'But haven't you just come from my place?'

'Um, yeah . . .' *Think!*

'Mu-um,' said Riley, yanking on his mother's arm.

'Excuse me, Riley, Mummy and Rachel are talking.'

'He's fine, go ahead, Riley,' Rachel said. Interrupt away, kid.

'I have to do a wee, Mum,' he winced, clutching at his crotch.

'Best not hold you up then,' said Rachel, relieved, unlike poor Riley.

'But you'll come with us?' Lexie persisted.

'You know, the thing is, when I got to your place, Tom was out the front, he was getting into his car, and well, we got talking, and you know, it must have been twenty minutes, half an hour, and now, well, I really am out of time. I was only dropping in to say hi.'

A car pulled up behind her, and Lexie looked past Rachel. 'Oh, here's Tom now.'

Rachel turned around. She hoped he had the sense to follow her lead.

The passenger window slid open and he leaned into view. 'Hi ladies, what's happening?'

Rachel came closer, ducking down to look at him. 'I was just telling Lexie how I called by to see her, and she wasn't there but you were out the front, getting into your car, and we were talking for ages, and well, now I'm out of time.'

'Oh, you should have said. Can I give you a lift somewhere?'

Good save.

She looked at her watch again. 'You know, that'd be great actually, thanks, Tom.' She turned back to Lexie. 'I'll call you soon about lunch, okay?'

Lexie looked a little bemused, but she raised her hand in a wave. 'Okay, bye guys.'

Rachel jumped into the car and Tom took off from the kerb with a toot of the horn. He turned out of the street before reaching over to plant his hand on her knee. 'Are you all right?'

'Tom,' she sighed, removing his hand. 'I don't think this is a good idea.'

'You don't think what's a good idea? Going to your place to talk?'

'Yeah, well, that's what I'm worried about, I don't know how much talking is going to happen.'

'See, you can't pretend there's not something going on between us.' He slowed the car to a stop as traffic bottlenecked ahead.

'That doesn't make it right.'

He turned abruptly to look at her. 'You think it's wrong?'

Of course she thought it was wrong. How could she not? Kissing and cavorting in his dead wife's house, what could be right about that? Annie was supposed to have been her friend.

'I think a lot of things,' said Rachel. 'What happened back there, with Lexie, for example.'

'What's the problem? We covered it.'

'Exactly, and we had to lie to a friend to do it.'

'Well, technically, you did the lying,' he said, a twinkle in his eye.

'Tom,' she chided, 'don't try and make light of this.'

He faced to the front as the traffic started to move again. 'I'm not making light, Rach, I just don't think we did anything wrong. Or that we're doing anything wrong.'

'I'm not so sure about that,' she said quietly.

'Come on, we're consenting adults. Why does this have to be so hard?'

She looked at him, amazed. 'I can't believe you're saying that. If you don't understand the enormous issues involved, then we really do have a problem.'

He straightened his arms out, clenching the steering wheel. 'So I suppose now we're going to talk about what's appropriate or not again? I thought I didn't have to do that with you.'

'It's not that simple, Tom. Other people are involved.'

She didn't want to even think about the way Catherine would react, but hitting roofs would surely be involved. And poor Lexie would just be confused; she had such unwavering loyalty to Annie, it would seem like a betrayal to her. And wasn't it? Surely there was some kind of statute of limitations on something like this? And Rachel bet it had to be longer than a few measly months. Annie deserved better. The knot of guilt in Rachel's stomach tightened another notch.

'Nobody's going to be able to handle this,' she muttered, least of all herself.

'It's nobody else's business,' Tom said bluntly.

'What about your daughters?'

She saw the first hint of understanding flicker across his eyes.

'It's too soon, Tom. And it'll be weird for them.'

'Okay, I agree,' he relented. 'It is a little too soon for the girls to process. So we just have to wait a while, keep it to ourselves, and then introduce the idea to them, slowly, and sensitively. That's possible, isn't it?'

'I guess,' she faltered. Again, this was heading in a direction she hadn't planned at all. They weren't supposed to be talking about how they were going to be together; they were barrelling along entirely the wrong track.

He was watching her. 'What is it, Rach?'

'There's just a lot more to it.'

'All right, what else?' he said in a businesslike way, as though they were running through items on an agenda.

Rachel sighed. They had to talk about Annie. She had to get Tom to talk about Annie. They couldn't just go on as though she never existed. It wasn't right. But not here in the car, it didn't seem . . . respectful somehow.

'We're nearly there, let's talk about it when we get inside.'

Ten minutes later, Tom was perched on the edge of her couch, a glass of water at hand, watching her expectantly. Rachel had pulled an armchair over to face him, with the coffee table between them — she needed to keep a little distance.

'So,' she began, 'all we've really talked about are the logistical problems involved in you and I –' Rachel couldn't believe she was about to say this '– being together, but I think that's the least of our problems.'

He was listening intently, waiting for her to go on.

'I'm a little nervous about bringing this up again because of the way you reacted earlier, back at the park.'

He sighed, sitting back and dragging a hand through his hair.

'See, you're annoyed already and I haven't even said anything.'

'I'm not annoyed,' he denied. 'Or maybe I am. I don't know. But I'll hear you out.'

'Okay,' she said. 'I'm sorry if it seemed like I was patronising you, or analysing your feelings, so I'll try not to do that.' Rachel looked straight at him. 'Which means you have to tell me what's going on with you.'

He frowned. 'What do you mean?'

She took a breath. 'You don't talk about Annie, you barely even mention her.'

He sighed loudly.

'Catherine said –'

'Fucking Catherine. This'll be good.'

'Just listen to me,' Rachel said firmly. 'Catherine said, and I have heard it elsewhere, that the more pain someone is in after a loss – that's any kind of loss, separation, whatever – the quicker they'll want to fill the gap with someone else.' She stared down at a stain on the carpet, she couldn't look at him. 'And I don't know if I can be that person, Tom,' she added quietly.

'You think that's all you are to me?' he said.

She shrugged, still not looking at him.

He sat forwards, leaning his elbows on his knees. 'Okay, well I think it's time we talked about us, before Annie.'

Her eyes flew up then. 'Tom, we were kids.'

'We weren't kids. Maybe we were young, but what I felt for you was real.' He paused. 'And you treated me like I was your brother.'

'That's not how I thought of you.'

'Yeah, well, not the night before you left.'

Rachel clenched her hands together. 'We were drunk, Tom.'

'Why do you always say that?'

'Because it's always true,' she said, looking up at him again. 'Both times we ... we were heavily under the influence.'

'Yeah, well, I could argue that it just helped us lose our inhibitions, express the way we really felt.'

She didn't answer that.

'I was in a pretty bad way after you left, you know, Rach,' he went on. 'I remember I woke up, it was nearly eleven and you weren't there, and I knew your plane was already gone. I rang the airport anyway, just to check.'

She looked at him. 'Did you think I wasn't going to get on that plane, Tom?'

'No, I knew you had to go,' he shrugged. 'I just hoped you also knew you had something to come home to. Someone.'

Rachel blinked back tears that were creeping into her eyes again. Why did he have to go and say that?

Tom sat back with a heavy sigh, folding his arms across his chest. 'And then I got nothing, for how many weeks? Not a word, till that crappy postcard arrived.' He shook his head. 'I told you, you broke my heart, Rach.'

'Tom ... I had no idea,' she said. 'I never suspected you were attracted to me.'

'So the making love part didn't give you a hint?'

Her cheeks went hot pink. 'It was the night before I left,' she said in a small voice.

'I know, it wasn't your fault. I should have done something a lot sooner. That you can blame on youth and inexperience.'

Rachel sat forwards. 'It was a long time ago, Tom, and we would never have worked out anyway.'

He frowned, considering her. 'Why do you say that?'

She hesitated. 'Well, because you were obviously meant to be with Annie, or else Hannah wouldn't be here, and Sophie wouldn't have you as her dad.'

He nodded faintly. 'Annie knew all about you, you know.'

Rachel's eyes widened. 'What?'

'She knew everything,' he said. 'She was cool about it; it was before we met, after all. And you behaved impeccably when you came back home, so she didn't have any reason to be jealous.'

Rachel's heart was pounding. It seemed so strange that someone else knew about something she'd barely admitted to herself. She wondered what Annie had really thought, if she had been a little jealous, if she hadn't completely trusted her, if she'd ever watched her closely around Tom.

Well, she wouldn't have seen anything. Rachel had kept Tom at a distance over the years; he was someone else's husband, they couldn't have the same friendship as before.

'I've never told a soul what happened,' she said.

'Not even Catherine?'

'Catherine'd be the last person I'd tell. You know she was a bit obsessed with you back then. I don't think it was that serious, it's more of a conquest thing with Catherine. But she was very jealous of poor Annie, in the beginning at least.'

Tom seemed uncomfortable at that, and a silence descended on the both of them. It occurred to Rachel that he'd diverted the conversation away from Annie to talk about them instead.

She looked at him, staring across the room out the window, apparently deep in thought.

'What are you thinking about?' she asked.

He roused, meeting her gaze. 'Nothing.'

She took a breath. 'Why don't you talk about Annie, Tom?'

'Because I don't have anything to say,' he said squarely.

Rachel frowned. 'What do you mean?'

'I mean there is nothing to say, nothing new to add,' he explained. 'I miss her, every day. But I can't dwell on that, Rachel. Talking about her, about what happened . . . it's just painful, that's all. The grief is always with me, I don't have to dredge it up all the time. It's not going to bring her back, it's not going to change anything. So what's the point?' He took a breath. 'I told you before, Rach, I can't let the rest of my life be defined by something so tragic, so fucking incomprehensible. I feel like it could swallow me up. I want to move on. I have to.'

'I just think that's harder to do if you don't deal with –'

'For Chrissakes!' he exclaimed, getting up and striding across the room impatiently. He turned around to look at her. 'I don't know if it's a gender thing, but Christ, it seems that all you women want to do is talk and talk and pick over the carcass and suck everything dry. It's okay to leave well enough alone sometimes.'

Rachel was too stunned to speak.

'What do you want from me, Rachel?' He held his arms out wide. 'Will you only be happy once I'm a broken, blubbering mess, curled up on the floor in the foetal position? Will that prove to you that I've grieved enough?'

'You don't have to prove anything to me,' she said, her voice faltering.

'Then what is it?' he went on, still angry. 'You want me to feel guilty because I have feelings for you? Well I can't. I can't help what I feel, so I refuse to feel guilty about it.'

'No, no, I'm sorry,' Rachel cried, getting to her feet. 'This is about me, I'm the one who feels guilty. I couldn't cry for Annie, Tom, I told you that. I couldn't cry, and when I did cry, that night after the funeral, it was for you. I never felt as close to Annie, all these years, she was so kind to me, but I know I was holding myself back, because you were with her, and you couldn't be my best friend any more.'

'Rachel . . .'

'I promise, I didn't let myself think of you like that, I didn't even realise I still did till the other night, and so yes, now I feel guilty.' She covered her face with her hands as the sobs rose up in her chest.

Then she felt Tom's arms close around her, holding her tight. 'It's okay.' He lifted her chin after a while so she had to look at him. 'You have nothing to feel guilty about, Rachel.'

'I can't help it, it just feels wrong.'

'Listen to me,' he said. 'Annie's gone. I loved her very much, but she's gone. And I just don't accept that what we had will be undermined or diminished somehow if you and I are together now.'

'But people will think –'

'Yeah, people will think they can dictate what's appropriate behaviour when they have no idea what they would do in the same situation,' Tom insisted. 'I don't see why I should put my life on hold to make other people comfortable.'

'What about the girls?' she sniffed.

'Of course, I realise they need some time. But I don't. I don't want to waste any more time, Rachel.'

She gazed up at him as he held her face, wiping her tears away with his thumbs.

'If this has taught me anything,' Tom went on, 'if it's left me with anything positive at all, it's that life really is short. I want to grab hold of happiness wherever I can find it. And it's here, right now, right in front of me.'

His eyes were glassy, staring into hers, and Rachel felt a rush of tenderness towards him.

'Don't we deserve to be happy, Rachel?'

She made a little noise in her throat as he brought his lips down onto hers. And as they kissed, Rachel let all her doubts, all her misgivings, rise up and float out across the rooftops to the ocean, because she did want to be happy, and finally, just maybe, she felt like she had a chance.

After a long while, Tom drew back to look at her. 'Okay, hold on,' he said. 'We're going to do this right.'

'What do you mean?'

He took both her hands in his. 'I would like to establish for the record that neither party is currently under the influence of alcohol, or drugs, or any other mind-altering substances,' he said, 'so any DUI charges are not going to stick, are we agreed?'

She smiled. 'We're agreed.'

He started to walk backwards across the room, drawing her with him. 'And I further wish to confirm that the party of the first part is not currently in possession of a plane ticket out of the country for tomorrow?'

She shook her head, still smiling, as they stepped into the hall.
'Passage on a boat to Tasmania?'

'Nope,' she said, changing direction so that now she was backing him into her bedroom.

'A train pass to the Central Coast?'

'Not even,' she said, bringing her hands up to circle his neck and kissing him soundly. 'There is one problem though.'

'What's that?'

She sighed. 'I'm still not on the pill.'

'Aha, reach into my pocket, my love.'

She raised an eyebrow. 'Which one?'

'Well, you can try them all if you like, for fun.'

She gave him a playful tap on the backside as he leaned in to kiss her again. 'Front, left,' he murmured, against her lips.

'Your left or my left?'

'Mine.'

Rachel slipped her hand into the pocket of his jeans and drew out a strip of condoms, leaning back from him to hold them up. 'Well you were very sure of yourself, mister.'

He gathered her close again. 'I'd prefer to call it "cautiously optimistic". I also wish to state for the record that my intentions were honourable. I didn't want a repeat of the previous unpleasant episode. I had no idea you were about to shatter my hopes and call into question my very motives, and that it was going to take me the best part of a day to convince −'

Rachel brought his face close to hers. 'You're going to have to stop talking so much.'

His lips sank into hers, and this time she was right there for every second, every sensation. She didn't resist as he removed her clothes, piece by piece, ever so slowly. And she didn't feel embarrassed as he gazed the length of her naked body, or awkward as he held her gaze, gradually lowering her onto the bed and nestling his hips between her thighs, before gently, almost reverently, drawing himself up inside her, pausing long enough to lean down and brush his lips and tongue against hers. Then, as their bodies surged and subsided against each other, Rachel arched back as wave after exquisite wave washed over her, until she felt him shudder and groan then collapse into her. She cradled him with her arms and legs, and they lay there, wrapped around each other, entirely spent, drifting slowly, sweetly, out of consciousness.

A muffled tune, Rachel knew it but couldn't name it, was creeping into her head. What was that? She wanted to block it, she didn't want to think, to come out of this.

'*Fuck!*' Tom almost leaped off her. 'That's my phone.'

Rachel blinked, squinting. He was already perched on the edge of the bed, slowly coming into focus. The tune stopped playing.

'What time is it?' he said urgently.

Rachel lifted her head but it felt cloudy. 'Um . . .'

He was digging in the pocket of his jeans. Rachel let her head drop back onto the pillow again as she fumbled for the sheet, covering herself. He'd found his phone and flipped it open.

'Shit, that was Hannah,' he said, pressing to call back and holding the phone to his ear as he reached around, gathering his things off the floor. 'Hello Han? Sweetheart, I'm so sorry, are you okay? You won't believe it, I fell asleep.' He was hastily and rather clumsily pulling on his clothes with one hand. 'No, no, tell Mrs Fleming she doesn't have to do that, I'll be right there, I'm leaving now, okay? No, I'm sure. Tell her I'm very sorry. I'll see you soon, bye darling.'

He flipped the phone shut and stood, pulling his jeans up.

'Is everything okay?' Rachel asked.

'Yeah,' he said, yanking his shirt over his head. 'I completely lost track of the time, I wasn't even thinking . . . so stupid,' he muttered, looking around the floor. 'My shoes must be out there,' he said on his way out the door. He reappeared a moment later, fishing his keys from his pocket. 'Okay, I better run. I'll see you later.'

Then he was gone. Rachel lay there, not moving, a dull ache rising up in her chest. She heard the front door open, and close again, but then footsteps came back down the hall. He appeared in the doorway, his expression contrite. 'I'm sorry, Rach,' he said, coming over to the side of the bed and leaning over her.

'It's okay, I understand, you have to hurry.'

'Are you sure?'

'Of course, go.'

'Okay.' He bent to kiss her quickly on the mouth. 'I'll call you later.'

She nodded. 'Drive safe.'

'I will,' he said as he headed out of the room. 'Bye.'

She heard his footsteps in the hall again, and then the door closed with a bang. She breathed out, but the dull ache was still there. She brought her forearm up to rest across her eyes. Don't cry, you silly baby. He had to go and pick up his daughter, he didn't have a choice. But she felt sordid, or cheap, or something. Empty probably. She was just being ridiculous. What was he supposed to do?

Her phone rang loudly into the silence. She reached over and grabbed it from the bedside table. 'Hello,' she croaked.

'Hi, it's me.'

'Oh, hi Catherine.'

'Don't sound so excited,' she retorted.

'Sorry, I'm a little foggy. I just woke up.'

'My god, what time did you get to bed last night?'

'No, I was having a nanna nap.'

'What's worn you out?'

'Sorry?'

'Sleeping such a beautiful day away. Honestly Rachel, you should be out getting some fresh air, and a bit of exercise wouldn't hurt.'

Oh, she'd burned plenty of calories this afternoon. 'I went for a long walk earlier.'

'Well, what do you know,' Catherine said. 'So how do you think it went last night?'

'Um . . .' She shuffled up to sit with her back against the bedhead. Last night? Was it only last night they were at Catherine's house? It seemed like several lifetimes ago. 'It was great, Catherine, it was a lovely night. Thanks.'

'What did Tom have to say?'

'What do you mean?'

'Well, I haven't heard from him. I thought he might have called to say thank you at least.'

Rachel sighed. 'He's a guy, Catherine. And he doesn't have Annie to do that for him any more. Give him a break.'

'Fair enough,' she relented. 'Well what did he say to you?'

'Why do you think I've spoken to him?'

'He drove you home,' Catherine reminded her.

'Oh, yeah.'

'So did he say anything?'

'Um, he said it was . . . great. They had a really nice time.'

'That's pretty generic. I went to a lot of trouble, you know.'

Rachel sighed inwardly. 'I'm sure he appreciated that.'

'Well, did he say anything about me? That it was good to talk to someone who knew what he was going through?'

For crying out loud. 'You don't know what he's going through, Catherine, none of us do.'

'I meant as far as the girls are concerned,' she said. 'I wanted him to feel that a dialogue has been opened, that he can come to me when he has issues, you know, about the girls, their schooling, anything.'

'I'm sure he knows that.'

'Did he say so?'

'Oh for Chrissakes, Catherine. Was this all about you? Or did you genuinely want to do something for them?'

'I'm just asking. What's wrong with you?'

'Nothing, sorry,' she muttered. 'I'm just tired.'

'But you've been sleeping all day.'

'I haven't been sleeping all day,' she retorted. 'I just haven't woken up properly yet.'

'Well, I've obviously caught you at a bad time.'

'Yes you have. So I'm going to hang up now, before I'm tempted to hang up on you.'

'Snippy, snippy.'

'Goodbye Catherine.'

Rachel sat up late watching bad TV, not wanting to admit that she was waiting for Tom to call. But she badly needed to hear his voice. She felt uneasy about the way things had ended today, and her mind was in a whirl, going off on tangents, revisiting all the issues, all the problems they were going to have, allowing doubt to creep back in . . .

At eleven she'd had enough. He must have forgotten, she

decided, brushing her teeth; out of sight was obviously out of mind. And that's the way it was going to be from here on in. They wouldn't be able to spend much time together, certainly not out in public, at least nowhere around here. Her office was out at Alexandria, while his was in the heart of the city, so they couldn't even meet up for lunch. And with the girls going back to school they wouldn't be off staying at their friends' places so much. Rachel had a dreaded feeling that their 'relationship' was going to consist of the odd booty call.

She fell into bed, but her mind was still racing. How were they going to gradually 'introduce' this 'idea' to the girls anyway? How could they let it unfold slowly when they were already sleeping together? They'd have to come up with some kind of fake act to create the impression they were just starting out. The whole thing was fraught, not least how she was ever going to deal with Catherine and Lexie.

The phone rang, giving her a start. It must be him. She picked it up.

'Hi.'

'Hi.'

Silence.

'Are you okay?' asked Tom.

'Sure.'

'Is it too late, am I calling too late? Were you asleep?'

'No, I wasn't asleep.'

'You sound a little sleepy.'

'I am, but I wasn't asleep.'

'I'm sorry I didn't call earlier,' he said. 'Soph was in a talkative mood, she wanted to tell me all about her weekend after Hannah had gone to bed. It was nice, really, I didn't want to rush her.'

'Of course not.'

'But now you're mad at me.'

'I'm not mad.'

'Rach, I'm sorry about what happened this afternoon. I was just thrown, and I know I wasn't very sensitive and I really am sorry, it won't happen again.'

'Of course it'll happen again, Tom. It'll happen again and again. And again.'

She heard him sigh. 'See, you are mad at me.'

'I'm not mad, I'm just being realistic.'

'Rachel, please don't let things slide back again.'

'What does that mean?'

'We finally got somewhere today, didn't we? Sorted out the bullshit?'

'Oh really? Is that what we did?'

'Rach –'

'No Tom, don't you see? We haven't got rid of the bullshit, we've boarded the bullshit express. I don't know how this is going to work.'

'We can make it work if we want to. Look, I know we're going to have to be ... discreet –'

'Discreet? There's a euphemism if I ever heard one,' said Rachel. 'Tom, we're going to have to lie to our friends, and you'll have to lie to your daughters, and we're going to have to sneak around and hardly ever see each other. What kind of a relationship is that?'

'It's all we've got at the moment,' he said plainly. 'But I'll take it. Because I love you, Rachel. And I don't want to lose you this time.'

Her heart cramped in her chest, and she could feel tears rising in the back of her throat. He loved her?

'Rach? Are you still there?'

'Yeah, I'm still here,' she said thickly.

'Are you crying?'

'No, I'm not crying,' she sniffed.

'I wish I was there with you.'

She released a tremulous sigh. 'Me too.'

'Can I come over one night this week?'

'What about the girls?'

'They're still off school for most of the week, they'll be doing stuff.'

'Okay.'

'I'll call you.'

*

February

They finally made a date for lunch for Lexie to face Catherine. It was Rachel who turned out to be the most difficult one to pin down, which was a first. It was just that Tom could almost always duck away for a couple of hours through the day on a weekend, even if he had to be home with the girls at night. And Rachel was far too selfish of what little time they had together to give it up for lunch with the girls. A disgrace to the sisterhood, she was well aware, but it wasn't a permanent situation.

She had to admit there was something incredibly seductive about this undercover caper, it had given her a little insight into why people had affairs. Of course she also knew she would get sick of it eventually; basically they spent the whole time in bed, but the sex was so damn good she wasn't going to complain about that. However, it was only half a relationship, or less to be entirely honest, and that felt like half a life, which was going to wear very thin before long, though Tom assured her that when it did, it would be the trigger for them to start to come out from the shadows. The idea still made her head spin, so she tried not to think about it. She would cross that bridge when she came to it, which for once was probably a reasonable strategy; there was no way of predicting how that would go, so why worry unnecessarily? Tom was always telling her that the girls adored her and that, given time, they would have no problem accepting her into their lives. He similarly reassured her about Lexie, reminding Rachel of what a sweet nature she had, that once she got used to the idea she'd only want them to be happy. Catherine was another matter entirely; Tom would just shake his head and change the subject at the mention of her name. But sometimes Rachel was aware that a tiny part of her was secretly gloating, that Catherine could throw all the histrionics she liked when it all came out, but it wouldn't change the fact that Tom wanted to be with her. It was so adolescent, yet strangely satisfying at the same time.

Today Rachel was particularly excited because Tom was staying over, for the first time since the girls had gone back to school. It was only fair to give them a few weeks to settle into a routine, and now their patience was being rewarded, with Sophie staying at a friend's and Hannah invited to a sleepover party on the same night. Tom wasn't dropping Han off until six and Rachel could hardly wait, so lunch with the girls was a perfect distraction.

They planned to meet at the Clovelly Hotel. Lexie had lined up her mother to mind the children; they were expected there later for dinner for Eric's birthday, so that had turned out well. Lexie offered to pick up Rachel, but it was a gorgeous day so she decided to walk, and Catherine was meeting them there. Rachel was first to arrive, which was another first in itself, and when Lexie rushed in breathlessly, fifteen minutes later, Catherine had still not shown up.

She stooped to give Rachel a kiss hello. 'Where's Catherine?'

'I don't know, she's not here yet.'

Lexie slid onto the seat opposite. 'Really? You don't suppose she got the date wrong?'

Rachel shook her head. 'I was talking to her only yesterday, she definitely knew it was today. I'm sure she'll show up soon enough.'

And she did – like a hurricane. Or something similarly wild and out of control.

'You can blame my daughter for my late arrival,' she fumed, as she reefed a chair out from the table and dropped into it, crossing one leg over the other with a dramatic flourish.

'What happened?' asked Rachel.

'I need a drink,' she declared, her eyes searching the table. 'What the fuck are you two drinking?'

'Mineral water,' Lexie offered meekly. 'We were waiting for you, because you always like to choose the wine.'

'I wasn't going to have a drink, just so you know,' said Catherine. 'I was planning an alcohol-free day, like all the authorities recommend. But that child has driven me to it.'

'Catherine,' Rachel said calmly, 'will you please tell us what happened?'

She took a breath, making quite a show of collecting herself. 'Alice went to a sleepover last night like a normal teenage girl,' she paused for effect, 'and she came home as an emu.'

'What?' Lexie and Rachel glanced at each other, mystified.

'You know, the ridiculous asymmetrical haircut, dyed jet-black, the tight black clothes from head to foot. The sullen attitude, though that's nothing new for her.'

'Oh,' said Rachel, getting it. 'You mean *emo*.'

'That's what I said,' Catherine dismissed. 'I was so furious, I could barely say two words to her.'

Rachel doubted that.

'Are we going to have something to drink?' Catherine demanded.

Lexie jumped up. 'I'll go. A bottle, yes? What would you like?'

'I couldn't give a fuck as long as it's alcoholic,' she snapped.

'Right.' Lexie grabbed her bag and skittered off towards the bar.

'So,' said Rachel. 'How did it end up with Alice?'

'I've grounded her for the foreseeable future, till I work out the wider consequences,' said Catherine. 'I might just have to keep her locked up until her hair grows out.'

Rachel thought about it. 'Wasn't she already grounded?'

'Yes she was,' Catherine said each word distinctly, like shooting bullets from a gun. 'And I should have stood my ground. But as I'm not an unreasonable person, and she behaved herself the night the Macklins came over, I gave in to her nagging and granted a reprieve. More fool me. Never again.'

Rachel thought carefully about what she was about to say. 'Well, I know it must have been a shock, seeing her like that. But,' she took a breath, 'as far as I understand, at her age, and considering her socio-economic background, it's a fairly innocent form of self-expression, a bit of a fad, a way to identify with a group.'

Catherine was glaring at her. 'Well that goes to show just how little you know, Rachel.'

Lexie rushed back to the table with a bottle of white wine and three glasses.

'That was quick,' said Catherine with begrudging gratitude, snatching a glass from her.

'Yes,' said Lexie breathlessly. 'The young man on the bar is going to bring over an ice bucket shortly,' she said, pouring wine into Catherine's glass, 'I told him I couldn't wait.'

'At least somebody's on the ball,' Catherine remarked, taking a good mouthful of wine and closing her eyes as it went down with a sigh. She opened her eyes again. 'Rachel here thinks that Alice is just playing innocent dress-ups.'

Wisely, Lexie made no comment.

'What you don't realise, Rachel,' Catherine went on, 'is that this is only the beginning. It'll be body piercing next, then tattoos, though at least she needs my permission till she's eighteen, which, needless to say, she will not get.' She picked up her glass again. 'But what's even worse, the self-harm will follow, and then the drugs. It's a slippery slope.' She shook her head before downing half the contents of her glass.

'Catherine, don't you think you're overreacting a little?' said Rachel. Someone had to stand up for Alice. 'You can't punish her for behaviour you think she might engage in later.'

'I'm not,' Catherine insisted. 'I'm trying to protect her from it.'

'So why is she being punished?'

'Because she cut and dyed her hair without my permission,' she said simply.

'Would you have given it?' said Rachel.

'What?'

'Would you have given her permission to dye her hair black and have it cut in that style?'

'No, of course not, that's the whole point.'

'Well, then, that's why she didn't ask you.'

'There was a saying at my school,' Lexie was nodding. 'It's easier to get forgiveness than permission.'

'Oh, I see, so it's *my* fault,' Catherine baulked. 'She's just rebelling?'

'Of course she is,' said Rachel. 'It's pretty normal behaviour.'

Catherine was shaking her head. 'It's so easy for you to sit there and pontificate, Rachel,' she sighed wearily. 'You don't have children of your own, yet you think you know how you would handle something like this. You have no idea how I felt when she came through that door, her beautiful long blonde hair gone, replaced with a hacked black mop.'

Rachel wondered if Catherine had ever told Alice her hair was beautiful; she could only remember her constantly harping at her to get it off her face.

Catherine poured herself another glass of wine. 'You know, incredible as this might sound, sometimes I envy you, Rachel.'

'Oh?'

'I know it seems like I have it all compared to you.'

Lexie pulled a face.

'But you don't have any of the hassles either,' Catherine went on. 'No husband to get on your nerves, no parents bothering you with their petty problems. You have a job you don't have to think about once you leave the office, and by the sounds of it, you don't have to think about it that much while you're there. You don't even have a big house to look after.'

Not that Catherine looked after hers, she paid people to do it for her.

'But most of all, you don't have a child that you've raised for seventeen years, on your own for a good part of it, only to have her turn around and hate you.'

Rachel knew she should say something, but nothing was forthcoming. Lexie was similarly mute.

'That's what you've got ahead of you, Lexie,' said Catherine finally, picking up her glass. 'Mark my words. Get yourself a real job. Because parenting is the most thankless thing you could ever do with your life.'

'Maybe we should order?' Lexie suggested.

'So Lexie,' Catherine resumed, once they had their food in front of them, 'you still haven't emailed me that information. There are a lot of jobs being advertised in your field at the moment, now that the year is underway. We really need to get on with this or you'll miss the window.'

Lexie calmly put her fork down on her plate and dabbed at the corners of her mouth with her napkin. She glanced across at Rachel, who gave her an encouraging wink.

'Okay, well, the thing is, Catherine,' she began, 'it's not really my field.'

'Yes it is,' said Catherine. 'This is exactly the kind of work you were doing before.'

'Yes, but what I'm saying is, I don't want to go back to lab work.'

'Oh? Well, why didn't you say so?' She picked up her glass.

'I don't know what else you're qualified for ... Are you thinking about retraining?'

'No,' said Lexie. 'I'm very qualified for what I'm doing.'

'Oh, not this again? What do I keep telling you?'

'That being a mother is a relationship not a job,' she chanted. 'Yes, I know that's what you believe, Catherine, but I happen to disagree. When did mothering become so worthless? We went from a time when it was expected, when women had no choice, and now we have the choice, it's considered a waste of time, something you can outsource. Well, if I had the money, I'd outsource the cleaning and the ironing, but I don't want to outsource raising my children.'

'Are you suggesting that's what I did with Alice?' asked Catherine, one eyebrow raised accusingly. 'That's terribly simplistic, Lexie. Just because you put a child into day care doesn't mean you forfeit your role as a parent.'

'I'm not saying that, and I'm not judging you, Catherine,' she said. 'That's the whole thing, I respect the choices you made that worked for you, so why can't you give me the same respect? I'm good at what I do. Sure, it can get a little mindless at times, but I make the most of it. I have lots of interests and hobbies.'

'Have you ever tasted her cupcakes?' said Rachel. 'To die for.'

'I'm not just talking about domestic stuff like that,' Lexie persisted. She was on a roll. 'I take care of my mind and my body. I read, I keep up with current affairs, and I keep fit walking Riley to school and back most days, which is setting a very good example for him. My children have a routine, our life is much less stressful because I don't work outside the house. Scott has enough stress in his job for the both of us.'

'So Scott's work has to take precedence?'

'Don't put that spin on it, Catherine. It's not that Scott's work is more important.'

'Oh, you misunderstand me,' she said. 'Scott's work is obviously vital. He's left to take on the entire load of financially supporting your family while you get to take care of "your mind and your body" and flit about ... just like Annie always did.'

Rachel's ears pricked up then.

'Annie didn't flit about!' Lexie protested. 'She was completely devoted to raising Sophie and Hannah. You only have to look at those girls, they're a credit to her.'

'And what about Tom?' said Catherine. 'Doesn't he get any credit? After all, he was the one footing the bill the whole time for her lifestyle choice.'

'You can't call it a lifestyle choice.'

'That's what Tom called it.'

Rachel frowned. She remembered Tom talking about choices a while back ... She remembered sensing his frustration at the time.

'Sounds like you've got inside info,' Rachel said, trying to sound casual.

Catherine tilted her head in a coy fashion. 'Oh, well, Tom had a few too many drinks at a Law Society function last year, it was before Annie died, and he said some things.'

'What kinds of things?' Lexie asked defensively.

'Look, it's probably not fair for me to talk out of school, confidentiality and all that, but you get my drift,' she dismissed. 'How is Tom doing anyway?' she asked Lexie. 'Do you see him much?'

'No, not really.' Lexie was relieved to change tack, she didn't like Catherine's 'drift'. 'I was worried about him for a while there. I told Rachel that I often saw his light on in the middle of the night, and he seemed to just hang around the house on the weekends when the girls weren't there. But now he never seems to be home unless they're home.'

'Hmm,' said Catherine, her eyes narrowing. 'I wonder if he's seeing someone now.'

Lexie groaned. 'Let's not go there again.'

Catherine glanced at Rachel. 'Look at you, you're blushing. What's going on in that little head of yours?'

'Nothing,' she stirred, 'and I'm not blushing.'

'She's ... glowing,' Lexie jumped in. 'I was going to say, you look great, Rachel. Doesn't she look great, Catherine?'

Catherine considered her. 'Actually, she's right. Have you done something with your hair?'

Rachel shook her head. 'No, in fact I'm overdue for a cut.'

'Your face looks less bloated or something, have you lost some weight?'

Catherine, master of the backhanded compliment.

'I've just been getting more exercise,' Rachel shrugged.

'Well, you should get going while the going's good,' said Catherine, taking a chug of her wine. 'Have you checked out all the arrows you've been getting?'

'What?'

'On Rendezvous. Some of them aren't too bad, why aren't you at least giving them a go?'

'Why are you looking on my site, Catherine?'

'Why are you avoiding my question, Rachel?'

She breathed out. 'Look, I'm just not interested, I don't think it's right for me. I'd rather click with someone than click on them.'

Lexie giggled. 'That's very clever.'

Catherine didn't seem to think so. 'You've decided this after one date?'

'Yeah, well, one was enough,' she said plainly. 'I don't want to waste any more of my time on married men and losers.'

'What else have you got to do with your time?'

You have no idea, Rachel thought, just a little smugly, picking up her glass and taking a sip.

'Oh, speaking of the time,' Lexie said, looking at her watch. 'I might have to get going.' She bit her lip. 'Would you girls excuse me while I make a call?'

Lexie walked inside the hotel, finding a quiet spot in the foyer, and dialled the café.

'Bean East,' Scott answered.

'Hi honey, I'm just finishing up here with the girls.'

'Okay.'

She could tell she wasn't getting his full attention.

'So I was thinking I might come by and hang out there till you're finished, and then we can drive over to Mum's together.'

'I've got my car here, Lex.'

'I realise that, but you could follow me back to our place and we could leave it there. It's on the way.'

'Look, I don't know when I'm going to be able to get away. You should go on ahead.'

'I don't mind waiting for you.'

She heard him sigh. 'To be honest, Lex, I've been run off my feet today, I'm exhausted. And by the time I finish up here, maybe I'll just go home to bed.'

'You can't do that,' she protested. 'It's Eric's birthday.'

'No one's going to miss me,' he said.

'I'll miss you,' Lexie insisted. 'The kids'll miss you.'

'Don't be unreasonable, honey.'

'I'm not being unreasonable! You're the one being unreasonable, Scott.'

'Look, I don't have time for this now, Lexie. I still have customers.'

And then he hung up! Lexie was stunned for a moment. She'd had quite enough of this. She had a good mind to go back to the table and have a few more drinks with the girls, enough so that she couldn't drive. And then Scott would have to come and pick her up.

But she wasn't going to do that. She didn't want to let Catherine know what was going on, and besides, it was manipulative and childish and she needed to handle this like an adult. Lexie thought about her options. She scrolled down to her mother's number and pressed *Call*.

'Hello Lexie, dear,' Sally said when she picked up. 'Are you on your way?'

'Oh, Mum, I'm sorry, I was going to ask ... Well, Scott's run off his feet, they're short-staffed again, and he's going to be really late if I don't go and give him a hand.'

'Of course, darling.'

'Are you sure? The kids aren't in the way while you're trying to get ready?'

'Now don't you worry about a thing here,' Sally reassured her. 'They've been absolute angels. Mia had a lovely long nap, and Riley has been helping me in the kitchen. I think he takes after his daddy.'

Not so much. Scott never cooked with him, he wasn't around enough. It was Lexie who let him help out in the kitchen.

'They're a credit to you, Lexie.'

She felt a lump in her throat. Somehow her mother had the

knack of saying the right thing at the right time, even if she had no idea she was doing it. 'Thanks Mum. I'll buzz you when we're on our way.'

'I can't bear the thought of going home,' Catherine confided to Rachel after Lexie had said her goodbyes in a flurry and left. 'I know I'll just want to yell at Alice every time I look at her with that ridiculous haircut,' she groaned.

'Then don't,' said Rachel.

'What, look at her?'

'I was thinking more don't yell at her.'

Catherine sighed heavily. 'I know you believe I'm too hard on her, Rachel, but I really am only trying to protect her.'

'You can't protect her from everything, Catherine. You have to let her make her own mistakes.'

'That's what terrifies me.'

'But why?' said Rachel. 'The worst thing that ever happened to you also gave you the best thing that ever happened to you.'

Catherine was shaking her head. 'Alice isn't like me, she wouldn't survive.'

'Maybe you underestimate her.'

'I really wish that was the case,' she said, draining her glass. She hadn't stopped drinking, or rather guzzling, since she arrived.

'How did you get here today, Catherine?' Rachel asked.

'Martin dropped me off,' she said.

'Is he coming back to get you?'

'Mm . . . ' She seemed to be contemplating something. 'Hey,' her eyes suddenly lit up. 'Why don't we have a girls' night in? We can pick up some Thai food and a couple of bottles. It'll be fun, you and I haven't had a night together in *ages*.'

Rachel winced. 'Sorry Catherine, I can't. I'm . . . I have plans.'

'Oh?' she frowned. 'Who with?'

'Um, people from work.'

'You don't even like the people you work with, you always make excuses not to go out with them.'

That was true. Bugger.

'Well, I haven't always liked the people I work with,' Rachel began, 'but, you know, we have quite a high staff turnover –'

'I wonder why,' Catherine snorted, taking another drink.

'– and lately we've had a few younger people start, and, you know, they're a lot of fun. And they were talking about checking out this new club tonight, and, well, they ended up inviting me to come along.'

God, she'd better keep track of what she was saying. This was the problem when you made up lies. You couldn't remember the details later. She'd better not start making up names, she was hopeless at remembering names.

'Honestly, Rachel, you really need to start acting your age,' Catherine drawled. 'You're always chumming it up with the young folks. They were just being polite when they asked you out tonight, they don't really want an old thirtysomething tagging along with them to a club opening, cramping their style. They won't care if you don't show up.'

'Well, I'll care!' Rachel exclaimed. Now she was getting defensive about a fictional scenario. That was it, she'd had enough of Catherine for one afternoon. The only way Catherine seemed to be able to relax was with a drink, but when she drank too much – which was becoming the norm – she just became unpleasant. She certainly could never be called a happy drunk. Watching her now, slumped in her chair, her face all ruddy, Rachel felt a little sorry for her.

So she wasn't going to get into an argument with her. 'I have to get going, Catherine,' Rachel said, standing up. 'Do you want to ring Martin, or shall we see if there's a taxi out front?'

Lexie parked her car and walked briskly down the street to the café. There were still a few stragglers at the tables outside, but as she got closer she could see that inside was almost empty.

As she marched straight in, she could also see there was no one clearing the tables, wiping them down, making it obvious they were about to close. There was a girl Lexie had never seen before; she was dressed like a waitress, wearing the café's logo on her apron, but that was all that suggested she actually worked here.

She was leaning against a wall, yarning away to a table of what were obviously her friends. She didn't even look up when Lexie walked directly around the counter into the kitchen area.

Scott had his back to her, so she grabbed an apron from a hook on the wall and started to tie it around her waist.

'Hi hun,' she said breezily.

He turned abruptly. 'Lexie, what are you doing here?'

'I guess I'll start with the washing up.'

'What?' he frowned, coming closer to her. 'You're not doing the washing up.'

'Well, someone has to.' She looked around. 'Where's Josh?'

Scott shrugged. 'He had tickets to something tonight. I let him go early to get ready.'

'Are you kidding me? Josh can take off when he has something on, but you can't?'

'Lexie, it's a little different. I own the business.'

'And Josh is your right hand,' she reminded him. 'You can't run this place on your own, with one waitress,' she dropped her voice, 'standing out there chatting up the customers.'

'There were another couple of casuals on over lunch, but they knocked off already.'

'You need to develop a better roster system,' said Lexie. 'If you were going to let Josh go home early, then one of those casuals could have stayed on for a longer shift.'

'Lex,' he said with a hint of condescension in his voice, 'I've been running this business for a long time, I think I know what I'm doing.'

'Despite all evidence to the contrary,' she said, looking around the mess of the kitchen. 'Anyway, we can talk about this later. We're wasting time.'

She made a move towards the sink, but Scott blocked her.

'I'm serious, Lex,' he said. 'You're not doing the washing up.'

'Fine, I'll start clearing the tables, you wash up.' She glanced out into the café. 'Or get Flirty Girtie out there to do it.'

'Lex –'

'I'm not going to discuss it, Scott. We have plans tonight, we made a commitment, and I'm not going to let you welch on it.' She took a breath. 'The kids haven't seen you all weekend, Riley doesn't get to spend your day off with you any more now that he's at school. You have a family, and we can't take second place to the café all the time.'

He looked a little taken aback. 'You're kinda cute when you get all riled up.'

She folded her arms, glaring up at him. 'Don't patronise me, Scott. Here's what's going to happen. I'm staying till you close. I've already phoned Mum and told her I was coming to give you a hand finishing up for the day, and you know what? She didn't have a stroke, and she didn't say you were a bad provider, she just said, "We'll see you when you get here, darling!"' Lexie chirped, imitating her mother. 'So what do you want me to do? Clear the tables, or shall I put on those rubber gloves and start the washing up?'

His expression had hardened. 'Just for the record, I don't like this, Lex,' he said seriously. 'I don't appreciate being cornered.'

'Neither do I,' she returned, staring up at him defiantly.

Now he really did look cornered. 'Well, you're not washing up,' he said, hanging on to some authority.

'Fine, then I'll do the tables.'

Autumn

Rachel stepped off the bus into the pouring rain. No, this wasn't pouring, it was bucketing down. The clouds that had been threatening to open up all day had finally made good on their threat, dumping the full force of their weight in a downpour of biblical proportions. Rachel didn't mind the change so much after a hot, sticky, stifling day, but why did it have to hit only moments before she was about to get off the bus? She broke into a run, but she pretty quickly realised it was pointless. She was already drenched through to her skin. So she slowed to a walk, holding her face up to the rain. It was quite refreshing actually.

She'd had a lousy day. Lloyd had been more persnickety than usual; Rachel had not thought it possible. But in his vast administrative wisdom, he had decided that too many mistakes were being made on the invoices lately, and so he had developed a laborious double-checking procedure, which Rachel was certain would end up wasting more time than the odd mistake had ever done. But what did she care anyway? Every day she came closer to packing it in. She would have thought that having something fulfilling in her life would make work matter less, but that's not the way it was panning out. Instead it seemed to bring everything into sharper relief. It was like teaming a designer dress with scuffed, chainstore shoes, or placing a new armchair beside a battered couch, or wearing real gold next to a tarnished fake.

And Tom was the real thing, solid, eighteen-carat. Rachel's stomach did a flip right now just thinking about him. She couldn't get enough of him ... literally. Though they talked on the phone every day, they hadn't seen each other all week, and the weekend was looking impossible. Sophie had a big assignment; she was going to be based at home for the duration, with all her friends in lockdown over the same assignment. Hannah was having her best friend, Ellie, over to stay, which meant Tom couldn't duck away even for a short time, and he'd also promised Sophie a long-overdue driving lesson, which would have to wait until Ellie went home. So he was going to be tied up for the entire weekend, while Rachel was free for the entire weekend. She tended to keep her weekends free now so that she was available on the off-chance ... That sounded so pathetic, but she kept telling herself it was only temporary. And even if Tom only had half an hour spare – when he was supposed to be doing the grocery shopping, or popping out first thing in the morning for milk and the newspaper – that half-hour made her whole weekend. Sometimes Rachel even liked the fact that no one knew about them; they existed in their own little bubble when they were together, they didn't have to share their time with anyone else. Except when there was no time, like this weekend.

Oh bugger, was that hail?

Fortunately she was not far from her block, and she took off up the street, squealing occasionally as pebbles of hail ricocheted around her. They were only tiny yet; Rachel just wanted to get under cover before they got any worse. She rounded the corner and raced up her driveway to the awning at the entrance of the building, taking a moment to catch her breath. There were none of the dramatic golf-ball-size hailstones the papers loved to report; instead it looked like someone had split open a bean bag on a balcony above, the little white balls bouncing playfully after they hit the ground. Rachel pushed on the security door; it was open, as usual. She stepped into the foyer, dripping, her shoes squelching as she mounted the stairs, which actually made her smile. Now that she was out of it, she decided it wasn't so bad. In a minute or two she would change into dry clothes, which was always such a cosy, comforting sensation after being caught in the rain. Then she would pour herself a drink and sit and watch the storm head out over the ocean.

She fished around in her bag for her keys and, retrieving them, she stuck the key in the lock, but the door gave way before she'd even turned it, which was odd. Before she had time to process what was going on, Tom was standing in front of her.

'Surprise!' he announced.

And she screamed.

'Rach,' he laughed, drawing her inside. 'It's okay, it's only me.'

'Oh my God,' she breathed, her heart racing in her chest. 'You scared the shit out of me, Tom!'

He was still laughing as he gathered her into his arms. 'You're soaked,' he said, recoiling.

'What are you doing here?'

He pushed the door closed. 'I wanted to surprise you.'

She was still catching her breath. 'Were you also trying to give me a heart attack?'

'I'm sorry, honey. Look at you,' he grinned down at her. 'You look like a drowned rat.'

'Sweet talker,' she returned. 'You still haven't said what you're doing here?'

'Sophie texted me at lunchtime with a likely story about how three of them were going to stay at Zoe's and work on their assignment together. So I did the stern father thing and told her it was okay as long as she was home by midday tomorrow and that she stays put for the rest of the weekend.'

'What about Hannah?'

'Well, once I'd heard from Sophie, I did a switch with Ellie's mum, so I'll have them next weekend instead.'

'Did you know all this when you called me today?' asked Rachel.

He looked a little sheepish. 'Not for sure. I wanted to check you were free before I talked to Ellie's mum, but I didn't want to tell you what I had in mind in case it didn't pan out. And when it did, I realised I could surprise you. I didn't mean to give you a fright.'

Rachel considered him. 'Does this mean you can stay the night?'

'Yes it does.'

She smiled, reaching her arms up around his neck. 'Then you're forgiven.'

As they kissed, she felt his fingers hook under her top, slowly easing it up. 'We really should get you out of these wet things,' he said in a low voice, his mouth close to hers, as Rachel dropped her bag on the floor and raised her arms again. Tom pulled the top up and over her head, tossing it aside. He smoothed his hands over the damp fabric of her bra. 'You really are wet through,' he murmured.

'Indeed.'

His mouth covered hers and he brought his arms around her, scooping her up so her feet left the floor and striding into the bedroom. He lowered her to the floor again, tugging at the zip of her skirt, before slowly sliding it down. But the wet fabric clung to her, not moving, so Tom dropped to his knees, running his lips and his tongue across her belly as he peeled the skirt all the way down. Rachel gasped. She raked her fingers through his hair and drew him up again. 'Come here, you,' she said, pushing him down onto the bed and straddling him. She started to unbutton his shirt, from the bottom up, while he lay back, gazing up at her. She loved the way he looked at her; he made her feel as though she was incredibly sexy, and Rachel hadn't felt like that in a very long time. She got to the last button and opened his shirt back, lowering herself down to press her body into his, skin against skin. That was almost her favourite part. Almost. He wrapped his arms tightly around her as their mouths locked and their urgency started to build. She felt his hands on the catch of her bra –

Rachel jumped as a knock sounded at the door.

'Don't answer it,' Tom whispered, their faces close.

They didn't move, didn't make a peep, though Rachel's heart was beating so hard she wouldn't be surprised if it could be heard all the way outside.

Another three knocks sounded, loud and clear. 'Rachel, I know you're in there, I just saw you walking into the building.'

It was Catherine. They gave each other a bewildered look.

Rachel sighed. '*Fuck.*'

'Not any more.'

She burrowed her face into his neck to stifle a giggle.

'Rachel!' Catherine called again, like an angry schoolteacher, before thumping the door three, no, four more times.

Rachel lifted herself upright. 'Okay,' she sung out. She looked down at Tom, mouthing 'Stay here' as she climbed off him.

'Where else am I going to go?' he whispered.

She held her finger to her lips as she grabbed her robe from the hook on the back of the door and slipped it on. She stepped out into the hall, closing the door firmly behind her.

Rachel wrapped the robe around her as she hurried up to the front door and opened it. Catherine was standing there, poised to speak, but Rachel cut her off at the pass.

'You saw me walk into the building? What, are you carrying out surveillance on the place?'

'Don't be so paranoid,' Catherine said, sweeping past her, brandishing a bottle of champagne. Rachel groaned inwardly. How was she going to get rid of her? She closed the door and followed in her wake, down the hall into the living room.

'I saw you running up the street as my taxi pulled up on the other side,' Catherine was explaining as she dumped her bag in an armchair. 'What took you so long to answer the door?'

'I was just getting out of my wet clothes. I was drenched through.'

'Yeah, I noticed. I tried to call out to you to wait, I had an umbrella. I left it out there on the landing, I hope it's safe,' she said, frowning as she glanced up the hall. 'Your security door doesn't seem to close properly, you know.'

Yes, unfortunately. Rachel tied the sash around her robe. 'What are you doing here, Catherine?'

'Do I have to have an excuse to visit my best friend?' She leaned forwards to touch cheeks with Rachel and kiss the air. She'd been drinking, Rachel could smell it.

'I have had the worst day,' she said, tearing the foil from the neck of the bottle. 'You remember that gold-digger, Alannah Cresswell, I told you about? Her settlement came through this week, and it's customary for the partners to take the client out to lunch after such a big win. So I've just sat through two hours with that conniving little tart, while she flirted with all the partners and they lapped it up, because she's blonde and perky, and they haven't had to put up with her for the past few months.' She popped the cork off the bottle. 'So I decided to come and get drunk with you.'

Rachel shrugged apologetically. 'Catherine, I can't, I've got plans tonight.'

'You're kidding?' Her face dropped. 'How come you've suddenly got a social life? What's going on?'

'I've always had a social life, Catherine. You don't know everything I do and how I spend my time.'

Like, for instance, that she was hiding a man in her room that very moment.

'What are you grinning about?' Catherine was watching her suspiciously. 'You look like the cat that got the cream.'

'Nothing,' said Rachel. 'Look, I suppose I have time for one drink, and one drink only, but then I really have to get ready.'

'Well, it appears I'm the beggar and you're the chooser,' she said, a little miffed.

Rachel padded off into the kitchen. 'I'll get some glasses.'

'I see you've tidied up a little around here,' Catherine called from the other room.

Rachel had been somewhat more attentive to the housekeeping now that she was entertaining, so to speak, on a regular basis. She also found it quite therapeutic when she got twitchy waiting for the phone to ring.

'Gorgeous flowers,' Catherine remarked, leaning over a vase of tulips as Rachel came back with the glasses. 'From an admirer?'

She couldn't collect her wits in time, her face froze with her mouth open, but nothing came out.

'Oh my God,' said Catherine, watching her with a look of surprise laced with admiration. 'I was only kidding, but they are, aren't they?'

Rachel sighed, but she was still mute, apparently. Catherine grabbed a glass out of her hand and filled it with champagne.

'Why didn't you tell me?' she said, handing the full glass back to Rachel and taking the other one. 'We really do have something to drink to now.'

She actually sounded genuinely pleased for her. It was a nice change.

'It's only early days, I didn't want to make a big deal.'

'Tosh,' said Catherine. 'It is a big deal, this is so exciting!' She held her glass up in a toast. 'To you and – what's his name?'

Rachel froze again.

'Rachel?' Catherine prompted. 'He does have a name?'

She glanced around, looking for a hint, a cue, something. Her eyes landed on the square of carpet in the doorway to the kitchen. 'Matt,' she said finally. 'His name is Matt.'

'Ma-*tthew*, please, Rachel,' Catherine corrected her. 'Matt makes him sound like a plumber. He's not a plumber, is he?'

'No, Catherine. But what would be wrong with that anyway?'

'Well, granted, they do make good money, but please, you know the kinds of places they have to crawl into.' She grimaced. 'They say they never get it all out from under their fingernails.'

Rachel pulled a face, before taking a good gulp of her champagne.

'So tell me all about him.' Catherine put the bottle down on the coffee table and made herself comfortable in one of the armchairs. 'Where did you meet?'

Oh, God, now she had to start making up details. Actually, the trick was probably to avoid making up too many details, keep it as close to the truth as possible. Then hopefully when it all came out she wouldn't look completely ridiculous.

'I actually knew him a long time ago, back at uni,' said Rachel, perching on the arm of the couch, making it quite clear she wasn't settling in.

'Then I must know him as well.'

'He wasn't in your year.'

'Still, I might know him. What's his last name?'

Oh shit. Rachel glanced around the room for another prompt, trying not to look obvious. Catherine reached for the bottle again, and Rachel got a fleeting glance of the label. 'Hardy . . . ing. Harding,' she announced.

'Matthew Harding,' Catherine mused. 'He's not one of the Point Piper Hardings, is he?'

'How would I know?' Rachel watched Catherine refilling her glass. 'Hey, I said one drink.'

'I'm only topping it up,' she dismissed. 'Anyway, I haven't heard of a Matthew Harding, he is working as a lawyer?'

'Uhuh . . . for legal aid.' This was turning into a miniseries.

'That'd be right,' Catherine shook her head. 'You realise he'll have no money to speak of, Rachel?'

'See how much we have in common?'

'What have I always told you?' she sighed. 'It's just as easy to fall in love with a rich man as a poor one.'

'I thought you didn't like gold-diggers?'

'That's entirely different, I said fall in love, not take them for everything you can get.' She sat forwards. 'Anyway, seeing as we're sharing, I've met someone too.'

Rachel blinked. 'What are you saying? You're married. Remember Martin?'

She shrugged. 'The spark's gone.'

'There was a spark?'

'Oh, there was something, certainly he used to be more enamoured of me, which helped. Now he just annoys me.' She sipped her drink. 'Then a few months ago, last year actually, I was at a conference, and there was this man . . . We've known each other a long time too, I think there's always been a mutual attraction, but we were both married.'

'You still are,' Rachel reminded her.

Catherine ignored that. 'So we got to talking, and turns out we were both feeling pretty disgruntled with our lot, and we commiserated, and well, one thing led to another as they say, and we ended up in bed together. It was pretty heady stuff, I think it caught us both by surprise.'

'So, what? Are you telling me you're having an affair with this guy?'

'No, no, nothing's happened since the conference. The situation is quite complicated.'

'You don't say.'

Catherine looked at her. 'Listen Rachel, I'm an attractive woman, I've got a great body – and not just "for my age". That's such an insulting turn of phrase.' She curled her lip, before taking a mouthful of wine. 'I want someone who appreciates me as a woman. I want a bit of excitement in my life. I think Martin would get more excited if he could fillet and cook me.'

'You know perfectly well he adores you.'

'Well, he bores me,' she shrugged.

Rachel was shaking her head. 'So you're going to dump him? Just like that?'

'No, I have to wait for the right time . . .' Catherine had a dreamy look in her eyes. 'When all the planets align.'

This was turning Rachel's stomach. 'Isn't that the doomsday scenario?' she snapped.

Catherine stirred. 'What's that?'

'If all the planets lined up there'd be chaos across the world.'

'I don't think so,' she said. 'Anyway, it's just an expression. What I'm trying to say is that I have to bide my time, till the circumstances are right.'

Rachel couldn't listen to any more of this. Catherine clearly had no shame, but how had it come about that she thought it was okay to say this stuff to Rachel?

Because Rachel didn't challenge her on it. Oh, perhaps vaguely, on occasion, but not nearly enough. She got to her feet abruptly. 'I really have to get ready now, Catherine.'

'Oh. Well that's all right, I'll hang around.' She stood up, picking up the bottle. 'Let's move the party into your room, I'll help you pick out something to wear.'

'No!' Rachel blurted, standing in front of her to block her.

'Why, what's wrong?'

'I just . . . I don't like an audience while I'm getting ready,' she insisted. 'And besides, I haven't even showered yet, and now I'm running late. I said one drink, Catherine.'

She sighed dramatically. 'Fine, I know when I'm not wanted.' She handed Rachel the bottle. 'Have you got a stopper? You and *Matthew* can finish this off later.'

'Thank you.'

She picked up her bag and Rachel walked her up the hall and opened the door.

'I expect to meet him sooner rather than later,' she said. 'I get approval rights this time, so you don't end up with another Sean.'

Rachel wouldn't credit that with a response, she just turned her cheek to receive another air kiss from Catherine.

'Ah, it's still here.' She picked up her umbrella where it stood propped by the door. 'Bye then, talk to you soon.'

Rachel closed the door and breathed out, leaning back against it for a moment as she listened to the click of Catherine's heels on the terrazzo stairs fading away. And then, faintly, the sound of the security door on the ground floor. She would have felt more comfortable if she was sure it had actually locked, but she wasn't going to run downstairs in her robe to check. She walked down the hall and opened the door of the bedroom. Tom was lying back on the bed, one arm tucked underneath his head. He looked across at her with an expression of melancholy, probably mirroring her own. She climbed onto the bed as he opened his arm out so she could cuddle in close into him.

'Hi there, Matthew Harding.'

He sighed a kind of half-hearted laugh as he closed his arm around her.

Rachel looked up at him. 'I don't want to do this any more, Tom.'

'I know.'

'Did you hear Catherine talking about the guy she picked up at a conference?'

'Mm.'

'We're not like that, are we?'

'Of course we're not,' he said, kissing the top of her head.

'Then I don't want to have an affair with you any more.'

He shifted onto his side, bringing his face level with hers. 'Listen to me closely, Rachel. I love you, and I chose to be with you. I just want you to remember that when the shit hits the fan.'

Her face dropped. 'Now you think it's going to go badly?' she said. 'You're always trying to reassure me that it'll be fine, as long as we handle it right.'

'I hope so, but we can't control everything,' said Tom. He stroked her hair from her forehead. 'I wish we could go away and live our own lives and everyone else could just mind their own business.'

'What about the girls?'

'I'm not talking about them, you know that. But I guess it's time to start working on them,' he said, resolved. 'Come home with me tomorrow.'

'What? No, I can't do that.'

'Rachel, we have to get the ball rolling.' He propped himself up on one elbow, looking down at her. 'We'll have a barbecue in the afternoon. It'll be casual, relaxed. You'll just be an old family friend coming over for a meal.'

She looked at him doubtfully, and he leaned down to kiss her.

'Do you want to hide like this forever?' he asked.

Rachel shook her head.

'Well, once we get the girls onside, we won't have to any more. And I don't give a damn what anyone else thinks.'

'Okay,' she said finally. 'I'll come. But here's the deal – no flirting. No touching. No eye contact.'

'No eye contact?'

'I'm just saying that this time, and for the meantime, we have to behave the same way we've always behaved around them.'

'Okay, but I'm pretty sure I've usually made eye contact with you.'

'There's eye contact and there's eye contact, you know what I'm saying, Tom?'

'Not really,' he said, suppressing a grin.

'Stop teasing.'

'Okay, so that I've got it absolutely clear, we better sort out exactly what's allowed and what isn't.' He shifted to position himself above her. 'I guess, for example, this is not acceptable,' he said, nuzzling into her neck.

'Definitely not,' she breathed.

'What about this?' he murmured in her ear before teasing her lobe between his teeth. That always did her in.

'No way,' she managed to say.

'So I guess this is out of the question,' he said, as his hand slid down across her belly, and then . . . Rachel let out a squeal.

He lifted his head to look at her. 'Out of bounds?' he said, a glint in his eye.

'Tomorrow, absolutely. Today . . . go for your life.'

The next day

Tom would be back to pick her up any time now. He'd left over an hour ago to collect both the girls, and he was going to tell them that he'd run into Rachel yesterday, and she'd asked after them and so he invited her over for a barbecue. Then they would stop at the supermarket for supplies and come by her place on their way home. Rachel implored him not to overdo the details; she wasn't comfortable lying to the girls, and besides, it just made it easier to get caught.

She was inordinately nervous. It was stupid, she loved Sophie and Hannah, she'd always got on well with them. And she'd always got on well with Tom, so it shouldn't seem odd or strange, socialising with them as a family. But it occurred to Rachel that this was the first time she and Tom had been around anyone since they had got together. And she wasn't sure how she was going to handle it, if it would be obvious, if they'd slip up somehow.

But she had no more time to think about it, because that was Tom now, pranking her phone. She grabbed it, and her bag, and her keys, and hurried out of the flat and down the stairs. When she came out of the entrance, she could see his car parked across the drive, and Hannah waving from the back seat. That was a good sign. But as she drew closer she noticed that Sophie was sitting hunched over against the far window, her arms folded, her expression grim. It might not even have anything to do with her, but Rachel's heart sank.

She opened the door and climbed into the front seat as Tom and Hannah both greeted her. Sophie remained silent.

'Hi,' Rachel said brightly. 'Thanks for coming to get me.'

'No problem, it was right on our way,' said Tom, keeping his eyes firmly on the road. She sensed maybe he was a little nervous too.

'It's so great to see you both,' Rachel said, craning around to look over to the back seat. 'How've you been?'

'Good thanks, Rachel,' said Hannah.

Sophie still didn't say anything.

'Sophie,' said Tom, 'I believe Rachel's addressing you as well.'

She sighed loudly. 'I'm fine, thank you for asking.'

Rachel turned to the front again, catching Tom's eye. But they both looked away quickly.

It was a mercifully short car trip, which was just as well: the conversation was strained, to say the least. Hannah seemed fine, but she gradually picked up on the vibe and became more subdued as a result.

As soon as they pulled up in the drive, Sophie got out of the car and pranced into the house ahead of them. Tom threw a sidelong glance at Rachel, before climbing out of his seat and marching straight in after Sophie. Rachel hesitated, maybe she should give them a minute. Then suddenly the door swung open beside her. It was Hannah.

'Come on, Rachel. What are you waiting for?'

When they walked through the front door, Sophie was halfway up the stairs.

'. . . but we have a guest,' Tom was saying.

She turned around to look down at him. 'Well I didn't ask her!'

'Sophie.'

'Dad, you knew I had this big assignment, and you picked me up later than you said, and now you expect me to entertain someone you invited over?'

Rachel flinched.

'What I expect is for you to mind your manners, young lady.'

Her eyes flickered to take in Rachel standing just inside the door. 'Sorry,' she muttered. 'Is it all right if I come down when dinner's ready, so I can at least get some work done?'

'Fine,' said Tom. 'As long as you bring a better attitude with you then.'

She turned and stomped up the stairs and out of sight. Tom looked around at Rachel. 'Sorry about that.'

She shrugged. 'She must be anxious about that assignment.' She looked down at Hannah, placing an arm casually around her shoulders. 'So looks like it's up to you and me to make the salads, kid.'

'I'm an excellent salad maker,' Hannah said proudly. 'Aren't I, Dad?'

'Yes you are,' he said, ruffling her hair as he walked past. 'I'll just get the things out of the car.'

Rachel caught up with all of Hannah's news while they chopped the vegetables for the salad. Mostly it was gossip from school, girlie stuff. But she also talked about teachers she liked, subjects she enjoyed. Tom hovered in the background, topping up Rachel's drink, coming in and out from the backyard as he prepared the barbecue.

It was all very relaxed and normal, but Rachel could not shake the feeling that she was somehow trespassing on Annie's domain, using her things, preparing dinner with her daughter. It was easier to keep Annie out of the equation when it was only her and Tom, at her own place, but it was impossible here. Especially with Hannah's constant, rather unsubtle reminders: 'No, Mummy uses this cutting board for vegetables . . . that knife for tomatoes . . . No, you don't do it like that, Mummy always said you have to tear the lettuce leaves . . . This was Mummy's favourite salad bowl, her and Dad got it on their honeymoon . . .'

'Are we going to eat outside?' said Tom, popping his head around the back door, holding a pair of tongs. 'It's pretty nice out here.'

Tom had even gone back to looking like Annie's husband again.

When Sophie came downstairs to join them she complained she'd be eaten alive by mosquitoes, so Tom lit every citronella candle and mozzie coil he could find, and finally they were seated around the outdoor table eating their meal.

'How's the assignment going, Soph?' he asked.

She shrugged, picking at the vegetable kebabs Tom had cooked for her specially on a separate hotplate.

'What's it about?' Rachel tried next.

'*King Lear.*'

Tom and Rachel exchanged a smile. 'As flies to wanton boys, are we to the gods; They kill us for their sport,' they recited in unison.

'What was that?' Hannah pulled a face at them.

'Rachel and I both studied *King Lear* for our HSC, we used to play duelling quotations.'

'Did you go to school together?' she asked.

'No, we met at uni straight after we'd finished school,' Tom explained. 'I knew Rachel before I knew your mum.'

Hannah shrugged. 'I never knew that.'

'I'm sure I've told you.'

'Musta forgot.'

'So, ask us anything, Soph,' he said, turning to her. 'You have two old hands here at your disposal.'

'It's different now.'

'Shakespeare's different?'

She sighed. 'We don't study it the way they did in your day.'

Ouch, there was that phrase again.

'What do you mean?' asked Tom.

'We have to imagine we've just seen a production of *King Lear* where the genders have been reversed, and then write a review about it for a journal.'

Tom was listening, obviously confounded. 'So you have to imagine King Lear is Queen Lear, and the daughters are her sons?'

She nodded. 'And the other characters as well. You have to discuss one character where the gender reversal works, and one where it doesn't.'

'What's the point of that?'

'It has to do with exploring gender constructs in literature and applying a postmodernist framework, or something like that.'

'Again, what on earth is the point?'

'Don't ask me,' said Sophie. 'To pass the exams, I guess.'

Tom was shaking his head. 'Shakespeare would be spinning in his grave. King Lear as a woman . . .'

'Maybe it's not so weird,' said Rachel. 'After all, all the female parts were played by men in Shakespeare's time.'

'Why?' Hannah asked.

'Because women weren't allowed to act on stage.'

'That's so dumb,' she declared. 'But I guess it was like, a thousand years ago, and everything was dumb back then.'

'Do you know,' said Tom, 'Rachel's been to places where women are still not allowed to walk the street unless they're covered from head to foot, and in the company of a man.'

Hannah screwed up her face. 'Why would you go somewhere like that? It doesn't sound like much fun for a girl.'

Rachel smiled. 'Don't worry, I never stayed in those places long.'

'Where else have you been?'

'All over,' she said. 'Europe, Africa, South America –'

'Did you go to Bolivia?' Sophie broke in, suddenly interested.

'Bolivia?' Rachel frowned, shaking her head. 'No, I didn't get there. I travelled through Brazil and Argentina and Chile, but I think Bolivia was considered pretty dangerous at the time.'

'Why the interest, Soph?' Tom asked.

'I'm thinking about majoring in international studies, as part of a law degree, and maybe doing an exchange year in South America.'

'You haven't mentioned that before,' he said.

'Well, we had this former student come to the school,' she explained. 'You know, supposed to motivate us for the HSC, but it was so totally cool what she's doing. She just got back from her exchange year in Bolivia, and now she's going to specialise in human rights.' Sophie paused. 'I've always thought I'd probably do law, but I mean, no offence, Dad, corporate law is so not what I want to do.'

'No offence taken, it's not really what I want to do either.'

'Your dad used to want to save the world back when we were at uni,' said Rachel.

'Like Superman,' Hannah giggled.

'Is that true?' Sophie asked him.

'That, or become world surfing champion,' he said. 'But I had more chance of saving the world.'

That raised a smile from Sophie. 'So why did you go into corporate law?'

He seemed to be considering how to answer that. 'Well, I thought I'd try it for a while, get some money behind me . . . Your priorities have to change when you have a family to support, Soph.'

She was looking at him curiously.

'You should follow your dreams while you can, Sophie,' he went on. 'When you're young you've got the whole world at your feet. Anything's possible.'

The conversation flowed a little more easily after that, though Sophie remained reserved. When they all appeared to have finished eating, Tom checked that no one wanted any more food and started to clear the table.

Rachel got to her feet. 'I'll help.'

'No, Rachel, sit. You're a guest.'

'Don't be silly,' she dismissed, gathering up the plates.

'Can I be excused, Dad?' said Sophie.

'No you may not,' he said. 'You got out of helping prepare dinner, the least you can do is help clean up.'

She pulled a face, but she didn't argue. Hannah helped as well, and they transferred everything back into the kitchen in a couple of trips.

'Now can I go upstairs?' Sophie asked.

'After the kitchen's done,' Tom said calmly.

'I have homework!' she shrilled.

'And you also have chores.'

She made a growling sound and turned around to the sink. Rachel had to bite her lip to stop herself from telling Tom just to let her go, she would clean up, it was all her fault anyway. Rachel had thought it was going to be easier than this, that they might even have fun. But her very presence here was creating tension, and there was only one way to put an end to it.

'Um, well, dinner was great, thanks,' she began tentatively. 'But I think I might get going.'

Tom turned to face her. 'Oh . . . do you have to?'

'Yeah, I do, Tom,' she said meaningfully. 'Gotta get the bus . . . you know.'

'You're not getting the bus,' he said, patting his pockets. 'Let me just grab my keys and I'll give you a lift.'

'Tom, no, I'll be fine,' she insisted. 'The bus stop is up the road.'

But he was shaking his head. 'It's dark and you'll have to wait for ages at this time of night on a weekend, Rach. It'll take me five minutes to drive you home.'

She hesitated. 'I don't want to put you out . . .'

'We could call her a cab,' Sophie suggested over her shoulder.

'Or I could be a polite host and drive our guest home,' Tom said sternly.

'Or, better still,' she turned around from the sink, 'you could be an *awesome* dad, and take this chance to give me a driving lesson, and we'll both take Rachel home. You know, kill two birds, and all that.'

'No way, Sophie.'

'Dad, come on. I have to get so many hours up for my logbook, I should be driving, like, every chance I can get.'

'Sophie, two minutes ago you were complaining about having to do chores instead of homework, and now you want to go out for a drive? I said I'd take you for a lesson tomorrow, and I will.'

'Dad –'

'Sophie, that's enough,' he said. 'I'm not putting Rachel through that, or leaving Hannah alone this late while we go for a driving lesson.'

She pulled a face. 'You said it'd only take five minutes.'

'Which isn't long enough to record in the logbook,' he returned. 'Tomorrow I'll take you for a whole hour.'

'But Dad –'

'Drop it, Soph.'

As they backed out of the driveway and turned up the street, the reality of the situation began to sink in for Rachel. Life with Tom would mean taking on one soon-to-be young adult, about to embark on her HSC, with God knows how many issues yet to surface; and one soon-to-be teenager, with all of that ahead of her. Hannah was delightful, but clearly she needed a lot of attention. The prospect felt a little overwhelming.

Tom steered around the corner. 'That went okay,' he said hopefully.

'You think?'

He glanced at her. 'You don't?'

She shrugged.

'On a scale of one to ten?' he persisted.

'You don't want to hear the figures.'

'Rach, come on, it wasn't that bad,' he said. 'You and Hannah were getting on great, and Soph warmed up eventually.'

She could hear a tinge of hurt in his voice. How could she tell him that she found it hard to listen to Hannah's running commentary about her mother? It wasn't as though there was anything wrong with that, it was entirely natural for her to talk about her mother. Rachel just wanted Tom to understand how it felt for her. And as for Sophie, she was lukewarm at best, for about five minutes. It occurred to Rachel that she couldn't talk to anyone about Tom, and now she couldn't talk to Tom about any of this. She suddenly felt very alone.

'Hannah's a sweetheart, Tom,' Rachel said finally, in an effort to mollify him. 'But I was thinking, maybe you should just let it go if Sophie acts up like that again when I'm around.'

'But aren't we trying to behave like normal?' he frowned.

'Yeah . . .'

'Well, I wouldn't let her get away with that kind of behaviour normally, Rach. She's more likely to suspect something if I pussyfoot around her.'

'I guess,' Rachel nodded, thinking about it. 'But maybe she already suspects, maybe that's why she was acting that way. I've never seen her carry on like that.'

'You haven't been around her enough lately, don't take it to heart,' said Tom. 'She runs hot and cold, she can be an absolute angel one minute, and then she turns into a she-devil.'

Rachel didn't believe for a second that Sophie's behaviour this evening was merely due to hormones. But those female hormones brought with them a fair dollop of intuition. Maybe women did overthink things, as Tom had suggested, but at least they actually gave some thought to their feelings, their misgivings, their fears. And Sophie had every reason to be fearful of what Rachel's presence in the house that night signified. She was not wilful or bratty, she was a sixteen-year-old girl whose emotional antennae had been sharpened since the death of her mother. She knew that going to her school formal on her mother's birthday was fraught; she knew that an old friend of her father's coming over for a casual dinner was probably anything but.

'How did she react when you told her I was coming over?' Rachel asked Tom.

He took a moment to answer. 'Oh, she was fine about that. She was worried about her assignment, that's all.'

He had definitely hesitated then. So now he was lying to her, or fudging the truth anyway. Just as she couldn't tell him what upset her tonight, he was not about to tell her what the girls' reaction had been to her coming. They were both only trying to save each other's feelings, but this was not a good development. And Rachel didn't know what to do about it.

They were silent the rest of the way to her place. Tom was probably as wary as she was to risk saying anything else. When he pulled up outside, he cut the engine and turned to her, taking her hands in his.

'It's going to be okay, Rach,' he said. 'We made it past the first step. You know that Chinese saying – a journey of a thousand miles begins with a single step.'

'Goodie, only a thousand miles to go!'

He gave her that slightly hurt look again, so she quickly leaned over to kiss him. And as he responded, and Rachel lost herself in the moment, her doubts drifted away from the forefront of her mind till she was barely even aware of them. Before long they were steaming up the windows.

'I could come up,' he murmured, his lips barely leaving hers, 'if we were quick.'

Rachel pulled back abruptly. 'Are you out of your mind, Tom? Sophie will have the stopwatch on you. Down boy. Home!'

'Okay,' he agreed reluctantly. 'Maybe I can find some time tomorrow to pop over?'

'Tom,' said Rachel, 'you have to take Sophie for that driving lesson, and you need to spend time with Hannah. You and I had last night and most of today, what's left of the weekend is for the girls.'

He sighed. 'You're right, I know.' He held her face in his hands. 'I can't wait till this is all out in the open and we can be together all the time.'

But as she strolled up the driveway to the entrance, Rachel knew it wasn't that simple. She was never going to be able to stay at that house. It was hard enough using Annie's salad bowl, let alone sleeping in her bedroom. In her bed. It didn't seem as though Tom had even thought about any of that. But on the other hand, it was probably very important for the girls to stay in the house, to maintain the memories of their mother. Of course it was. So where did that leave Rachel?

They were on a very long road, of a thousand miles at least; but what was missing from that image was all the debris strewn about that could trip you up, or even block your way altogether, making it impossible to get any further.

Rachel suddenly yearned for their safe little bubble. Maybe it was the only place where they could be a couple, because Rachel was beginning to doubt how they were going to travel in the real world.

The following week

'So, how's Matthew?'

'Who?' Rachel asked. She was distracted. Catherine was calling from her car on her way home from work, so she had her on speaker phone. Rachel hated when she did that. Her voice echoed back at her the whole time, and she felt self-conscious about being broadcast into Catherine's car, like a drive-time radio presenter.

'I was asking after your new boyfriend, Matthew,' Catherine reiterated. 'He hasn't already ditched you, has he?'

'No, just no one calls him Matthew.'

'Well, I certainly will be.'

Of course she would. Catherine was a complete pedant about

calling people by their full name, like it was somehow superior. She used to insist on calling Tom Thomas, until he had to point out to her that his name wasn't Thomas at all, he had actually been christened Tom.

'Is there something specific you were calling about, Catherine?'

'In fact there is. I have had a fabulous idea,' she said. 'You know how we should be making an effort to include Tom, keeping him busy . . .'

Rachel was doing her bit.

'. . . So I was thinking that we should have a night out, book a decent restaurant – you can leave that to me – and you can bring your Matthew as well so we can all meet him.'

Rachel needed a minute to compute that. 'I didn't catch all that, what did you say?'

'We should all go out to dinner one night, and I am including Lexie in this, you'll be pleased to know. But not the children. I'm talking about a sophisticated, adult night out, with partners.'

'And you want to ask Tom along?'

'That's right. And your Matthew.'

Jesus Christ. 'I don't think that's a good idea, Catherine.'

'Why not?'

Because Matthew was the love child of a carpet square and the label off a wine bottle.

'Well, don't you see?' Rachel began, trying to think of a way out of this. 'You want to include Tom in the group . . . but he'll be like the third wheel, or actually the seventh wheel, which is not going to make him feel included, it will probably only make him feel worse.'

'Oh, but I haven't explained the whole scenario,' said Catherine. 'Martin is going overseas on business shortly, for at least a couple of weeks, so I thought that would be the perfect time to do it. You know what it's like when Martin and Scott get together, it's all food talk, I don't think Tom has ever really fitted in with them. So with Martin away, and your Matthew in his place – another lawyer, in fact – it will be a completely new dynamic. And we'll be an even six, Tom won't be the odd one out, I'll be his partner!'

Rachel was dumbfounded. She couldn't imagine how Tom was going to take it.

'Well, um . . . I don't know, I have to see if Matt is free. He's a very busy person.'

'For godsakes Rachel, why do you think I'm calling you a couple of weeks in advance? We've got a lot of busy people to coordinate, but I have a range of dates, so I'm confident we'll find something to suit everyone.'

Great. 'Okay,' she said weakly.

'So do you have a pen? I'll give you the dates. You talk to your Matthew, and I'll call Lexie, and Tom, and we'll narrow it down. This is completely doable, Rachel.'

Oh, it really wasn't.

Catherine pulled her car into the garage and turned off the engine. Today had been a good day, and she was quite charged about her plan. A drink was certainly in order. She gathered up her things and walked through into the house. Martin was sitting reading the paper at the dining-room table, a glass of red and a small bowl of olives at his elbow.

'You haven't started dinner?' she enquired. She was feeling quite upbeat, so she stooped to give him a kiss on the cheek as she placed her briefcase down on the floor.

He turned his head slowly to look at her. 'I wasn't sure what time you'd be home, and Alice wasn't interested. She's eaten already.'

'Not instant noodles again, Martin?' she chided.

'It's all she'll eat.'

'That doesn't mean you should let her have them.' Catherine crossed over to the cabinet to get a glass. 'You shouldn't buy them in the first place.'

Martin sat back in his chair. 'I only buy them because you put them on the list when we run out and she complains. Do you want me to ignore that in future?'

Hmm, he was in a mood. Catherine poured herself a glass of wine from the bottle on the counter. 'Do you want a top-up?'

'Yes, thank you,' he said.

She carried the bottle over and handed it to him, before taking a seat opposite. She took a long drink. Red was not her preferred drop, but it would do for now. She'd open a bottle of white after this.

'I suppose she's been up in her room all afternoon?'

He nodded, topping up his own glass.

'And she won't be doing any study,' said Catherine. 'She'll be on MSN, or Facebook, or whatever, wasting time.'

Martin shrugged disinterestedly.

'This grounding is not going to have the desired effect if she can just hole up in her room, connected with all of her friends anyway.'

He met her eyes directly. 'You have given her internet access, a television, a mobile phone, what do you expect?'

Catherine frowned. 'She needs the internet for her homework.'

'And the television?'

'Well, I'm certainly not going to watch the tripe she wants to watch down here on the main set.'

'So, what are you going to do?' he dismissed with another disinterested shrug.

Catherine considered him. 'What are you so stroppy about?'

He sighed. 'You're always complaining that she spends too much time in her room, online, so do something about it. Restrict her access.'

'How am I supposed to do that? We have wireless internet, she can access it anywhere in the house.'

'You're a strong woman, Catherine, I'm sure you could impose sanctions, you just have to be prepared to enforce them.'

Catherine shook her head with a snigger. 'She's grounded for the entire term, have you forgotten? I think I know how to handle my own daughter.'

'Then don't bring me into it,' he said squarely.

'Fine, duly noted. What is wrong with you this evening, Martin?'

He sighed, picking up his glass. 'Problems at work.'

That was a bore. She hoped he wasn't going to go on about them, but she supposed she should ask at least.

'Anything major?'

'Major doesn't begin to describe —'

'Just get to the point, would you, Martin?' she said, feeling a little uneasy.

'That merger looks like collapsing,' he said flatly.

'Which merger is that?'

'The reason I was going to Singapore next month.'

Catherine's face dropped. 'Is the trip off?'

'More than likely, the way things are going.'

'Well that's no way to deal with it. You obviously need to go over there in person and do something.'

'Catherine, I'm not a rainmaker, you know that. I'm the guy who sorts out the details. At this stage, there will be no details to sort out. And what's worse, if this fails, things aren't looking good for the firm.'

Catherine cared less about the firm than she did about a week or two with Martin out of her hair. 'I think you should insist. Take a delegation over there, show them some balls.'

'It's not that simple, Catherine. I'm more concerned about what's going to happen if things keep going the way they're headed. We rely on the growth of these major markets, and the markets are collapsing like dominoes.'

Catherine certainly didn't need this downer, she'd been having a good day up until now. She stood up. 'You're with one of the major consulting firms on the planet, Martin, it's not going under. You're always such a pessimist.'

And with that she walked smartly over to the fridge and took out a bottle of white. She picked up a fresh glass from the cupboard and headed for the terrace. 'Excuse me, I have to make a call.'

Lexie had everything set when the phone rang. No, don't let it be him! She picked up the phone on the second ring, not wanting it to wake the kids.

'Hello?' she said urgently.

'Hello Lexie, Catherine here.'

She breathed a sigh of relief. 'Oh, hi Catherine. How are you?'

'I'm just fine, thanks,' she returned. 'I'm calling about making a date to get together.'

Lexie wondered if that was Scott's car now. She walked up the hall, listening. 'What was that you said? A date?'

'Yes. You were absolutely right that we have to take care of Tom now, include him, make him feel part of the group.'

'Uhuh.' Lexie opened the front door and peered out. It wasn't Scott after all.

'So, I'm giving everyone plenty of notice, and I'm going to book somewhere really special for us all to go out to dinner.'

Lexie leaned against the doorjamb. 'How special?' she said warily. Special usually meant expensive, in Catherine-speak, and the last thing she needed right now was to give Scott another thing to feel anxious about. She could picture him, sitting in a swanky restaurant, staring at the prices on the menu, trying not to hyperventilate.

'Don't worry,' said Catherine. 'There are quite a few affordable restaurants I have in mind. I just want to make it nice for Tom. For all of us.'

'Okay.'

'So I'm hoping to organise it for a couple of weeks' time.'

Lexie didn't answer, there was a car turning into the street.

'Are you still there, Lexie?'

It was Scott this time. She flew inside, closing the door. 'Um, yes, I'm here, but I have to go, Catherine.'

'All right, just let me give you these dates.'

Jeez. 'Can you put them in an email?' said Lexie.

'You don't always read my emails, Lexie.'

She always read them, she just didn't always answer them. 'I promise I'll check, Catherine. Put all the details in an email and I'll get back to you, I promise.'

'Okay then.'

'I have to go, bye,' she said, hanging up. She scooted down the hall and put the phone back in its base. On second thoughts, she picked it up again and switched it to silent. She didn't want them to be disturbed. If someone really needed to get in touch, if it was really important, like a family emergency, they'd try their mobiles. Lexie dashed over to the table and lit the two taper candles, just as she heard Scott's key in the front door. She smoothed out her hair and her skirt, and stood up straight with a big smile, facing towards the hall and the front door. It swung open and Scott appeared in the doorway. He didn't look up as he stepped into the house and closed the door behind him. But then something must have seemed amiss. No little feet running to meet him, soft music drifting in from the living room, dim lighting. He peered down the hall, and Lexie beamed back at him.

'What's going on here?' he said, as he walked tentatively towards her.

She gave a coy shrug as he came all the way into the room. She had already lit dozens of candles around the room; the table was set with flowers, their good crockery and crystal glasses; dinner was in the oven, and champagne was chilling in an ice bucket.

'Oh shit!' Scott exclaimed.

That wasn't the response Lexie was hoping for.

'Have I forgotten our anniversary?' he asked.

She smiled then, walking up to him and taking his hands in hers. 'Honey, it's only March, we were married in September.'

'Oh, yeah, that's right,' he sighed out. 'Well I know it's not your birthday —'

'Scott, do we need a special occasion to have a nice, adult night together, just the two of us?'

He smiled sheepishly. 'Yeah, these days we do. Where are the kids, by the way?'

'They're already in bed. Riley had swimming lessons after school, and he's always so tired after that, and Mia didn't get her afternoon nap, so they were both falling asleep in their dinner. Don't be cross.'

'Why would I be cross?'

'Well, not getting to see them.'

He gazed down at her with a look in his eyes she hadn't seen in a while. 'You look beautiful, Lex,' he said, leaning closer. 'And you smell beautiful.' He sighed. 'And I smell like a kitchen, and I'm all grimy.'

'Go,' she said, 'have a shower, take your time, relax.'

'Are you sure?' he said, glancing across to the kitchen. 'Something smells good over there as well.'

'It'll keep,' she insisted. 'Go on, take a shower and get out of your work clothes, you'll feel better.'

*

This was all going exactly to plan, Lexie was thrilled. She'd put enough thought into it. She had rung Josh this afternoon to make sure there had been no last-minute hitches and that they would be finishing up at a reasonable time. She didn't put Mia down for a nap, which meant she had to enlist Riley to help keep her awake when she started dozing off in the car seat on the way home from swimming lessons. She wanted to make absolutely sure both of the children would go off to bed early, and they wouldn't hear from them again.

When Scott came back down the stairs, he was wearing one of his best collared shirts and the jeans Lexie had bought him for Christmas.

'Look at you,' she said with a little swoon.

'Well, I wanted to look good for my girl.' He drew her into his arms. 'This was a really nice idea, Lexie, we don't get enough time together.'

'No, we don't,' she murmured as his lips came down on hers and her insides dissolved. He still had it. But there would be plenty of time for all that later, for now she had to stay on task.

She stepped back to look at him. 'Would you like to open the champagne while I serve dinner?'

Lexie had decided to attempt a rather complicated French recipe which involved slow-cooking a piece of beef for most of the day. Sweets were really her specialty, but she always enjoyed a challenge.

'This looks amazing, Lexie,' Scott remarked once they were sitting at the table, their glasses full, their meals in front of them.

'I get a little nervous cooking for you,' she admitted.

'What do you mean?' he asked. 'You cook for me all the time.'

'Hmm, but you usually do the special stuff.'

He cut into the meat and tasted it. 'It's fantastic,' he pronounced.

'Really?'

'Really.'

She smiled widely. 'So, how's work?'

'We don't want to talk about that.'

'Yeah, we do,' Lexie said firmly. 'And that's exactly what we're going to talk about.'

He met her eyes then. 'What are you saying?'

'I want to talk about the business, Scott.'

'Let's not spoil such a lovely night.'

'We don't have to spoil it. I just want to know what's going on. I'm your wife, I want to share it with you. Now, the kids aren't around, and we've got a nice meal in front of us, and a glass of wine, so don't you spoil it by having a pout.'

He took a deep breath in and out. 'All right. What do you want to know?'

'Well, have you heard any more about the rent going up?'

'The owner's got his accountant checking the books before he makes a decision.'

She nodded. 'Okay, so have you thought about what you'll do if he does decide to increase it?'

'Lexie, I really don't want to worry you with this.'

'Scott, please, I want to know.'

He shrugged. 'We might have to open seven days, Lex.'

'No,' she said flatly. 'That's not an option. You cannot work seven days a week, Scott, we'll have no family life. It's not acceptable.'

'We might not have a choice.'

'There's always a choice.' She took a breath. 'I could go out to work.'

'No!'

'But if things are that bad, it's a better alternative than you working seven days,' she insisted.

'But I don't want you to have to go to work while the kids are young.'

She glared at him. 'How very 1950s of you, Scott. So you'd rather I'm alone in the house with the kids, seven days a week, scrubbing floors –'

'No,' he said, raising his voice. 'For Chrissakes, Lexie, I wish you didn't have to do any of that.'

'Scott, you have to stop treating me like I'm some fragile china doll.'

'I know you're not fragile, I was in the room when you gave birth, remember?' He gazed at her across the table. 'You're the strongest person I know, Lexie.'

She stared at him. 'Me? You think I'm strong?'

He nodded. 'You grew up with everything, and you gave it

all up to be with me. You moved into this little house, we had no money, you patched things together and painted and put up with crap, and you never complained. You're always so happy. And I know that all you want to be is a mum, it's more important to you than anything. I can't give you a big house, Lexie, and trips overseas, but if I work hard I can at least give you that, the chance to live your life the way you want to.'

Lexie's heart felt so full she thought it might burst.

'Oh, Scott,' she said, getting up and coming around the table to him. She held his face in her hands, looking into his eyes. She was barely taller than him even though he was sitting down. 'You're wrong, you know, or at least partly wrong,' she said, lacing her fingers through his hair. 'Being a mum isn't more important to me than anything – you and the kids are what's most important to me. Don't you know that?' She leaned in to kiss him, and he drew his arms around her, holding her close.

She slipped down onto his lap. 'We have to find a way through this together, honey,' she went on. 'So no more heroics. I'm your partner, you have to share it all with me, the good and the bad.'

'I was only trying to protect you,' he said.

'I know that, and I love you for it, but I'm not a child, Scott.' She brushed her lips against his. 'And I want to help, I want to get involved in the café,' she said, breathily. 'Isn't there some way?'

She planted a trail of little kisses all the way down to his neck as she felt for the buttons of his shirt, slowly undoing them. Scott released a moan, suddenly taking her face in his hands and kissing her urgently.

'There's dessert,' Lexie murmured against his lips.

'Later.'

April

'Rachel,' said Lloyd, standing directly behind her, so close that the hairs on the back of her neck stood on end.

She swivelled her chair around, pushing it away from him at the same time.

'My office,' he said, his tone grave, before turning on his heel and striding away.

Rachel groaned. He was such a drama queen, so full of his own importance, even though he wasn't. Important. She stood up and traipsed after him, past the rows of cubicles. When she got to his office she walked straight in and stood inside the door. He was already at his desk, pretending to be completely engrossed in something on the computer screen. He made a few clicks on the mouse and then turned to look at her.

'Take a seat.'

Jeez, how long was this going to take? Rachel sat down heavily, crossing her legs.

He rested his elbows on the desk in front of him, lacing his fingers together. 'As part of my constant and ongoing commitment to improving efficiency at Handy Home Health Care, I have lately undertaken random performance reviews . . .'

And been studying self-help management manuals, obviously.

'To cut to the chase, quite frankly, Rachel, your performance leaves much to be desired. Since the implementation of the new invoicing procedure, your rate of errors has not decreased in line with the rest of the staff. Your turnover is tardy, your statistics and record-keeping are patchy at best, and your phone manner is often . . . disinterested, to say the least. And while I do not wish to be a tyrant about these things, you have been taking too many personal calls. In summary, your performance is well below the standard we strive for at Handy Home Health Care.'

Rachel paused for a moment, taking all that in. 'You're right,' she said finally.

'Pardon?' he blinked. He was probably not prepared for total acquiescence.

'You're absolutely right, Lloyd,' said Rachel. 'I haven't been doing my job to the best of my abilities, and you know why I think that is?'

'Why?'

'Because I just don't like it. I don't like the work, I don't like the place, I don't really like many of the people. So I think it's time for me to move on.'

'I beg your pardon?' Lloyd was blinking furiously now.

'I quit.'

'You can't just quit.'

'Yeah, I can. I can just quit.' Why hadn't she thought of this before? She could already feel the proverbial weight lifting.

'But you are required to give notice,' he said pompously.

'Of course. No problem. Two weeks, isn't it?'

Lloyd was scowling at her from across the desk. 'On second thoughts, that won't be necessary,' he said. 'If you don't want to be here, far be it from me to keep you. In fact,' he said, getting to his feet, 'I would like you to leave immediately. I will personally escort you to your desk, you can have five minutes to clear it out and vacate the building.'

Rachel frowned at him. 'What, are you worried I'm going to steal sensitive client information —'

'No further discussion will be entered into. Please proceed to your desk, Ms Halliday.'

'Lloyd, are you trying to pull a swiftie and fire me instead so you don't have to let me serve my notice?'

'Incorrect,' he replied crisply. 'I always adhere to the rules and regulations as set out with the utmost stringency. You will receive the appropriate remuneration, but your services are no longer required in the office. Your continuing presence here will only be bad for morale.'

Rachel walked out of the building ten minutes later. She felt free, unencumbered. She wasn't even carrying the infamous cardboard box under her arm, like a character in a movie. When she went to clear out her desk she realised there was nothing there to take. She wasn't going to steal the stationery, she couldn't anyway with Lloyd breathing down her neck. She had no photos, no personal knickknacks; there was a packet of Tic Tacs, a tube of hand cream that she never used, and a magazine in the top drawer, all of which fitted quite easily into her handbag.

So what now? It was after eleven, maybe she could go into the city and meet Tom for lunch? She thought about surprising him, but if he wasn't available she didn't want to schlep all the way into the city for nothing. And it's not as though she could just walk straight up into his office, she'd have to call him from outside the building, so it wouldn't be much of a surprise anyway. She took out her phone and dialled his mobile.

'Tom Macklin.'

'Hi, it's me.'

'Oh, sorry, honey, I didn't look at the screen. Hey, how are you?'

'Unemployed.'

'What?'

'I quit my job.'

'Really?'

'Yeah, really.' And the reality was just hitting her.

'Are you okay?' asked Tom. 'What happened?'

'Picture me as a camel and Lloyd piling on the final straw.'

'Where are you now, you sound like you're out on the street?'

'I am,' she confirmed. 'He was kind enough to escort me from the building.'

'Rach, did you quit or were you fired?'

'No, I quit, but Lloyd took it to heart.'

'He has to let you serve out your notice.'

'I know that,' said Rachel. 'It's all covered, he just doesn't want me in the office, bad for morale. I don't know how morale in there could get much worse, mind you.'

'Are you sure you're okay?' he asked.

'Yeah, I'm fine,' she assured him. 'It's time, I've been wasting away there.'

'You've been wasted there, I know that much.'

She smiled. 'Listen, what are you doing for lunch? I could come in and meet you in the city.'

'Damn, sorry, hun,' said Tom. 'I've got a lunch meeting in . . .' he must have been checking his watch '. . . half an hour.'

'Never mind, thought it was worth a try.'

'What are you going to do?' he asked.

'Whatever I feel like, I suppose.'

'I'll call you later, maybe I can leave work early, after the meeting, that'd give me an hour or two before I have to pick up Hannah.'

'Okay.'

'I'll see what I can do.'

*

Rachel caught the bus towards home, but as it pulled in to Bondi she decided to get out there. She had time to kill, she could get some lunch, wander round the shops – though she'd better not buy anything. It was all very well to throw in her job, but she still needed an income. She barely had any savings to speak of, and she had rent to pay. And bills. And she had to eat. She hesitated as she walked past a noodle bar. Maybe she shouldn't buy lunch after all.

But she was being ridiculous; she had another few weeks' wages coming, between her severance pay and leave owing, and that gave her plenty of time to find a job. She could probably walk straight into another admin position, but she didn't think she could stand it. She still didn't know what she really wanted to do with the rest of her life, or even the next part of it, but what she did know was that she needed to do something different right now.

And then she saw it. It was like a sign. Actually, it was a sign, propped in the window of one of those juice bars that seemed to be everywhere these days.

**HELP WANTED
APPLY WITHIN**

Half an hour later Rachel sat opposite 'Mel' – according to her name badge – as she read through her application. She was the manager, as well as the owner, Rachel was pretty sure. She looked about her own age, quite short but sturdy, with intense dark eyes and what Rachel assumed was a wild mane of dark hair tucked underneath her cap, on account of the frizzy curls escaping at the back.

'Your experience is all office administration,' Mel remarked after a while.

'Yes, that's true, more recently,' said Rachel. 'But prior to that I travelled extensively for many years, working as a waitress and a bartender, right across Europe, in holiday resorts, all kinds of places. I can do this job.'

'But why would you want to?'

Rachel blinked. 'I'm sorry?'

Mel looked at her squarely. 'This is a casual position, the pay's not great. With your experience you could get a better paying office job with some kind of future. I own and operate this franchise, and I employ casual staff to support me. But it's my show. There's absolutely nowhere to go here – you make juice, you sell it, you clean up afterwards.'

'Suits me,' said Rachel. 'I just left an office job that I hated by the end. I'd like to do something completely different, in a more relaxed environment.'

'Hey, don't let the ads fool you,' said Mel. 'The ones with all the zany people dancing around, juggling fruit and laughing hysterically. We get busy, flat out in fact, especially over holidays and weekends.'

'Of course, I understand that.' Rachel paused, thinking about how to explain herself. 'The thing is, I'm tired of pushing papers around, sitting at a desk, sealed up in an airconditioned box all day. I want to work somewhere with a bit of life, and energy, and deal with people face to face instead of on the phone or through the computer. I'm desperate for a change of scenery, and look at this,' she said with a sweep of her arm. 'I can see the ocean from the counter, I can smell it! I'm sure it's busy, hard work, I'm not afraid of hard work. But I can't help thinking it has to be less soul-destroying than what I've been doing.'

Mel had listened closely to her spiel, and now she seemed to be mulling it over. 'Can you do weekends?' she asked finally.

'I can do absolutely any time.'

She frowned then. 'Have you just broken up with a boyfriend?'

'No, not at all.' And then it struck Rachel, she could actually mention Tom to this woman. She'd be able to talk about him freely here. It was suddenly the most attractive thing about the job. 'Actually, I have a wonderful boyfriend.'

'No need to skite.'

Rachel looked at her. 'Is that going to go against me?'

A little smile crept onto her face then. 'Nuh, I'm not that bitter and twisted. Though, to be honest, I'm a little sick of hiring young things with their long legs and their tits up to here.' She cupped her hands in front of her. 'And always with the lip balm, these girls, what's that about?'

'I believe it's one of the lesser known effects of global warming,' said Rachel. 'I've heard they're going to establish a lip dryness index, or LDI, to help predict the rate of icecap melt.'

'Ah, now that makes sense,' Mel nodded. 'That's why they're texting all the time, sending their data back to the lab.'

'Obviously.'

Mel made a face. 'Drives me mad,' she said. 'You don't text, do you?'

'Well, I have been known to text,' said Rachel. 'But I'm not a habitual texter. I control it, I don't let it control me.'

'Very good,' said Mel. She leaned forwards. 'Look, it's only a casual position, so it's going to be up to you. You work hard, the customers like you . . .'

'Stay off the lip balm . . .'

'And the texting,' she nodded, 'and you'll get as many shifts as you want.'

Rachel smiled. 'When can I start?'

Mel didn't want to throw her in the deep end by putting her on over the weekend, so she told her to come in Tuesday. Mondays were quiet, so Mel took the day off and left the running to her senior.

'I say "senior" lightly, she's all of twenty-three, but she's got a brain in her head at least. She's doing a Masters degree so her time's flexible. Before she came along, I hadn't had a day off in three years.'

After she left Mel at the juice bar, Rachel decided to take a stroll down onto the beach, conscious of a distinct spring in her step. This morning she'd caught that awful smelly bus to that awful stuffy building, with no idea it would be the last time she was ever going to have to do that. She felt like running and jumping into the ocean, but unfortunately she wasn't dressed for it, and Bondi was a little too public for skinny-dipping.

Her phone started to ring and she fished it out of her bag and flipped it open. It was Tom.

'Hi!' she almost sang.

'Hi, I'm on my way, are you home yet?'

'No, I'm at Bondi.'

'Oh, okay, whereabouts? I'll pick you up.'

She didn't feel like going home. 'You know, Tom, I've just come down onto the beach, it's really lovely. Why don't you meet me here?'

There was a pause. 'You don't want to go back to your place? I've only got an hour or so.'

She bristled a little. 'So this is just a booty call?'

'What? No,' he insisted. 'I just thought you'd be worried about being seen out in public together.'

Sure you were. 'Look, it's not like we're going to do anything, we'll just go for a walk.'

Was that a sigh? 'Okay, I'll see you soon.'

Rachel hung around where she had a view of the carpark, and soon enough she saw Tom's car pulling into a space. She waved when he got out and looked around. He spotted her and waved back, then he dipped down again out of her line of sight. He was probably taking off his shoes. Rachel ambled slowly back towards the ramp onto the beach, till she saw him appear again, taking the steps down from the carpark. He crossed the esplanade and started down the ramp, barefoot.

'Hey,' she said, smiling.

He looked awkward, glancing around as he came closer. 'You're sure no one's going to see us?'

'So what if they do?' she said. 'We're friends going for a walk.'

He shrugged. 'I would have liked to kiss you at least.'

'Nice to see you too,' Rachel said loudly, reaching up to offer him her cheek.

He bent to kiss it. 'Not quite what I had in mind,' he muttered.

'But all you're going to get.' They started to walk across the sand towards the shoreline. 'So guess what?' she began.

He looked at her, waiting.

'I got a job,' she said proudly.

'What?'

'I got a job,' she repeated.

He looked confused. 'I don't understand. You just quit your job and you've already found another one?'

'I know, isn't it great?' she said. 'I was walking along the street, right here in Bondi, and I saw a "help wanted" notice in a window, so I went in and applied.'

'What kind of job are you talking about?' he frowned.

'At the juice bar, just up there,' she said with a backwards wave of her arm.

He stopped then to face her. 'You're kidding?'

'No,' she said simply. 'The woman who owns it seems really nice, we clicked right away, and she gave me the job.'

'At a juice bar?'

'Uhuh,' Rachel nodded, walking off again.

He caught up with her. 'And that's really what you want to do?'

She shrugged. 'For the meantime.'

He took hold of her arm to stop her. 'Rachel, don't you think you're rushing into this? How will you ever find something you really want to do if all your time's taken up working at a juice bar?'

'But that's the beauty of it,' she explained. 'I'll just be a casual, so I'll have plenty of free time to work out what I want to do, apply for jobs, or maybe I'll even do some training, I don't know. But in the meantime I can pay the rent.'

'If money's the problem, I can help you out, Rach.'

She pulled a face. 'No way, Tom. I can support myself.'

'Working at a juice bar?'

'Yeah, for now.' Again, Rachel turned to walk on down towards the water. He was beginning to irritate her. If he said 'At a juice bar?' with that tone of disbelief one more time . . .

'Won't this mean you'll have to work weekends?' Tom asked as he fell in beside her again.

'Of course, that's their busiest time.'

'What about our time?' he said pointedly.

'Well, maybe you'll have to work around me for a change.'

'What's that supposed to mean?'

'Just what I said.'

'Rach, I have to work full-time, I don't have a choice. You and I have barely enough time together as it is; if you work weekends, when are we going to see each other?'

'Don't worry,' she said. She was really getting annoyed now. 'It closes at six. I'll still be available nights for your booty calls.'

They had reached the shore and Tom turned to look at her. 'Okay, that's the second time you've used that expression, Rach,' he said. 'What's the matter?'

She sighed. 'You know how miserable I was in that job, Tom. I would have thought you'd be happy for me.'

'I am, really, I'm glad you quit,' he said. 'I just don't know why you're in such a rush to take the first thing that comes along.'

'I'm not in such a rush.'

He gave her a dubious look. 'Rach, you quit your job and took another on the same day, all on a whim.'

'It wasn't on a whim,' she defended.

'Oh, I see,' he said, folding his arms. 'So after careful research of the job market, you decided that becoming a casual at a juice bar was a good career move?'

'Jesus, you sound like Catherine,' she sniped. 'What would you prefer I do, Tom? Sell my soul to work for a faceless corporation, even when it goes against every principle I ever held and I hate every minute of it?'

He glared at her. 'I can't do much about that right now, you know that. I don't have the choice to flit about and take a job like I'm still a backpacker without a care in the world. I have a family to support.'

'Fine, I understand that. I wasn't the one who started criticising you for your choices.'

'I wasn't criticising you,' he insisted. 'I was only saying you shouldn't rush into this, take your time to find something that works for all of us.'

She shook her head and gave a wry laugh. 'You really think we have a hope of finding an arrangement that works for all of us? Do you have any idea just how complicated this is?' She paused, giving that a moment to sink in. 'I can't put my life on hold while everyone else sorts themselves out. I might just do what suits me for a change.'

'For a change?' he scoffed. 'Are you kidding? You've always done exactly what suits you, Rachel, you've never taken anyone else into consideration.'

'Yeah well, that's because I haven't had anyone in my life who gives a damn about what I do.'

'You do now,' he said loudly.

She stared up at him, breathing hard.

'Look, I know what this is about. You're afraid –'

'Don't psychoanalyse me, Tom.'

'I was there, don't forget, for the missed calls,' he went on, 'the forgotten birthdays, the cancelled visits. I never left you alone then, and I'm not going to leave you now.' He paused, gazing steadily at her. 'I know this is hard right now, Rach, but it's temporary, and we will get through it. I'm not going anywhere, Rachel. I'll always be here for you.'

She was trembling. 'As long as I fit in with you. As long as I'm available at your beck and call.'

'Rachel –'

'It's true, Tom, and I'm over it. I'm getting on with my life.'

'And where do I come into that?'

She took a breath. 'I don't know.'

'What are you saying?'

'I honestly don't know,' she repeated, raising her voice and her hands at the same time. Tom was just staring at her, he looked like he was in shock or something. Rachel couldn't stand it, she turned abruptly and set off at a brisk pace along the shoreline.

'Rachel!' he called.

She stopped but she didn't look back at him.

'Don't just walk away,' he pleaded. 'You can't say something like that and just walk away.'

'We can't talk about this now, Tom,' she called back over her shoulder. 'You have to go to pick up Hannah.'

'Then let me drive you home, at least.'

She turned halfway around. 'I'm not going home.'

'Where are you going?'

'Wherever I feel like.'

She walked off again, faster than before. What the hell just happened? She hadn't planned any of that, it had just come out. And now she felt sick in the stomach. She didn't look back, but she knew he wasn't following her. He couldn't, he did have to go pick up Hannah. There wouldn't be enough time to have it out, they didn't have that luxury.

Eventually Rachel did look back, and she could just make him out, striding back up the steps to the carpark. Her heart cramped uncomfortably in her chest as she turned and walked on, watching the waves lap onto the shore ahead of her. Why did he have to bring up all that stuff about her parents, it had nothing to do with anything. Yes, Tom had been there for her when they'd let her down, she'd cried on his shoulder, he'd even cancelled a date one night because he didn't want to leave her alone.

But he was the one making excuses, pinning the problem onto her so that he didn't have to admit how impossible this situation was. It was crowding in on her, and she had no one she could talk to about it. Rachel felt she'd go crazy if she went home now to sit alone in her empty flat. But what were her alternatives? Talking to Catherine would be inviting a lecture; she judged, she had no compunction whatsoever telling Rachel exactly what to do, and she fully expected her to follow her advice to the letter. There was always Lexie, but apart from the fact that Rachel wouldn't go anywhere near her place right now, Lexie was not someone Rachel felt she could pour her heart out to, not about something like this. Though in truth, she wouldn't be pouring her heart out to anyone – that was the whole problem, she couldn't.

So she might just as well go to Catherine's. At least she'd be sure to get a drink there.

Half an hour later Rachel rang Catherine's doorbell. She was unlikely to be home yet, it was still too early, so she supposed she'd have to camp out on the front porch. But then she heard footsteps approaching and the door swung open. It was Alice. Her face lit up, and Rachel felt like crying.

'Hi Rachel! What are you doing here?'

She swallowed. 'Well, just passing . . . I guess your mum's not home yet?'

'No, but come in,' she said. 'She'll be home soon.'

Rachel stepped into the hall and Alice gave her a hug. 'I haven't seen you in ages.'

'And I haven't seen this new "do",' she said, giving Alice's hair a tweak.

She pulled a sheepish face. 'I suppose Mum told you all about it.'

'What do you think?' Rachel considered her. 'It's kinda cool. I think you've pulled it off.'

'Mum hates it.'

'You didn't actually expect her to like it, did you?'

Alice smiled. 'I'm glad you're here. I get so bored since I've been imprisoned for the term of my natural life.' She started down the hall. 'Do you want a drink or something? Mum always has wine in the fridge.'

Rachel would have loved nothing more than a glass of wine, but somehow she didn't think it was appropriate to sit here drinking in the company of a seventeen year old. 'Just water'll be fine, thanks.'

She sat up at the kitchen island bench and Alice got them both a bottle of water out of the fridge, handing one to Rachel as she perched herself on a stool.

'So what's the goss?' said Alice.

'Ah, well, lots actually. I quit my job and got a new one, all on the same day.'

'Awesome.'

'I know, I rock.'

Alice giggled. 'What's your new job?'

'I'm going to be working down at the juice bar at Bondi Beach.'

'That is so totally cool!' Alice exclaimed, her eyes wide. 'I love that place, everyone from school wants to work there.'

'Well, now you have someone on the inside, I'll see what I can do.'

She giggled again.

Rachel took a swig of her water. 'So, what's the goss with you?'

She groaned. 'Zilch. I'm in Year 12 and I'm grounded. I totally have no life.'

'No boyfriend I should know about?' Rachel raised an eyebrow.

'Sure, like I'd have a boyfriend.'

'What are you talking about?' Rachel chided. 'You're gorgeous, I'm thinking you must be carrying around a big stick to beat them off all day.'

She pulled a face. 'There's no way I'm going to have a boyfriend until I'm out of here.'

'What do you mean?'

'I wouldn't bring a guy home here, can you imagine the way Mum would go on?' Alice shuddered. 'She thinks she's a MILF, and she so isn't, she's too highbrow. MILFs dress like their teenage daughters, and they're totally embarrassing anyway.'

'I thought it was cool if your mum was considered a MILF?'

'No way,' Alice shook her head. 'Gross fifteen-year-old boys like MILFs, and trampy Paris Hilton–type girls, because they're like role models of what they want to be when they grow up. Everyone else thinks they're lame as.'

Alice had a good head on her shoulders, Catherine should appreciate that.

'Well, at least you have a lot of time to study while you're in lock-up,' said Rachel. 'How's it going?'

She shrugged. 'I just can't wait for it to be over.'

'Do you have any idea what you want to do?'

'Kinda. I'd like to do Communications, but Mum says it's the "BA of the new century". She thinks it's like, totally worthless and I'll just end up working at McDonald's.'

Rachel considered her. 'What would you want to do with a Communications degree?'

'I dunno . . .' Alice screwed up her face.

'Come on, your dream job. If someone said you could do whatever you wanted to do, no restrictions, what would it be?'

She squirmed on her stool. 'Seriously, I don't know.'

But Rachel noticed that her cheeks were flushed and she couldn't look her in the eye. 'Yes you do,' she urged. 'Come on, you can tell me.'

Alice looked at her. 'You won't say anything to Mum?'

This was delicate. 'As long as it's not prostitution or drug-running.'

'Rachel!' she squealed, laughing.

'Come on, out with it.'

She took a deep breath. 'Okay, but you're not allowed to laugh.'

'I wouldn't laugh at you, Alice,' Rachel said seriously.

She bit her lip. 'Well, I like to write.'

'Really?'

'See, you think I'm totally lame.'

'No I don't,' Rachel insisted. 'Why would you think that?'

'It's a total wank to say you want to be a writer.'

'Not if you can write. Can you?'

'I dunno,' she shrugged.

'Do you do much writing?'

'Some.'

'Show me.'

'No way, Rachel!' she exclaimed.

'Why not?'

'It'd be *so* embarrassing.'

'But if you want to be a writer, someone's going to have to read your work eventually. So start with me. I can't write to save my life, but I read heaps, so I wouldn't criticise you because I could do better, but I can tell you if it's any good as a reader.'

Alice gave her a doubtful look. 'You wouldn't tell me, you'd just say it was good.'

'No I wouldn't.'

'You so totally would. You're too nice, Rachel.'

She laughed. 'I'm *so* not. I'm like, a total bitch.'

Alice laughed then. 'You so totally are not.'

'The thing is, I would be honest,' Rachel said seriously. 'I promise.'

Alice was looking at her curiously. She nearly had her.

'And if I don't think it's any good, then we never speak of this again. We never had this conversation.'

'Okay,' she agreed. 'But you can't tell anyone, no matter what you think. And if you don't like it, just don't say anything. And if you go all gushy, then I'm going to know you're making it up.'

'Deal.'

Rachel followed Alice up to her room and sat on the bed while she scrolled through files on her laptop, umming and aahing and pulling faces, nearly showing her something about a dozen times, then changing her mind at the last second. Rachel sat patiently; she knew if she pushed her there was every chance she would change her mind.

Finally Alice seemed decided. 'Okay. Here it is, but I so totally can't watch you while you read it. I'll be in the bathroom.'

She thrust the laptop at Rachel and jumped off the bed, darting off to the bathroom and closing the door.

Rachel settled herself amongst the cushions and began to read. It was heavy on the typical teenage angst, but what else was she going to write about? It's not as though she'd travelled the world or had a baby or a great love. Though there was a fragment about a faceless father which Rachel found quite poignant.

But it was evident that she could write. She was only young yet, she needed to develop confidence in her voice, and she needed a good editor. But it was honest. And it was funny. It was really funny, and clever. That was what struck Rachel most of all.

She got up off the bed and went over to the bathroom, knocking lightly on the door.

'Yes?' came the tentative response.

Rachel pushed the door open. Alice was sitting in the corner, on the tiled floor, hugging her knees to her. Rachel needed to put her out of her misery.

'Hey sweetie,' she said. 'I hate to be the one to break it to you ... But guess what, you can write.'

'You're just saying that,' she said in a small voice.

'No, I'm not,' Rachel said plainly. 'I promised, didn't I?'

Alice stared at her.

'Didn't I?'

She gave her a faint nod.

'So do you trust me?'

She nodded again.

'You know what I liked most about it?' said Rachel, not waiting for a response. 'It's really funny, it's poignant and sweet, but it's really funny. You've got your own voice, Alice, and as far as I understand, that's the most important thing for a writer to have.'

Alice allowed the tiniest trace of a smile to creep onto her face.

'I'm trying to remember something we talked about that night Sophie and the Macklins were here,' Rachel went on, leaning against the vanity cabinet. 'There's a unit in the HSC where you can do a creative piece, is that right?'

'Yeah,' she nodded.

'You didn't think you were good enough?'

She shrugged. 'My teacher wanted me to do it.'

'Then why didn't you?'

Alice groaned. 'Because then Mum would have had to read it.'

'I think if she read anything like this she'd be very impressed.'

'No she wouldn't. She'd want to analyse it, and edit it, and she'd be asking me what I meant by this or that. I can write what I really want to write if I don't have to think about showing it to her.'

Alice definitely had a point, Catherine would tend to be hypercritical, and overanalyse, which Rachel imagined could be crippling for a young writer. She wished Catherine could see that she'd get a lot further with Alice if she just backed off a little.

'Can I ask you something, Rachel?'

'Sure.'

'Do you think Mum might be going through menopause?'

'What?' said Rachel. 'God, I hope not, we're too young for that.'

'That's what I thought,' she sighed.

'Why do you ask?'

'Just the way she's been acting. I mean, she's always been a control freak, but lately she's gotten heaps worse. I can't do anything right any more. She's just so critical. Some of the girls at school are going through the same thing, but their mums are older. I just wondered if because she had me so young, and she didn't have any more babies, she might go through it earlier?'

'I don't think that's how it works, chook.' Rachel thought about it. 'You're right about the same age as she was when she had you, you know. Maybe it's stirring up old feelings for her.'

'About how I ruined her life?'

'No, you were the only good thing to come out of the whole sorry business. Don't you ever forget it.'

Just then they heard the front door.

Alice's eyes widened. 'That's Mum,' she gasped. 'You can't say anything about the writing, you promised.'

'Don't worry, I'm not going to,' she assured her. 'But I hope one day you will. You might be surprised by the reaction.'

'Alice, are you up there?' Catherine called a moment later as they both appeared at the top of the stairs. She frowned. 'Rachel, what are you doing here?'

'I had the afternoon off, so I thought I'd drop in,' she said, starting down the stairs.

'I'm going back to my homework now,' said Alice, turning away.

'Drink?' Catherine asked rhetorically.

'Why not,' said Rachel, following her into the kitchen.

'So why have you got the afternoon off?' Catherine asked absently, opening the fridge.

'I quit my job.'

That stopped her in her tracks. She turned around. 'You quit? That's fantastic. This definitely calls for a drink!' She clapped her hands together. 'Now we can find you a decent job.'

'I got a job already,' said Rachel.

Catherine frowned at her. 'When did you quit?'

'Today.'

'So did you already have a job lined up?'

'No, I got the job today as well.'

'Okay.' She slid a bottle out of the fridge and closed the door, turning to face Rachel. 'From the beginning.'

And so she related the events of the day, while Catherine proceeded to open the bottle and pour champagne into two glasses, and finally slam the bottle down on the bench as Rachel got to the punchline.

'A juice bar!' she exclaimed. 'You have got to be kidding me, Rachel.'

'What's so bad about that?'

'Well, for one thing, you're not a teenage girl.'

'That actually worked in my favour.'

'It's a juice bar, what kind of career path are you on? I've never known anyone to work their way down.'

Rachel pulled a face. 'Look, Catherine, I need an income, and this won't be regular hours, I won't be travelling as far, and it'll give me time to figure out what I want to do. And I won't go into debt in the meantime.'

'So it's only temporary?'

'I don't see myself retiring there.'

Catherine shook her head as she picked up her glass. 'Well, at least I'll drink to you getting away from that other place.'

'Thank you,' said Rachel as they clinked glasses.

'Let's go out onto the terrace,' Catherine suggested.

Having a drink at Catherine's was like going to a nice bar: she always had good wine and incredibly good nibbles. When they were seated at the outdoor table, the champagne chilling in a bucket beside them and a plate of antipasto between them, Catherine resumed her line of questioning.

'Does your Matthew know about this new job yet?'

Rachel hesitated. Maybe she could talk about Tom after all, using his alias. Though she would have to be careful.

She nodded. 'He's not very happy about it, he doesn't like the idea of me working on weekends.'

'I can understand that.'

'Yeah, well, it isn't very fair. He wants me available at the drop of a hat whenever he has a free hour he can fit me in.'

Catherine frowned. 'I thought you said he was with legal aid?'

Rachel looked up. 'Yeah, so?'

'One thing that comes with the low pay is regular hours at least,' she said. 'Why can he only give you an hour here and there?'

Oh bugger. 'It's complicated.'

Catherine's jaw dropped. 'Oh my God, he's not married, is he?'

'No,' Rachel assured her. 'But he was, until relatively recently, and there are kids involved, so we have to be sensitive.'

Catherine was listening to her, Rachel could almost see the cogs turning in her brain.

'Is it really over, do you think?' she asked.

'Oh, it's really over, she's not coming back.'

'So *she* was the one who left?'

Rachel nodded, this was getting weird. She drained her glass, and reached for the bottle.

'Did he know it was coming?' Catherine persisted.

Rachel shook her head, filling her glass.

'So it was a shock?'

'I guess,' she said, passing the bottle to Catherine. 'Yeah, it was a shock.'

'He was still in love with her then?'

Rachel nodded faintly. She hadn't thought about it quite like that before. But of course Tom was still in love with Annie; he had to be, feelings don't just evaporate. Could someone be in love with two people at the same time? She picked up her glass and gulped down half of it.

'God, Rachel,' said Catherine, refilling her glass. 'I don't know why you'd choose to get caught up in such a mess.'

She stared down at the paving. 'Because I love him.'

'You hardly know him.'

'I knew him years ago, remember?'

Catherine stuck the bottle back in the ice bucket. 'I've never heard you talk about him before and suddenly he's the love of your life?'

'Maybe,' she said quietly.

Catherine was watching her. 'How does he feel about you?'

'He says he loves me.'

She shook her head. 'I don't know, Rachel, this sounds like serious rebound territory to me.'

Rachel could feel a lump rising in her throat. Catherine was right, that's exactly what it was. Good old Rachel, a safe harbour to sit out a patch of rough weather. 'So what should I do?'

'Don't ask me,' Catherine shrugged. 'I can't tell you what to do.'

'What are you talking about, you always tell me what to do,' Rachel insisted, her voice breaking. 'You have to tell me what to do, I've been dealing with this all on my own, and someone just has to tell me what to do.'

'Hey,' Catherine said, reaching over and covering Rachel's hand with her own. 'It's not like you to get so emotional.'

Rachel sniffed, shrugging.

Catherine considered her thoughtfully. 'And you're not someone who's easily infatuated either. I never remember you having a crush all the way through high school.'

Rachel was wondering where she was going with this.

'You really do love him, don't you?'

She nodded. She really did. 'What am I going to do?'

'Hang on to him for all you're worth,' she said plainly.

Rachel wiped a hand across her eyes. 'You think so?'

'I do. I mean, it's going to be a bumpy ride, and I'm not saying it'll work out. Chances are it probably won't.'

'Then why should I risk it?'

'Because it makes life worthwhile,' Catherine declared. 'You know, Rachel, come to think of it, that's your whole problem. You won't take risks.'

Rachel could smell a lecture coming on.

'Oh, I know you looked like the big adventurer taking off overseas,' Catherine went on, 'but I always knew you were just avoiding real life. It was easier than trying to figure out what you were going to do with yourself,' she added. 'And Sean was the classic risk-free choice, but that backfired because he nearly bored you to death. All the jobs you've had, including this new one, they're all about playing it safe, doing something you can't possibly fail at.' She shook her head. 'You know, a lot of people with your background would channel their feelings of, I don't know, is it abandonment? Neglect, perhaps? Anyway, they would either become ambitious and driven, or go to the other extreme and their lives would be complete trainwrecks. But you've gone another way entirely, you consistently fly under the radar. It's very interesting psychodynamics.'

'Well, I'm glad you find my case so intriguing,' Rachel said dryly. 'You still haven't convinced me why I should stick with, um . . . Matt, when apparently it's inevitable I'm just going to get hurt.'

'I didn't say it was inevitable,' she corrected her. 'The fact is, you're already in too deep, you can't save yourself by jumping ship now. I mean, if you did get out, this minute, it would hurt, am I right?'

Rachel nodded.

'But there is a chance it'll all work out, so you can't give up, because what if it's your only chance?' She picked up her glass. 'Let me tell you, you'd regret that for the rest of your life.'

'Is that how you think about James?' Rachel asked.

'Oh, my God, why have we suddenly switched over to the history channel?'

'You started it,' Rachel reminded her. 'I was just wondering if he was your only chance.'

She shook her head. 'Don't be crazy, Rachel, I was a child.'

'Still, have you ever been in love since, like you were with him?'

'I was a child,' she repeated, slowly and insistently. 'I'm not denying I had some very intense feelings, but it was teenage hormones, sheer infatuation. What the hell do you know about anything when you're seventeen? You only have to look at Alice; if she told me she was in love now I'd take it with a grain of salt.'

'Does she ever ask about him?'

'About who?'

'About her father.'

'Not any more. She was curious around twelve or so, for a couple of years, but then she lost interest again.'

Rachel was pretty sure she hadn't. 'What did you tell her?'

'You know the story.'

'I know the real story, but you didn't tell her that.' Rachel had long been sworn to complete and utter secrecy; she was under strict instructions never to breathe a word of it to Alice, and if Alice ever broached the subject with her, to direct her to her mother for answers. 'I don't think you ever told me the story you gave her.'

'If you didn't know, you didn't have to lie,' said Catherine.

'But I did know the truth, so –'

'Oh Rachel, you know what I mean,' she dismissed. 'Look, for Alice I kept it simple. I said I was on holidays with my family at a caravan park, that I hooked up with a boy, one night we went down onto the beach, he had alcohol, I didn't handle it, one thing led to another . . . blah, blah, blah. I never saw him again, and I only knew his first name. I made it James, so at least she knows that much about him.'

'That's a horrible story, Catherine,' Rachel grimaced.

'Well, I took the opportunity to make it a cautionary tale. I'd have told her it was a virgin birth if I could have gotten away with it.'

Rachel was shaking her head. 'I don't understand why you wouldn't just tell her the truth. It doesn't put you in a bad light at all, Catherine. It's quite a romantic story, almost Romeo and Juliet–like.'

'Oh, please,' she frowned. 'James was no Romeo.'

'I just think it would be a whole lot better for Alice to have a picture of her mother and father as young lovers forced apart by unsympathetic parents.'

Catherine sighed. 'Maybe if James had ever attempted to make contact, even just a phone call to see if I was all right . . . And I wouldn't want Alice to get it into her head to try and find him. If he couldn't care less about me back then, and there's never been a single word since, how do you suppose he'd react to her showing up? Especially as he believes I had an abortion.' She shook her head. 'No, what she doesn't know can't hurt her. That document my parents signed disavowed her very existence. If I was going to tell Alice the whole truth, I would have to tell her that part as well. And there's nothing romantic about that.'

Fortunately Martin came home at some point, and he made them something more substantial to eat so at least they had food in their stomachs to soak up the alcohol. It developed into quite a bender, but at around eleven Rachel was still lucid enough to know she had to stop, and that she had to leave. Catherine tried to talk her into staying the night, but Rachel insisted she wanted to go home. She preferred to get over her hangovers in the privacy of her own flat, to her own timeframe.

Besides, there was something she needed to do tonight on the way home, she didn't want to put it off. She was fully aware that she was tired and emotional, but she kept seeing Tom's face on the beach today as she walked away. He'd been through enough, she didn't want to cause him any more pain. She wanted to let him know she was in, boots and all, that she would be there for him as well. That she wasn't going anywhere. And she wanted to do it now, tonight, while she was under the influence of alcohol-fuelled bravura, before she chickened out tomorrow and her risk-averse self came back to the fore.

For that reason, she flatly refused Martin's offer of a lift home, but thanked him for calling her a taxi. Rachel gave the driver Tom's address as they pulled off up the street. 'But I only need to stop there for a minute,' she said slowly and deliberately, trying not to slur her speech. 'Then we'll go on to Bronte.'

She directed him to pull up just short of Tom's place, on the other side away from Lexie's, and then she stepped out of the taxi and picked her way carefully in the dark towards the front gate. Thankfully there was a light on inside; she didn't know what she would have done if the house had been in darkness. Still, she didn't want to knock at the door and risk alerting the girls. She took out her mobile and managed to find Tom's number and call.

'Hi Rachel?' he said when he answered.

'Yes, it's me, Rachel.'

'Why are you whispering?'

'Because I'm out the front.'

'What?'

'I'm outside your house. I didn't want to knock in case I woke somebody.'

A moment later the door opened and Tom peered out. Rachel tottered unsteadily the rest of the way up the path and straight into his arms.

'I'm so sorry about today, Rach,' he said, holding her tight.

'No, no, *I'm* sorry,' she insisted, drawing back to look at him. 'That's why I came, to tell you I'm sorry, and I know I don't like risks, it's something to do with my psycho . . . something, but even if it's going to be a trainwreck, I want to be on it.'

He smiled indulgently at her. 'Have you been drinking, just a little, maybe?'

She shook her head. 'No, I've been drinking quite a lot. But I know what I'm doing. And I know what I'm saying. I love you, Tom, I love you so much,' she said, her voice becoming little more than a squeak.

'Hey, it's okay,' he said, gathering her close again. 'I love you too, Rach. Everything's going to work out.'

She leaned her head on his shoulder, gazing up at him. 'You really think so?'

'I know so,' he assured her, running his fingers around her hairline. 'Where have you been tonight anyway?'

'Catherine's. She actually had some helpful things to say.'

Tom frowned. 'You talked to her about us?'

'No, no, I talked about . . . oh, damn, what's his name? The doormat guy.'

'Matt Harding?'

She looked up at Tom, wide-eyed. 'You know him?'

He smiled, kissing her forehead. 'I think I better take you home. How did you even get here?'

'Oh damn, in a taxi, he's waiting right over there.'

Tom glanced across to where she was pointing. 'Okay, I'll go and send him off, and then I'll drive you home.'

Rachel pulled herself together. 'No, Tom, you can't . . . the girls are here. I'll be fine, I just wanted to make sure we were okay.'

'We're okay,' he said, 'and it's going to get better, I promise, Rachel.'

She looked up at him. 'I just get scared it's all going to end badly.'

He held her face in his hands. 'I know you do, but I'm not going to let that happen, okay? Trust me.'

And then he kissed her for a long time, and Rachel kissed him back, wanting so very badly to believe him.

'What was that?' she said suddenly, pulling away from him.

'What?'

'I thought I heard a noise.'

'I didn't hear anything,' said Tom. 'Are you sure you're going to be all right?'

'I'm sure.'

'Okay then, let me walk you to the taxi, at least.'

Bean East

'Lexie, here you are, I've been waiting for you,' said Scott a little impatiently as she walked into the kitchen at the café.

She glanced at her watch. It was the same time she usually got here. 'What's the problem?' she asked, putting her things down on the bench.

'Some guy showed up today with a delivery of paper products, not the regular guy from our regular supplier. He said the order had been placed by a *Mrs* Dingle.'

'Yeah,' she nodded. 'I was going to mention –'

'Going to mention?' He was obviously annoyed. 'Lexie, you can't just go changing things willy-nilly.'

'I'm not,' she chided. 'We're talking about paper cups and napkins, cleaning supplies, that kind of thing. I would never touch the food side of things, Scott. Well, not without discussing it first.'

The fact was, Lexie had a lot of ideas about the food, she was brimming over with ideas ever since Scott had finally relinquished the books to her. She had taken to her new role with relish. Once she had a handle on the way things worked, she started to compare suppliers and find more competitive deals. She had already cut overheads by eight per cent, and she'd barely got started. Her next plan was to take them carbon neutral and largely organic. Not only was it right for the planet, Lexie was all too aware that it was a good marketing strategy in this area. People around here lapped up that kind of thing.

'I don't know, Lex,' Scott had remarked when she'd mentioned it to him. 'I think I've taken organic as far as I can and still be cost-effective.'

Lexie begged to differ. He used organic olive oil and free-range eggs as staples, and he had a fresh produce guy who supplied some seasonal organic fruit and vegies, but Lexie knew they could do better. And she loved the challenge. The fact was, there were so many programs and government grants to assist businesses in going greener, but Scott had never had the time to look into any of them, he wasn't even aware of what was on offer.

But Lexie had the time and the motivation. Her mother was minding Mia for a couple of hours, two mornings a week, which Lexie mostly spent at the café. Then every afternoon while Mia was down for her nap, she had ample time to keep the books up to date, make calls, research. She was still able to walk Riley to school and back, and take him to his swimming lessons, and organise play dates, all as normal. And now Scott was finishing work at a reasonable hour, and the family had more relaxed time together. Lexie didn't know why they hadn't thought of this sooner.

'I just think you should talk to me about some of this stuff first,' Scott was saying.

'If I have to come to you with every little thing,' said Lexie, 'it's going to negate the reason I'm here in the first place, which is to take some of the load off you.'

'Yeah, but . . .'

She sidled over and leaned against him. 'Yeah but what?'

'I'd been using the other guys since I started,' he muttered. 'I happen to think loyalty means something.'

'So do I,' said Lexie, 'and I think it should be rewarded. I haven't dropped any supplier before going to them and asking them what they can do for us. Most of them have been prepared to drop the account ultimately, before dropping their prices.'

Scott didn't seem convinced. 'Well, what if the new guys aren't up to scratch? What if they let us down, late deliveries, that kind of thing?'

'I'll be monitoring all that, of course, Scott,' she assured him. 'I'm not going to let anything disrupt the smooth running of the café. That's why I'm here.'

He stood there sulking. Sometimes she saw where Riley and Mia got their stubbornness from. But they were children. She nudged him. 'Come on, stop having a pout,' she cajoled. 'Scott, I want you to be able to concentrate on the kitchen, that's your strength. You're a fantastic, creative chef, and you've been bogged down in all these details. Now you don't have to be.'

'I did build this business, Lexie.'

'I know that. And I get to step in and smooth out some of the rough edges. It's easy for me.'

She felt a slight uneasiness about having to tiptoe around his ego like this. Fact of the matter, Scott was not all that great at the business side of things, Lexie had discovered. He'd made some poor decisions, nothing too serious; but worse, he ran every day by the seat of his pants. His staff roster was a nightmare, it was one of the first things she pulled into shape. The staff loved him because he was so easygoing, but he found it hard to be a boss. And so, naturally, they took advantage. Well, not any more. They'd be dealing with Mrs Dingle from now on, and she was not such a soft touch. Lexie surprised herself sometimes, she didn't know where she was getting all this chutzpah; maybe it was all these years practising on the kids.

Her mobile started to ring. 'Oh, I better get that,' she said, diving into her bag and grabbing her phone. She flipped it open, throwing an apologetic smile at Scott as she ducked out of the kitchen. She'd rather not have him standing over her if this was something to do with work.

'Hi Lexie.'

But it was only Catherine. 'Oh hi, Catherine, how are you?'

'Fine thanks. Look, I won't keep you, I'm at work. But I just wanted to let you know that the night out I was planning is off.'

'Oh, to be honest, Catherine, I'd forgotten, I've been so busy,' said Lexie. 'Did we even have a date yet?'

'Well, not really, I had a couple in mind, but it doesn't matter now.'

'Okay then. Still, we haven't all got together in such a long time.' She realised it had been since before Annie . . . 'We should try to do something.'

'I suppose.'

Catherine sounded particularly flat. She must have been really disappointed that her plans had fallen through. Perhaps there was something Lexie could do about that.

'You know,' she said, 'I might just organise a barbecue at our place. Something more casual, and then we won't have to get a babysitter.'

She thought she heard a sigh. 'Surely that's too much trouble for you, Lexie?' Catherine said.

'You know what, Catherine?' Lexie replied. 'I honestly feel like I could handle anything these days. I'm having such a ball working at the café, you should see how I'm pulling things into shape . . .'

'Oh, I have a call on the other line,' Catherine interrupted her. 'Sorry, I have to go, Lexie.'

'Sure, I'll get back to you as soon as I've made a date for the barbecue. It'll be fun!'

Catherine did not have a call on the other line. She hung up the phone with a groan. That was not exactly the outcome she'd intended. She sat back in her chair, resting her head back and closing her eyes. She was tired already and it was barely midmorning. She blamed Martin; ever since the merger had fallen through he exuded negative energy. He was morose and unmotivated, he didn't even seem to have much interest in cooking. If Catherine said she wasn't hungry, he didn't argue. He'd just make himself a sandwich and go and watch television.

Alice was not much better; she'd set up camp in her bedroom and rarely ventured out. She even took food up there. Catherine couldn't be bothered arguing with her any more. The term was nearly over, it would be a relief when her grounding was up. The house felt like a mausoleum. There was no life, no energy. Catherine was beginning to hate going home.

At least she wouldn't have to tonight, she was heading straight to a Law Society cocktail party after work. She would have had time to call in home to change, but instead she brought some clothes with her – a dressier blouse, shoes and jewellery – and she could freshen up in the executive bathroom. It was just as easy.

Of course she couldn't help wondering if he'd be there, but she wasn't going to get her hopes up. He hadn't made any attempt to follow up on what had happened that night. The next morning there had been all the tired clichés – 'This should never have happened ... it will never happen again ...' But things had changed since then, and Catherine had exercised admirable restraint waiting for him to make the first move, which she felt was appropriate under the circumstances. But all for what? To be so roundly ignored? It had occurred to Catherine that his painful moral code applied to her as well, and although he was free now, he wouldn't approach her while she was not. For the first time, she was seriously considering suggesting to Martin that they take a break, they were on the brink anyway. She just didn't like to free-fall; she would prefer to have some indication that he was interested. If he was there tonight, it would give her a chance to finally confront him, though she would have to be careful and pick her moment. She couldn't risk a public scene. But surely she was owed some kind of explanation?

He wasn't here. Although Catherine was not surprised, she was nonetheless disappointed. And she was bored. It was the same old faces, the same old tired anecdotes; the air of self-importance in the room seemed particularly stifling tonight. So Catherine did what one does at a boring cocktail party, she drank cocktails. She was standing in a group of fellow family-law practitioners discussing the ramifications of a recent piece of legislation, when someone came up behind her.

'Catherine Rourke?' a vaguely plummy voice enquired. It had such an incredulous note to it that Catherine was intrigued to find out who the voice belonged to. She turned around to see a heavy-set, middle-aged man with a round, pale face; his hair had receded almost as far as the eye could see. She couldn't place him, though there was something familiar about him.

'You look incredible, Catherine,' he remarked in that faintly English accent. Had she met him at a conference overseas?

'The years haven't been as kind to me, I'm afraid,' he went on.

Those eyes. The voice was throwing her though.

'You don't remember me, do you?' He gave her a sheepish smile. 'I guess I shouldn't be surprised. I look like . . . this, and you don't look much older than you did at seventeen.'

It felt like all the air in the room had suddenly been sucked out and the walls were closing in on her.

'James?' she managed to say, her own voice barely able to project all the way out of her throat.

He was nodding faintly, his eyes fixed on her. 'It's been a long time, Catherine.'

She was trying to take in enough oxygen, but the air felt so thin, so insubstantial, it was making her dizzy.

'I haven't seen you at one of these before,' she said finally, composing herself. 'Have you been practising law all this time?'

He nodded. 'But in the UK. We came home just last month.'

'We?'

'My wife and I, with our two boys,' he explained. 'What about you, Catherine? Are you married, any children?'

She swallowed. He just assumed she'd had the abortion. Of course he would. 'Yes, I'm married, we don't have any children.' That wasn't a lie – she and Martin had not had children – not that she was overly concerned about lying to James. But she was certainly not going to tell him about Alice.

'We should catch up, have lunch sometime,' he was saying.

'Sure, sometime.' She was beginning to feel a little woozy. She knew what was coming. 'But if you'll excuse me right now.'

He opened his mouth to say something, but Catherine turned and headed for the exit. She walked quickly down the corridor and into the ladies' room, relieved that no one was at the basins. She slipped into a cubicle and flushed the toilet to mask the sound of her throwing up. She heard another toilet flush, so she closed the lid of hers and sat down, waiting for them to leave. She heard the tap running, then stop, the hand dryer, and finally footsteps and the creak and whoosh of the door as it opened and closed again. Catherine stood up and walked out to the basins where she rinsed her mouth and splashed a little water on her face. She couldn't go back out there. Fortunately she didn't have to, she'd left her briefcase in the cloakroom.

When she was safely back out on the street, Catherine took out her phone and scrolled through the numbers, finally pressing *Call*. 'Hi it's me,' she said. 'Are you alone? Are you expecting anyone, going anywhere?' She sighed. 'Can you spare me half an hour?'

Rachel answered the door about twenty minutes later. Catherine had sounded weird on the phone, but she was working her first Saturday shift tomorrow, so she hoped this wasn't going to turn into a big one. Well, it couldn't. She was just going to have to be assertive.

'What's wrong?' she asked at the sight of Catherine's harried expression.

'You're not going to believe this.'

It was a shock all right, and it was a measure of just how much Catherine had been thrown by the encounter that she asked for a glass of water first before Rachel got her a drink.

'You wouldn't recognise him, Rachel,' said Catherine, nursing her glass as she sat on the couch, her shoes kicked off and her feet drawn up underneath her. 'He's almost completely bald, and he's fat.'

'Really, how fat?'

'You know, well padded, paunchy.' She shook her head thinking about it. 'He's got so old.'

'We've all gotten older, Catherine. You still have a mental picture of him as a seventeen year old, it was bound to be a shock seeing him in his mid-thirties.'

'I'm telling you, he has not aged well. He said so himself.' She paused to take a drink. 'And he's got this toffee accent because he's been working in the UK. The whole thing was very strange.'

'I can imagine,' was all Rachel could offer.

'He asked me if I had children, do you believe that?' Catherine went on. 'Not a hint of shame, awkwardness, of any emotion even. He absolutely assumed I went ahead as his father instructed. He didn't even blink when I said I had no children.'

'Why did you say that?'

'Rachel, do you think I was going to stand in that room, with all those people around, and say, "Yes, I have a daughter actually, she's seventeen. You do the math."'

'Fair enough,' Rachel agreed. 'So what are you going to do?'

Catherine looked up at her. 'What do you mean?'

'Well, he's back in the country, sounds like there's a chance you might bump into him from time to time.'

'I can keep out of his way,' Catherine dismissed.

'He could easily find out about Alice.'

'How? He'd have to have some suspicions, and he certainly didn't appear to.'

'But he might find out accidentally,' said Rachel. 'If he moves in the same circles, it's bound to come out eventually.'

Catherine pressed her lips together, thinking about it.

'What if he's settling down in the eastern suburbs somewhere?' Rachel went on. 'You could run into him on the street, anywhere, with Alice right beside you. How would you explain her?' She realised her mind was beginning to work in different ways since her life had become so steeped in subterfuge and secrecy. Agent 99 would be proud of her.

'I don't know,' Catherine said finally. 'He suggested we get together for lunch sometime, catch up.'

'Maybe you should,' said Rachel. 'You could get his side of the story, might put things in a different light.'

'He doesn't have a side,' said Catherine. 'He did what his father told him to do.'

'Isn't that what you expect of Alice?' Rachel pointed out. 'In fact, hasn't she been grounded for the past couple of months for that very reason?'

'I was having his baby, you think it's a reasonable excuse that he didn't want to risk being grounded?'

'I think he was a seventeen-year-old kid.'

Catherine stared at her.

'You've been living a lie for a very long time, Catherine,' said Rachel, aware of the whiff of hypocrisy in what she was saying. 'To be brutally honest with you, I think Alice deserves to know the truth.'

Catherine swallowed. 'But what if he . . . I can't risk her getting hurt.'

'Maybe this has all happened for a reason,' Rachel suggested. She felt like she was channelling Annie. 'Maybe it's finally the right time to do the right thing.'

The following day

'You did good, girl,' said Mel. 'You got through your very first Saturday with flying colours.'

They had closed to customers twenty minutes ago and now they were cleaning up. The sixteen-year-old casual, Minxie – her actual name, Mel and Rachel decided her parents should be shot – had fled on the dot of closing, and although Rachel's shift had officially ended she wanted to make a good impression. Besides, she had nothing to rush home to. And she'd enjoyed herself today; she'd actually even had fun at times, and she hadn't had fun at work in a very long while. She'd forgotten how much she enjoyed dealing face to face with people, regular happy people, down at the beach, wanting nothing more serious than a fruit juice or a smoothie. Though it had to be said that some of the customers took their selections very seriously, and Rachel had no doubt such customers would irritate over time. Along with the ones who just couldn't make up their minds, faced with such an overwhelming choice. Still, it beat answering phones at Handy Home Health Care, and Mel was the absolute diametric opposite to Lloyd, thank goodness. Rachel had amused herself from time to time, trying to imagine Lloyd dealing with the orders, his officious clipboard at the ready. 'No Rachel, it's Banana Berry Blast, not Berry Banana. Your product knowledge leaves much to be desired.'

'So how about a celebratory drink?' said Mel.

Rachel was up to her elbows in sudsy water at the sink. She handed Mel a juicer bowl. 'You're not talking about something involving fruit, are you?'

'Only the fermented grape kind,' she winked, wiping the bowl with a tea towel.

'In that case, I'd love to.'

Mel considered her. 'What about your Mr Wonderful? You won't be missed on a Saturday night?'

'He's got kids, he's with them tonight.'

She raised an eyebrow. 'What, are you allergic to the little darlings?'

'It's not that,' Rachel shook her head. 'It's . . . a long story.'

'Can't wait to hear it,' Mel said with a glint in her eye.

They finished up and headed for the local pub. Coming straight from work they were hardly dressed to go anywhere more upmarket, not that Rachel would have wanted to. Laidback was definitely her preference. Mel bought the first round and sat down opposite Rachel at a table outside in the beer garden. It was a gorgeous, clear autumn evening; the air was heavy with the scent of sea salt. It occurred to Rachel that she really didn't get out enough, and that sitting at home in case Tom dropped in had its limitations.

'So, out with it,' said Mel. 'I want to hear the curious tale of Mr Wonderful. And don't leave anything out.'

Rachel smiled. 'His name's Tom, actually.' She took a breath. This felt like confession, but in a good way. 'And up until last spring, he was married to one of my best friends. Then she died.'

Rachel waited while Mel picked her jaw up off the table. And then she proceeded to relate the whole tale, from woe to go, without leaving out anything. It was liberating, it was a relief, and it was complicated, to say the least. Mel had to stop her at one point to go and get them more drinks.

'That's quite a story,' said Mel when Rachel had finally brought her up to date. 'And you seem so normal.'

'I'll take that as a compliment.'

'As you should,' said Mel. 'What I want to know is, is Mr Wonderful wonderful enough that you want to take on this whole palaver?'

Rachel took a moment, sipping her wine. 'Yeah, he is.'

'Well, here's cheers to you,' she said, raising her glass.

They toasted. 'So what about you. Is there a Mr Wonderful in your life?' Rachel asked her.

Mel grunted. 'Not so much. I'm having what they call a dry spell.'

'So how did you come to be running a juice bar?' asked Rachel. 'Did you break up with a boyfriend?'

'Why do you ask that?'

'You asked me the same question when I applied for the job.'

'So I did,' Mel nodded. 'But no, it wasn't a broken heart that led me to this, it was a broken spirit. I used to work at the top end of town for an investment bank, in the days when that still held some cachet.'

'I remember those days,' Rachel nodded.

'Yeah, well they weren't all bad. I bought my own apartment, a very nice one, right here in Bondi. And I bought myself a hybrid car, because despite being a loathsome investment banking type, I had my principles.'

'Good for you.' They toasted again.

'Of course that meant I hated my job for the most part,' she went on. 'So I plotted my escape. I bought my little piece of the franchise, but I kept on the existing manager and the staff. Then when I could smell the crash coming, I bailed. I cashed in my share options while they were still worth something and I paid off my apartment and gave my manager notice. With a glowing reference, I might add, so he walked straight into another managerial position. I made sure of that.' She took a long, slow drink of her wine. 'Some of the people I worked with were not so lucky. I know of three guys who worked for the bank who committed suicide when the crash finally came.'

'Wow,' said Rachel quietly. 'That's rough.'

Mel nodded, staring down at the table. Rachel wasn't sure if she should draw her out, ask her about it, if she'd known any of them personally.

'Another round?' said Mel, moving to get up. She obviously didn't want to talk about it.

'Don't you dare, it's my shout,' said Rachel.

By the time she returned to the table, Mel's mood had picked up. 'So, what shall we drink to?' she said. 'Love in all its manifestations?'

'I guess,' said Rachel, raising her glass to Mel's. 'But I reckon you still owe me a story.'

'Oh, I've got nothing on yours,' she said.

'Come on,' Rachel urged.

'I've had the odd "prospect" over the years,' Mel assured her. 'But after a while, the flaws always float to the surface. And I'm not a hard bitch, I'm not just talking about the guy only, I'm talking about the inherent flaws in every relationship.' She paused to take a drink. 'You don't see eye to eye on this and that, he doesn't listen, you don't squeeze the toothpaste tube the right way, then there's the whole minefield over the toilet seat,' she groaned. 'It's all stupid stuff, but you end up breaking up over it.'

Rachel was trying to remember what used to bother her about Tom when they were living together . . . Surely there was something . . . Maybe because they weren't actually a couple that kind of stuff just didn't get to her in the same way.

'Anyway,' Mel continued, 'I don't know whether it's because I'm getting older, or what it is, but nowadays I just feel less and less inclined to try, because it seems like no matter how great things are at the start, it's bound to come down to that screaming match over the toilet seat.' She took a sip of her wine. 'Though just between you and me, I worry that I'm making excuses, that I'm just intrinsically relationship averse.'

Rachel thought about it. 'I don't know. My friend, Catherine, she said that my problem with relationships is that I'm risk averse.'

'What?' said Mel. 'You're currently in the relationship equivalent of midair acrobatics without a safety net.'

Rachel grinned. 'Let me qualify. *Up until* Tom, I've been risk averse, according to Catherine. That's why she thinks he could be the real thing.'

'I thought your friends didn't know about you two?' she frowned.

'Oh, sorry, Catherine doesn't know it's Tom. I had to make up an alias.'

Mel winced. 'That's quite a tangled web you're busy weaving there.'

'Tell me about it.'

'Have you thought about how you're going to unravel it?'

'Well, the plan is to take it gradually,' said Rachel. 'Tom reckons that we should start to spend more time together, quite openly, but innocently, or platonically, I guess you'd say. And then we're kind of hoping that people will come to the obvious conclusion and start making mention of it themselves. You know the kind of thing – "Oh, you're seeing a lot of Tom" . . . "Is there something going on with you and Tom?" . . . "You and Tom are becoming quite an item."' She looked directly at Mel. 'What do you think?'

'Are you intending to hand out those snappy one-liners to your friends on little cards?'

Rachel pulled a face at her.

'What can I tell you?' said Mel, holding out her hands. 'You can't keep all of the people happy all of the time, yada yada. Some of your friends will be fine, no doubt, they'll be happy for you. Others'll take issue, but that's the thing. It's their issue, not yours.'

'That's what Tom says,' Rachel nodded.

'Ah, who cares what people think in the end,' Mel declared with a wave of her hand. 'At least you can quit all the sneaking around. It must be exhausting. You can have some normality finally.'

Rachel gave a wry laugh.

'What?'

'I don't know if we're ever going to have much normality.'

'Why do you say that?'

Rachel couldn't believe she was finally going to be able to talk about this out loud to someone. 'Think about it. Okay, it's out in the open, everyone knows, most importantly his daughters know, and so what do we do then? Have sleepovers at his house, in her bed?'

'Eew,' Mel grimaced. Then she shrugged. 'So, he'll get a new bed. You'll go shopping for a bed together, it'll be your bed.'

'And then we put it into her room?'

'Hmm,' Mel thought about it. 'Is there another room you could use? Can some rooms be changed around, maybe?'

Rachel shook her head. 'The place doesn't really allow for it, but it's not just that. The thing is, it's Annie's house. If you knew her, if you saw it . . . She was a very distinctive woman with a very distinctive style. The house is all her.'

'Well, that's not all that unusual,' Mel offered. 'Not many blokes are into interior decorating, you realise.'

'It's more than that.' Rachel twirled her glass by its stem. 'Does anybody actually do this? Start a new life with a new woman in the dead wife's house?'

'There's your answer. He has to sell up, obviously. You can find your own place to start your new life.'

'But I don't think that'd be fair to the girls. They shouldn't have the memories of their mother pushed aside like that.'

'Snap.' Mel drained her glass. 'You did say it was complicated.'

'I did.'

They sat silently for a while as the buzz carried on around them; the music played, guys put the word on girls, girls accepted, or knocked them back. Like all the gin joints in all the towns . . .

'See, this is what I'm saying,' Mel said finally. 'It's like every relationship is doomed. It all starts off fine, and then you settle down and the cracks start to appear.'

'Well, that's just depressing,' said Rachel.

Monday

Catherine arrived at work, still shell-shocked. She hadn't slept well, and she'd felt like a caged lion all weekend. She paused at Brooke's desk with a perfunctory 'Good morning' as she was handed her messages. She walked on slowly, glancing through them. She stopped suddenly, taking a few steps back to Brooke's desk.

'This one,' she said, 'from a James Barrett, did he have anything else to say?'

'No,' said Brooke. 'He asked for you, I said you weren't in, he gave me his details, asked if you could call back.'

'Hmm.' Catherine proceeded through to her office, put down her briefcase and sat in her chair. She flicked through the rest of her messages, but she wasn't actually reading any of them. She was still thinking about James. And what Rachel had said. But she had to control how this played out.

She stood up and walked back out to Brooke's desk. 'Brooke, if Mr Barrett calls again, tell him I'm in a meeting.'

'Of course, Catherine.'

She went to walk away, then she turned back again. 'Actually, Brooke, always check with me first. You know the drill.'

Brooke nodded. 'I'll say you're in a meeting, let me just check if she's available.'

'Good.'

Catherine went back to her office and closed the door. She wanted to know if he called. If he kept calling. Just how persistent he was prepared to be. Because this was too important. If she was going to risk opening this particular can of worms, as Rachel had suggested, she had to be absolutely sure about James, that she could trust him, that he was someone who would do the right thing.

Saturday

'Hi,' said Rachel, surprised, as she turned around to serve the next customer. 'What are you doing here, Tom?'

Mel looked up. 'Ah, so Mr Wonderful, we finally meet.'

'Why'd she call you that, Dad?'

Tom put his hands on Hannah's shoulders. 'My daughter, Hannah,' he said, by way of introduction. 'And I'm guessing you're Mel, Rachel's new boss?'

'Yeah,' she said, recovering. She looked directly at Hannah. 'Doesn't everyone call your dad Mr Wonderful?'

Hannah frowned, glancing sideways up at her father.

'It's true, Han,' he said. 'I get it all the time, everywhere I go.'

'La-*ame,*' she rolled her eyes.

He grinned, looking at Rachel. 'Hannah and I were wondering if you were having a break any time soon?'

She hesitated, glancing at Mel.

'As a matter of fact, she's due for one right now,' said Mel.

'Are you sure?' Rachel asked her.

Mel turned around, her back to Tom and Hannah. 'Oh, quite sure, I owe you for the foot-in-mouth thing just now,' she said in a low voice. 'And by the way . . . *hot!*'

'Okay,' said Rachel, smiling across at them. 'Let me make you some drinks first. What would you like, Hannah?'

They waited for Rachel to wash her hands and shed her apron, and then they walked across the road to the reserve overlooking the beach, where they found an empty bench to sit down.

'You're not having juice?' Tom asked, watching Rachel open a bottle of water.

She shook her head. 'I'm all juiced out.'

Hannah giggled, slurping through her straw.

'So Lexie called,' Tom went on, 'about the barbecue next week.'

Rachel nodded. 'I'm looking forward to it. We haven't all got together for such a long time.'

He gave her a meaningful look across the top of Hannah's head while she was focused on her smoothie. 'Yeah, it'll be a good chance to catch up.'

She knew what he was getting at, they'd already talked about it. The first time they would all be together as a group – their 'coming out' party. Rachel vacillated between feeling enormous relief and sheer terror, as though she was standing on the edge of a cliff, about to take a step off. When she'd said that to Tom, he'd reassured her that he'd be holding her hand on the way down. Rachel wasn't sure that was such a comforting idea.

'So, do you want to ask Rachel, Han?' Tom was saying.

Rachel looked at them.

'No, you do it, Dad,' Hannah said, nudging him.

'Okay then. Well, we wanted to know if you'd like to come over tonight after work to watch a DVD? Just me and Hannah,' he added quickly. 'Sophie's going out.'

That did make it more appealing, but still Rachel hesitated. 'I wouldn't be imposing on a father and daughter night?'

'No way!' Hannah jumped in. 'It'll be two against one if you come with us to pick the DVD. Dad's totally hopeless.'

He pulled a face. 'And there I thought I was Mr Wonderful.'

Hannah snorted. 'Yeah, right. That lady was nuts.'

'Oh, don't mind her,' said Rachel. 'She says that to all the good-looking guys.'

Hannah screwed up her face. 'Dad's not good-looking.'

'Thanks, Han.'

'Oh, Daddy dear,' she patted his leg. 'You know I love you. But let's face it, you're no Zac Efron.'

Rachel laughed.

'I don't even know who he is,' said Tom. 'Should I be offended?'

Rachel shook her head. 'No, he's about eighteen, and let's face it,' she winked at Hannah, 'there's no one like Zac Efron.'

'Tell me about it,' Hannah sighed.

'So what do you say, Rachel?' Tom asked. 'Will you join us tonight?'

'Okay,' she said. 'I'd love to.'

'Yay,' said Hannah, giving her a hug.

Tom looked across at her, smiling broadly. And Rachel smiled back, because he looked so happy.

'Okay, are you finished with that, Han?' he said to her. 'I'll take these to the bin.'

He collected their containers and sauntered over to a bin nearby. Hannah turned to Rachel with an urgent expression on her face.

'Do you like my dad?' she asked quickly, her voice hushed.

'Of course,' Rachel said uncertainly.

'No, you know, *like* him. 'Cause I think he *likes* you, and I'd hate him to get his heart all broken, after Mum and everything, so if you think he's gross or something, then let me know and I'll put him off.'

Rachel wanted to hug her. 'I don't think he's gross, Han. Not at all. Actually, I think he's pretty wonderful.'

Hannah's whole face broke into a smile.

Rachel sat there, her heart racing, as Tom walked back towards them, feeling for the first time like this could actually work. And she was going to be part of a family.

'What are you two grinning about?' he asked.

'Me and Rachel were just talking about which DVD we're gunna get and we're totally agreed on *He's Just Not That Into You*.'

Tom nodded, frowning. 'Is there a movie title in there somewhere?'

Monday

Lexie heard Scott coming down the stairs. He'd been in bed all day, and she was just finishing Riley's bedtime story. She had put Mia to bed a little earlier, trying to keep things as quiet as possible upstairs. Scott hadn't been feeling well since Saturday night, but she hadn't been able to talk him into not going to work yesterday. Josh had had the good sense to send him home early, and he'd looked dreadful when he walked in the door. His face was drawn and pale, his eyes sunken, and he was shivering. He said Josh had overreacted, but Lexie told him he was being ridiculous. She only hoped that he hadn't spread it to the customers. Lexie had packed him off to bed right away, but he was worse this morning. The café was closed Mondays, so she didn't have to argue with him to stay at home, but he couldn't have gone to work. He was aching all over, and he'd kept up a high temperature all day. It was all Lexie could do to get him to take Panadol at regular intervals, but at least he'd stayed in bed.

'Daddy!' Riley exclaimed as Scott slumped into the room. He went to jump off her lap, but Lexie held him back.

'No, Riley,' she said firmly. 'Daddy's not well.'

'It's okay,' Scott said as he lurched at the sofa, falling into it.

But Lexie held onto Riley. 'No, sweetheart, Daddy's really sick, you can't go near him or else you might get sick too.' She shifted him in her lap to face her. 'And if you get sick, you'll have to miss school tomorrow, and then you know what you'll miss?'

He looked at her wide-eyed. 'The petting zoo?'

Lexie nodded. 'That's tomorrow, sweetheart, you know how much you've been looking forward to it.'

'But I could still go.'

'But then you might make the animals sick as well,' Lexie pointed out.

He sighed, looking plaintively over at his dad.

'Mummy's right, mate,' Scott croaked. 'Blow me a kiss and I'll blow you one back.'

Riley looked dubious. 'But I might catch it from you, Daddy. You better not.'

Scott gave him a weak smile. 'Will you still blow me a kiss anyway?' he asked. 'It might make me feel better.'

Riley nodded emphatically before blowing him a highly staged kiss.

'Okay,' said Lexie, 'I'll just get him off to bed. Do you need anything? I made you some soup.'

He waved her off. 'I can get it.'

'No,' she said. 'Just sit there, I'll be back in ten minutes.' She scooped Riley off her lap and stood up. 'Don't move,' she ordered Scott.

And he hadn't, when she returned. Though he had turned the television on to some kind of dance show.

'What on earth are you watching?' she asked as she came over to the sofa.

'I have no idea,' he said. 'But it's making my head spin.'

'I don't think you can blame that on the TV.' She leaned over him and held her hand to his forehead, but he brushed it away.

'I'm fine, feeling a lot better,' he said, then broke into a fit of coughing.

Lexie's stomach lurched, watching him. She sat down on the coffee table opposite him, passing him a box of tissues. The coughing fit eased, and he slumped back against the sofa, catching his breath.

'Okay,' she said. 'I've called your mother –'

'Why did you do that?' he frowned.

'Because she's the only one who can stop you from leaving the house tomorrow.'

'Lexie,' he said, 'I'll be fine by tomorrow.'
'No you won't.'
'The café can't run itself.'
'No, Josh and I will handle it.'
He sat up then. 'No way.'
'Way,' said Lexie. 'What else are we going to do?'
'I'll go to work as usual.'

Some hideous rap song was playing in the background, distracting her. 'What the hell is that?' Lexie snapped, grabbing the remote and pressing the mute button. She turned back to Scott. 'It's all arranged. Your mother will be here at seven, and I've called a friend to pick up Riley for school –'

'This is crazy, Lex, you can't run the café.'

'Oh, and you can, the state you're in?'

'One more night's sleep and I'll be good to go,' he said, and then he broke into another coughing fit.

Lexie sat there, trying to be calm, letting him ride it out, telling herself he didn't have an undiagnosed heart complaint, he just had the flu. But she couldn't deny feeling anxious, she'd even double-checked the family history with his mother. Lexie knew that Jenny realised what she was worried about, but she didn't make her feel stupid for asking.

'Okay,' said Lexie when he'd recovered. 'Would you like some soup?'

'Lex, I know what this is about,' said Scott. 'You're overreacting because of what happened to Annie.'

She shook her head. 'I'm not going to deny this is bringing up some uncomfortable feelings,' she said. 'But I don't think you're going to die, Scott. However, you are sick and you need at least a couple of days off.'

'Not going to happen, Lex,' he said. 'Josh can't run the place on his own.'

'He won't have to, he'll have me.'

Scott gave her a doubtful look. 'You're a good cook, Lexie, but you're not a chef.'

'No, but Josh is, and I can cook, and I can follow orders,' she said. 'Unlike you.' She stood up. 'Your mother will be here at seven, you can argue your case with her. I'm going to get you some soup.' She reached down and grabbed the remote again, tossing it onto his lap. 'There, watch your stupid show.'

Wednesday

'Thank God for netball training,' Tom murmured, nuzzling into Rachel's neck.

The netball season had started last week, affording them a midweek tryst, which was just as well because they hadn't had much other time together, apart from last Saturday night with Hannah, which, Rachel had been happy to admit, had turned out beautifully. Now that she had her little matchmaking plan in place, Hannah had quit the incessant talking about her mother, and Rachel felt much more at ease with her. Being in the house itself was another matter, but she did feel more relaxed this time. Especially as they just ordered in pizzas and ate them at the coffee table while they watched the movie. Rachel didn't step foot in the kitchen the entire night.

'Three more big sleeps till Saturday,' said Tom after a while as he rolled over onto his back, drawing Rachel with him. 'Thank Christ, I don't think I can do this for much longer.'

She propped her chin on his chest, looking up at him. 'You don't think one night is going to change everything, do you, Tom?'

'No, but we'll be on our way.' He shifted so he could face her fully. 'Are we together on this?'

'Mm.'

'So, on Saturday night at the barbecue, in front of everyone, I'm going to be very attentive ...'

'Not too attentive.'

'I'll top up your drinks, laugh at your jokes, even though that in particular will be a bit of a stretch.'

She nudged him.

'And I'll be a little affectionate –'

'Not too affectionate,' she warned.

'No, just in a friendly way. And I'll offer to drive you home.'

Rachel was pensive.

'What's wrong?'

'Nothing, I'm just nervous, I guess.'

He held her close and kissed her. 'Look, it's going to be fine. If everyone has the same attitude as Hannah, we'll be home free.' He paused. 'And in the end, nobody else matters anyway if the girls are okay with it.'

'Yeah, well, don't count your chickens, we haven't got Sophie onside yet.'

Tom shook his head. 'You worry too much, Rach. She'll be fine. When it's all out in the open I'll actually be able to talk to her about it, and I can reassure her that nothing's going to change.'

He still didn't get it. And Rachel had not been able to bring herself to broach her very real concerns about how on earth they were going to conduct this relationship once they were 'out'. She'd ended up deciding that maybe she should just take one thing at a time; that she would cross that bridge when they came to it. And although that approach had not always worked for her, she still hadn't managed to come up with anything better.

Tom raised his arm to check his watch. 'I have to go,' he sighed regretfully. He kissed her lightly on the lips before unravelling himself from her arms to sit up. Rachel shifted to get up as well.

'Don't get up, honey,' he said. 'I can let myself out.'

She shrugged. 'I don't like lying here in the afternoon, watching you go. It makes me feel . . .'

'What?' He frowned, turning to look at her.

'Oh, I don't know . . . a little sleazy or something, like you're going to leave the cash on the hall table on your way out.'

He seemed shocked. He leaned across her. 'Rachel, have I made you feel like that?'

'No, not at all,' she assured him, stroking his arm. 'It's me, and it's not a big deal, it's just an image in my head from the movies probably.' She kissed him. 'Go, or you'll be late.'

He got up reluctantly and Rachel slipped on her robe while he dressed. She walked him to the door and he drew her into his arms and held her close. The truth was, she always felt so lonely after he left. She had travelled around the world on her own; it had never bothered her living by herself, being single. She had actually felt more alone when she was with Sean. But it was different with Tom. So different. Despite all the issues, deep down in her heart Rachel felt like they were meant to be together. That they were always meant to be together, and that this was finally their time.

But of course, if she took that to its logical conclusion, it meant that Annie's death was all part of some cosmic plan to bring her and Tom together, and that just brought up all Rachel's guilt again, and she'd end up thinking that they were not meant to be together at all, and that something bad was going to happen.

Tom drew back from her. 'Look at that frown. You have to stop worrying so much, Rach,' he chided. 'There's only one thing I'm worried about.'

'Oh? What's that?'

'How I'm going to keep my hands off you on Saturday.'

She smiled. 'Self-control, Tom. You can do it.'

'Okay, but do me a favour and try not to look too gorgeous?'

Rachel laughed then. 'I'll give it a shot, but you know, what can I do? I'm irresistible.'

'Yes you are,' he said, leaning in to give her a soft, lingering kiss. 'I love you,' he said seriously. 'See you Saturday. First day of the rest of our lives.'

Thursday

'Hi Lexie.'

She turned around from the sink. 'Jenny! Hi,' said Lexie, slipping off her rubber gloves. 'What are you doing here? Is everything all right?'

'Of course, love,' she assured her. 'I just thought I'd call in on my way home. Scott insisted that I didn't need to stay till you got home, that he'd be fine with the kids for the rest of the afternoon.

And he will be, today really made the difference. He's over the worst of it.'

Lexie breathed out with relief. 'Oh, I'm so glad. I can't tell you how grateful I am for your help this week, Jenny. We couldn't have done it without you.'

'Nonsense, happy to help any time, love,' she said. 'I don't get to spend enough time with your two, or with my son for that matter, the way he works.'

Lexie nodded. 'No wonder he got sick,' she said. 'Listen, have you got time for a coffee?'

She did, so Lexie made them both a cup and led her mother-in-law to one of the booths at the back of the café. She placed a small plate of cupcakes down on the table between them.

'These look just like those beautiful little cakes you make, Lexie,' said Jenny, picking up one. 'You should think about selling yours here.'

She grinned. 'They are mine.'

'Really?'

'I had a freezer full of them when Scott got sick, so I thought I'd see how they went,' she explained. 'We've had a special going all week, a dollar extra with coffee. They've been selling like . . .'

'Cupcakes!' Jenny quipped. 'Well, good for you. You seem to have really taken to this.'

'You know, I have, I really have,' said Lexie. 'I mean, I feel torn, I miss the kids so much, I could never do it full-time. But now that we've proved we can hold the fort without Scott, I'm going to try and get him to share the load, and take some regular time off.'

Jenny smiled, shaking her head. 'Good luck with that.'

Lexie looked at her. 'What is it with him? You know how I adore him, Jenny, but God, he can be stubborn.'

'Always has been,' she agreed. She took a sip of her coffee. 'Oh, he was a bugger of a kid, so independent and headstrong, he wouldn't accept help, couldn't be told. I always put it down to him being the youngest of four. He had to prove he was just as capable as his big brothers.'

'How did you handle it back then?'

'Two ways, depending. If you can get him to think something's his idea, that works best, but it's not always possible. The other way is just not to give him a choice.'

Lexie was nodding faintly. 'That's what I had to do this week, when I rang you about coming over. I didn't discuss it with him first, I just told him what was happening, and that he could argue with you if he didn't like it.'

Jenny was smiling. 'And he knows better than to try that.'

'I don't know how you did it with four of them.'

'Five of them altogether, if you include their father,' she reminded Lexie. 'You know it's a funny thing the way men work, really. They're happy to have you run their lives, they couldn't remember what day it is without you. But step foot on their territory and they get so antsy.'

'That's exactly what happened with Scott,' Lexie agreed. 'As soon as I wanted to help out at the café, he got all defensive.'

Jenny nodded. 'Same with John when I took over the books for the business, years back. Truth is, he was making quite a shemozzle of things, it was just as well I stepped in when I did, we might have lost the house.'

Lexie's eyes grew wide.

'Don't you ever say a word,' said Jenny. 'He still doesn't know to this day. I had to negotiate with the bank, keep all our creditors at bay and put the hard word on all the laggards who owed us money. John was such a softie, he let people take advantage of his good nature all the time.'

Lexie was shaking her head in disbelief. 'That's just what Scott's like. He had the staff walking all over him.'

'The secret is to work on them gradually,' said Jenny. 'I've learned a lot living with all these men. You have to reassure them their whatsits are not going to drop off if you take the reins occasionally.'

Lexie had to laugh at that, but underneath she felt a little uncomfortable about the idea of having to handle Scott with kid gloves. It was all right for Jenny, she came from a different era, but Lexie wanted her and Scott to be true partners, to be equals. She didn't want to play games, or manipulate him, even though she knew she'd been guilty of that in the past, on occasions. From here on in she wanted to be completely honest and upfront about everything.

*

As she headed home later, Lexie was relieved that Scott was all better, for his sake and hers. She was tired right through to her bones, and she was so looking forward to a day off tomorrow. Not that you could call it a day off as such; she would have Mia, and a lot of housework to catch up on, as well as shopping and preparations for the barbecue. But it was the kind of work she was used to. She didn't know how Scott did it, six days a week, on his feet for most of the day.

From now on he wouldn't have to. There were so many options available to them. Lexie could work one whole day, or a couple of half-days. Or she could take over in the afternoon a few days a week so Scott could knock off early, pick up Riley from school, have more time with the kids.

As she pulled into the driveway she felt the tension lifting up and floating away out to sea. She understood why Scott appreciated that feeling so much, coming home, and she would never begrudge it again. But from now on they were going to share everything, be partners in every sense of the word. Lexie was feeling positive about the direction they were taking. Scott getting sick had actually been a good thing, in a way, speeding up the process.

But as she unlocked the front door and stepped inside, Lexie wasn't met with the sounds of children playing, the smell of dinner cooking, she was met with utter silence. 'Hello?' she called, walking down the hall. 'Anyone home?'

The place was empty. She realised the other car wasn't in the driveway when she pulled up; she'd assumed without really thinking about it that it was in the garage. Lexie's heart started to race as she searched for her phone in her bag. He's just gone up the road to get milk or bread or something, she told herself. Though why wouldn't he have called her to pick up whatever they needed while she was out? Maybe he just wanted to get out of the house. His mother had said he was fine, back to normal. She dialled his mobile and he picked up after a couple of rings.

'Hi hun,' he said. 'What's up?'

'Where are you? I just got home.'

'I brought the kids down to McDonald's for tea.'

'Oh,' Lexie was thrown. 'Why?'

'I didn't feel like cooking.'

'I would have cooked.'

'Ah, you've done more than your share of cooking this week. And I wanted to give the kids a treat.'

'Are you down at Coogee?' Why wouldn't he have called her? She was up the road from there.

'No, we're at Bondi,' he said.

'Well, why didn't you wait for me?'

'You don't like McDonald's,' said Scott.

No, and she didn't like the children eating it either. She could have brought them something a little more wholesome from the café if he wanted to give them a treat, then at least they could have eaten together. She couldn't help feeling left out.

'How much longer are you going to be, do you think?' she asked.

'Oh, maybe another half an hour or so, we're still eating,' said Scott. 'You should relax for a while, hun, have a shower, put your feet up.'

'Hmm.'

'Do you want us to bring you anything?'

'No thanks, I'll see you when you get here.'

Lexie hung up the phone and looked around the room. It was a little untidy; at least he could have straightened up before he left. She picked up a couple of mugs off the coffee table and walked over to the dishwasher, but when she opened it she saw that it hadn't been emptied. She sighed. She felt tired and grimy and she did not feel like unstacking the dishwasher right now. She put the mugs in the sink. Scott was right, she should relax, not make such a fuss; it was okay to leave a few things lying around the house, just like it was okay for the kids to have the occasional treat. But as she walked up the stairs to get ready for her shower, Lexie was glad things would be back to normal tomorrow.

'Oh no, I'm not going back to work tomorrow,' Scott announced when she mentioned it later. They had got the kids bathed and into bed, and Lexie was outlining her plans for the next couple of days.

'I'm sorry?' she blinked. 'What do you mean you're not going to work?'

He was sitting on the sofa with his feet on the coffee table. 'I think I could use another day off, make sure I'm really over this.'

'Okay,' she said carefully. 'But like I was just saying, I was going to shop for the barbecue.'

'I can take care of that.'

'Then it's not really a day off, is it?'

'It'll still be easier than going in to the café,' he said, picking up the remote control and switching on the TV.

Lexie felt cornered. If she said it was just as hard, then he could argue what was the difference? And if she insisted that he go to work and let her handle the household stuff, as though she couldn't trust him with it, she'd never get him to agree to taking regular time off. She had to go with the flow for now; this transition phase was likely to be a bit tricky, but it would be worth it to get some balance into their lives.

But right now Lexie felt quite unbalanced, watching him search the channels before settling down to a Gordon Ramsay repeat. Well then, fine, if she was going to be working again tomorrow, she needed to make up some more batches of her cupcakes. She hadn't planned to tell Scott yet, she'd intended to introduce the idea next week, when he was back at the helm, and when she would have the time to bake up a full week's supply. But seeing as he was prepared to leave the running of things to her, she obviously didn't need to consult with him; she'd make her own decisions about what she served at the café when she was in charge.

Having Gordon Ramsay throwing tantrums in the background didn't do much to salve Lexie's mood, and pretty soon she was banging cake tins and slamming cupboard doors.

Scott got up off the sofa and came over to the kitchen. 'What are you doing, Lex?'

'Making cupcakes,' she said bluntly, without looking at him.

'Why?' he asked. 'You should be relaxing, you've been on your feet all day. We can live without cupcakes for a few days.'

'I'm not making them for us, I'm making them for the café.'

'What are you talking about?' Scott frowned.

Hmm, now she was getting his attention. 'We've had a special going all week, coffee and a cupcake for a dollar extra. It was a huge hit.'

'And this is cupcakes you've been making at home?'

'Yeah. What's wrong with that?'

'Well, for one thing, this is not a commercial kitchen, Lexie. Someone gets sick, they find out that food sold at the café was prepared in a kitchen that has never been inspected, and is not subject to the same standards and ordinances, then we're screwed.'

'No one's going to get sick from my cupcakes, Scott.'

'They don't have to get sick from a cupcake, but if they get sick at all, and report it, we get a visit from a food inspector. Do you realise the risk you're taking?'

'Fine,' she said. 'I'll make them at the café in future.'

'We're not set up for it, there's not enough bench space. We're not running a bakery, Lexie.'

'Then I'll make them after we close,' she said. 'A couple of nights a week, maybe. They're selling really well, it's worth it.'

'They're selling well because you're undercharging.'

'No I'm not, I worked out what the ingredients cost.'

'Did you include your labour, electricity, water . . .'

She just stared at him.

'It's not a school cake stall, for Chrissakes, Lexie! You don't know what you're doing.'

She put her hands on her hips. 'And you couldn't be happier, could you?'

'What are you talking about?'

'Ever since I've got involved in the business, you just can't stand it. You can't bring yourself to admit that maybe I'm actually making a difference. You'd rather work seven days a week, till all hours, than admit that things were getting out of hand and you needed help.'

'What are you implying, Lexie – that I don't know how to run the business?'

'Oh you can run it, just not all that well.'

He glared at her. 'Oh, is that right?' he said. 'So you come in, change suppliers, make a few cupcakes, and you think you've got the whole thing whipped, eh?'

'I'm not saying that,' said Lexie. 'I just don't understand why you're so precious about everything. You wouldn't even show me the books till I virtually begged you, but this is my life too, Scott. It affects me, it affects our children, it affects our future. But you have to have total control, even when it's getting beyond you. What are you so worried about? That your balls are going to drop off if you share the load?'

He was shaking his head, obviously angry. 'You know what, you think I'm doing such a bad job, then go ahead, it's all yours.' He raised his arms in surrender.

'Don't be ridiculous, Scott,' she said.

'No, I mean it,' he said, walking away. 'Do whatever you want. I don't give a shit.'

Friday

Catherine stepped out of the lift and walked down the corridor to her office. As she rounded the corner to Brooke's desk, she came to a dead stop.

Brooke leaped out of her chair, her expression apologetic and not a little fearful. 'Catherine, Mr Barrett was hoping to get five minutes with you first thing.'

James was sitting on the clients' waiting couch, his briefcase on his lap. He nodded, 'Good morning, Catherine.'

She just gave him a steely glare.

'Excuse me while I check my schedule,' she said curtly, before continuing on to her office, with Brooke scampering along in her wake.

'Close the door,' she snapped as she dropped her briefcase on her desk.

Brooke did as she was told. 'I'm so sorry, Catherine. He just walked in. I said you weren't here, but he insisted on waiting,' she said breathlessly. 'I didn't know what to do.'

Catherine turned around to face her. It wasn't Brooke's fault.

It's not as though she could have ordered him to leave, called security, even if that's what Catherine would have preferred. So now she had to take control.

'It's fine, Brooke. Go back out, wait till I send for him.'

Brooke left the office, closing the door behind her. Catherine sat down in her chair, taking a deep breath to compose herself. She sat forwards and opened her briefcase, as she normally would, withdrawing the documents she needed for the day. She snapped the briefcase shut again and placed it on the floor beside her desk. What did she usually do next? Her hands were shaking as she went over her schedule. Bastard. Pushy bastard. Used to getting his own way. What if he knew something, what if he had found out about Alice, like Rachel had suggested he might? She refused to be cornered this way. She had to control the situation. She reached across the desk for the stainless-steel jug that Brooke filled with iced water every morning. It was full, she had managed to get that much right. Catherine poured herself a glass and sipped from it slowly, thinking. She would hear him out. She would not give away anything, or admit to anything. She would also be careful not to assume anything.

When she felt calm and in control again, she leaned forwards to press the button of the intercom. 'Send Mr Barrett in, thank you, Brooke.'

She stood and walked to the door, opening it as he arrived. She nodded.

'Catherine, thanks for seeing me,' he said.

Like I had a choice, she felt like saying, but she didn't. Instead she just said, 'Take a seat.'

He walked past her and sat down in a chair opposite her desk, putting his briefcase down beside him and crossing his legs.

'So, what brings you here, unannounced, James?' said Catherine as she took her seat.

'Well, you wouldn't take my calls.'

'And clearly you wouldn't take a hint.'

He took a breath. 'Catherine, I'm not trying to upset you, I was only hoping to talk, catch up. It feels as though there's unfinished business between us.'

'What makes you think that?'

'The very fact that you won't take my calls,' he said plainly.

She bristled. 'I'm a busy woman, James.'

'I appreciate that, Catherine. I just . . .' he hesitated, before shaking his head. 'My wife always says I won't leave things alone.'

Christ.

'It didn't seem to bother you eighteen years ago,' she sniped.

He looked up then, blinking. Shit, why did she say that?

'But it did, Catherine,' he insisted. 'I guess that's what I wanted you to know. I mean, I was just a kid, really, we were both kids. And I know I should have got in touch, but I was upset.'

He was upset? Everything was handled for him, he should have been relieved.

'I snapped out of it after a couple of weeks, and I tried to look for you,' he went on. 'I waited at your school, around the bus lines, but I never saw you again.' He paused. 'To be honest, and I don't mean to sound overly dramatic, it's always haunted me a little, Catherine.'

She couldn't breathe. She couldn't speak. What did he want from her? It didn't seem that he knew about Alice. Or did he? What the fuck was he doing here?

'I suppose I've just always wondered if you were okay,' he said finally.

She took a moment to find her voice, and her nerve. 'Look around you, James, I'm doing just fine. You don't need to wonder any more.'

He stared at her for a moment. Catherine stood abruptly. 'Thanks for stopping by, but now I really have work to do.'

'Of course,' he nodded, getting to his feet. 'Thanks for your time.'

She went to the door and opened it. He walked towards her and put out his hand. 'It was good seeing you again, Catherine. I expect our paths will cross in the future.'

She took his hand and shook it. 'I expect they will. Bye James.'

He left the office and Catherine closed the door again. She walked back to her chair and sat down before her legs gave out on her.

*

That afternoon

Catherine had no sooner walked in the door than Alice was in her face.

'Mum, you know how I asked if I could go to that under eighteens dance party tomorrow night? And you were still deciding? Well, now Sophie Veitch wants to come –'

'Sophie's going out with you?'

'Well, only if I'm allowed to go,' said Alice. 'Tom said if it's okay with you, then it's okay with him.'

'Did he now? Why didn't he just give me a call?' said Catherine. 'I don't bite.'

'Whatever.' Alice pulled a face. 'I had to talk to you first anyway, or else you wouldn't have known what it was about.'

'Okay, can you go over it for me again?' said Catherine, walking through to the kitchen.

Alice followed her, rattling off what sounded like very convoluted arrangements, while Catherine poured herself a drink. They were going to someone or other's place to get ready, and her mother was driving them to the venue, and someone else's mother was picking them up, but she would be dropping them at one of the other girl's places where they would stay the night, because they all couldn't fit at the one house.

'Why don't you and Sophie just stay at our place?'

Alice shrugged. 'You don't like me bringing anyone back to sleep over when you've been out.'

That was true. If there was a chance she might have a hangover the next day, Catherine didn't care to have an audience. 'When are we talking about?'

She groaned. 'Tomorrow night, Mum. You're going to be at Lexie's, remember?'

'Oh, that's right,' said Catherine, half to herself, gazing across the bench at her daughter, into her eyes. Her father's eyes. That was the only thing she had inherited from him, his blue eyes. People often remarked upon it, because in every other way she was very much like Catherine. But Catherine's eyes were brown, and Alice had the same clear blue eyes that had looked at her across her desk this morning.

'Mum?' Alice prompted her. 'Are you all right?'

Catherine snapped out of it. 'Yes, darling, I'm fine, it's just been a long week.'

'So what can I tell Sophie?'

Catherine didn't have the energy to make Alice jump through hoops this time; she had just finished serving her longest grounding ever, she should give her the benefit of the doubt. She had to admit it was good to see her out of her room and excited about something. Besides, she definitely wanted to encourage this friendship with Sophie.

'Tell Sophie yes, she can tell her father it's fine with me. But you have to make sure I have the names of the parents and the phone numbers of the various places you're going to be,' she called after Alice, who had let out a whoop as soon as Catherine had uttered the word 'Yes', and promptly raced out of the room and up the stairs.

'Did you hear all that, Alice?'

'Yeah, sure Mum, no worries.'

That evening

'What's going on, Scott?'

Lexie had just walked in the door after another exhausting day. She hadn't spoken to Scott since last night; she left the house before any of them were up this morning. She also left a list for him. If Scott thought running the house was the easy option, and he really did intend to leave things at the café up to her, then she had a right to certain expectations here at home. But she was tired and cranky. This was feeling less like a transition phase and more like they were marking out battlelines. And she really was not up to going to war.

'Nothing's going on,' Scott answered her.

'I can see that,' she said, looking around. The house was a mess, the kids were playing outside, and he was standing at the kitchen bench, opening a beer. He looked up.

'What's your point?'

She took a breath. Patience. 'Well, have you thought about dinner, and the kids have to have their baths . . .'

'Chill, hun, it's a Friday night,' he said, taking a swig of his beer. 'Want a drink?'

'No thank you,' she said, dumping her bag on the bench. 'Did you get the shopping done?'

'Nah,' he said, turning to flick his bottle top into the bin, so he missed the look of shock on Lexie's face.

'It was such a beautiful day,' he went on. 'I took Mia down the beach, and we ended up staying there all morning. Then we came back for a nap, then we had to go pick up Riley, and when he got wind we'd been to the beach he was upset that he'd missed out, so I took them both down this afternoon.'

Lexie was beginning to seethe inside. 'Scott, have you forgotten we've got people coming tomorrow night?'

'Don't stress,' he said. 'It'll all get done.'

'Yeah, because now I'm going to have to do it all tomorrow.'

'No, you won't. I'll handle it.'

'How are you going to organise a barbecue and clean this house while you're at the café all day?'

'I'm not going to be at the café, you are.'

'What?' she blinked. 'Look Scott, I never said I wanted to take over full-time, that was your idea. I just wanted us to share a little more of the load.'

'So, this is sharing,' he shrugged. 'I was talking to Dad today and they're pouring a slab for his new shed tomorrow. They could use another pair of hands, so I said I'd go round and help.'

Lexie had to physically give her head a shake to take all that in. 'Why did you say you'd do that when you know we're having a houseful of people over that night?'

'It's six of us for a barbecue, Lexie, stop making such a big deal about it. I never get to help Dad out, I'm always working. I really want to do this.'

'Fine, I'll just have to ring everyone and tell them it's off tomorrow night.'

'Don't be so dramatic, Lex,' he chided. 'Everything'll get done. I'll be at Dad's for the morning, I'll do the shopping on the way home, and I'll have the whole afternoon to clean up and get ready.'

'But just look at this place,' she insisted. 'Do you realise what has to be done around here? The floors, the kitchen, the shower . . .'

'No one's going to be taking a shower tomorrow night, Lexie.'

'But they'll use the bathroom. It still has to be clean.'

'I don't think it's a priority,' he shrugged. 'You're going to have to give up some control about the way things are done around here, Lex, if we're going to be "sharing the load".'

'So this is how you get back at me?' she said.

'What do you mean?'

'You do a really bad job around the house, and I'll give up "interfering" in the café and everything will go back to the way it was.'

'I don't think I did a really bad job today,' Scott said plainly. 'I had a fantastic day with my kids, I was there for them one hundred per cent, and not just for the fun stuff. They were fed decent food, Mia had her nap, Riley was picked up from school on time. So the house is a little messy. I don't remember you ever saying that housework should take precedence over the kids.'

'Of course it doesn't.' Lexie was feeling cornered. 'But certain things still have to get done.'

'Lexie, you don't want my input in how you run the café –'

'I never said that.'

'Whatever,' he dismissed. 'You're going to have to accept the way I run things here at home. That's the only way this is going to work.'

'Fine, you're right,' said Lexie. 'But I'd rather do the home shift tomorrow, you can go to the café.'

'Sorry, I'm already committed to helping Dad.'

'So we're not even going to discuss it?'

He shook his head, walking from the room. 'There's nothing to discuss.'

*

Saturday night

Rachel jumped off the bus as soon as the doors swished open. She was so late. It had been an incredibly busy day at work; one of the juniors had called in sick – probably hungover – so they'd been run off their feet all day, which meant cleaning up also took longer. By Rachel's calculations, she should have been home and in the shower already around the time she was just getting on the bus. And then disaster struck, literally – they were majorly held up by an accident that happened almost right in front of them. Fortunately no one was seriously hurt, but they were blocked in, the driver couldn't detour, so they had no choice but to wait until tow-trucks arrived to clear the cars out of the way. Rachel considered getting off and walking the last few blocks, but it turned out the driver was some kind of OH&S nazi, and he refused to open the doors while the bus was in the middle of the road, despite the fact there was no through traffic with the road completely blocked by the accident.

Tom kept messaging to find out what was taking her so long, and he even offered to come and get her, but she messaged back that it was no use, he wouldn't be able to get through either. She had toyed with the idea of going straight to Lexie's, but she'd promised to bring a potato salad and it was waiting in her fridge at home, and she really needed a shower and a change of clothes. By the time she'd done all that, and waited for another bus to Clovelly, she was very late, and quite breathless when she finally knocked on the Dingles' front door.

'Hi,' Lexie said when she opened it. She looked a little flat, not her usual ebullient self. Rachel hoped she wasn't cranky with her for being so late.

'I'm really sorry I'm so late –'

'Don't worry about it,' Lexie dismissed. 'I got your message, you poor thing, stuck on the bus all that time.'

'I brought the salad,' Rachel offered, holding it up.

'Thanks for that,' she sighed wearily, taking the bowl from Rachel and leading her down the hall. 'The house is a mess, please don't look at the bathroom especially. I did manage to clean the toilet when I came home. I asked Scott if he'd done that at least, and you know what he said? That it looked all right to him.'

Rachel gave her an encouraging smile. 'I'm sure everything's fine, Lexie. Besides, we're all here to see each other, not to inspect the house.'

Lexie walked around the bench into the kitchen. 'Scott's barely lifted a finger. The most he managed was to get to the butcher's.'

'He didn't work again today?' asked Rachel.

'No, I had to, he seems to have gone into semi-retirement.' Lexie picked up a knife to resume chopping vegetables. 'Scott assured me he'd handle everything, then I get a call at four – four o'clock this afternoon, Rachel – to say he was just leaving his parents' place and he'd only have time to get to the butcher's, could I pick up salad stuff, bread rolls ... everything!' She waved the knife in the air.

Rachel had never seen Lexie like this.

'He knows better than anyone what the café's like on a Saturday afternoon. Josh, bless him, offered to finish closing or I never would have got out of there. And then I come home and the place is a shambles, nothing's been cleaned, and Riley's rearranged the living room and made tunnels and cubbies out of the sofa cushions and blankets that he's dragged from the linen cupboard. But Scott's completely oblivious; he's got stuff spread from one end of the kitchen to the other, making a special "rub" for the meat that he'd read about and wanted to try.' She actually growled. This time she slammed the knife down onto the chopping board, right through the middle of a cucumber. Rachel couldn't help think she was imagining it was something else.

'Would you like some help, Lexie?' she asked tentatively.

'No, you've been working all day too,' said Lexie. 'What are you drinking? Let me get you a glass.' She turned around to the cupboards behind her.

Rachel drew out a bottle of wine from the cooler bag she'd brought, and Lexie set a glass down in front of her.

'You're going to need to catch up to that lot out there,' she said, cocking her head towards the back garden. 'Scott's drinking beer like it's going out of style, after being sick all week. Of course, Catherine's having no trouble keeping up with him, she's already half-tanked.'

'I know she had some unexpected news last week, it's probably thrown her a bit,' Rachel offered in an attempt to calm things over, but Lexie didn't even seem to take it in.

'And Martin, well he's in the doldrums, big time, I don't know what's going on there. The whole night is turning into a disaster. It was supposed to make Tom feel included. He probably wishes we hadn't bothered.'

'I'm sure he doesn't feel that way, Lexie.'

'You should go outside, he'll be happy to see your face, I reckon.'

Rachel hesitated. 'Are you sure I can't help somehow?'

'You'll help most if you go out and make nice with Tom.'

She should be able to manage that.

Rachel picked up her glass and wandered out through the playroom and into the small backyard, where the four of them were sitting in a half-circle. Tom's face lit up when she appeared and he leaped out of his seat.

'Hey, Rach, it's great to see you,' he said, throwing his arms around her. 'It's really great to see you,' he muttered in her ear. 'You have no idea.'

Rachel pulled back from him. 'It's nice to see you too, Tom. How have you been?'

'Good, really good,' he said. 'You look fantastic, Rachel, what have you been doing with yourself?'

'Yeah, you do look great,' said Scott expansively, standing up to greet her with a kiss.

'I should come here more often,' Rachel remarked. 'All these compliments. I blame working in the juice bar, it's like an enforced detox. I seem to live on carrots and celery and watermelon.'

'Well, it certainly agrees with you,' said Tom, gazing at her with a kind of proud glint in his eye. Don't overdo it, Tom.

'Oh stop,' she joked, 'you're going to make me blush.'

'Then her face goes all red and blotchy,' Catherine broke in, standing up to join them. 'She's not so pretty then, let me tell you.'

'Hi there, Martin,' Rachel said, craning to see around Catherine, who was standing right in front of him. 'How are you?'

'Don't ask, he's likely to tell you,' said Catherine, linking her arm through Rachel's. 'I'm just borrowing her for a sec, boys, girl-talk,' she said, drawing her away.

'Okay,' said Rachel uncertainly. 'But can I just grab a chair? My feet are killing me.'

'No, I'd rather stand,' Catherine said, dragging her down to the back fence. 'Every time I sit down Mia thinks it's an invitation to climb all over me,' she grimaced. 'She's like a cat – you know how they always go for the one person in the room who doesn't like cats?'

Rachel wanted to get whatever this was over with so she could sit down. 'What did you want to talk about?' she prompted Catherine.

'James showed up at my office yesterday, just like that, unannounced and uninvited.'

She had obviously been drinking heavily, her speech was so slurred that 'unannounced and uninvited' had proved quite a challenge to get her tongue around.

'Has he found out about Alice?' Rachel asked.

'I don't think so. I don't think he has any idea, quite frankly.'

'Then what did he want?'

'It was weird,' said Catherine. 'He said he felt like we had unfinished business.'

'That is weird. Did he explain himself?'

'Not exactly,' she said. 'He told me he was upset way back then, but that he did come and look for me at school after a few weeks, but he couldn't find me.'

'That must have been after you'd left,' said Rachel. 'But why is he telling you all this now?'

'That's what I don't get.'

'And you're sure he knows nothing about Alice?'

'He doesn't seem to,' she said. 'Unless he's playing some kind of sick game.'

Rachel looked at her. 'What are you going to do?'

Catherine sighed. 'I don't know.'

'But you have to do something,' said Rachel. 'Don't you?'

'Do I?'

She nodded. 'It's all going to come out eventually. I don't know why he's making a move now, but you're going to have to find out what he's up to, or at least what he knows, and you're going to have to prepare Alice.'

'You're probably right. I'm just not sure in what order.'

'What do you mean?'

'Well, if I confront him and reveal all, and he starts making demands, then I'll be forced to tell Alice, and what if she baulks at the idea of meeting her father? But if I tell her first, and he doesn't want to know about her, then she gets rejected.'

Rachel thought about it. 'Catherine, when you take custody cases to court, what's the underlying philosophy, the bottom line for the judge in making their decision?'

'The needs of the child, always.'

'There's your answer,' said Rachel simply. 'James can make all the demands he wants, but it's ultimately up to Alice. You have to talk to her first.'

Catherine raised an eyebrow. 'You're getting smart in your old age,' she remarked. 'Where's your Matthew by the way, wasn't tonight all about meeting him?'

Rachel blinked, gathering her thoughts. 'No, I haven't even had the chance to tell Lexie about him, so I couldn't just show up with him, and besides, he was busy, and anyway then Tom would be the odd one out –'

'Okay, okay,' said Catherine. 'I suppose we'll meet the phantom boyfriend eventually.'

Interesting choice of words.

They wandered back up the yard to join the others. Catherine raised her glass. 'Martin, my glass is empty.'

'That's nice, dear,' he replied without looking at her.

'Miserable sod,' she muttered.

'Can I get you a drink, Catherine?' Tom offered.

'Well, aren't you the gentleman?' she returned. She went to pass him her glass, but changed her mind. 'Oh never mind. I have to go to the bathroom anyway.' She tottered off inside, a little unsteadily.

Rachel looked up at Tom. 'Where's Hannah tonight?'

'Actually, a friend called her this afternoon and asked her over for the night, so seeing as Sophie and Alice weren't going to be here, I let her go.'

'Oh? Where are they?'

'They're both going to an under eighteens dance party. Catherine approved, so I figured it must be okay.'

Rachel nodded. 'I've heard those under eighteen events are really well supervised. I'm sure she'll be quite safe.' She paused to sip her wine. 'So you're on your own tonight?'

'Yeah . . .' He dropped his voice. 'Do you think anyone would notice if we disappeared next door for half an hour?'

'That's a good one, Tom,' she laughed loudly.

'What's so funny?' said Scott, looking over at them.

'Just a joke I heard at work,' said Tom. 'It's not really worth repeating.' He placed an arm lightly around Rachel's shoulders. 'You know Rach, she's easily amused.'

She elbowed him.

Lexie appeared at the back door. 'Scott, now that Rachel's here we really should get the barbecue going.'

'I'll just finish my beer,' he said, raising it.

'Do you need a hand with anything, Lexie?' Tom asked.

'No, Tom, thanks.' She glared at her husband. 'I think the kids should be put to bed before the adults eat, Scott.'

'Do you want me to cook the barbecue or deal with the kids?' he returned evenly.

'Either one would do,' she sniped.

'Soon as I finish my beer, love,' he repeated.

Tom and Rachel glanced awkwardly at each other.

Lexie sighed loudly. 'Riley, Mia, inside now!'

It was at least another hour before they were all seated at the table inside. The food was delicious, the wine flowing, but the atmosphere was strained to say the least. Rachel was not sure how their plan was going; she had a feeling she and Tom could have slow danced naked on the table and it would have gone unnoticed tonight, so wrapped up was everybody else in their own dramas. Still, she was quite enjoying Tom's attention, and the flirting was fun. She even felt a little smug, considering everyone else at the table seemed to be at each other's throats. But she also couldn't help a niggling doubt that once their private little bubble burst they wouldn't be any different. She wanted to believe they would, but it had been a bit of a jolt to witness Lexie and Scott going hammer and tongs at each other tonight. It reminded her uncomfortably of her own childhood. No one ever seemed to stay happy. Tom and Annie were almost the only happy couple she knew, but who knows what might have happened to them? They were frozen in time now, like a legend – the last happy couple left in the eastern suburbs. How was Rachel ever going to compete with that?

'Funny thing is,' Lexie was saying, waving a wineglass as she spoke, 'Scott seems to think the house cleans itself, and the clothes wash themselves. I don't know what he thinks I've been doing with myself all this time.'

'It's what I've been trying to tell you, Lexie,' said Catherine. 'It's not a valued job. No one takes it seriously. You might as well have a cleaner doing it, for all the thanks you get.'

'Catherine's an expert on hired help,' Martin piped in. 'She hasn't lifted a finger around the house as long as I've known her.'

'But see, Lexie does it all so much better than I ever could,' said Scott. 'And it turns out that now she can even run the café better than me. Apparently I've been doing it wrong all these years.'

Rachel felt Tom's foot nudging hers, then sliding up her ankle; at least she hoped it was Tom's foot. She looked across the table and he was gazing at her with a bemused grin. She moved her foot against his. They could be alone together at her place right now, but instead they were reduced to playing footsies under the table.

Lexie started to clear the plates, and Tom and Rachel both jumped up to help. 'No, sit, you're guests,' she said, glaring at Scott. But he didn't budge.

'Yeah, really guys, let her do it all herself,' said Scott. 'She's going for the title Superwoman of the Year, or is it Martyr? I keep forgetting.'

Lexie stomped over to the kitchen and started clattering the plates noisily into the dishwasher.

'Tom, can you grab another bottle out of the fridge while you're up, darling?' said Catherine.

'You're opening another bottle?' said Martin.

'Yes. I'm sure I'll have help drinking it. You're having white, aren't you, Rachel?'

'Yes, but I still have half a bottle,' she said. 'Do you want some of mine?'

Catherine curled her lip. 'Probably not. I'm sure we'll get through another bottle.'

'I'm sure *you* will,' Martin muttered.

'Lay off, would you, Martin? It's a Saturday night, it's party night.'

'So what was your excuse Friday night, and Thursday night, and Wednesday –'

'Okay, we get it, you can recite the days of the week, backwards even,' Catherine sneered. 'Tom, you haven't talked about work at all this evening,' she said, placing a hand on his arm as he reached past her to fill her wineglass.

'It's Saturday night, Catherine, party night, like you said,' Tom reminded her. 'No one wants to hear about work.'

'Oh, but I do,' she gushed.

'You never want to hear about my work,' said Martin.

'Because yours is boring.'

'So is mine,' Tom assured her, returning to his seat.

'Is your firm affected by this economic downturn as well?' Catherine asked. 'That's all Martin can talk about.'

Tom looked at him. 'You guys are US-owned, aren't you? Things must be a little precarious right now.'

Martin nodded, leaning forwards. 'It looks like we may not have any choice but to close our Australia-Pacific operations altogether.'

'What?' said Catherine. 'You never mentioned that.'

'Because any time I bring it up you cut me off.'

'But if they close, what happens to you?'

'There'll probably be a position for me somewhere. Not in the UK or the US, they're shedding staff over there. But it's probably worth keeping a presence in China, so we might open an office there.'

Catherine snorted. 'I'm not going to China.'

'What will you do, Martin?' Rachel asked.

'Probably join the office in China,' he said squarely.

'Dessert everyone,' said Lexie as she planted an enormous platter in the centre of the table. It was some kind of layered cream confection, covered in berry fruits.

'Wow, look at this,' said Tom.

'It's fantastic, Lexie,' Rachel added.

'To my wife,' said Scott, raising his beer bottle as he gave her backside a slap. 'Is there anything she can't do?'

Lexie's face was turning red with barely suppressed rage; it looked like she just might blow. But before she could come out with anything the doorbell rang. She frowned. 'Who could that be at this time of night? Scott, maybe you should go.'

He sighed loudly and got to his feet. 'Excuse me everyone. Apparently I am useful for something after all.'

Tom and Rachel exchanged a glance across the table. Straight after dessert she was going to call it a night — she would apologise that she was tired, she'd been on her feet all day — then Tom would offer to give her a lift home. Hopefully that would give Catherine and Martin the hint and they would leave Lexie and Scott to what was surely going to be a mighty reckoning. Rachel didn't think she could stand much more of this. Especially when she could have Tom all to herself, for the whole night. This 'coming out' thing was feeling vastly overrated right now.

Scott came back down the hall, an odd expression on his face. 'Tom, Catherine,' he said.

Tom rose from his seat. 'What is it?'

Just then Alice and Sophie stepped forwards into the room, along with a woman Rachel didn't know.

'What's going on?' said Catherine, standing up.

'Hello,' said the woman, 'I'm Olivia's mother, Carolyn. I don't think we've met.'

Tom came around the table. 'Sophie, what's wrong?'

Rachel noticed then that Sophie was quite pale, almost green actually, and she was squinting at the light. Tom held her by the shoulders. 'Have you been drinking, Soph?'

Catherine strode over. 'Alice, what have you done?'

'Nothing!' she protested.

'Hello, Carolyn, I'm Catherine,' she said, shaking the woman's hand.

'And I'm Tom, Sophie's dad,' he added. 'Thanks for bringing them home. Do you know what happened?'

'Can I sit down, please?' Sophie said weakly.

Scott grabbed a chair from the table and turned it around for Sophie to sit on. 'Would you like a seat?' he asked Carolyn. 'Can I get you anything?'

'No, thank you,' she said. 'Olivia and her friend are out in the car. I can't stay, I just felt I shouldn't leave them on their own. We tried Alice's house first, but there was no one home.'

'You knew we were out, Alice,' said Catherine. 'Why did you make Olivia's mother take you home when you knew there'd be no one there?'

'I think that was probably the idea,' said Carolyn. 'We tried Sophie's place next, then they finally admitted you were all here next door.'

'You shouldn't have had to run around like that, Carolyn,' said Tom. 'I would have come and got them.'

'I was picking them up at the end of the night anyway,' Carolyn explained. 'Apparently Olivia and the others got separated from Alice and Sophie, then Alice messaged her that they were outside and couldn't get back in. There are no pass-outs after nine pm at these events, they were going to have to wait around till it was over. Olivia was worried after a while and that's when she called me. When I got there, we couldn't find them at first, and they weren't answering their phones. Eventually they came out from the toilets, Sophie had been sick, I'm afraid.'

Tom sighed, rubbing his forehead. 'I can't tell you how sorry I am you had to be involved in this, Carolyn.'

'Look, it's fine, it happens,' she said. 'I'm just glad security didn't pick them up first. They're very strict about alcohol consumption on the beach, not to mention they're under-age. You might have had to collect them from the local police station.'

'Hmm, and I might have been tempted to leave Alice there,' Catherine grunted.

Tom shook his head. 'Well, we're very grateful to you, Carolyn.'

'No problem,' she said. 'I'll leave you to it.'

'Thanks again,' said Catherine.

'I'll see you out,' Scott said, walking Carolyn up the hall.

'Okay, miss.' Catherine turned around to face Alice. 'You've got some explaining to do. Where did you get the alcohol?'

'Where do you think? The house is full of it.'

'Don't you get smart with me, young lady,' Catherine snapped back. 'I'm mortified, Tom. I should never have trusted her. I thought she'd learned a lesson from being grounded so long, but obviously not. You just couldn't wait to get out and do the wrong thing again, could you, Alice?'

Tom crouched down in front of Sophie. 'I don't understand, Sophie. What's going on? Why did you do this?'

Her head was bent, her eyes downcast. 'I don't want to talk about it,' she muttered.

'You don't have a choice,' he said firmly. 'This is unacceptable, Sophie. You know better.'

'Don't be too hard on her, Tom,' said Catherine. 'I'm sure she would never have done something like this without Alice putting her up to it.'

'Why do you always think the worst of me?' Alice cried. 'What have I ever done that's so bad?'

'That's enough, Alice,' said Catherine.

'No, really, Mum,' she persisted. 'What have I done?'

'Isn't this enough?' she snapped. 'Tom entrusted Sophie into your care, and look at how you repay that trust. By stealing alcohol from the house, dragging Sophie away from the dance and making her sick.'

'It was her idea,' Alice blurted.

'What?' said Tom.

'Don't make Sophie take the blame,' Catherine shrilled.

'Sophie,' said Tom. 'Is it true what Alice is saying, this was your idea?'

She was slumped forwards, her hair hanging over her face.

'Sophie, answer me!'

She looked up then. 'I don't have to answer to you.'

'I beg your pardon?'

'You don't tell us anything that's going on. You keep stuff from us all the time.'

Rachel suddenly felt nervous.

'What are you talking about?' he asked.

No, don't ask her. Not here. Take her home. Rachel had a bad feeling about this.

Sophie lifted her face to look her father in the eye. 'I know about you and Rachel.'

Tom stared at her, dumbstruck.

'You've been sneaking around, lying about where you're going and what you're doing, but I'm not stupid, Dad. You're sleeping with one of Mum's best friends,' Sophie accused, her voice breaking. 'It's sick.'

Rachel froze. She couldn't breathe, her eyes blurred, she couldn't see anyone, but she could feel Lexie staring at her.

'Rachel?' she said in a small voice.

'You slimy, cheating snake,' said Catherine. What did it have to do with her?

'Catherine, don't,' Tom said, straightening up and turning to face her.

Rachel blinked a couple of times, willing her eyes to focus again. Catherine was standing right in front of him. 'You fucking player,' she was saying.

'Don't do this, Catherine. Not here, not in front of the girls.'

'Don't do what? Out you for what you really are?' she said. 'What, were you going to try Lexie next?'

'Stop it, Catherine.'

Rachel felt sick in the stomach.

'What's she talking about, Dad?' Sophie asked nervously.

'Let's just say your father certainly gets around,' said Catherine. 'He and I –'

'It was one night,' Tom interrupted loudly. 'Once only. We were very drunk. It was a mistake.'

Sophie got to her feet, glaring at her father, shaking her head. 'When was this?'

Oh my God. The conference. Tom was the guy Catherine met at the conference. But that was before Annie . . .

'Sophie . . .' Tom put his hands on her shoulders.

She shook them off violently. 'No!' She pushed him away and fled up the hall. Tom followed straight after her and a moment later there was a loud slam of the door. An eerie quiet descended on the room.

'So there was no Matthew, I take it, Rachel?' Catherine said finally, her voice twisted with bitterness. 'How long has this been going on with Tom?'

Rachel wasn't going to be put through an inquisition, especially not by Catherine. She still felt sick in the stomach, and now she was finding it hard to breathe. She had to get out of here. She went on automatic pilot, crossing the room to pick up her bag. There were other things, a salad bowl, a cooler bag, but she didn't care about them right now. She knew all eyes were fixed on her, watching her, following her.

'Rachel?' Catherine persisted as she walked past her.

She ignored her, pausing in front of Lexie and Scott, but she couldn't meet their eyes. 'I'm sorry.' She tried to think of something else to say, but nothing came. So she just said it again. 'I'm sorry.'

She felt Martin at her side. 'I'm leaving now, Rachel, can I give you a lift?'

'No . . . thank you.' She walked up the hall, numb. Her hand was shaking as she opened the door and stepped out, closing it quietly behind her. The air was cooler outside. She breathed it in and it hurt her lungs. She could hear voices, and she glanced over towards Tom's place. The door was open. She felt compelled, her legs carried her down the path and over to his front door. She stood on the front step; she couldn't see them, but she could hear them clearly now.

'Of course I loved your mother,' Tom was saying. 'I did a bad thing, a terrible thing, but it was a mistake. I was really drunk. Come on, Sophie, look at you tonight, surely you can understand people do stupid things when they're drunk? It never happened again.'

'What about Rachel?'

'That didn't start until after . . . a while after.'

'I don't understand.' She was crying. 'How could you replace Mum like that, so soon?'

'Oh, Soph, I could never replace your mother.'

Rachel could hear her sobbing. 'I've been so scared. I didn't know why you were being so secretive. I thought you were going to run away with her.'

'What?' Tom sounded shocked. 'Why would you think that? You and Hannah are more important to me than anything in the world. You're my family.'

'But I'm not.'

'Sophie, you are my daughter every bit as much as Hannah is. Don't you know that? Don't you think of me as your father?'

'Yes.' She was still sobbing. 'But I started thinking, maybe with Mum gone, you might try and find my real father, so you wouldn't have to be responsible for me any more.'

'Oh, my God, Sophie.' The shock and distress in his voice was palpable. 'I wouldn't give you up for anything, don't you know that? You think because your mum's gone that could change? That it could ever change?' There was a long pause, and eventually Sophie was quiet. Tom was hugging her, Rachel imagined, soothing away her tears. After a while he spoke again and his voice was calmer.

'I fell in love with you the same time as I fell in love with your mum. You were a package. I honestly couldn't cope with losing you as well, Sophie.'

Rachel stepped away from the door and walked quietly down the path, as Martin's car pulled away from Lexie's house. She turned in the opposite direction. She didn't want to go up to the main road, she'd take the coastal walk. It probably wasn't the safest route this time of night, but she had to clear her head, away from cars and traffic, where she could look out at the ocean.

'Rachel! Wait!'

She turned around to see Alice running towards her.

'Can I come home with you, please?' she said as she drew closer, breathless.

'No, Alice, you can't,' said Rachel. 'You have to go with your mother.'

'I don't want to go with her,' she protested. 'I don't have to do anything she says, ever again.'

'Yes, you do,' said Rachel. She saw Catherine stepping out onto the footpath outside Lexie's.

'Please, I won't be any trouble,' Alice pleaded. 'Let me go home with you.'

'No, Alice. You can't come with me.'

'Why not?'

Rachel swallowed down the lump in her throat. 'Because you have to sort this out with your mother.'

'No,' she cried.

'Alice, listen to me,' said Rachel, taking her by the shoulders. 'Sophie would give anything to have her mother back. And I would have given anything to have a mother who cared about me.'

'She doesn't care about me.'

'Of course she does, Alice. She loves you more than anything. I know it doesn't always seem like that to you, but she does. And you're old enough now to make it work. Talk to her, tell her how you feel. Make her listen to you.'

Alice just stared at her, her eyes glassy.

'It's going to be all right, chook. I'll always be here for you, but she's your mum, and you have to go with her now.'

And then she turned and walked quickly up the street.

'Alice,' Catherine called to her. 'Come along now.'

Lexie was watching from the doorway. Alice stood where she was, and Catherine walked up to her. She couldn't hear what was said, but eventually Catherine took Alice by the arm and led her down the street in the other direction. Lexie stepped back inside and closed the door. She walked slowly down the hall to the living room. Scott was clearing the table, he glanced up at her.

'Go to bed, Lex,' he said. 'I'll clean up.'

She didn't say anything; she walked through the kitchen to the playroom and locked the sliding doors to the backyard, turning out the lights. Then she came back into the kitchen, where Scott was standing at the sink. 'Leave it,' she said.

'No, I'll do it.'

She took his hand. 'Leave it.'

She led him through the kitchen and up the hall to the stairs, turning out the lights as she went.

'Lexie . . .'

'Shh.' She started up the stairs. At the landing she pushed open the door to the children's room and peered in; they were both sleeping peacefully. She closed the door and turned around. Scott was standing there, watching her.

She brought her arms up around his neck. 'I love you, Scott,' she said.

He sighed, drawing his arms around her and holding her tight. 'I love you, too, Lexie, so much.'

'I'm sorry,' she said tearfully.

'I'm sorry too.'

'Please make love to me.'

'Absolutely.'

The next day

Tom had been calling all day. Rachel didn't answer the phone, she wasn't ready to talk to him yet. But he didn't seem to get the hint.

'Rachel, come on, pick up, I know you're there. We have to talk. You can't just ignore me.'

Oh, but she could, for now anyway. After five similar messages, each a little more desperate than the last, she pulled the cord out of the wall. Then she turned off her mobile when it kept ringing out. She checked her text messages after a while, and there was a steady stream, all from Tom.

When can I see you? We have to talk. Call me. I love you.

You can't ignore me forever. You have to let me explain.

RACHEL!!! CALL ME!

I'm coming round. See you soon.

That was obviously him now, buzzing the security door downstairs. It was annoying, but he couldn't keep it up for long, someone would get the shits eventually and come out to see what was going on.

It stopped. Rachel breathed out. She went into the kitchen to put the kettle on. But then she was startled by loud knocking on the door of her flat. Blasted security door, someone must have let him in.

'Rachel!' he called, followed by another couple of loud knocks.

She walked back into the living room, her heart pounding in her chest.

'You're not leaving me any choice,' he called, and then she heard a key in the lock. She walked over to look up the hall as Tom came through the front door, closing it behind him.

'You can't just barge in here like that!' she cried.

'I can, I have a key, remember,' he said bluntly, striding right up to her.

'Then give it back,' said Rachel, holding her hand out.

'Not until you listen to what I have to say.'

'Excuse me?' she frowned. 'You've got no right to walk in here making demands, Tom.'

'I just want to talk to you, Rachel, please,' he said plaintively.

'Then give me the key,' she insisted, glaring at him.

He sighed, taking his keys out of his pocket. He twisted her house key off the ring and handed it to her.

'Okay,' she said calmly. 'Now leave.'

'Rach, come on, you have to hear me out.'

'No, I don't,' she said, walking across the room away from him. 'I don't have to hear you out, I don't owe you anything, Tom.'

'So you never really loved me this whole time?'

Rachel spun around. 'What the fuck? Where do you get off putting this whole thing onto me?'

'I'm not, I just think if you loved me you'd want to hear what I had to say,' he said plainly. 'But you'd rather take Catherine's drunken ramblings over my word.'

'I remember, Tom, her going on about the guy she slept with at the conference, the guy she was going to leave Martin for.'

'That was all in her head.'

'Are you going to try and tell me you didn't sleep with her?'

'No, I'm not. But the only person I have to apologise to for that is Annie, and I already did.'

Rachel wasn't expecting that. 'You did?'
He nodded.
'Annie knew?'
'Yes,' he said. 'I couldn't live with myself, I had to tell her.'
She stared at him. 'How do I know you're telling the truth?'
'For Chrissakes, Rachel, why would I lie?'
'You've been lying all along.'
'I didn't lie to you, it had nothing to do with us. It was none of your damn business, to be honest.'
She flinched at that. 'Fine. Then we have nothing more to say to each other,' she said. 'So leave.'
'Rachel,' he held his hands up. 'It is your business now. Of course it's your business now, after what happened last night. You have to give me a chance to explain.'
She stood there, breathing hard.
'Please,' he said. 'I promise I'll go if you still want me to, once you hear me out.'
She stood for a while longer, considering her options. It's not as though she could physically evict him.
'All right, fine.' She dropped down into the armchair furthest away from him. 'Go ahead.'
He sighed heavily, walking over to the couch and sitting down. He mustn't have slept much, he looked dreadful.
'I don't know where to start,' he said.
'Well, you could start with how you came to sleep with Catherine,' she retorted.
'But that's not where it started,' he said, looking at her. 'You have to understand, I was going through a bad time last year, even before that. I hated my job, I'd hated it for years. I was working longer and longer hours, and I was getting no time with the girls, or Annie. I felt like I didn't have a life.'
Rachel frowned. 'You've talked about this a lot, you know, Tom. Why haven't you ever done anything about it?'
He shrugged. 'Every time I brought it up with Annie, she just didn't seem to hear me,' he said. 'I mean, she'd sit there, she'd listen while I'd tell her how miserable I was, that I couldn't bear going in to work every day. And she'd act like there was no way out.' He paused. 'It was strange, she was so . . . sympathetic in a

way, but it was as though there was nothing that could be done about it.'

Rachel could picture Annie, being so understanding, listening to him. That's how she always was. She never pushed solutions, she just listened. 'Maybe she was waiting for you to work it out for yourself?'

'I tried. I started to throw up options, other jobs I could do, maybe something in legal aid, or with a government agency, where the hours would be better and I might be able to do something I believed in. Annie would look right into it, do the sums, and then she'd say it wasn't possible. We just couldn't maintain things the way they were without my salary.'

'Did you ever put it to her that maybe you didn't need to maintain things exactly the way they were?' said Rachel. 'That she could have gone out and got a job, for example?'

He sighed heavily, holding his head in his hands for a moment. Then he looked up again. 'I don't know,' he shook his head. 'Maybe I should have pushed it more. It's hard to explain . . . The way she was about it, I would have felt selfish if I suggested anything like that. She just asked me to hang in there for a few more years, get the girls through school, and then I could do whatever I wanted, she promised.'

He stared out across the room. 'But Han had just started high school . . . it would be another six years. I felt trapped. I mean, I loved her, and I knew she loved me, but there was this gulf opening up between us.' He shook his head. 'Annie just thought it was all about work. So when this conference came up, she encouraged me to go, have a break, connect with other lawyers, I might get a new lease . . .'

He sat back, breathing out.

'Catherine came on to me the first night, I could tell what she was doing but I held her off, ignored her pretty much,' he said. 'Then the second night . . .' He sighed. 'I got really drunk.' He looked directly at Rachel. 'I'm not making excuses, but she came on pretty strong. And I guess I was flattered by the attention. By someone who wanted me, not my pay packet. Which is shallow, I know.'

Rachel didn't think it was that shallow.

'She seemed to understand exactly how I was feeling, she said all the right things, things I'd been waiting to hear Annie say.' He drifted off for a moment, thinking. 'But when I woke up in her room the next morning, I freaked. I couldn't believe what I'd done. I told her it was a mistake, it should never have happened. But she kept calling me.'

'Is that why you confessed to Annie?' Rachel asked.

He shook his head. 'I'd already decided to tell her, I was too riddled with guilt. But after what happened, I wish I hadn't told her.'

Rachel frowned. 'How did she take it?'

'She was shocked. No wonder, I was shocked myself. She couldn't understand how I could do that, with Catherine of all people.' He took a breath. 'But mostly she was just . . . bewildered, I suppose you'd call it. You see, I think Annie believed the fantasy as much as everyone else, that we were the perfect couple, and that's why she had literally been unable to see how unhappy I was. It rocked everything she believed in. She was completely disillusioned – with me, and our marriage, and herself. I didn't want her to feel that way, but she wouldn't talk about it, she said she couldn't, she needed time to process it . . .'

There was a long pause till finally he spoke again, his voice ragged. 'And then she got sick.'

Rachel drew her breath in sharply. She hadn't realised exactly when all this had happened. Tom was visibly distressed. He had to wipe his eyes before he continued.

'When she . . . when she died,' he went on, his voice hoarse, 'I lost it. I was so torn up with guilt, convinced it was my fault somehow, if only I hadn't told her . . .'

'Tom . . . no . . .' was all Rachel could say.

He looked at her. 'I haven't told anyone this, but I snapped at the hospital, I went a little nuts, they had to give me something to calm me down. That's why it took so long before I was able to call the girls, before anyone knew what had happened.'

Tears sprung involuntarily into Rachel's eyes. And that's why he had so much trouble talking about it, talking about Annie. He probably thought he'd lose it again if he dared to open up, scratch under the surface.

'The guilt was eating me up, Rachel,' he said. 'I honestly didn't know how I was going to be able to stand it.' He paused. 'And then, you were there for me ... and you let me be myself. And you loved me for myself. You helped me let go and heal, Rach. I couldn't have done that without you.'

She stood abruptly. 'But I didn't know about any of this.' She turned her back to him, looking out the window at the brick wall of the next block.

'Rachel,' he said, his voice sounded so tired, 'I know that. Of course you didn't know. You haven't done anything wrong.'

She turned around. 'Sophie's never going to see it that way.'

'She will, given time.'

'Give her a break, Tom. She lost her mother, so suddenly and tragically, and you just haven't been there for her, for either of them. I understand why, and what you've been going through. And I'm glad I could be there for you, and that we've had this time together, but it's been borrowed time. We can't do this any more, Tom.'

Something shifted in his expression. 'What are you saying?'

'Nothing you haven't said yourself,' Rachel said plainly. 'It didn't matter what anyone else thought, but this had to be okay with the girls.'

'It's okay with Hannah.'

'Because Hannah's never going to imagine you'll send her packing off to her real father.'

He looked a little stunned at that.

'I heard you and Sophie talking last night, at least some of it.'

'She knows that's not going to happen, Rachel,' said Tom.

'Maybe on one level, but that's how insecure she's feeling, poor kid. I know what that's like, I was around the same age. My parents chose jobs and partners and pretty much anything over me, and it broke my heart, Tom.'

He shook his head. 'So that's what this is really all about,' he said, getting to his feet. 'This is your stuff again, Rachel, running away from a relationship, from uni, from life, when it all gets too hard.'

She stood there, trembling, her eyes filling. 'You think that's what I'm doing? That this is about me? I'm not twenty years old any more, Tom, I've figured out a few things. I know that you love me, and I do love you, so much, and I want to be with you more than anything, but this is not about us. I promise I'm not taking the easy way out.' Her voice broke. 'This doesn't feel easy to me. Walking away from you feels like the hardest thing I've ever done.'

He crossed the room and caught her up in his arms as she collapsed into tears. 'I'm sorry, I'm so sorry,' he said, holding her close. 'I love you, Rachel, I just don't want to lose you. We can find a way to make this work.'

She drew back, wiping her eyes with her hands. 'It's not that simple, Tom. Sit down, you have to listen to me.'

They sat facing each other, Tom rested his arm across the back of the couch, stroking her shoulder.

'This is not just about Sophie,' Rachel began. 'We had all these grand plans about "coming out" to everyone so that we could be together all the time. But how was that ever going to work?'

He frowned. 'What are you saying?'

She looked at him directly. 'Did you expect me to sleep with you in Annie's bed?'

'No, of course not.'

'So what were we going to do?'

He hesitated for a moment. 'Well, I'm not sure, I hadn't really thought about it.'

'I know,' said Rachel. 'You haven't thought about anything much, Tom. You've been telling me how unhappy you were with your life, but what have you done except latch onto me and expect me to slot into that same life? I suppose in a few years' time you would have got drunk one night and slept with someone else because you felt trapped and unhappy.'

'Rachel,' he protested, 'that's not fair.'

'I'm just saying, I can't be a replacement for Annie,' she said. 'You said it yourself.'

'I didn't mean . . . I was just trying to reassure Sophie that no one was ever going to replace her mother.'

'I understand that, Tom. I know I can't replace Annie, and that's the thing, I don't want to. I don't want to live Annie's life with you.'

'We don't have to, we'll make our own life together,' he said. 'Maybe we should sell the house –'

'Maybe you should,' Rachel agreed. 'Maybe that would be the very best thing for all of you. But you have to decide that together, you can't do it for me, Sophie will resent it.'

'And Sophie will get over it,' he snapped then, getting to his feet and walking away, annoyed.

'What if she doesn't, Tom?' said Rachel. 'What if she acts out, like the other night. You think a little under-age drinking is as bad as it's going to get? She could make life hell for us if she chose to, and nobody would win in that scenario. Not you and me, not Hannah, and certainly not Sophie. But far worse than that would be if she decided to withdraw, go inside herself, fly under the radar.' Rachel took a breath. 'She has no one else, Tom. No one. You have to try and understand what it's like for her, you've always had people around you who love you, who would do anything for you. My God, your parents drove through the night to be with you after Annie died. Now you have to be that person for Sophie. She needs to know you're going to be there for her.'

He turned around to look at her. 'Okay, I get that. But why can't I be there for her and still be with you? Isn't it better for the girls if their father is happy?'

She was shaking her head. 'You know what, I think that kind of attitude is a cop-out from adults who want to justify selfish behaviour. It's bullshit,' she said. 'Sophie said the idea of us together was "sick". You're not going to convince her otherwise right now by showing her how happy I make you. And Hannah thinks we're in a romantic comedy – as long as I tear the lettuce the way her mother did, and use her bowl, and fit right in, Hannah will be fine. Because she's trying to patch up her life, that's all she knows how to do at her age.'

Tom was quiet, his head bent, listening.

'You ask a kid what matters to them most,' Rachel went on, 'they're not going to say their parents' happiness. That's not their responsibility, Tom. They need to know that it's their happiness that's important, that they matter, that someone would miss them if they weren't around.' She swallowed down the lump rising in her throat. 'I didn't have that till I met you, you know.'

'Rach . . .' He walked back over to the couch and sat, taking her in his arms and holding her close.

'I don't think I knew until I went away how much you meant to me,' she said tearfully, leaning against his chest. 'And then it was too late. You met Annie. We just can't seem to get the timing right.'

He drew back to look at her. 'Well, that's the thing, Rach, it is just timing,' he said. 'I know I have to focus on the girls right now, but then –'

'No, Tom,' she stopped him. 'That can't be in the back of your mind, marking off days on the calendar like you're serving time. That's not going to work.'

He leaned his forehead against hers. 'I don't want to leave you alone, Rach. I said I wouldn't, I promised.'

'I know you did, and it's not your fault, it's no one's fault. We have to do the right thing now.'

'I wish we could go back, before everyone found out, at least we could still be together.'

She lifted her head to look at him. 'But Sophie knew, remember?'

Tom sighed. 'What are you going to do?'

'You don't have to worry about that. You just worry about the girls. They need you, Tom, they need their dad.'

Rachel didn't know how much time had passed since Tom had left, but the flat was in darkness now. She was still sitting in the same spot on the couch, curled up, hugging herself. She should probably get up, make some dinner. But she wasn't hungry. Odd that, how you could feel so completely empty inside, but food was the last thing you wanted.

She told Tom not to keep in touch; she didn't want updates, she didn't want to have to counsel him, it would be too hard. It had to be a clean break. As if there was such a thing. Breaks were painful and messy and hard. There was no way to fast forward through the next few days, weeks and months, to when it might, she could only hope, get a little easier. No, Rachel knew she had to live through every moment of this. And what was worse, she had to do it without Tom.

She had never felt so alone.

That night

Scott had got up early and gone to work without waking anyone in the house. The kids had even slept in a little. Lexie enjoyed just pottering about, taking the morning slowly, spending time with her children. After she put Mia down for her nap, and Riley was ensconced in front of a DVD, she attacked the house in earnest, catching up on a week's worth of housework. It actually felt restorative. Maybe she had a tendency to veer towards perfectionism, but it just felt like God was in his heaven and all was right with the world when her house was in order. In the late afternoon, she bathed the children in the sparkling clean bathroom and made them their favourite pasta dish for an early dinner, so they were already asleep when Scott arrived home.

She met him at the door with a kiss and a hug. 'You didn't have to go to work today, I would have gone.'

'No, you deserved a break,' he said. 'Kids in bed already?'

'Yeah, you've had plenty of time with them lately, and you're off tomorrow, so I wanted you to myself tonight.'

He smiled. 'Sounds good to me.'

She led him down into the living room. 'Do you want a drink, a beer?'

He shook his head. 'I had enough to drink last night.' He dropped into the sofa. 'That was some night.'

Lexie sat next to him, side on so she could face him. 'I'm still in shock about Tom. It's bad enough about him and Rachel, but to think he slept with Catherine before Annie died. They were so happy, they were the perfect couple. Why would he do that?'

'You don't know what goes on behind closed doors, love.'

'Oh, come on, Scott, I'm sure Annie didn't know anything about it, she was crazy about Tom.' She sighed. 'I just don't know how I feel about him now.'

Scott looked at her. 'I'm not going to make excuses for him, can't understand it myself. But I will just say that Catherine would be pretty hard to fight off if she wanted you bad enough, I reckon.'

'Doesn't excuse it, Scott.'

'No it doesn't,' he agreed. 'But he did say it was a mistake, and it only happened once.'

'With Catherine,' she said. 'Now it's Rachel.'

'That's not the same thing,' said Scott. 'You can't say he was cheating with Rachel.'

'Then why did they have to sneak around?' said Lexie. 'It just doesn't sit right. If they thought there was nothing wrong with what they were doing, surely they could have been open about it?'

Scott shrugged. 'But look at the way you're reacting,' he pointed out. 'You're one of the most understanding people I know, Lexie, and you're judging them.'

'I'm not judging them!' she protested. But Scott just looked at her. 'Okay, I'm judging them,' she sighed. 'It just seems . . . weird, I don't know. He was married to her friend.'

'But didn't Tom and Rachel have some history together?' Scott asked. 'They knew each other long before he met Annie, right?'

Lexie nodded.

'Well, I don't know if it's all that weird,' he said. 'I was thinking about this today, and you know what I reckon? If Annie had been sick for a while, if she knew she was going to die, let's say, I reckon she's the type who would have been looking out for somebody for Tom.'

'You think?'

'Yeah, you know that way she had about her?' he smiled faintly. 'That whole new-age thing, that there was a reason for everything. I always liked Annie, she was a lovely person, but I did think she was a little loopy, you know.'

Lexie couldn't help smiling now. 'Did you?'

He nodded. 'And I reckon she would have been looking out

for someone for Tom, and Rachel would definitely have made the shortlist.'

Lexie shrugged. 'I guess we'll never know.'

'Tell me this, do you think if she's up there somewhere, floating around, she'd be upset about the two of them being together?' he asked. 'She'd be pissed off about Catherine, but I think she'd be okay about Tom and Rachel.'

Lexie thought about it. 'Maybe you're right, but it just seems too soon, that's all.' She looked at Scott. 'I mean, if I died, could you imagine finding someone that quickly?'

'Oh no, you're not going to get me to go there,' Scott shook his head. 'That's what's known as a minefield.'

Lexie nudged him. 'Oh, come on, tell me the truth, I want to know.'

He took her hand and held it to his heart. 'Lexie, if anything ever happened to you, God forbid, I would never lay eyes on another woman ever again. In fact, I'd go into a monastery. And I'd have myself castrated.'

'Good answer,' she said, leaning over to kiss him soundly on the lips. 'I love you, Scott. I'm so sorry about the way I carried on last night.'

'No, you were only reacting to me being such an arsehole,' he said. 'I'm sorry, Lex, I was completely out of line. It's just, when you started changing things, and fixing things, it felt like you didn't think I'd been doing a good job. And then when you said as much . . .'

'I was just angry that night,' she insisted, 'and tired and cranky, and I went for your sore spot.'

'What sore spot?'

Lexie looked at him. 'Scott, you know you're very sensitive about being seen to provide for your family.'

'What's wrong with that?'

'Nothing, nothing at all, it's sweet. But sometimes I think you should just get over it. You've supported this family since Riley was born, you don't have to prove anything any more.'

He sighed. 'Lexie, this is hardly the life your parents had in mind for you.'

'You have the wrong idea about my parents, Scott.'

'No, I don't,' he said plainly. 'They're good people, I know that, they love me because you love me, but Lexie, admit it, they would have preferred you ended up with someone who could give you the kind of life they'd given you. That's what parents want for their kids. There'd be something wrong with them if they didn't.'

Lexie thought about it. 'Well, it doesn't matter . . . This is the only life I want for myself, because you're in it. I couldn't be happy with more money or a bigger house if I didn't have you, so it's a moot point. Okay?'

'Okay,' said Scott as he brought his arms around her and drew her close.

'And you know what else?' she said, cuddling into his chest. 'I love working with you, Scott, I love being involved in the business. Do you think we can find a way to make it work?'

'I'm sure we can.' He smiled at her. 'It's funny, before I met you I always thought I'd probably marry someone in the industry and that we'd end up running a restaurant together.'

'You used to talk about that when we first met,' said Lexie. 'Not the part about marrying someone in the industry.'

'No, because you were a lab assistant.'

'Which is not so different to someone who works in a kitchen, when you think about it, Scott.'

He shrugged. 'I guess.'

'So why did you drop the restaurant idea?'

'It was only a vague dream.'

Lexie rested her head back in the crook of his arm, looking up at him. 'Tell me about it.'

'What do you mean?'

'Tell me about the restaurant you would have had with your other wife, you must have had some kind of picture in your head,' she urged.

He shrugged. 'I don't know.'

'Scott, we have to start telling each other everything,' said Lexie. 'Hopes, fears, dreams, frustrations – everything. We've stopped doing that. We've stopped talking. And look what ended up happening. We can't let things ever get that bad again. I don't want to become one of those couples, at each other's throats all the time.'

He stroked her hair. 'I don't either,' he said. 'The way I treated you this last week . . . I don't know what was wrong with me. I couldn't seem to stop once I got started. You didn't deserve that, you were only trying to help.'

'Yeah, but I was manipulating the situation, instead of being honest with you.'

'No,' he denied.

'I'm just saying, we have to be totally open and honest from now on, okay?'

'Okay,' he said, leaning down to give her a kiss.

'So, tell me, did you dream of owning a big swanky place in the city?'

He pulled a face. 'No, never.'

'Well, what did you imagine?'

He stared out across the room, thinking about it. 'There was this guy, Todd, I haven't thought about him in a long time. He was the sous chef in the first place I ever worked when I was an apprentice. Lovely guy, much too gentle a temperament to ever become a head chef in a busy city restaurant, and he knew it. So he and his wife moved up to Bellingen, and they opened a restaurant there. A couple of years later I called in to see him when I was on holiday up that way.' Scott shook his head, remembering. 'I'd never seen anything like the set-up they had. They'd converted this rambling old house on a huge block of land, and they actually lived upstairs, above the restaurant. They had three little barefoot kids running around the place, and they grew their own vegetables and herbs, and they had chooks. They made everything on the premises, bread and pasta . . .'

Lexie sat up again, facing him, her eyes wide. 'What, you mean everything on the menu?'

He nodded. 'Just about. And they sold stuff as well: bottled sauces and preserves, that kind of thing. They had this whole little cottage industry going.'

'It sounds wonderful,' Lexie sighed.

'Yeah, it was,' he agreed.

'Couldn't we do something like that?'

He shook his head with a smile. 'It's only a dream, Lex.'

'What do you mean "only a dream",' she argued. 'They did it.'

'But we couldn't.'

'Why not?'

'Well, for a start, we couldn't do it in Sydney, it'd be too expensive, and you wouldn't want to move away from your family,' he said simply.

'Oh, wouldn't I?' she returned. 'What else wouldn't I want to do, Scott?'

He frowned, considering her. 'You'd actually consider moving away from your family?'

'I wouldn't be moving away from my family, I'd be moving *with* my family.' She took hold of his head with both hands. 'God, Scott, when are you going to get it? You're it, you and the kids, you're everything to me.'

He still looked uncertain. 'You wouldn't miss your mum?'

She sighed, releasing his head again. 'Of course I'd miss her. But she'd visit, and we'd visit. This is about us, Scott, and our family, and what's right for us.' She paused, biting her lip. 'And there's something I've wanted to tell you for a long time.'

He looked worried. 'What is it?'

'I want another baby.'

Now he looked shocked.

'But you don't?' she sighed.

'No, it's not that, honey,' said Scott, 'I'd have a houseful. But that's the problem. We have a houseful now.'

'I know,' she agreed. 'That's why I've never said anything. I knew it wasn't possible the way things are, and I didn't want you worrying that you couldn't give me what I wanted.' Then she smiled faintly. 'But if we were to move . . .'

He was gazing at her with a kind of disbelief in his eyes. 'You'd really think about moving away from Sydney?'

'You know what, Scott, I've lived my whole life in about a ten-kilometre radius,' said Lexie. 'The hospital where I was born, the house I grew up in, where I went to school, uni, got married, had my own kids, all in shooting distance. Maybe I wouldn't want to go quite as far as Bellingen, but I think moving away could be a wonderful thing for us, Scott. Isn't it worth looking into at least?'

*

Monday

Catherine had decided to take a few days' leave, perhaps even the whole week. She hadn't had any time off in ages, and she wasn't scheduled in court; there was nothing so urgent she couldn't catch up on it later. Martin was in the guestroom when she made it home Saturday night, and he packed his bags Sunday and moved to a hotel. They exchanged not more than a few words, his to the effect that he'd have his lawyer get in touch with her in time. Catherine felt bad about the way it had happened, but it had to happen sometime. And strangely enough it felt good to be free. She'd always been accustomed to having a man in her life, but she and Martin had not been in sync for a very long time, and she hadn't realised how draining that had become. And she certainly didn't need Tom and all his complications; Rachel was welcome to him. Catherine had tried to call her yesterday to debrief, but she couldn't get past the answering machine. After the dust had settled, the more she thought about Rachel and Tom together, the more it seemed absolutely right. Normal. Natural, even. Good luck to them. She could see why they'd kept it under wraps from the general public, sake of appearances and all that, but Catherine didn't understand why Rachel would think she couldn't confide in her, instead of making up that whole Matthew Harding fiasco.

But she had more pressing concerns right now. Alice had locked herself in her room since Saturday night and refused to acknowledge or respond to Catherine whatsoever during her brief trips to the kitchen, or as she left the house this morning for school. In reality, Catherine should have been the one on her high horse, considering the debacle of the dance party; her own actions, involving another consenting adult more than six months ago, were none of Alice's business.

Except Catherine didn't really believe that. She shouldn't have blurted it out the way she did in front of Alice and Sophie; she wondered if Tom would ever be able to forgive her. But it was the heat of the moment, the shock, and she'd had a little too much to drink, which didn't help. But that wasn't her fault, the whole evening had been quite stressful ... Still, Catherine felt a deep, nagging dread about the irretrievable impact this could have on her relationship with Alice. If she didn't sort this out, she sensed she might lose her forever. She had to find a way to open a dialogue with Alice again, and it occurred to Catherine that this might be the right time to tell her about James. If she could demonstrate to Alice that she was prepared to be open and honest, perhaps they had a chance of rebuilding their relationship. Or even building a better one.

As she'd thought over it all day, Catherine had gradually felt lighter; the stress of lying, suppressing and avoiding all these years had obviously been draining. So by the time she heard Alice at the front door, home from school, she was quite reconciled about what she had to do. She hurried up the hallway to meet her head-on.

'I have to talk to you, Alice,' she said.

'Well I don't have to talk to you,' Alice replied airily, not making eye contact as she walked straight past her into the kitchen.

'I think you're going to want to,' Catherine persisted, following her. 'This is not about what happened on Saturday night, this is about something much more important.'

'Says you,' she retorted, slipping her backpack off her shoulders and dumping it on the floor before heading for the fridge.

Catherine decided she was just going to have to come out with it. 'I spoke to your father the other day.'

Alice stepped back from the fridge door, turning her head towards Catherine but not actually making eye contact. 'You don't even know who my father is.'

'Yes, I do,' said Catherine. 'I haven't had any contact with him for over eighteen years, until just recently. The thing is, I never told you the full truth about him.'

'My, what a surprise,' she said dryly. 'So why are you bothering now?'

The fridge started making that beeping noise like a truck reversing.

'Could you please close the fridge door,' said Catherine, 'and pay attention to what I have to say?'

Alice grabbed a bottle of water and closed the door, slumping onto a bar stool. Catherine could tell she wasn't really taking her seriously yet; she was intrigued, but not convinced.

'His name is James,' she went on, 'just as I always told you, and his surname is Barrett. He was my boyfriend at the time. I didn't want to give you more details about him in the past because I was trying to protect you.'

Alice pulled a face. 'From what?'

'I'll get to that. Now that he's turned up again, I want you to know the whole truth, so you can make a decision about what you want to do.'

She frowned. 'Did he ask after me?'

Catherine hesitated. 'Not exactly.'

Alice rolled her eyes. 'So I suppose if I say I want to see him, there'll be some reason that I can't.'

'There are complications –'

'No! Really?' Alice scoffed. 'Such as, you're making this whole thing up?'

'No, I'm not, Alice. I promise you, I wouldn't do that about something like this.'

She was shaking her head. 'Well, if this is the truth, that means you made the other story up, so obviously you'll make up whatever bowl of crapola suits you at the time.'

'Well I'm not making this up,' Catherine repeated. 'And I'll prove it to you.'

Alice looked at her. 'Okay. Call him up now, let me talk to my dear papa.'

'I can't do that.'

'Oh and why do you think that is?' she said, channelling Catherine at her sarcastic best. 'Could it be that he doesn't exist?'

'No,' Catherine sighed. 'He just doesn't know you exist.'

Alice finally relented to hear her out. Catherine knew she had to tell her the whole story, she couldn't edit anything out, even though she found it excruciating to have to mention that an abortion was ever on the table.

But Alice just sat there, listening, not asking any questions, not making any comments.

'So,' Catherine said finally, 'what are you thinking?'

Alice shrugged. 'What do you want me to say?'

'Whatever's on your mind. The truth.'

'Okay. Then I don't understand why you're telling me all this now.'

'Because, like I said, he's back in the country and –'

'But why now, why today?' Alice persisted. 'This totally feels like you're trying to distract me from what happened the other night.'

Catherine blinked. 'That's not what I'm doing, Alice. I thought this would be important to you, and I wanted to show you that I was prepared to tell you the truth, so that it could open a dialogue between us –'

'Okay, dialogue opened,' she cut her off. 'Let's start with what happened the other night.'

'If that's what you want,' Catherine said calmly. 'What happened between Tom and me was probably a mistake, like he said.'

'I'm not talking about that, I'm talking about *what happened the other night*,' she repeated, emphasising each word.

Catherine wasn't following her.

'How could you blurt that out in front of Sophie?' she demanded. 'It just keeps going round and round in my head, and I don't understand how you could do that. It was so mean.'

Catherine wasn't expecting that. She took a deep breath. 'Things happen in the heat of the moment. I didn't think it through, it just came out.'

'Admit it, Mum, you were just so jealous of Rachel, that Tom chose her, and you had to find a way to ruin it.'

'No, I just –'

'What? What excuse could you possibly have for doing that? I keep thinking about poor Sophie, and everything she's been through. She didn't need to hear that as well.'

Catherine sighed, but kept her composure. 'You're right. And I wish I could take it back,' she said. 'It was unforgivable.'

Alice shook her head in frustration. She got up and walked over to the window, staring out at the back garden.

'What do you want me to do, Alice?' Catherine asked. 'I would apologise, but I don't think they're going to want to hear that from me.'

'Probably not,' she muttered without turning around.

Catherine felt like this was just a distraction now. Of course she felt awful about what had happened, but there was nothing she could do about it now. This wasn't turning out the way she'd planned, and it wasn't getting them anywhere.

'So,' she said after a while, 'do you have any thoughts about the other thing we were talking about? Do you think you might want to meet your father, or have anything to do with him?'

Alice turned around slowly then, leaning back against the windowsill. 'You know, Mum, right now it's hard for me to see any great advantage in having another parent in my life. One's bad enough.'

'You want to throw insults at a single mother? Go right ahead,' said Catherine.

'I never thought worse of you because you were a single mother, or because you had me when you were a teenager,' said Alice. 'You were the one who seemed ashamed of that, and resentful that I ruined your life.'

'No Alice, you didn't ruin my life,' Catherine insisted. 'How could you think that?'

'You've always been so disappointed in me.'

Catherine took a deep breath. This wasn't the time for platitudes and pretence, she had to be completely honest with her. 'It's true, but not in the way you think. You don't disappoint me, Alice. You are beautiful, and funny, and smart, and I've just wanted you to be everything you can be, and so any disappointment I've expressed has to do with that.'

'But don't you know you can't put that onto me?' said Alice. 'I don't want the same things you do. I don't want to be a lawyer.'

'Well, I realise that, Alice,' said Catherine. No surprises there. 'But what do you want to do?' she added tentatively.

'I don't know,' she shrugged. 'And that doesn't mean I'm hopeless, Mum. Heaps of my friends don't know what they want to do.'

Catherine nodded. 'I understand, but the HSC is getting close, you'll have to put in your preferences for uni soon. You're going to have to make some decisions.'

'I'm thinking I might take a year off.'

Catherine hated the whole trend towards 'gap' years. It was indulgent, and she'd seen too many bright, capable kids lose their focus entirely. It's exactly what had happened to Rachel. But she knew she had to play this carefully. If she reacted too strongly, it would only make Alice all the more determined.

'Well, we'll see,' she said. 'But you still have to apply for uni so that you can defer it for a year. That's the way it works.'

'But I don't even know if I want to go to uni.'

Catherine took a breath. 'Look Alice, I'm trying to be understanding here, but I am entitled to some say if I'm going to be supporting you while you figure out what you want to do.'

'Who said you're going to be supporting me?' Alice said squarely.

Catherine was taken aback by that. 'Who else is going to?'

'I'll support myself, get a job, then I can move out.'

Catherine swallowed. This was getting worse, but she mustn't take the bait. 'But what if you decide to go to uni later, Alice, how will you manage then?'

She shrugged. 'If I work for a certain amount of time I'll be considered independent, and then I can get student support from the government.'

Catherine grimaced; she'd obviously looked into this. 'I had to do that, Alice,' though in her case it was the single parent pension, 'because I didn't have any choice. But there's no need for you to live on welfare. Look, I'm going to sell this place, I can buy an apartment somewhere that suits you, maybe near the beach, wherever you want.'

'Mum, don't.'

'I just don't want you to make any rash decisions.'

'I'm not going to,' Alice insisted. 'That's the whole point. I don't want to apply to uni when I don't even know what I want to do. I don't want to get stuck. I'm young, Mum, I have time, that's one thing I do have. And I want to take my time. You're just going to have to accept it, because you can't make decisions for me any more once I turn eighteen.'

Catherine sighed, dropping her head in her hands. So it had finally come to this. She looked up again after a while. 'This has been my nightmare, you know,' she said. 'That you'll walk away after your HSC and live your own life, and I'll be lucky to get a phone call on my birthday.'

'Mum,' Alice groaned. 'I'm doing this, well, for a lot of reasons, but only one of them is about getting away from you.'

Catherine laughed then, she couldn't help it. 'That's supposed to make me feel better?'

Alice was smiling now as well. 'And another is because I think we might have a much better chance of getting on if we don't live together.' She walked back over to the kitchen and picked up her school bag. 'That's about as much D and M as I can handle for one afternoon. And I've got homework.'

Catherine watched her saunter off over to the stairs. 'You still haven't said what you want to do about your father.'

Alice turned to look at her. 'I don't know yet. But I'll figure it out myself. It's my decision, Mum, and you're going to have to respect that.'

Bean East

Rachel got off the bus at Coogee Beach and started up the street towards the café. When she'd called earlier, Scott had told her Lexie would be in around ten. Rachel had missed her on the home phone this morning; she gathered she was already on the school run. She had to talk to her, and she had to do it in person. She wasn't sure how Lexie felt about the fallout on Saturday night, though she got some idea from her brief exchange with Scott. He was fine, very friendly, reassuring, which was a relief. But when she asked him to let Lexie know she was planning to call in this morning, he said, 'I think it might be best if I don't tell her in advance.'

'Why, so she's not tempted to hide when I get there?'

'Something like that.'

Rachel sighed.

'Don't worry,' he'd assured her. 'You know what a softie she is. She'll be fine once she sees you.'

Rachel walked up to the café, past the tables on the footpath, and stepped inside. It was not terribly busy, there was only a smattering of patrons, so at least she didn't feel she was getting in the way. Scott was first to spot her; he was so tall he easily saw over the dividing wall to the kitchen.

'Hey,' he said, not announcing her name. 'Come on through, Lexie's up the end there. Lex, you have a visitor,' he called.

Rachel went to the gap in the counter as Scott walked up to her, wiping his hands on a tea towel. Lexie was sitting on a stool in a corner at the far end of the galley kitchen. She had a pile of papers on the bench in front of her and the telephone in her hand, though not to her ear. She must have been about to make a call. When she turned around and saw Rachel, she hung the handset back in its cradle on the wall. 'Hi,' she said quietly.

'Hi Lexie,' said Rachel.

'Well, I'll leave you two to it,' Scott said with an affectionate pat on Rachel's shoulder as he retreated to the other end of the kitchen again.

'Would you like a coffee or something?' Lexie asked.

'If you're having one.'

'Sure, why don't you go find us a table and I'll bring them out.'

She was being polite, but reserved, which was fair enough. Rachel walked over to a booth at the back of the café where they could have some privacy, and soon Lexie appeared carrying two cups of coffee. She set them down on the table and slid into the booth opposite Rachel.

'Thanks,' she said. She took a sip of her coffee and set the cup back in its saucer. 'Okay Lexie, I might as well get straight to the point. I came here to apologise for the scene on Saturday night, to begin with.'

'You didn't create the scene, Rachel,' she said.

'Still, I feel partly responsible.'

'Tom's already been in to apologise.'

'Oh, he has?'

She nodded. 'He and Sophie.'

'Right,' Rachel nodded. He wouldn't have brought up everything in front of Sophie, it would have been all about the girls' misdemeanours. 'Well, I guess I just wanted to see if everything was okay, with us, you know, considering . . .'

'. . . you've been sleeping with one of our best friend's husbands?'

Well, that was certainly giving it to her straight.

'Tom was one of my best friends, before Annie came along. Just so you know,' said Rachel. 'And the other thing you should know is that we're not going to see each other any more.' She felt a thickening in her throat as she said that.

'Why not?' Lexie asked.

'We just decided that it's not the right time. Tom needs to establish a new life for himself with the girls. I'd only get in the way.'

Lexie shook her head faintly. 'That seems a shame.'

Rachel sighed. 'Wow, Lex, I thought you'd be pleased.'

'Pleased?'

'Well, you obviously didn't approve. I guess you felt betrayed on some level.'

Lexie sighed heavily. 'You know, Rachel, I probably felt most betrayed because you didn't think you could tell me.'

'I didn't tell anyone,' Rachel assured her. 'Catherine didn't know either.'

'What has she had to say about all this?'

'I haven't seen her, haven't spoken to her. And I'm not planning to.'

Lexie frowned. 'Really?'

Something had shifted irrevocably. From her messages Rachel construed that Catherine didn't get that at all, she thought it was business as usual. Which only made Rachel more resolved. She'd had enough. Every moment she'd ever spent feeling guilty about Tom was obliterated by the cold hard fact of Catherine's premeditated betrayal. Rachel wasn't excusing Tom's part in it, but Catherine had deliberately seduced a close friend, who was married to another close friend, when he was down and vulnerable. What had she hoped to achieve? Quite obviously she had no qualms tearing their marriage apart so that yet again she had a man waiting in the wings once she was ready to leave Martin. While that was never going to happen with Tom, of course, what it said about Catherine was beyond what Rachel could tolerate any longer.

'I think we've grown apart over the years,' Rachel started to explain, 'and we've never really stopped to think about it. I mean, you can have different tastes, like different music, movies, that stuff doesn't really matter. But at the core of a friendship, surely you have to have some kind of shared values? And I just don't understand Catherine any more. I don't understand her motivations, her actions, and I don't agree with them. It makes it difficult to relate to her.'

'But you've been friends such a long time.'

'Maybe too long.' Rachel picked up her cup and sipped her coffee. She didn't want to rubbish Catherine to Lexie, that was between the two of them. 'So anyway, like I said, I just wanted to apologise for Saturday night.'

Lexie shook her head. 'Listen, Scott and I owe everyone an apology as well. We acted like a pair of five year olds, it was a disgrace.'

'Are you okay now?'

'We are, you know,' she nodded, a smile forming on her face. 'Better than ever, to be honest.' She paused. 'We're actually thinking of selling up and moving to the country.'

Rachel blinked. 'You're kidding? Where did this come from?'

'Totally out of the blue,' she exclaimed. 'It's been a dream of Scott's for a long time, but he thought it could never happen so he never told me. And when I got it out of him the other night, I can't explain it, but it felt so right. It was like a light bulb going on, making everything clear. We were up half the night talking, and on the internet all day yesterday, looking up restaurants for sale. We're going up to Orange next week to check some places out.'

'Wow, that's quick.'

'I know,' said Lexie, holding up her hands, like it was a surprise to her as well. 'But you know, why muck around? Life's short.'

'Yes, it is.'

Lexie sighed. 'Well, now I feel like a hypocrite.'

'Why?'

'I thought you and Tom were ... well, wrong, because it seemed like it was too soon ... But what do I know?'

'Don't worry about it.'

Lexie looked at her. 'Do you love him?'

Rachel could feel her throat tightening. There wasn't any point evading the question, but she didn't trust her voice, so she just nodded.

Lexie reached over and took her hand. 'I'm sorry it hasn't worked out,' she said. 'You know what Scott told me?'

Rachel shook her head.

'He reckons that Annie would have been happy for you two to be together.'

'Did he?'

She nodded.

'What do you think?' asked Rachel.

Lexie took a moment. 'I think Annie would say, if it's meant to be . . .'

Wednesday

Catherine was sitting in the restaurant, positioned so she could see the door, preparing herself. She had made sure she got here a full fifteen minutes early, so there was little chance James would be the first to arrive. She needed time before she had to face him to get centred in the surroundings so she would be in control of this meeting.

She could barely believe what she was about to do, and there was still a chance she may not, it depended on how the conversation went. Alice had come to her again that same evening; she'd decided they should test the waters. No point putting off the inevitable, she'd said, trying to sound offhand. 'Might as well suss him out,' she'd added. 'But don't give anything away until you're sure about him . . .' She reminded Catherine of a child hiding behind a curtain, peering through a chink, intrigued and fascinated by what she might find out, while at the same time terrified that she would be discovered. So she trusted her mother to judge the situation and do what felt right. That was pretty amazing in itself, that Alice trusted her judgement, at least a little, at least insofar as this was concerned. The only proviso Alice had made was that her mother refrain from drinking. That had pulled Catherine up, especially the way Alice put it. She wasn't being smart or derogatory, she just said it straight. 'Maybe it will go better if you don't have anything to drink.' It was sobering, quite literally.

So the plan was to get his side first. Weigh it up, analyse it, analyse him. Catherine was good at that, it was what she did every time she sat a client down for the first interview, to help her decide how to proceed with a case. With James, she had to decide if he was going to be open to hearing the truth. But before that, if she even wanted him to know the truth.

James arrived promptly at one, as a punctual lawyer would. He glanced around and spotted her immediately. He didn't wait to be shown to the table, and Catherine watched him as he made his way over. Something in his gait, the way he held himself, took her right back. He might look a lot different on the outside these days, but somewhere inside was the seventeen-year-old boy she remembered. She hoped so anyway.

He came to the table as Catherine went to stand. 'Please, don't get up,' he said, pulling his chair out and sitting down. He gave her a cautious smile. 'I was so pleased to get your call, Catherine. Though a little surprised, I have to say.'

'Well, I suppose your visit brought up some unfinished business for me as well.'

'Good then,' he nodded. 'This will give us a chance to clear the air. Shall we order a drink?'

'Not for me,' she said. 'But please, you go ahead.'

'No, I'm fine.'

Catherine felt inordinately nervous. 'Then why don't we order our meals first?' she suggested. 'Get that out of the way.'

He agreed, and they picked up the menus and read quietly until the waiter came along. Catherine ordered a salad, while James went for steak with a rich sauce. No wonder he had that paunch.

The waiter poured water into their glasses, picked up the menus and left them alone.

James leaned forwards. 'So, what exactly is on your mind, Catherine?'

She took a breath. She'd rehearsed this, but that didn't make it any easier. At least she could get him to do the talking for now. 'I suppose I was intrigued by something you said the day you came to my office.'

'Oh? What was that?'

'You said that you were upset after your father's visit to my house all those years ago. That was the word you used, "upset", and I wondered why.'

'Well . . .' He looked slightly surprised by the question. 'I suppose I would have thought that was obvious.'

Catherine realised she was going to have to be a little more direct. 'James, at this point it would be helpful if you could explain your side of what happened, without making any assumptions about how it might have been for me.'

'All right.' He seemed to be thinking about what he was going to say. 'This is a little awkward. Please,' he looked at her, 'don't think for a moment that I don't believe in a woman's right to choose. I do, absolutely. And we were so very young. It was not an easy situation.'

Easier for him.

He hesitated. 'I suppose it was the circumstances that upset me. My father, what he did, I didn't know . . .'

Catherine frowned. 'You didn't know he came to my house?'

'No, I was aware of that, of course,' he said quickly. 'I'm sorry, it probably seemed very weak or cowardly to you, Catherine, but I was terrified, absolutely terrified. I had all that bravado back then, thought I knew everything about everything, and in the end I was just a frightened boy. That's why I went to my parents first. I should have known my father would take over, that was his way. But he made sense, he said the adults needed to discuss it, that we couldn't make the decision on our own because it was going to have ramifications for everybody. And besides, how could we be expected to make such a big decision at our age? He wasn't being condescending, he was actually kind, in a way. He said he would take care of it.'

Hmm. There wasn't any discussion, but he certainly did take care of it.

'I have to admit I was relieved,' James went on. 'But then, I didn't realise what he was going to do.'

'What do you mean?'

'Look, I don't want to judge you –'

'Just tell me what you're talking about,' Catherine insisted.

'Okay.' He paused to take a drink of water. 'He said he intended to discuss the options – having the baby, adopting it out, or . . . well, terminating the pregnancy.'

Catherine felt like screaming. He didn't present any other options, he'd said there were no other options as far as they were concerned. But she had to stay calm, let James explain what he knew before she gave anything away.

'Go on,' she urged.

'What he didn't tell me, was that he would also offer you . . . the payment.' James paused, breathing out heavily. 'I'm an adult now, I see things differently. I understand, really. But at the time, I was just . . . hurt, to be honest.'

'Hurt?'

He nodded. 'That you would take the money.'

Catherine was completely confused. 'So you were hurt and *upset* because he offered to pay for the abortion?'

James looked confused now. 'No, that he offered to pay you to stay away from me.'

'What?'

Right then the waiter returned with their meals. James was staring at her, clearly thrown by her reaction. Catherine was stunned, incensed, outraged . . . But she needed to hold it together, find out exactly what he meant, not fly off with accusations that might only put him on the defensive. She took a couple of deep breaths, and when the waiter left she looked steadily across the table at him.

'Please, go on, James,' she said. 'Explain to me exactly what your father told you he did.'

'All right.' He reached for his glass and took another sip of water. 'He said that he told you, and your parents, that we would do the right thing, meet our obligations, whatever you decided. But this was the part I didn't know about. He said he wanted to assess . . .' he hesitated. 'These are his words, not mine, Catherine.

He wanted to assess exactly what kind of girl you were, so that I would know the truth about you. So he offered you a substantial sum of money if you had the abortion, as long as you never made contact with me again and didn't respond to any contact I attempted. He said you jumped at it – his words again.'

Catherine felt as though the room was spinning. She looked down at her salad, she thought she might be sick.

'Excuse me,' she said, standing up suddenly.

'Catherine, please don't leave,' James said, getting to his feet.

'I'm not, I just have to go to the bathroom.' She rushed off; her legs were shaking so badly she wasn't sure they would carry her, but somehow she made it to the bathroom, and straight into a cubicle, where she closed the lid and sat down. She was still shaking, her hands were clammy and she could feel a film of perspiration on her face. She tried to breathe slowly and deeply, to stop herself from hyperventilating, as she struggled to make sense of what she had just heard. It felt like her whole life had been predicated on a lie. A callous, calculating, destructive lie. Every decision Catherine had made, every relationship she'd had, everything . . . had all been in reaction to that one event in her life, when she had felt so small and so powerless that she had vowed no one would ever have that kind of power over her again.

And the man sitting out there now was as much a victim as she was, and he had a daughter he didn't even know existed.

Catherine sat there for a long time, though she didn't feel all that much calmer by the time she stood up again. At least her legs were not shaking, however, as she walked to the over and washed her hands. She dabbed her face with a damp napkin, staring at herself in the mirror. Tears pricked at the corners of her eyes. No, no, keep control, you can't fall apart here. She wished she could transport herself to Rachel's flat and talk it all over with her before she had to go out and face James again. She still had no idea how he would take the news. He had a family of his own, a wife and children. She wasn't even sure that she'd tell him everything today, she supposed she would have to play it by ear. But she knew now that, eventually, she would tell him. And that her life was going to change forever.

She walked sedately back to the table, and James got to his feet.

'Catherine, are you all right?' he asked, concerned.

'Yes, of course,' she said, her voice sounding surprisingly calm. 'Please, sit down.'

'Can I get you something?' he asked. 'A drink?'

She realised she wasn't going to be able to do this without a drink. She knew she'd promised Alice, but she'd be careful. Just one.

'Yes, all right,' she said. 'White wine, please.'

He motioned for a waiter and ordered them each a glass, and then he sat down, watching her with an anxious frown. 'Catherine, I'm beginning to feel like I don't have the whole story.'

'You certainly don't,' she said, meeting his eyes. She could see the seventeen year old, and she could see Alice. 'I don't quite know how to say any of this.' She was about to tell him his father was a cold, heartless, despicable liar; maybe he wouldn't believe her, she hadn't thought of that.

'What is it, Catherine?' he urged. 'Really, you can say anything.'

'That's not the way it happened,' she began.

The waiter arrived with their drinks, and Catherine picked up her glass and took a long sip. She put it down on the table again.

'Please, Catherine, go on,' James urged.

'Your father, he had papers.'

'What do you mean, papers?'

'Just hear me out,' she said. 'He said that your "liability" did not go beyond paying for an abortion, because that was the only alternative he, and by extension you, were prepared to accept. He added a small sum for what he called "damages"; it was by no means substantial, James, let me assure you. He wrote the cheque to my parents, and he made them sign papers to the effect that we relinquished all claim on you and your family. As far as he was concerned, that was the end of it.'

Now James picked up his glass and took a gulp.

'I suppose my parents might still have those papers somewhere, if you want proof,' Catherine added.

He was shaking his head. 'I believe you.'

'For what it's worth,' said Catherine, 'I believe you too, what you understood of it.'

'I appreciate that.' He sighed deeply. 'My father was used to getting what he wanted, by whatever means. When he told me what he'd done, or what he said he'd done, I was furious. We didn't speak for weeks. But he didn't care, he'd proved his point, he said. It was for the best.' James shook his head. 'I have to say, it was never the same between us after that.'

Catherine was watching him. 'Where is he now?'

He looked at her. 'He passed away almost two years ago.'

'I'm sorry,' she said automatically.

'You have no reason to be.'

He seemed to become lost in thought. Catherine looked down at the table. Neither of them had touched their food. She couldn't eat now anyway. She took another sip of her wine and put the glass back down on the table. She felt calmer now. But she still had questions of her own.

'James,' she said.

He came out of his reverie and looked across at her.

'It's strange that we've never bumped into each other all this time. Where did you go to uni?'

'Well, in London, of course.'

'What?'

'I told you, we only got back a couple of months ago.'

'But I thought . . .' she paused. 'When exactly did you go to London?'

'Just after I finished high school,' he explained. 'My father took a job, the whole family packed up and went there to live. My wife is English, our boys were born there. But after my father died, my mother wanted to come back home. She'd always missed Australia.' He paused. 'Elizabeth, that's my wife, decided we should come with her. Her parents had both died years before, and she had one brother living in the US. She said family was more important, and we should be close to my mother.'

He was a good man. A decent man. Catherine wasn't thinking 'what if', in terms of the two of them. But she couldn't help thinking what if Alice had had him in her life.

'Catherine,' he said, getting her attention. 'I want to say how sorry I am for what my father did, and that I'm sorry for the way that it happened. But what I'm most sorry about is that you had to go through that on your own. It must have been truly awful.'

She looked across the table at him. She had to tell him now, she couldn't bear any more lies, any more deception. If she didn't say it now, she would have to find another time, broach it all over again. That was not an option. It had to be now.

'James, I didn't go through with it.'

'Pardon?'

She took a deep breath. 'I didn't have the abortion.'

His face went a whiter shade than it already was.

'I'm sorry,' said Catherine. 'I realise this is a shock, and it's not the best place to tell you, but I just can't lie any more.'

He waved his hand, dismissing that. 'So you actually gave birth?'

She nodded. 'To a girl. A very beautiful girl.'

'Oh my God.' He seemed to be catching his breath. 'Do you know what happened to her? Have you had any contact with her over the years?'

'I'm sorry?'

'Well, you know, I'm just thinking, quite often adoptions are open these days, or isn't there a register so if the child wants to make contact –'

'James, I didn't give her up.'

He stared at her. 'But you said . . .'

Catherine realised then, she remembered what she'd told him at the Law Society function. 'Oh, I'm sorry James. I don't have any other children, none with my husband. I didn't want to blurt it out to you that night.'

He was obviously in shock now. 'Oh my God,' was all he could say, his voice barely making it out of his throat.

'Look, it's okay, I know this is a shock, you don't have to –'

He waved his hand again to stop her. 'A girl, you said?'

'That's right.'

'She'd be going on eighteen,' he said quietly, almost wistfully. 'You know, I never stopped wondering. And when I met you that night, I went home to Elizabeth and I said, "That's that. I finally know."'

'Your wife knew about this?'

'Of course,' he said. 'It's not the kind of thing you keep from your wife.'

Catherine was impressed. He really was a decent man. And his wife sounded pretty decent as well.

'Her name is Alice.' She suddenly felt like she could tell him everything, and not only that, she wanted to tell him everything.

'Alice,' he repeated. 'What's she like?'

Catherine thought about it. 'She's very bright, she can be very funny, and she's quite strong-willed, definitely has her own mind.'

'She's like you then, at that age,' said James.

Catherine supposed she was, in some ways.

'Do you have a picture?' he asked.

'Yes, of course,' she said, reaching for her handbag. She took out her wallet and flipped it open, passing it to him across the table. 'That was taken about a year ago.'

He was just staring at it. 'Oh, she is beautiful. She looks just like you.'

'She has your eyes.'

He looked up, and those eyes were filled with emotion, and gratitude . . . and now they were filling with tears. And involuntarily, and quite uncharacteristically, Catherine's eyes filled with tears as well.

They both laughed then, embarrassed, taking up their napkins at the same time, dabbing at their eyes.

The waiter returned to their table. 'Was there anything wrong with your meals?' he asked, looking at the untouched plates.

'No, nothing at all,' James assured him. 'We just decided we weren't hungry after all.'

'Shall I take them?'

'Yes, please.'

'Can I bring you anything else?'

James glanced at Catherine and she shook her head. 'No, thank you.'

He removed the plates and left.

James sighed deeply. 'Do you mind if I ask . . .?'

'Anything,' said Catherine.

'Does she know about me?'

'Not until just recently,' she said. 'She only knew her father was called James, and he was a one-night stand. Under the circumstances, I didn't want her to know any more than that, I didn't want her to go looking for you.'

'I understand.' He nodded. 'What does she think now?'

Catherine shrugged. 'She's curious, but wary. She has no expectations, after all this time. To be honest, I think she's still taking it all in.'

James leaned forwards. 'Look, I can't make any promises till I talk to Elizabeth –'

'James, it's fine, this is a difficult situation,' Catherine assured him. 'You have children of your own.'

'And now I have a daughter,' he said with a kind of wonder in his voice. 'Elizabeth is a wonderful woman, she's kind and understanding. She'll be fine with it. We just have to work out the best way to proceed.'

'So you would like to meet her?' Catherine asked.

'Of course,' he said without hesitation. 'If that's all right with you, and if it's all right with Alice?'

Catherine felt a deep sense of relief she hadn't felt since … probably since before those two lines had appeared on that pregnancy test.

'It's all right with me,' she assured him. 'Let's just take it a step at a time. Give everyone the chance to adjust to the idea.'

'You're right, I know,' he said. 'We have to work out the best way to introduce it to our boys.' He paused, before looking across at her. 'But I have to admit, Catherine, suddenly I'm quite anxious to meet her. I've missed out on so much of her life, I feel like I don't want to miss out on any more.'

James insisted on taking care of the bill, and they stepped out onto the street into the bright sunshine. Catherine turned to face him.

'So, we'll keep in touch. Call me after you've talked it over with Elizabeth.'

He looked at her intently. 'Thank you, Catherine. Thank you so much for telling me. You didn't have to.'

'Yes, I did.' She put out her hand. 'We'll talk soon.'

He took her hand, and then suddenly he leaned forwards to give her a quick, slightly awkward hug. He stepped back again, looking a little abashed.

She smiled at him. 'Bye James.'

'Bye Catherine.'

She turned and walked down the street in the other direction. She walked almost a block before she had to stop and think about where she was actually going. Where had she parked the car?

No, she remembered now. She had decided to get a cab in the end, in case there was an issue parking. She didn't want to have to dash out in the middle of things to put more change in a meter.

Catherine was brimming over, she could hardly wait to tell Rachel all of this. But not now. She checked her watch, Alice would be getting home from school and she had to tell her first. And Catherine was going to tell her everything. She had wondered about that, whether she was going to have to edit details to protect her, play it safe. But she felt overwhelmingly positive; the kind, understanding Elizabeth would be kind and understanding, and everything was going to work out, she knew it in her bones. She so wanted to tell Alice that her sweet, eminently decent father's eyes had welled up with tears when he'd looked at her photo. Alice should hear that, every girl should get to hear that. And Catherine couldn't wait another minute. She stepped out on the kerb and hailed a taxi.

Bondi Joost

Rachel had arrived for her shift at eleven and she hadn't stopped since. It was her first shift of the week, and she was so glad to be here. And especially glad it was busy. She thought she would go crazy if she spent one more hour at home alone in the flat. Apart from visiting Lexie the other day, she hadn't stepped foot outside. She just didn't have the energy or the motivation. She missed Tom so badly it was crippling. She had to keep reminding herself this was her decision, and it was the right decision. And somehow she had to find a way to move on with her life.

So it was good to be at work. She didn't have a moment to feel sorry for herself. They were inundated as busload after busload of Japanese tourists poured into Bondi. Apparently it was Golden Week in Japan, Mel managed to explain in short bursts, when more Japanese people were on holiday than at any other time of the year. And most of them came to Sydney, and all of them came to Bondi Beach.

There was finally a lull after three, and Rachel turned to the mess and started washing up.

Mel came out from the back. 'Thank God that's over for today.'

Rachel just gave a faint shrug, murmuring, 'I'll say,' as she concentrated on dismantling one of the juicers.

Mel busied herself around her, stacking things on the sink, wiping down benches.

'Hey, I just remembered,' she said suddenly. 'How did the big coming-out party go?'

Rachel wasn't prepared for that; she stammered something incomprehensible, and then unexpectedly and quite overwhelmingly she burst into tears, sobbing over the sink.

'Oh my God,' said Mel. 'Are you okay?'

But Rachel couldn't speak.

'Here.' Mel moved her away from the sink, glancing over her shoulder to make sure no customers were waiting. 'Take off your gloves,' she ordered. 'Go out the back.'

'No, it's okay,' Rachel whimpered.

'No, it's not,' Mel said flatly. 'Hand over the gloves.'

Rachel pulled off the rubber gloves and Mel passed her a tea towel. She trudged out to the storeroom and dropped down onto an upturned milk crate, crying into the towel. A moment later she felt a hand on her shoulder. She looked up.

'God, what happened, Rachel?'

She sighed tremulously. 'It's a long story.'

'Dammit,' said Mel. 'And it's still a few hours till closing.'

Rachel wiped her eyes. 'I'll be okay, just give me a minute.'

'No, you're going home.'

'I don't want to, really, Mel, I'd rather be here.'

Mel pulled over another crate and sat down to look at her. 'Are you sure?'

She nodded. 'I'd rather keep busy.'

'Jesus, Rachel, what the hell happened? Can you at least give me a hint?'

'Tom and I broke up.'

'Oh no,' she said, rubbing Rachel's shoulder. 'Okay, that's it, we're going out for a drink after work.'

'No, I don't want to drink.'

'Jeez, this really is serious.'

Rachel swallowed. 'I'm just afraid if I start drinking I won't be able to stop.'

'Okay,' she nodded. 'We'll go for a coffee, or a walk on the beach or something. But you stay out here as long as you need to.'

'I'll be okay in a minute.'

'Whatever you want, all right?' Mel said kindly, getting up again. 'It's not going to get that busy again, there won't be any more tourist buses, just the after-school mob. So do whatever you need to do.'

For the rest of the afternoon Rachel manned the sink and Mel handled the customers. Her shift should have ended at five, so with her staying on for the extra hour, washing up and cleaning everything in sight, Mel could pull down the shutter on the dot of six and close.

'So what do you want to do?' she asked Rachel.

'Maybe a walk?' she said weakly. 'A walk on the beach might be nice.'

'Whatever you say.'

So they walked across the road and over the bridge and down the steps onto the beach, and by the time they made it to the shoreline, Rachel had filled Mel in on everything that had happened on Saturday night, and since.

'Seriously, the stuff that happens to you,' Mel said when they finally plonked down on the sand, facing the water, 'you should write a book.'

Rachel grunted. 'No thanks, then I'd have to relive it.'

'Good point.'

Rachel had to admit, though, she did feel better getting it all off her chest without having to edit herself, or worry whose feelings she might be treading on. Mel was blissfully uninvolved, the best kind of sounding board.

'And you don't think there's any hope for you and Tom down the track?'

'I can't think like that, Mel. He has to work himself out, do the right thing by those girls.'

'Well, you're very noble, that's quite a sacrifice you're making.'

'I'm not so sure,' Rachel shook her head. 'In fact, Tom said something to me, that it was just my stuff, that, as usual, I was walking away from a difficult situation. And maybe I am. I never learned how to deal with conflict. My parents hated each other, my mother became vindictive and my father withdrew. I think maybe I've taken after him.'

'Who knows?' said Mel. 'We think we can put together why we do things like pieces in a puzzle, and it'll all fit in the end, it'll all make sense. But it's like when they finally mapped out the human genome. Everyone got so excited, they'd be able to predict everything about a person, but the scientists baulked at that. The myriad combinations of genes, and the myriad effects of the environment, and a whole lot more we don't even understand makes it impossible to predict anything with absolute certainty.' She looked over at Rachel. 'You'll never know for sure why you react the way you do, Rach, even if your gut instinct is a little skewed, in the end it's all you've got. And you have to be true to yourself.'

Rachel sighed. 'Well, my gut tells me I can't stand by and watch Sophie self-destruct, if I have anything to do with it.'

'And I'm saying . . . noble.'

Rachel looked at her. 'Well, you know what, between you and me, Mel, being noble sucks.'

Mel laughed. 'What can I tell you, good guys always come last.'

'Why is that? Who made up that rule?' Rachel wanted to know. 'I don't pretend to be a saint, but you try and do the right thing, do unto others, all that, and yet the people who only look out for themselves, they seem to get everything they want.'

'Maybe, on a superficial level, but would you really want to be like that?'

'Why not? Maybe that's where I've been going wrong. I need to put myself first.'

Mel shook her head. 'You couldn't do it, Rachel.'

'How do you know?'

She looked squarely at her. 'Because you're giving up the man you love for the sake of his daughter's wellbeing. You don't have it in you to put yourself first and screw everyone else, and it wouldn't make you happy.'

'Well, this doesn't either,' Rachel sighed.

They sat staring out at the water. The sun had disappeared behind them and there was a distinct chill rolling in off the ocean. Rachel drew her jacket around her.

'So what are you going to do now?' asked Mel. 'You can't hide out in my juice bar forever, you know.'

Rachel gave her a startled look.

'Don't worry,' Mel said quickly. 'You'll always have a job there, but the thing is, you really shouldn't. You're too smart for this.'

'Ho, you should talk,' Rachel came back at her. 'You're way smarter than me, and you own the place.'

'Exactly,' she said. 'And I have a five-year plan. A couple more shopfronts in my name and I get to live like a sheik, travel, survey my empire from afar. I've got it all figured out.'

Rachel was smiling. 'I didn't know that. Good for you.'

'So what are you going to do with yourself, Rachel Halliday?'

She shook her head. 'Everyone keeps asking me that, and I have no idea.'

'Well,' Mel said with conviction, 'we're both bright women, I reckon if we put our heads together we should be able to come up with something.'

'What do you have in mind?'

'Don't ask me,' she shrugged. 'Isn't it more important what you have in mind?'

'Pardon?'

'What do *you* want to do, what do you like to do, what are you good at?' she fired off. 'If you could do anything you wanted to . . . dream job . . . what would it be?'

Rachel smiled slowly. 'No one's ever asked me that before.'

'Well it's about time you asked yourself.'

*

May

> Hi. Can i see you? Please. All
> above board. Just want to see you
> before we leave. Call me. T.

Rachel had been staring at the text message for some time now. She wasn't sure how long. This was the first time she'd heard from Tom. He'd taken her at her word and not made any contact. Not a word. And now this.

What did it mean? Leave? Where was he going? Where were *they* going? Up the coast, perhaps? For how long? Why would he need to see her if they were just going up the coast to visit his parents? Why was she asking herself all these questions when she could just call him?

Her stomach was twisting into knots; it had just about leaped out of her throat when the message first arrived. She still hadn't been able to steady her hands as she sat there, staring at the screen.

Okay, this was crazy. He just wanted to see her, it was all 'above board', whatever that meant. And he was leaving, somewhere, for some indeterminate length of time. And he wanted to see her. Couldn't hurt.

Yes, it could.

But the opportunity to see his face was overwhelming. Rachel pressed the button to call before she thought about it any longer.

'Hello, Rachel?'

She wasn't prepared to hear his voice. Which was pretty silly, since she'd phoned his number.

'Rachel, are you there?'

She cleared her throat. 'Yes, I'm here.'

'Hi.'

'Hi Tom,' she said, trying to sound normal, though she doubted she was pulling it off. 'How are you?'

'I'm okay. It's good to hear your voice.'

She made a kind of strangled noise to indicate agreement, acknowledgement, something or other.

'So you got my message?' he asked.

'Yeah, I did,' she croaked. She cleared her throat again. 'Um, you're leaving? Going somewhere?'

'That's right, but I'd rather talk to you about it in person,' he said. 'Do you mind? Would it be all right to come around and see you? I wouldn't stay long.'

'Well, when?'

'I can come now.'

She took a breath. 'Oh, I dunno, Tom, it must be nearly nine.'

'Yeah, I know,' he said. 'But I don't have much time.'

Her heart was beating hard in her chest. What was this about?

'Look, I'm sorry if I sound mysterious,' he went on, 'but I don't want to talk about it over the phone. I promise it won't take long.'

She wasn't prepared for this, she'd had no time to steel herself.

'Rachel, please?' he said finally. 'I think you might change your mind if we put it off.'

He was right about that.

'Okay,' she willed herself to say.

'Thanks,' he said. 'I'll be there in, say, twenty minutes? See you then.'

And he hung up before she could say anything. Change her mind, put in a protest, call it off. He knew her too well.

What the hell. Rachel looked down at herself. Oh for godsakes, she had to change. She raced into her room and wriggled out of her baggy tracksuit pants and grabbed a pair of jeans out of her wardrobe, wriggling into them. She was panting like she'd been for a jog. Stupid. Calm down. She pulled off her oversized sweater and tossed it aside. She sniffed under her arms. What did it matter what she smelled like? But she felt all clammy . . . She ran over to her dressing table and grabbed a can of deodorant, spraying under her arms and then across her chest for good measure. She glanced at herself in the mirror. Oh God, she looked so flustered. She pulled the elastic out of her hair and shook her head, running her fingers through her hair. She looked at herself again. Makeup? No, she hardly ever wore makeup, especially not sitting around at home. She'd look ridiculous.

She crossed back over to the wardrobe, flicking through the hangers, till she landed on a plain black long-sleeved T-shirt. That would do; she didn't want to look like she'd got changed specially, this could be something she'd wear around the house. She scuppered back down the hall, pulling the T-shirt over her head. She picked up her dinner plate and glass off the coffee table and ran them out to the sink. She turned on the tap, too hard, and water sprayed up all over her.

'*Fuck!*'

Calm down! Rachel leaned against the sink for a moment, catching her breath. She picked up a tea towel and dabbed at her top. Blast, she would have to change it. Back in her room, flicking through the hangers in her wardrobe again, she started to panic. The black top was perfect – neat, unassuming, clean . . .

The security buzzer sounded. What the? That wasn't twenty minutes. Bugger. She ran out to the hall and pressed the button to release the security door, not bothering to check, she knew it wasn't going to be anyone else. She dashed back into her room and yanked the first thing off the hanger. Crap! It was the green top. She didn't have any time. She pulled it on, shook out her hair again and walked out of the room as she heard his knock.

Rachel took a breath and forced herself to take slow, steady steps to the door. Her hand was shaking as she reached up and turned the lock. The door swung back. And he was standing there.

'Hi,' said Tom.

'Hi.' She stepped out of the way and he walked in, stooping to give her a quick kiss on the cheek.

'It's good to see you, Rach.'

She nodded. 'Go through,' she said, turning to close the door again. She followed him down the hall, gazing at his back, the caramel curls at the nape of his neck, his broad shoulders. Oh God.

He walked into the living room and turned around to face her, looking straight into her eyes. It felt as though a lightning bolt shot through her.

'Please, sit,' she somehow managed to say. 'Can I get you something? A drink?'

He shook his head. 'No, I'm right.' He crossed over to the couch and sat down as Rachel dropped into the armchair closest, twisting her legs up underneath her and clasping her arms around herself like she was attempting some weird yoga pose; the Coiled Spring, perhaps.

Tom sat forwards, resting his elbows on his knees. 'How have you been, Rachel?'

'Fine, good, nothing to report.' She gave a nervous laugh. Deflect, deflect. She did not want to talk about herself. If she talked about herself she might end up saying that she missed him so much that sometimes she didn't know how she was going to get through the day. Then the next day would be a little better, and the day after, then something would send her plummeting again, a pair of blue eyes across the counter, or a couple walking arm in arm ahead of her. And then she'd wonder how come they got to be happy. And what had she done to deserve this? And then she'd get angry, and worse, bitter, and it would take days before she could pull herself out of that dark pit again.

So no, she did not want to talk about herself.

'Um, how are you?' she said instead. 'How are the girls? Is everything all right?'

He nodded slowly, clasping his hands together. 'They're good, thanks. We're all good. We've made some big changes.'

'Oh?'

'Yeah.' He paused, thinking. 'I wanted to thank you, Rachel. You were right, about everything.'

Somehow that wasn't reassuring right now.

'I've spent a lot of time with the girls,' he went on. 'We've talked and talked, there were so many things I wasn't aware of . . . And we've discussed a whole lot of options and possibilities. And, well, look, you don't want to hear all the ins and outs, but the thing is, I've put the house on the market and we're going away for a while.'

'Oh,' said Rachel. 'Where to?'

'We've got round-the-world tickets. We're off to do the backpacking thing I never got to do all those years ago.'

She hadn't expected that. She didn't know what she was expecting, but not that. 'Wow, Tom,' she said quietly. 'That's wonderful. I'm really happy for you.'

He nodded. 'Yeah, it's great, really, the girls are very excited.'

'How long are you going to be away?'

'Well, you know how those tickets work, you have a year to

use them. But I don't think we'll go for quite that long, it'll be too disruptive to their schooling.'

'Oh, of course, school,' said Rachel. 'What are you going to do about that?'

'Well, it doesn't matter for Sophie, because she's already a senior, so she's not legally required to attend school.'

Rachel frowned. 'So she's quitting?'

'Not exactly. She'll have to do Year 11 over, but she can go to a senior college, so it won't feel so much like she's repeating.'

'And Hannah?'

'We had to jump through a few hoops with the education department, but she was considered a special case because of her mother. So they've given us units of work for her to complete while she's away, which should be a challenge,' he added wryly. 'But Sophie has promised to help.'

'And Hannah's okay with that?'

He nodded. 'She's had her moments – you know what their friends are like to them at that age. But her sister is very persuasive. She's been the driving force behind this whole thing.'

'So I suppose you're going to South America?' asked Rachel.

Tom smiled faintly. 'Yes we are, as a matter of fact. Sophie wants to check it out. And quite frankly I'm happy to be checking it out too, if she does decide she wants to do the exchange thing later.'

Rachel's head was buzzing, trying to take it all in. 'And what about your job, Tom?'

'That was the easiest decision,' he said plainly. 'I quit.'

'But how will you live?' she blurted. 'Sorry, that's none of my business.'

'It's okay.' He paused, sitting back. 'Thing is, Annie had a life-insurance policy. It was something she insisted on, way back. She said if anything ever happened to her I'd need help with the girls. And she was right. I just couldn't bring myself to cash it in before now. But this is for the girls, so . . .'

Rachel nodded. 'You don't need to explain, Tom.'

He shrugged.

'So when do you leave?' she asked.

He took a breath. 'End of the week.'

Her heart dropped into the pit of her stomach. 'I see.'

'Rachel, there's so much I want to say to you . . .'

'No, Tom, it's probably better if you don't say anything,' she said firmly. 'I'm happy for you, I really am, please know that. This is an amazing thing you're doing. A lot of people wouldn't have the guts.'

'I'm only doing it because of you,' he said. 'You forced me out of here, made me face up to my responsibilities and connect with my daughters again. I had been keeping them at arm's distance, because I just didn't know how I was going to be able to love them enough to make up for their mother. And I've finally realised I don't have to do that, I just have to be their dad.'

Rachel smiled faintly. 'I'm so glad, Tom.'

'That was an extraordinary, selfless thing you did for us,' he went on. 'You know, I hope you don't mind me saying, but Annie would be very impressed.'

She shrugged. 'I think she'd be pretty impressed with you right now as well.'

He was staring at her with a wistful look in his eyes. 'Rachel, I wish . . .'

'No, Tom. Let's not.'

'Okay,' he nodded. 'You're right, I know. But you do understand why I wanted to tell you in person? I didn't want to just disappear without the chance to explain.'

'Of course, and I appreciate that.'

He looked at her intently. 'And I also wanted to make sure . . . Well, are you going to be okay, Rach? I worry about you.'

'Hey, don't. I'm fine, I'm good. I'm making plans, I'm getting on with it.' She really didn't want to talk about herself. And the longer they sat here, the more dangerous the territory they were likely to tread.

'So . . .' she said, uncoiling herself and getting to her feet.

Tom stood up as well. 'I'll get out of your way then.'

He followed her up the hall and she turned to face him at the door. 'Thanks for coming, Tom. You go have a fantastic time. Give the girls my love.'

He had a strange look on his face and his eyes were glassy. 'Rachel, would it be okay . . .'

'What?'

'Well, would a hug be . . . inappropriate?'

She breathed out. 'Of course not.'

He took her in his arms and they held each other close. So close, Rachel could feel his chest heaving, his heart beating against her.

'Tom,' she said after a long while had passed and he hadn't moved.

'I can't let go,' he said.

'Yes you can.'

'I can't.'

'You have to,' said Rachel, looking up at him. 'You've got a plane to catch.'

They stared at each other, and Rachel didn't know who moved first, but all of a sudden their mouths were locked and they were kissing, deeply, and then frantically. And they were pulling at each other's clothes, and stumbling back down the hall to her room. They fell onto the bed and they made love like it was the last time either of them ever would.

Afterwards, Rachel rolled over onto her side and Tom curled into her back, holding her close.

'I love you,' he said.

'I love you too.'

'I don't want to go, Rachel. I don't want to leave you.'

She shifted, turning her head around to look at him. 'You have to, Tom. But can you do me a favour?'

'Anything.'

'Stay until I fall asleep.'

He brought his hand up to cup her face, kissing her gently. 'Of course.'

Rachel turned around again and he moulded himself into her back, wrapping his arms around her and resting his cheek against hers.

That was the last thing Rachel remembered. The next morning, she woke up alone.

*

Winter

Rachel strolled up towards the cemetery gates, clutching a small posy of flowers. It felt a little weird coming here again. She could never pass this way without thinking of Annie. It was strange to imagine her here, buried under the ground. Sometimes it felt a little creepy, other times it was comforting.

Today she was meeting Lexie and they were going to visit Annie's grave to inspect her newly laid headstone. Rachel hadn't realised how long these things could take, but she'd never known anyone who'd died before, so how would she know? Apparently Tom had recently been in touch with Lexie; he'd been notified that the headstone had finally been laid and had asked if she wouldn't mind going to check it out for them. So Lexie had called Rachel; she didn't want to go on her own, which was quite understandable.

She wasn't waiting at the gates when Rachel arrived, but as Lexie was even less punctual than she was, Rachel didn't really expect her to be. And it wasn't long before she spotted her, bustling her way up the street, wrapped in a coat and gloves and scarf and a beanie. It was cold today, but she was perhaps overdoing it.

'Hi,' Lexie called out as she approached, her face all pink from the cold air. 'I'm so sorry, Rachel, I didn't want to keep you waiting.'

'It's fine, Lexie, I've only been here a few minutes.'

'That's good.' She came right up to her, giving her a hug. 'Oh, damn,' she said, stepping back. 'I meant to bring flowers too, it completely went out of my mind this morning. I got caught up trying to figure out how to use the camera on my phone.'

'What for?'

'I want to take a photo, for Tom and the girls.'

Rachel nodded.

'So, how are you anyway?' Lexie asked.

'Good, thanks. Everything's good.'

'Have you heard from the uni yet?'

'Any day now.'

'Well, I'm sure you'll be accepted,' she said reassuringly. 'So . . .'

Rachel looked at her, wondering what they were waiting for. They could walk and talk.

'I heard from Tom, like I told you,' said Lexie. 'They're all doing really well, trekking their way across Europe. Have you had any word from them at all?'

She shook her head. 'It's better that way.'

'Of course,' said Lexie, giving her arm a pat. 'He did ask after you. He always asks after you.'

Rachel nodded. She really didn't want to know. It was best not to know what he was doing, or where he was, because then she might be tempted to work out their route, count down days, imagine what might be when he came back. And that was when she hit dangerous territory. Because there were no guarantees. Tom could be in a very different place now, and not just geographically. Rachel had had to accept that once they were apart, and he gave himself the space to grieve properly for Annie, he might not feel the same way about her. She had been his safe harbour and now he had set sail. Anything was possible.

But nothing had changed at this end; Rachel still ached for him, every day. She tried to keep herself busy, keep her mind off him, but that was difficult working part-time at a juice bar. She simply had to get into this course, or she didn't know what she was going to do with herself.

'And how are your plans coming along?' she asked Lexie, changing the subject.

'Everything's full speed ahead. We close on the restaurant in Orange in less than a fortnight, can you believe it?'

'So your house must be on the market already?'

'No, we've decided to rent it out,' she explained. 'Everyone, both sides of the family, told us we were mad giving up real estate in Sydney. And the bank seemed to agree. We had enough capital from the sale of the business, so, blah blah, with the house counted as part of our "portfolio",' she gave a little shriek at that idea, 'everything went through without a hitch.'

'So when do you move?'

'Oh, it'll take a couple of months yet,' she explained. 'Actually renting the house makes things a lot easier. We can stay here while Scott travels back and forth organising the renovations and setting everything up. And then we can move when it suits us, which will be a lot less stress in the end.'

'Still, it's a big move, Lexie,' said Rachel.

'But I'm just so excited,' she said. 'I can't tell you. I'm busting to get up there and get started. We've got so many plans.'

Rachel smiled. 'I'm really happy for you guys. Even though I am going to miss you.'

'Oh, we're going to miss you too,' said Lexie. 'That's why you have to come up and visit as often as you can.'

'Oh, I think I'll have to get in line behind all the family.'

'You will get priority whenever you say the word.'

'Thank you,' said Rachel. 'That's very sweet. I'll look forward to it.'

Lexie nodded, glancing around. It seemed as though she was stalling, maybe she felt uncomfortable about visiting the grave. She was so close to Annie, and the last time she was here she had been in quite a state. But it had to be done, so Rachel decided maybe it was up to her to move things along.

'So,' she said, 'shall we do this?'

Lexie frowned, checking her watch. 'In a minute,' she said vaguely.

Rachel was beginning to wonder what was going on, when she heard a faint toot, and then a car swept around the corner in front of them. Catherine's car. They watched as it pulled up across the road.

'Lexie,' Rachel sighed.

'Oh, please don't be cross, Rachel,' she said, turning to her. 'I just thought we should all be together for this, it seemed like the right thing.'

'I'm sorry,' she said. 'I don't think I can stay.'

Lexie grabbed her arm. 'Please, Rachel.'

'Lexie, you know I haven't talked to her in all this time.'

'I know, and you won't ever have to again, if you don't want to. But let's just do this one last thing together. For Annie.'

'You think Annie would want her here?'

Lexie shrugged, biting her lip. 'I'm sorry, I shouldn't have butted in. But you two have been friends for such a long time, it just seemed wrong to end it without even a word to each other.'

They heard the beep of a remote lock and looked over to see Catherine walking across the street, carrying a huge arrangement of flowers in her arms. Typical. It was too late, it would be awkward now whatever Rachel did.

'Fine,' she sighed.

'Oh, thank you so much,' Lexie gushed. She rushed forwards to meet Catherine, while Rachel hung back where she was. She had actually talked to Catherine once, over the phone. She'd finally decided, after Tom left, that she had to put an end to the constant stream of messages. Catherine had gradually realised that Rachel was deliberately avoiding her, and her messages had evolved from cheery 'We have to debrief' to 'What's going on?' to 'Please, Rachel, pick up. What's wrong?'

So she had spoken to her, though only briefly. She basically told her she needed a break, some space, time out. Catherine had been a little taken aback.

'Time out? What are you talking about?'

'I just can't be around you right now, Catherine.'

'If this is about the Tom thing, I know I handled that badly on the night, but really, isn't that all in the past now? I heard you two even broke up. You couldn't still be jealous, surely?'

And that pretty much said it all. The fact that Catherine could reduce everything down to that, as if jealousy was the issue here. There was no point trying to explain it, Catherine could rationalise her way out of anything, and even turn it into a shortcoming on Rachel's part. And Rachel had had quite enough of that.

But now she was walking right up to her, dressed in a long black coat and large, dark Jackie-O sunglasses, looking the part of the grieving friend. How dare she? After what she'd done.

'Hello Rachel,' she said, her tone appropriately sombre.

'Let's get this over with, shall we?' said Rachel, turning on her heel and walking into the cemetery.

Lexie took it upon herself to provide a running commentary as they made their way along.

'So Rachel's enrolled in a teaching degree,' she began.

'That's great,' said Catherine. 'What kind of teaching?'

Rachel didn't respond.

'High school,' said Lexie.

'Won't that take years?'

'Normally, yes,' Lexie continued. 'But Rachel's applied for this special fast-track program, because there's a shortage of school counsellors, and they want to attract mature-age people with some life experience. They pay for the training and everything, and they have a mid-year intake so she can start straightaway.'

Lexie was fudging a few of the details but it was close enough.

'That sounds wonderful, Rachel,' said Catherine. 'I can't believe we never thought of this before. It's perfect for you.'

Rachel still didn't say anything, but that was okay, her spokesperson was ready with a response.

'I know, it's *so* perfect, isn't it? She's always had that connection with teenagers.' She paused. 'By the way, how are things going with Alice and her father?'

Rachel's ears pricked up, despite herself.

'Actually, they couldn't be better,' said Catherine. 'We're taking it slowly, a step at a time. James came to our house for their first meeting, so Alice would feel comfortable in her own surroundings. That went really well, so then he took her out to lunch, and they had coffee just last week, so she could meet his wife. This weekend is the big one, she's going to their house to meet her half-brothers.'

'Isn't that amazing,' said Lexie, shaking her head. 'She has brothers, I didn't even think of that. How is Alice handling all of this?'

'Pretty well, actually. She's been quite mature about it. She gets a little nervous at each new step, but I have to say James has been so sensitive, so caring. She already seems to trust him.'

Rachel felt a huge sense of relief wash over her. Alice had another parent to love her, she had siblings. She wasn't an only child any more.

'She seems, I don't know . . . happier in herself,' said Catherine. 'She's buckled down to her studies, and she even won a short-story competition. Little minx has been writing stories for years, never shown me a thing. Still won't. A teacher submitted her story for the competition, it'll be published in the paper. She said I can read it then.'

'Do you know where we're going, Lexie?' Rachel said after they had walked quite a way into the cemetery.

'Oh, yes, I have a map,' said Lexie, pulling a piece of paper out of her handbag and consulting it. She looked around. 'I think it's this way.'

They found the grave easily enough, the map was quite straightforward. Rachel would never have found it otherwise, she hadn't been back since the funeral, and she certainly hadn't been paying attention that day. As they approached, the site looked very neat; they probably did some tidying up when they laid the stone. The three of them stood quietly at the foot of the grave, reading the epitaph.

'*Mother, wife, friend,*' Lexie read aloud after a while. '*Forever young, forever loved.*' She paused. 'It's very simple. I guess I expected . . .'

'What, Lexie?' Rachel asked.

She shrugged. 'Well, more, I suppose. Something to say how wonderful and amazing Annie was.'

'How can you express that in a few words carved on stone?' said Catherine. 'And they all end up sounding the same – "beloved" wife, "adored" mother, "loving" friend, or some variation on that. I think this is very dignified.'

Rachel slipped her arm through Lexie's. 'You know what Annie was like, she hated having a fuss made of her.'

Lexie smiled then. 'You're right, it's perfect.' She took out her phone and aimed it, taking a couple of shots.

Catherine stepped forwards to place her floral arrangement on the grave. While it was huge and excessive, at least it was all native flowers, which Annie would have loved: proteas and banksias and bottlebrushes. And it would last for ages. Unlike Rachel's little posy of cottage flowers that would be wilted by tomorrow. She bent down and laid them beside Catherine's arrangement. Still, they were pretty, and they'd reminded her of Annie when she saw them in the florist shop.

'Catherine,' Lexie said after a while, 'remember how you had that idea that we should be inspired by Annie's death to do something with our lives?'

Catherine nodded.

'Well, I guess we have, maybe not the way you intended, but we've all changed, so much has changed.'

'It certainly has,' said Catherine, and Rachel could feel her looking at her.

'I think she's resting in peace,' Lexie said finally. There was a long pause, and then suddenly she turned around. 'Well, I have to run.' She leaned over to give Catherine a peck on the cheek, and Rachel a quick hug, and she was scooting along the path away from them before they'd even registered she was gone.

Rachel sighed inwardly. That sweet demeanour hid a whole lot of cunning. 'Well, goodbye Catherine,' she said, walking off in the same direction.

'Rachel, hold on,' said Catherine, hurrying to catch up to her. As usual she was wearing ridiculous heels, while Rachel was in flat boots. She could easily outpace her.

'Can I give you a lift home?' she called after her.

'No thanks.'

But Catherine was not giving up that easily. 'Rachel, Alice has been asking after you. She's wondering why we haven't seen you lately.'

'I'm sure you'll make up something. Give her my love,' said Rachel, striding ahead.

'You really don't want to have anything to do with me any more, do you?' she said breathlessly, trying to keep up. 'Rachel, can you please at least help me understand why? Is it all because of what happened with Tom?'

Rachel sighed, coming to a halt. 'You just don't get it, do you?'

'No,' she said, catching up. 'So explain it to me.'

'How can you even come here? Show your face here?'

'Lexie asked me to come.'

'Catherine!' she scolded. 'You know what I'm getting at. You were quite prepared to risk ruining their marriage to get what you wanted. And then, even after Annie died, the way you threw yourself into organising the funeral . . . What the hell was that about? Did you actually imagine Tom would fall into your arms afterwards?'

She shrugged. 'Wishful thinking, I guess.'

Rachel shook her head. 'You just have no shame, do you? If you want something, you go for it, you don't care who gets hurt in the process, because you are always number one. And you know what shits me most about that? It's that people like you do seem to get it all.'

'Well, I didn't get Tom.'

'You were never going to get Tom,' she said plainly. 'But what you don't seem to realise is that you destroyed their last weeks together. What happened nearly tore Annie apart, and Tom has had to carry that guilt ever since. Can you imagine what that's been like for him?'

At least that seemed to affect her.

'Is that why it didn't work out between you two?' Catherine asked.

Rachel shook her head, breathing out. 'You wouldn't understand.'

'Try me.'

'You know what, Catherine, I don't want to. I don't want your opinions, or your judgement, I've had quite enough of that to last me a lifetime.'

'I see.'

'The thing is, I'm okay, because I know I made the right decision for the right reasons. And sure, I've ended up alone, but at least I can live with myself.' She paused. 'I'm not like you, Catherine, I don't need a man to feel okay about myself, at any cost. I don't want to go trawling the internet. I could never be with a married man, no matter how much trouble his marriage was in.'

'Okay,' Catherine said, raising her hands. 'I get it. I'll back off about you finding someone.'

'That's not the point.'

'Then what is?' she implored. 'We've been friends for a long time, we've always been able to tell each other everything.'

'No we haven't,' Rachel shook her head. 'That's what's so ironic. You know, we boast how we've got it all over men, we have such intimacy, such quality relationships. But when it comes down to it we can't say the really hard stuff.'

'I think I've always been able to,' said Catherine.

'But I haven't been able to tell you I didn't always appreciate what you said or agree with you.'

'So go ahead. Say what's on your mind.'

Rachel folded her arms, considering her. She really should say this, it was her last opportunity. 'You drink too much.'

Catherine blinked. 'Where did that come from?'

'I've been watching it for a while now, and a good friend would say something. Actually, no, a good friend wouldn't, that's the problem. So I'm telling you now. You drink too much.'

'Rachel, everyone drinks too much –'

'No Catherine, some of us drink too much sometimes,' she said. 'But you have a problem, and you should do something about it before you hurt anyone else.'

'Well,' she said, crossing her arms. 'When you decide to open up, you don't hold back, do you?'

'I should have said something a long time ago,' said Rachel. 'Not only about the drinking, but the affairs, and just the way you use people, Catherine. But these things creep up on you gradually ... until suddenly you realise you're friends with someone you have no respect for any more.'

Catherine flinched.

'Look, I don't mean to sound morally superior,' Rachel said. 'Everyone makes mistakes. I have, I know I've made you crazy at times, and I know you've done a lot for me over the years. But I think we've gone as far as we can go.'

'What's that supposed to mean? You can't treat a friendship like it's got a use-by date.'

'I don't see why not, you can get a divorce when a marriage is over,' Rachel said plainly.

'Look,' said Catherine, 'whatever you may think of me, just hear me out for a minute.' She took a breath. 'I know I'm not perfect, Rachel, and I realise I've hurt people on occasion. I've come up against some pretty hard truths lately, and I've been dying to talk to you about it all. The whole story with James, you won't believe it. I've come to realise that most of my life has been a reaction to something that didn't even happen the way I thought it did.' She paused. 'Now I'm trying to work out how to go on with the rest of my life. Martin's left, and I'm not in any hurry to find someone else, for the first time ever. I'm focusing on Alice now. I think we're finally beginning to have a meaningful relationship. It's different, but it feels real. And she's certainly happier.'

'That all sounds good, Catherine,' said Rachel. 'I hope everything turns out for you. Now I have to get going.' She turned and started to walk away.

'So that's that?' Catherine called after her. 'We have so much history together, doesn't that count for something?'

Rachel paused, turning around to look at her. 'Maybe, but it's not enough,' she said. 'Give my love to Alice. She's the best thing you ever did, Catherine, never forget how lucky you are to have her.'

'Don't you want to keep in touch with her?'

'I'm sure she knows she can always call me,' she said over her shoulder as she started to walk away again.

'What about me?' said Catherine. 'Can I call you sometime?'

Rachel didn't look back. 'You can call. I just can't promise I'll pick up.'

Six months later

Rachel was lying in bed, thinking about getting up. Her results had been posted on the internet at some ungodly hour this morning, but she hadn't bothered to set an alarm. She wasn't in any particular rush to check them. Today was her first Saturday off in ages, so she figured she was entitled to a sleep-in. She had worked incredibly hard this semester, getting used to studying again, juggling part-time work, as well as a few weeks of prac teaching. She'd been so busy she'd hardly had time to think about Tom.

But that didn't stop her. She thought about him every day, him and the girls, wondering where they were and what they were doing. But she didn't have time to dwell, or mope, or pine. And that was definitely a good thing, because before she started the course, Rachel had worried she'd sink under the weight of the loss she felt. Mel had helped keep her afloat, and for that Rachel would forever be in her debt. But it was the course that had finally given her purpose, and direction, and so much more. She loved it, even when she found it difficult and infuriating, and she was up half the night struggling to figure out how on earth to write an essay again, let alone what she was actually going to put in it. But when she stood in front of a class of terrifying fifteen year olds for the first time, Rachel had her moment of truth. She finally knew what she wanted to do with her life.

The flutter of anticipation she felt about checking her results was gradually becoming more persistent, so Rachel decided it was time to get up. She had scored solid marks for all her assignments and received an excellent report for her prac, so she wasn't worried about passing, as such. And now she understood better than ever that grades were subject to bell curves and averages and statistics and whatever, and that she couldn't allow one little letter to detract from all the good work she had done, and more importantly, all that she had learned in the process.

So she turned on her computer as she passed it on her way to the kitchen, where she filled the kettle and plugged it in. Rachel peered out the window while she waited for it to boil. She couldn't see the ocean from back here, but the glimpse of sky between her block and the next was bright blue and clear. She reached over the sink to open the window and was immediately met with a gentle waft of salty sea breeze. Perhaps she'd wander down to the beach later, but she'd put a load of washing on first, and she should write a list and pick up some groceries on the way back. The kettle started to whistle. But first there was that small matter of checking her marks.

Rachel made herself a cup of tea and traipsed back into the living room, plonking down in front of her computer. She put her cup to one side and logged onto her uni account. She followed the links until finally her results appeared, listed on the screen. And she smiled.

She looked around for her phone, remembering it was in her bedroom, recharging. She went and unplugged it, wandering back out to the living room as she keyed in a message to Mel. She pressed *Send*, and sat down in front of the computer again. She picked up her cup of tea and took a sip, when her phone rang.

Rachel answered it. 'Hi Mel.'

'What are you doing texting me?' she demanded.

'I didn't want to interrupt you at work.'

'You think it's easier to send a text with sticky watermelon hands?' she said. 'You would think someone who earned two distinctions and two high distinctions would be smarter than that.'

Rachel laughed.

'Woohoo,' Mel exclaimed. 'Kudos. How many of those teachers did you sleep with?'

'I'll never tell.'

'So, how are you going to celebrate? What are you doing today?'

'Oh, I've got heaps to catch up on, washing, housework . . .'

'You are hopeless, Rach, you're all work, work, work.'

'And that's how I got two Ds, and two HDs.'

'And smug to boot,' said Mel. 'Look, you have to celebrate, you should join us tonight.'

'What are you doing?'

'Well, we were just going to stay in, have a quiet one, but –'

'Thanks anyway, Mel, but I'll be fine.'

'Jack wouldn't mind, he loves you.'

Rachel laughed. 'Jack is a gentleman, and he would never show that he minded, but I think he'd go for the "quiet night in" option.'

Jack and Mel had worked together years back, until Jack left to take up a job in the UK. He had come home a few months ago, a casualty of the GFC, and set about looking up old colleagues. They had been going out ever since, and Mel was trying very hard to ignore toothpaste tubes and toilet seats, because, she'd admitted to Rachel, she really liked this one.

'Don't be so sure,' Mel was saying. 'If I put it to him that he could have two girls for the price of one . . .'

'Okay, now you're just grossing me out.' Rachel heard a knock at the door. 'There's someone at the door, I have to go.'

'Yeah, that's the fella I sent around to sweep you off your feet. You can thank me later.'

'Goodbye Mel.'

'Call me if you change your mind about tonight.'

Rachel hung up as the knock sounded again. 'Coming,' she sang out. Whoever it was had already got past the security door, so it was probably a charity collector who'd been right through the block. She hurried up the hall and opened the door, and her heart stopped.

'Surprise!'

'Hannah, Sophie!' Rachel finally found her voice. 'You're back.'

'Well, dahh!' Hannah lurched at her, giving her a hug.

Sophie was not so forward, but she looked happy, and she was smiling straight at her. 'We just got back a couple of days ago.'

Where was Tom? Rachel wanted to ask, but she didn't think she could get the words out. Her heart was pounding in her chest, and she could feel the blood pumping through her veins, creating a weird rippling sensation throughout her limbs. It was a little surreal. She wondered for a second if she was dreaming...

But no, the girls were definitely real, standing large as life in front of her. Hannah had clearly hit puberty, she'd lost that little girl look, but Rachel wouldn't embarrass her by saying so. 'Have you gotten taller, Hannah?'

She positively beamed but Sophie answered before she could. 'Yeah, she thinks she's going to end up taller than me, but I'm not going to let that happen.'

Sophie hadn't grown or changed that much physically, but there was something different about her. Maybe it was her hair, obviously longer now, held back haphazardly in a clip with strands falling loose everywhere, very un-Sophie like. She seemed less restrained or composed somehow. She looked like an adolescent again.

'Well, come on in,' Rachel finally managed to say.

'No, thanks anyway,' said Sophie. 'We were just going down to the beach.'

'And we came to see if you want to come with us,' Hannah chimed in.

'Dad's just parking the car,' added Sophie.

And then he appeared on the landing below, and he was turning around to come up the last flight, and he looked up at her, and he smiled.

'Hello Rachel,' he said, looking right into her eyes as he climbed the last few stairs.

She wasn't sure at all that she was going to get her voice to work. But she could feel the girls' eyes on her, waiting for her to respond.

'Hi Tom. Welcome home.'

He stopped where he was, on the top step, leaning his arm on the banister. 'So, have the girls asked you yet?'

'Um, yeah, they did.'

'So what do you say?'

Rachel honestly didn't know how she was going to even put one foot in front of the other. 'Um, I don't know, I've got all this stuff I was going to do ...'

'Isn't Saturday the day for not quite getting around to things?' asked Tom.

How did he remember that?

'Please Rachel, you have to come,' Hannah urged.

'It was their idea,' Tom said, giving her a meaningful look.

Then Rachel felt Sophie's hand, slipping into hers. She turned her head to look at her.

'Please come with us, Rachel,' she said. 'It'll be more fun. You know what they say ... three's a crowd.'

ALSO BY DIANNE BLACKLOCK IN PAN MACMILLAN

Call Waiting

Ally Tasker feels trapped. Her dreams of a fulfilling life after art college didn't include cleaning up after bored school children and being a doormat for her high-flying boyfriend. Ally envies her friend Meg who has turned her art training into a lucrative job in graphic design, not to mention having a doting husband and gorgeous baby to complete the package.

But when Ally's grandfather, her sole relative, dies, she returns to the Southern Highlands home of her childhood where she must confront painful issues from her past that her safe life in the city has allowed her to ignore. Meanwhile Meg is not as happy as Ally imagines . . .

Sometimes you have to risk all you have to realise what is worth saving.

Wife for Hire

When she was a little girl, all Samantha Driscoll ever wanted was to be somebody's wife. She would marry a man called Tod or Brad and she would have two perfect children. But instead she married a Jeff and he's just confessed to having an affair.

Spurred on by supportive friends and her unpredictable sister Max, she finds the job she was born for: *Wife for Hire*. Sam manages everything from domestic help to renovations to social events for many satisfied customers.

However when Hal Buchanan is added to her client list but claims not to need her services, Sam realises that while she can organise many things in life, she is not so businesslike when her emotions are involved.

Almost Perfect

Georgie Reading runs a successful bookshop – with a name like that, she was born to. A fun-loving friend, loyal sister and adored aunty, life's pretty good for Georgie. Except her love life, that is. Nothing seems to go right and she's ready to give up.

On the other side of town, Anna and Mac appear to have the perfect marriage. But with every failed attempt at IVF their relationship suffers further and Mac doesn't know how much longer he can cope with Anna's pain and disappointment.

So when a stranger walks into Georgie's bookshop and they strike up a friendship, events are set in motion that no-one could imagine. What is the connection between the stranger, Anna and Mac? And what will the consequences be for everyone involved if Georgie allows herself to fall in love with him?

False Advertising

Helen always tries to be a good person. She recycles, obeys the water restrictions – she is even polite to telemarketers. As a mother, wife, daughter and nurse, Helen is used to putting everyone's needs before her own. But it only takes one momentary lapse of concentration to shatter her life forever.

There was no such momentary lapse for Gemma. Her customary recklessness leaves her pregnant, alone and estranged from her family, with her once-promising advertising career in tatters.

So when Gemma barges unceremoniously into Helen's life, things will never be the same again for either of them. Two very different women who have one thing in common – their lives have fallen short of their expectations. But is fate offering them a second chance?

Crossing Paths

With a hefty mortgage, a frustrating career as a newspaper columnist and a flailing relationship with a married co-worker, Jo Liddell is resigned to living a less-than-perfect life.

That is, until she crosses paths with Joe Bannister – a celebrated foreign correspondent returning home to care for his dying father. Against all her natural instincts, Jo finds herself falling for Joe, and with his help, begins to realise that she might deserve to be happy after all.

But when she decides to take the plunge and give love a chance, the results are catastrophic. And so Jo must fight hard for everything she has never believed in – success, self-acceptance, and above all, real love.